TO DUST YOU SHALL RETURN

T0160174

TO DUST YOU SHALL RETURN

FRED VENTURINI

KEYLIGHT BOOKS

Turner Publishing Company
Nashville, Tennessee
www.turnerpublishing.com

Cover design: M.S. Corley
Book design: Meg Reid

9781684426348   Paperback
9781684426355   Hardback
9781684426362   Ebook

Printed in the United States of America

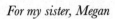

For my sister, Megan

PROLOGUE: THE MONSTERS

L ester Mansell had almost emptied his Sunday bottle of whiskey when a ghost emerged from the shimmering heat.

A ghost was all he could figure it for because even from a half-mile away, he could tell it was Geraldine's boy, Adam. The kid had been dead a long time, even longer than his momma, God rest her soul—doting wife, devoted cook, quick to give Lester what he wanted.

But Adam, her son from a long-dead husband, was a blight on the town of Harlow they had taken steps to wipe away years ago. Gerry, had she been alive, would have understood.

Lester guzzled the rest of his bottle and blinked, trying to make sure that his vision matched reality. His eyes were murky with the glaze of booze and clouded with cataracts, yet there was Adam in the distance, strolling up the driveway that had been turned to mud by a passing thunderstorm that morning.

He knew the boy by the cadence of his walk, an aloofness to his gait as if everything underfoot belonged to him. The way young boys tested their power over the world was always through cruelty, and through that cruelty, they'd usually discover the boundaries between right and wrong and downright depraved. Sometimes a few lashes with a belt helped the lessons stick. But not with Adam. No, sir, not him—he never cried, not once. And when the boy had taken to laughing during his beatings, well, that's when Lester Mansell had found himself trying other methods of punishment—methods that he never knew would please him until he'd tried them.

But Adam was broken from birth and never blamed his stepfather's actions for his own behavior. When the kid was nine, long before Lester had ever laid a hand on him, he had caught Adam in the barn with a litter of kittens, and—

Lester shook away the memory, blinking again, forcing beads of sweat loose as his forehead crinkled. They caught up in the creases around his eyes, and when he opened them, the sweat was burning, and Adam was closer. He had died at nineteen. He was a tall boy, just as tall as the figure who approached his porch.

His rocking chair had gone to rocking faster, and Moses, his German Shepherd, had disappeared, slinked away without so much as a sound. The storm had given way to a scorching August sun that baked up a humidity thick enough to stir with a wooden spoon. He sat there rocking, soaked in sweat tinged with alcohol, waiting for dark when it would be cool enough to sleep and wake up and start drinking again. The mines were long-closed now, and Harlow was hemorrhaging, a heart spasming out its last few beats after a vital artery had been blocked. Those who could work left, those who farmed stayed, and those too old to work who owned no ground and knew for damn certain their lungs were black as a starless night just stayed around to die drunk and alone.

The figure stopped at the porch steps. Even at that distance, Lester had to lean and squint to make out all his features—tall, slender, brown eyes that smoldered with some internal heat. The familiar crew cut was gone, replaced by curly locks the color of dead leaves.

"Come to pull me down to hell then, boy?" He tipped out the last few drops of whiskey and slung the bottle into the field, where it rapped against healthy stalks of corn. Not his, of course. Lester's ranch house had a few acres of tillable land that he'd sold to the Murrays, and that was enough to cover his daily bottle until the end of time.

Adam smiled, his teeth as yellow and jagged as the cornstalks would be by October. "You think I'm a ghost?"

"Demon's more like it, I imagine," Lester said. "Ain't much to take, though. I ain't but a sack of skin and guts, all of it soaked with whiskey. Punch a few holes in me, and then all the demons in hell can get a buzz." Lester laughed, feeling lightheaded. How long had it been since he laughed? The boy's emergence was a gift. Death was at his doorstep at long last. He'd been inviting him in all this time.

"You never saw me die," Adam said.

"No, sir," Lester said. "Just saw you take a deer slug to the chest out at Red Rock Ridge, saw you take another one in the back for good measure as you climbed off the edge and plummeted—oh, two hundred feet to the bottom. Never saw you buried, but I'll take Roy Carver's word for it. Couldn't stomach seeing you like that. You was my boy, after all, wasn't you?"

"It's Mayor Carver now," Adams said. "Isn't it?"

Lester grinned. Funny how the stench of death could make you feel so alive.

"Come to visit the woodshed one more time before we go?" Lester licked his lips.

Adam watched him, expressionless, his face a void. "I'm not a ghost," he said. "Nor a demon."

"Sheeit," Lester said. He got up from his rocker. His joints crackled. "We cut your ass down at Red Rock what now, fifteen years ago?"

"To the day," Adam replied.

What a mess that was—the year started with the collapse of mine six, and Adam was one of the workers swallowed up in it. He ended up as the only survivor, and what the boy did to survive was a pox that the town could only wash off with blood.

"Fifteen years, and yet you ain't aged a goddam day," Lester said.

"But I have," Adam said. "Some."

"Come to drag me into hell either way," Lester said. "So it ain't nothing worth fighting over. Come on inside. We'll toast to my demise, you and me."

The house was rotting along with the rest of Harlow. The boards creaked and groaned with each step, covered in brown spots where the roof leaked overhead. The spots shined with puddles from the storm; Lester had long given up trying to put out the buckets. Let the whole damn kingdom fall in around him.

He set tin cups on the table. Adam didn't take the cue to sit, standing at the head of the table instead, his palms resting on the oak planks. He examined the grain. It looked as if he was trying to remember something. His mom, perhaps. The table hadn't seen a fine meal since lupus got her back in twenty-six.

"Sit, boy," Lester said. "At least be a courteous guest before you try to kill me."

"A guest," Adam said, marveling at the words. "A guest in my own house. My mother's house."

"*My* house," Lester said. "Mine alone since the day you left."

"Didn't have much choice in the leaving," Adam said.

"That much is true," Lester answered, rummaging through the cupboard. He knew where the bottles were, of course, but what he really needed to remember was where he'd stashed his shotgun.

"I'll stand just the same," Adam said, just as Lester found the weapon. It'd sat there since he'd plugged a few deer during the winter, oiled up and ready, stored away from his stash of rifles specifically for him to serve up any rude guests with a bitter surprise of lead and fire.

"So be it," Lester said.

"I want to give you an easier shot," Adam said, just as Lester raised the gun. "You think I wouldn't remember where you store your shotgun?" He moved away from the table, offering up his whole torso—an easy, close-range, center-mass target.

Lester hesitated. He'd seen Adam shot like this before. Deer slug to the chest. Bloody, tattered clothes. He was dead. No away around it. Adam was dead. Who was this? *What* was this?

"It's me, Daddy," Adam said. "You always liked it when I called you that—but only after the spankings turned into something else, right, Daddy?"

Lester blinked the sweat away from his eyes. The house was a hotbox in the August heat, hot as the stoked pits of hell.

"You ain't a ghost," Lester said. "You're a goddam monster."

"You're the monsters," Adam said. "You, Mayor Carver, Baxter Murray, the whole lot of you." He took a step forward, daring him to shoot. Lester took a step back. "I've come to cleanse this place— to not only slay the monsters but teach those who would be taught and raise up those with blistered hands who have toiled in your service."

He came closer. Lester tightened his grip, ready to fire.

"Do you know what that is called? A being who can kill monsters? A force who is a dripping sword of righteous slaughter, whose hand is stayed by the cleansing tears of loyalty and redemption?"

A god. Of course that's what Adam wanted him to say, but Lester answered with a pull of the trigger. The barrels puked fire, the tin cans rattled, and Adam crashed to the floor, shreds of his cotton work shirt floating in the air. The slug had bit into his chest, a center-mass bulls-eye, a shot even a man blind-drunk and trembling couldn't have missed—and didn't.

Lester rested the shotgun on the table and looked upon it with the sweetness and endearment of a long-lost lover. He knew that the next pull of the trigger would belong to him, that the ghost lying dead on his floor wasn't real, but had torn off the scabs of all his sins, and even whiskey couldn't dull the snake of loathing that had uncoiled inside him.

And then, Adam rose to his feet.

"Come with me, Daddy," he said.

Adam dragged him to hell, all right. Literally dragged him—pulling along a man damn-near three hundred pounds as easily as one might carry an empty pail. Lester gave up fighting and made himself into the limpest weight possible, but it didn't matter. Adam had him by the ankle and pulled him through meadows of overgrown grasses that nicked at his skin, into the woods where the branches and sticker bushes lashed and cut him, into the mouth of darkness in those woods, a laid-open vein into the oldest of the mines.

Then, only darkness, the cool ground kissing his wounds, the sound of his body scooting along echoing off the damp walls along with the steady drip of water—wells and springs, above or below, he couldn't be sure.

Forever, all the way down. Down, down, down. Darkness like blindness. Colder, until he shivered, the booze wrung out of him, bubbling up in every stinking pore. The cold sweat made him a slimy thing, just another slug in the dark, the kind of thing that would scatter when the light hit it.

"You don't understand," Adam said. It felt like hours since he'd last spoke. "You never did understand. None of you did. You passed your judgments, you sentenced me...you executed me. All without understanding. But what I've been given? It's a gift I want to share, but only with those who truly and rightly understand what I went through. Only those who want to survive, and will pay the price to do it."

The dragging slowed. Lester sensed it before he heard it—he was not alone. Panicked breathing rattled off the walls. Whimpering. Crying. Vision was worthless, so the body had gifted him with hearing terror and confusion in amplified, maddening detail.

He didn't need a formal introduction to know the men who were trapped in the hole with him, and he knew exactly what Adam expected them to do to survive.

"I'll have you know my ordeal was worse," Adam said. "Much tighter quarters, while many of you have room to roam. I sucked water from dampened mud, whereas I have left you pails of fresh water to sustain you. And I was trapped with only three other men, not the feast you have to choose from."

Lester felt his ankle released, and his leg crashed to the ground, as lifeless and heavy as waterlogged firewood. He was exhausted and sick and needed a drink.

"I'm sealing the mine behind me, as this is the last of you," he said, louder now, so every inch of the mine could hear. How far would his voice echo? Hundreds of feet? Thousands? "My step-father, Lester Mansell, is here now. He hasn't been down here six days like the rest of you, and he's just as fat as you all surely remember him."

Moaning. Whispering. Crawling. Lester heard Mayor Carver's voice, an unmistakable rasp burnished by cigars and two decades of mine soot. *He's Roy Carver now*, Lester thought. *You done been de-elected, from the likes of it.* He couldn't make out what Roy was saying over Adam's footsteps, which fell like crunching thunderclaps, growing weaker as Adam got farther away, closer to the light that Lester knew he'd never see again.

Only then could he make out what Roy Carver was saying—at least, one word. The only word that mattered. *Hungry.*

No more footsteps.

Adam was gone, and the only things left were the monsters.

SALVAGE

CHAPTER 1

Curtis Quinn thought he was done with the temptations of city life, although St. Louis barely qualified.

In St. Louis, the traffic was driftwood, floating by on the way to somewhere else. The people who settled down there were tricked into thinking a dirty river, a monument, and a rising murder rate made you one of the big boys. New York, Chicago—cities like that were partnerships. They demanded that you add to the legend or get the fuck out. Nights in those cities were a current Quinn never fought, and he fed their gutters blood.

He sat on a bench near a rundown intersection, coffee in hand, waiting. Benoit was late, as usual.

Two gangbangers loitered near the traffic light. One was a dealer; one was in training. The lead dog was agitated, glancing over, pacing near the light. A big, calm white guy sitting on a bench with a coffee irked them. Certainly, they weren't so amateur to think he was a cop. If only they could see the gnarled vines of burn scars on the right side of his face, he'd just look like a retired hoodlum, not worth their attention.

The scars covered his upper arm, chest, and most of his torso. Most of the tattoos from his youth were melted away, a mess of ink and spider-webbed grafts. The only tattoo that mattered now was a griffin on the inside of his forearm—an eagle's head with prominent lion's ears, its feathered wings outstretched in mid-flight, the lion's haunches coiled and ready to explode. Yet the beast was shrouded by the bent limbs of a willow tree. Hidden in the leaves was the date of his marriage—6/14/92, five years ago.

The marriage wasn't licensed. The ceremony started with a kiss and ended with a dinner of cold chicken, and they got tattoos instead of rings. Kristina had suggested the griffin tattoo in lieu of a ring because of its supreme loyalty. Griffins took mates for life, and there was no "until death do us part." According to legend, if one griffin died, the other spent its life alone, never searching for a new mate.

I love you, Curtis, she'd said, sealing their marriage under the willow tree.

Kristina had used his real name often in the confines of their home and swore that one day she'd tell him her birth name. But now she was gone—and he intended to find her.

He waited, sipping his coffee. The lead dog on the corner was a snake of a kid wearing headphones around his neck, his pants sagging. He wore an N.W.A T-shirt. Quinn didn't dislike the group—they had a dislike for cops in common. But nowadays, Ice Cube was in the new George Clooney war movie. He probably called officers "sir." And Quinn himself—who had offed a few cops, crooked and otherwise, back in the day—was waiting to meet a cop. That was the thing about being a gangster—if you didn't end up dead, you ended up conforming to the comforts of the society everyone agreed upon, and that society thought cops were superheroes instead of the drug-running, coked-up, greedy, racist assholes Quinn had known during almost two decades in Chicago.

Lead dog finally started walking over. Quinn could tell by the kid's strut that he was packing. He couldn't get over their fresh, unspoiled faces, their confidence, their zest for the filth of the street corner. They hadn't been stitched up or shot, betrayed or busted. Life was good; life was perfect. Just hand over coke or grass or whatever the fuck they slung in East St. Louis, get some dough, go buy some new rims.

"What the fuck you doing here, man?" Lead dog squared off in front of him, just beyond grabbing distance, a tall kid with his hand hanging near the waistband of his jeans. The piece was likely tucked in the back of his pants, the nose of the gun probably covered in ass sweat. July was a broiling motherfucker in these parts, and the thunderheads boiling above them hadn't docked long enough to sweep away the humidity.

"Waiting."

The rookie grabbed his partner's shoulder. "Come on, TJ," he said. "Leave it be."

TJ brushed his hand away, and Quinn recognized the look in the kid's eye, that young blood craving his alpha status, ready to cut down an older, vulnerable lion in the pride.

"This doesn't have to turn bad, kid," Quinn said.

"That a threat?"

"Not anymore," Quinn said.

He looked at the sky. The swollen clouds were about to unleash a summer storm.

"That's right, that's right—this is a threat. Give me your wallet, man, and get to fucking steppin'."

"I'm meeting someone here, but you can have my wallet," Quinn said. "Old leather, ten bucks, and a fake ID. Yours if you want it."

He went to take a sip of coffee, and TJ batted it away.

"What the fuck you need a fake ID for?"

"I don't know—what the fuck you need my wallet for?"

TJ finally went for his piece. Quinn could tell it wasn't the first time the kid had drawn his gun, but still—not smooth. Clunky. Scared.

"TJ, what the fuck, man," the rookie said, looking around. Nothing. The traffic light clicked from green to yellow, yellow to red, with no cars there to pay attention.

"You're a real smart ass, you know that?" TJ said. "I don't give a fuck who you are. I just want your wallet now on sheer principle."

"I know who you are," Quinn said. "You're the type who doesn't last long. You got no instincts, no sense of risk and reward. Your partner there? I'll bet on him making rank."

"That so?"

"He's scared, but calm. He can tell I'm not afraid of having a gun in my face. He's starting to figure out that fucking with me isn't worth a few bucks and pointing a gun on a street corner. He's not reckless."

TJ smashed the butt of the gun into Quinn's temple. The kid was quick, and Quinn hadn't tried to dodge a punch in a long time. He felt the heat and thickness of blood on his cheek as he crumbled, sliding off the bench, crashing into the pavement.

A fat drop of rain splattered onto the pavement next to the steady drip of cranial blood. The concrete was hot on his palms as he tried to get to his feet, but by then, TJ had plucked his wallet.

"Shit, what do you know, he wasn't lying," TJ said, sliding out the ten-dollar bill. He tossed the empty wallet at Quinn. The bill-fold struck him in the back of the head, and then the rain came down in thick sheets.

Quinn got back onto the bench, tilting his head so the rain could wash away the blood. TJ and his trainee were gone, around the corner, in an alley—didn't matter. Steam clung to the roads as cold rain soaked the hot, sun-baked concrete.

Headlights pierced the smoke. Detective Scott Benoit finally pulled up in his Jeep Wrangler. Quinn got inside.

"Meet some of the locals?"

Quinn nodded.

"They dead?"

He shook his head.

"Shit. Do they know how close they just flew to the sun?"

Quinn glared at him.

"All right, easy—hey, you definitely need stitches. And on top of everything else, you're gonna owe me for a professional interior detail."

"Just drive," Quinn said, pinching his nose, the concussive headache drumming louder with each heartbeat.

Benoit looked like a guy with twenty ex-wives. Premature wrinkles bracketed his mouth.

"Fucking animals around here," Benoit said. "South Chicago with training wheels, man. Very underrated gang and crime problem out this way."

The rain choked the gutters, creating small rivers along the sides of the road.

"I got nothing to report, as expected," Benoit said. Quinn just watched the wipers dance. "Did you hear me? Dead end."

"You go to Vic's?"

"Talked to Vic himself. All I learned was that his bar's a shithole, you're a ghost, and no one knows anything about this Kristina girl."

Now on the interstate, they passed Busch Stadium, where Cardinal fans were bailing on the delayed baseball game, umbrellas sprouting in bursts of red.

"We both knew Vic's was gonna be a dead end," Benoit said. "But I owe you, so I did it. That drive fucking sucks. I hate Chicago."

"So where do we stand?" Quinn asked.

"Kristina's ten days gone," Benoit said. "You already know we're not gonna find her. Not alive."

Quinn said nothing, absorbed by the rain-battered windshield.

"It's not Nico—if he did this to punish you or draw you out, you'd know it was him."

Nico Coletti was Quinn's former employer, and his idea of a severance package was to have Quinn set on fire. For seven years, Quinn had dodged Nico and his men, staying hidden while his legend—and the contract on his head—continued to grow. When Kristina went missing, Nico was the only lead Quinn had, even if he knew, deep down, that Nico hadn't taken her.

"Maybe you should ask around," Benoit said.

"That won't do a damn bit of good."

"You don't think it's a different question if you ask it instead of me?" Benoit said.

"You're a cop," Quinn said. "So investigate."

"There's no missing persons report," Benoit said. "So there's no official investigation. Just me, making good on all those favors I owe you."

Quinn would have filed a report, but it was Benoit who refused to let him make such a dumb mistake. Quinn had nothing to offer—they weren't legally married, despite their years together, and Kristina wasn't even her real name. Quinn would just be serving himself up, warrants and all, on a platter. Then he'd eat through a slot in a cell door while Nico raced the state's attorney's office to see who could end him first.

"If you're stepping off, recommend someone," Quinn said. "Someone good. I'll pay."

"If someone took her, you shouldn't be the one paying, if you get my drift," Benoit said.

He pulled over two blocks down. The rain picked up, a frantic downpour. The wipers struggled.

"You find a lead, I'm happy to help," Benoit said. "I got some vacation days left. Until then, we're spinning wheels. Unless you ask around. Hard."

"When that kid dropped me," Quinn said, "I didn't feel a thing."

"That three-inch gash would suggest otherwise."

"I don't know if I didn't stop him and drop him because I didn't want to, or because I just can't anymore. And to do the shit you're suggesting, the shit I used to do—it takes a lot of both if you want to be effective."

Quinn opened the door. The full-throated noise of the storm filled the cabin. Benoit shouted over it.

"What you were," Benoit said, "you can't just lock that shit up and throw away the key."

"I'm not the one who locked it up," he said as he slammed the door.

CHAPTER 2

T he gas station at the edge of Harlow hadn't serviced a customer in decades. The fuel islands were dry, the price of gas frozen in time on the dials—forty-nine cents. The garage doors rattled in the wind, the fiberglass yellowed by time.

Now, it was just another outpost.

Beth Jarvis sat in the office with a ledger laid open in front of her. She sat beside a cash register, the old kind with raised keys, like a typewriter. The shelves were barren—no Snickers, no Juicy Fruit. No tire gauges or generic quarts of oil. A vending machine gathered dust in the corner, the light of dusk glinting off its empty silver spirals.

The front door opened, jingling the string of bells tethered to the knob.

Brad Reynolds greeted her and jotted his name in the ledger.

Beth reviewed the entry as he hurried for the door. "Wait," she said.

"I'd like to get back before dark," Brad said.

Beth picked up a rotary phone. She spun the numbers as Brad waited by the door, beads of sweat running down the bridge of his nose. The outpost didn't have air conditioning, and Beth had the box fan pointed at her desk.

"Beth Jarvis," Beth said into the phone. "Outpost south. I got Brad Reynolds. Two hours. Grocery shopping."

Brad continued to wait, his hand on the doorknob.

Beth hung up the phone. "One hour," she said, spinning the ledger around, an invitation for Brad to correct the entry. "Too close to dark."

A muted explosion rumbled in the distance. The glass in the station's windows shimmied, and the bells chirped, but neither of them flinched—they were accustomed to the sounds of TNT popping off at the dig sites around town.

"Never mind it, then," Brad said. "I'll go tomorrow." He rushed out, making sure to slam the door.

The bells hadn't even stopped vibrating when Galen Mettis walked in. Galen was a tall piece of rope, with muscle and tendons braided around thin bones. He always looked like he could slap his jeans and make a cloud of dust.

"Brad's looking fit to spit," Galen said.

"He wanted two hours and got one," Beth said.

"Fucker's always mad," Galen said. "Some men don't got the balls to boil over, so they kind of simmer all the time." He made a smoothing motion with his hand and cracked a smile. "So, what kind of action we got today?"

"Three out," Beth said. "Two back in already."

Galen twisted the ledger so he could read it.

"All right then," he whispered. "Morgan's on his way here. He's gonna take over."

"Morgan Albers?"

"The one and only."

"He's a full-on scout," Beth said.

"That's right," Galen said. "He's gonna train your replacement. I think you've rusted up in here long enough."

The last thing Beth wanted was to sound enthusiastic, but after weeks of marinating in an outpost, her mind was ready to chew on something other than her own thoughts. She managed the outpost ledger six shifts a week during the summer and four during the school year, sitting hours at a time, thinking about all she'd been told since she turned sixteen, and all that was yet to come this fall.

"I'll be back to pick you up in about an hour," Galen said. "We'll make a scout out of you yet."

Beth had never asked to be a scout. The entire apprenticeship felt wrong, like a betrayal of her family—her sister especially. But what inmate could say no to being trained as a guard? To know their routes and techniques? Their secrets?

"Thank you, sir," she said.

"I ain't your sir," Galen said. "The mayor's the only sir around here."

"And by his grace, we prosper," she said.

He took off his John Deere hat and ran a hand through his sweat-greased hair.

"Look," he said, hesitating a long time before saying anything else, massaging the bill of the cap before looking up at her. "I'm not all about that subservient bullshit. I do what I do out of loyalty to this town and its people. You can turn me in for blasphemy if you want, but if you're gonna apprentice with me, I want you to know you can talk plain when we're together."

"Of course," she said, stopping herself before another "sir" could leak out.

"I get it," he said. "You don't know me, and you can't trust me. Maybe one day you will. Maybe not. Makes no difference to me— now, you can be plain, or you can be silent. Just don't bullshit me, okay? That's rule one."

"Okay," she said. "I guess I'd never trust anyone I barely know."

"Not even the mayor?"

She said nothing.

"Good," he said. "That's a start. Kneeling to someone and trusting them are two different things, anyhow."

He left her alone, and for the next hour she watched the sun scurry toward the horizon, wondering about life outside of Harlow—and if a life on the run was any life at all.

On the twelfth night of Kristina's disappearance, Quinn finally got the call.

"We found a dead Jane Doe," Benoit said. "It's the girl in the photo you showed me. I'm sorry."

Quinn had braced hard for this moment over the past few days, rehearsing it so it couldn't dent him—but it did. He struggled to speak, stuck on the memory of her smiling beneath the willow tree, their willow tree, as they took their vows in the presence of no one but themselves, needing no God, gods, or government bodies to bless their union.

"This is a murder investigation now," Benoit said. "You'll see it on the evening news."

"Foul play," Quinn said, not a question but a realization.

"They left her face and hair and that's about it," Benoit said. He didn't need to spare the grisly details with a man like Quinn. "Her body was ravaged, man. Like a pack of lions got into her. No organs. No fingerprints. Just bone and gristle. But her face is perfect. Untouched. Although it seems like her teeth were removed."

"They don't want the body identified," Quinn said.

"The only lead we'll have is if someone comes forward to identify her—which I assume won't be you, seeing as you'd be a prosecutor's wet dream and you didn't even know her real name."

Kristina's journal was resting on her nightstand. She always trusted him not to read her private thoughts, yet it still surprised him that she never stored it in her drawer.

"Quinn, I'm sorry," Benoit said.

"Let me know if someone claims the body," Quinn said. "And if no one does, you let me know what funeral home is processing her remains."

He hung up the phone before Benoit could answer. He picked up her journal and brought it to the kitchen, placing it on the table, resting his hand on top of the leather cover.

After a long while, he got up from the kitchen table, leaving the unopened journal behind. He walked into the spare bedroom. The pink walls radiated, even in the dark, and he could still smell the freshness of the month-old paint.

Quinn rocked in their new glider and stared at the empty, half-assembled crib until the sun was down and up again.

Beth beat Trent to the cafeteria and staked out their regular seats, trying not to doze off while she waited. Since she began regular scout training with Galen, a full night of sleep was a rare luxury.

Trent strolled in late as usual. He was broad-shouldered from farm work, but had a softness to him. She could sense it in the way he took care of his hands. Even though he was assigned to dig site work now, he never had soot under his fingernails. And he was always smiling, beaming at her with the intensity of new love, even though they had dated over a year. She loved his smile but had come to see it as a lid he'd clamped onto something.

He sat down and opened his mini-cooler.

"What's the special today?" she asked.

"Turkey," he said, handing her a sandwich from the cooler.

She unwrapped it and took a huge bite. "Better than yesterday's," she said.

"I got the Nortel offer," he said. Nortel Community College was about eighteen miles south of Harlow, a holding bin for Harlow students until jobs popped up on the farms or at the dig sites.

"Everyone gets the Nortel offer," she said.

"Don't go degrading my pedestrian accomplishments—it's higher education."

"It's a high school with ash trays."

"It's two years away from dig sites and scouting shifts," he said.

"It's taking what they choose to give us."

"We choose to be together," he said. "Or at least I choose you—over anything and everyone else."

A smile felt too heavy to lift, but Beth tried anyway.

"I'm just tired," she said.

"You look tired," he said. "No offense."

"I think Galen's going to endorse me as a scout at Harvest, and I don't know how I'm supposed to feel about it."

He took her hand. She noticed a fresh callous on his upper palm.

"Your hands," she whispered, not knowing how to finish.

"Could be worse," he said. "Site two would be worse. No shade. I can't wait for the fall weather to break in for good. Bugs are horrible at site three, but we have some shade at least."

They finished off their sandwiches in silence. Then Trent withdrew a chocolate pudding cup from the cooler.

"You spoil me," Beth said.

"What? This is mine," Trent said. "But since your birthday is coming up…"

He broke the seal on the pudding and handed it to her.

"You always open the cup without tearing the foil," she said. "Quite a talent."

She tried to savor the pudding but couldn't help wolfing it down in four monstrous spoonfuls.

"About that birthday—you figure out what you want to do yet?" he asked.

"Take a nap," she said, but they both knew the truth. They were old enough, had dated long enough, and a birthday was special enough for a first time. She couldn't vanquish the thought of undressing Trent on a dirt road, flanked by corn stalks and tree lines, his tanned skin lit by a combination of the moon and his truck's dome light.

They'd already rehearsed for it, charting their territories, planting kisses and hands on places they meant to visit again. She knew he loved her, and she wanted to love him and seal it with a kiss and whatever bumbling passion that followed. Maybe she'd love him after. She didn't know how it was supposed to work and had no mother, no older sister to tell her.

Maybe she didn't love him because then she'd be anchored to him no matter what he said when she finally shared her secret with him—that she was going to run away from Harlow, as her sister had, that she never intended to turn eighteen and see the Harvest Ceremony or take the Oath.

If she escaped without him, how could she live knowing he was still here, in love with her, pounding that spade into hard ground, over and over, with ruined hands and a ruined heart?

"If you really want a nap, I'm thinking me and you, some blankets, just lie in the bed of my truck and nap under the stars."

"Sounds romantic," she said.

"For just a nap, it could be a little overkill, I admit," he said. "But what can I say? When I nap, I can nap so hard. I bet I can nap all night."

She threw the empty pudding cup at him. He caught it, and they both started laughing.

When lunch ended, they headed for their lockers. He held her hand, as he always did.

"I think I know what I want for my birthday," she said. "I just hope I'm brave enough to ask you before it's too late."

CHAPTER 3

Quinn waited in the empty embalming room, where the shining tools and clear hoses were used to prepare the neatly packaged dead. He had paid two grand to view Kristina's body alone in the bowels of the Winston-Day Funeral Home, and he refused to let her get anonymously cremated, or buried in a pine box.

She arrived from the medical examiner's office in a body bag. Wesley Winston, the funeral director, wheeled her into the embalming area on a gurney.

Quinn unzipped the bag. Benoit's description hadn't fully prepared him for the savage condition of her corpse. No skin remained below the neckline. Shards of bone gleamed through chunks of blackened tissue. Her innards were gone, leaving just a gummy bowl crowned by a naked ribcage. Her hands were cut off at the wrists.

Yet her face was unharmed. He leaned forward and kissed her on the cheek. It was cold and firm, like kissing a smooth rock.

"What do you make of this?" Quinn asked.

Winston crossed his arms and studied the body.

"She ain't talking," Quinn said. "You've been over every inch of her. Just tell me, all blunt-like. I heard it all before, and I've seen worse than this."

At that, Winston's eyebrows shot up. He took a long, steadying breath and pointed at Kristina's mouth.

"The teeth were taken out whole," he said. "No damage to the lips. Pliers, then. Very intentional. With the hands gone, you'd think they didn't want her identified."

"Yet they left the face alone," Quinn said.

"Not only that, but they cleaned her face and brushed her hair," Winston added.

"What about the rest of her?"

"I'm no coroner," Winston said.

"But you're one of the few who's seen more dead bodies than me. Take a guess."

"Take your pick—skinned alive? Fed upon by wild animals? Taken apart by some surgeon gone mad? There isn't enough left to examine, beyond her bone structure and what little tissue is left clinging to it."

Quinn handed Winston a rolled-up dress, white fabric with a pattern of red flowers. "Bury her in this," he said. She'd worn the dress the first day he met her, and then again later, on their wedding day under the willow tree.

"Beautiful," Winston said in practiced fashion.

"You put unknown people in cheap coffins, right?" Quinn asked.

"It's standard in situations like this," Winston said.

"It wasn't an essay question," he said. "How much for a good casket?"

"There are different degrees of good," Winston said.

Quinn pulled out a roll of hundreds. "Here's eight grand. That's enough for one of your nice caskets, with change left over for you to do two things." He reached into his jacket and pulled out her journal, enclosed in a Ziploc bag. "Bury this with her, and keep your fucking mouth shut."

"Forgive me, but why not just claim the body?" Winston asked. "You can grieve appropriately and be present when she's buried. You can put the journal in yourself before the casket is closed for good."

"Do I look like the kind of guy who's paying you to answer your questions?"

Winston shook his head.

"Fuck with me on this, and you become disposable. Do your job. Do it with honor, and this is the last time we see each other."

Quinn stroked Kristina's forehead. Her hair felt silken and alive. He put the journal next to her ravaged body.

"When will you bury her?" he asked.

"Tomorrow," Winston answered. "Usually, we don't prioritize these particular burials, but she's at the top of the line, thanks to you."

Quinn nodded, never looking away from his bride.

"I'm going to my office," Winston said. "You can let yourself out when you're finished."

When Quinn was alone with her, he waited, hoping the tears would come. They didn't, evaporated by the heated churning of his thoughts, a sickening hunger he hadn't felt in a long time threatening to swallow him.

Don't be that guy. Her constant refrain to him whenever she sensed the man he used to be was about to make an appearance.

Don't be that guy.

"I won't," he said, and kissed her for the last time. He lingered beside her. The world outside that door was one without her, and he wasn't ready. He had an old life to burn now and a weight to carry that he'd never be able to set down for the rest of his life. He forced himself away from her and headed for the door—let the descent begin.

The side door took him into an alley. Even in the shadows, the sun made his eyes ache.

As he turned the corner, he was adrift in thought, planning his exit from the normal life that hadn't lasted nearly long enough.

He'd dig up his cache of money and start a fresh identity further west. Maybe a cabin in Colorado somewhere, or something close to the ocean out in California. He'd never seen the Pacific, just the white teeth of the Atlantic gnawing at the New York coast. Maybe Florida—his mother told him that he had swam in the Gulf once when he was three years old. He didn't remember it. He barely remembered *her*, but maybe he would if he saw the beach again.

He glanced over at the entrance of the funeral home. A Toyota Camry was parked on the corner. The Camry itself didn't catch his eye, but the hail dimples on the roof did.

Quinn ducked across traffic to an adjacent street. He found a payphone and dialed Benoit.

"Someone's following her body," Quinn said.

Beth and her father, Marcus Jarvis, ate what they always seemed to eat for dinner these days—frozen things from cardboard boxes, heated up from their brick-like shape into something somewhat edible.

Beth didn't mind. Ever since her mother died, dinners got shitty and stayed that way. Her father was far from a cook, and even now, ten years later, he still hadn't bothered to learn.

Marcus was a listener, a guy who would grunt and tack on a "what can you do?" or "sounds about right" to any conversation. He was perfect at nodding in the right places, earning a kiss on the cheek, after which Mom would say, "Do I really talk enough for the both of us?" and they'd have a smile about it.

Beth was only seven when she died. Dad just came home one day and sat her down and told her that her mother was dead. Cancer. Beth never had a chance to tell her goodbye. She locked herself in her room for days, eating a steady diet of potato chips, feasting on reruns of *Full House*.

Kate, her older sister, was the only one who tried to penetrate his depressed veneer. She'd go into Dad's room and watch the Cubs with him, asking if Sammy Sosa hit another homer, asking about the standings, asking when the next game was on. She was much older than Beth—by then Kate would have taken the Oath—but the loss of her mother hit Kate harder than the secret truths of Harlow ever could.

Marcus put on his tough guy act, insulating himself from crying at the funeral services. He talked less and less as the years went on. Despite the growing distance, Beth never felt an icy vibe from her father. The man loved her in the lukewarm and silent way that fathers sometimes love their children.

"How was school?" Marcus asked, forking a piece of microwaved lasagna into his mouth.

"Fine."

"Trent?"

"They have him at Dig Site Three," Beth said.

Marcus was handling his fork in an unwieldy, pincer-like grip. Beth got a better look at his hand—a gash ran across his palm. Stitches crisscrossed the wound.

"Changed the oil on the truck today and had a lapse of clumsy," he said, noticing her curiosity. "You gonna eat or what?"

"No. I want to talk about Harvest," Beth said.

Marcus considered answering for a moment, then shook his head.

"This is bullshit," Beth said. "I need to know, Dad. They're making me a scout, and I'm starting to hear things. Things about the Oath, the Mayor. Low men. High servants."

"Stop it," Marcus said. "You've got a birthday coming up. Let's not spoil these last few days."

"I'd hate to spoil it. Everything's just so great around here."

"These are the last few days of not knowing," Marcus said. "Soon, you'll be an adult. You'll make your own decisions, and I can't stop you, but when that day comes, you'll have to own them. I won't be able to protect you anymore."

"From who?"

"From you," Marcus said.

"I guess we'll see," Beth said. "I'll move across town. It's not like I'm actually living with another person. You just microwave stuff and ask how school went."

She failed to get a rise out of her father, who kept picking at his lasagna. Beth reached out and smacked her father's plate off the table, the lasagna exploding on the linoleum, slinging maroon-colored sauce all over the fridge.

Beth waited for her father to respond. Marcus gently put his fork down and looked up at his daughter, his eyes glassy.

"They found Kate," Marcus said. "Couple days ago."

They never talked about Kate anymore—not since Beth learned the truth about her last year. At least part of the truth, anyway, when she was finally old enough to know that those who ran were punished.

For years, Beth thought Kate had died in a car accident not long after Mom passed away, but after she turned sixteen and her father told her the truth about Harlow, he also revealed that Kate had escaped over seven years ago. The sister Beth thought was dead was alive out there, and Beth relished the thought of following in her footsteps, perhaps even finding her. The two Jarvis girls, together, the only ones brave and strong enough to escape Harlow for good.

Yet they'd found Kate. They'd brought her back to Harlow.

"What did they do to her?" Beth asked.

"She's dead," Marcus said. "That's all you need to know. That's all you're gonna know. At least from me."

She couldn't look at him, staring into the grain of the table, not wanting to let the grief take hold, not in front of him. She let the anger scorch it away.

"You said they'd never find her," she said.

"I was wrong," Marcus said. "I make mistakes. I've made them with you. You come to grips with Harvest on your own terms. You hear me? There's a before and an after. You treasure the before while you still got it."

Marcus went to the sink and soaked a wash rag, looking out the kitchen window.

"Don't you run," Marcus said. "Move across town if you got to. I won't stop you. But don't you run away, you hear me? I can smell it on you—that itch to flee. You got your mother's stubbornness and your sister's sensibilities. Just know I'm not the only one who can smell it. Stay here, stay with Trent. Stay with me."

"Eighteen means I make my own decisions," Beth said.

"Fair enough, but just know your sister made her own decisions, too," Marcus said. He stooped down and started wiping up the spilled food.

Beth watched him struggle with his wounded hand, wanting to hold onto the anger, feeling it slip as she blinked away a starburst of tears. "Dad," she said, but didn't finish. Instead, she knelt down to help him.

CHAPTER 4

Quinn drank coffee in a rundown diner a half hour east of Saint Louis. Six cups later, Benoit finally arrived, looking more haggard than usual. He loaded up his own mug of coffee with a suffocating amount of cream and sugar.

"You do know this sounds like you finally lost it," Benoit said.

"I know what I saw," Quinn said.

"If you thought someone was following her remains, I'm shocked that you didn't pull him out of his car and leave his entrails on the concrete."

"He's not the perp," Quinn said.

"Driving out to these little hellholes isn't the best use of my time as a resource. I have a job to do."

Quinn had a yellow legal pad on the table. He moved his finger over his notes, squinting.

"You don't know this, but I was watching the precinct when all this went down," Quinn said. Benoit's eyebrows shot up. "I wanted to see who came and went from the coroner's office, from the police department. Hoping for a lead—a bent cop I knew from back in the day. Maybe one of Nico's men. Something. Anything."

"I just lost confidence in my brothers in blue, not noticing your gigantic ass stalking the place."

"Because I didn't want to be noticed. That, I'm still good at. I got nothing out of it, anyway. But I did see a silver 1997 Toyota Camry with Illinois tags."

"Useless. The Camry is a common vehicle, and Illinois tags are all over St. Louis."

"I didn't remember that car until I saw another Toyota Camry in front of the funeral home. 1997. Silver. Illinois tags."

"Same plates?"

Quinn shook his head.

"The top of the car had hail dimples and a deep scratch in the bumper. It was the same car. But they bothered to change the plates out," Quinn said. "Whoever left her body in that condition didn't want her identified by anyone other than a friend or loved one. That's why they left her face intact and destroyed the rest. She's bait."

"Jesus," Benoit said. "They'll regret that if they reel your ass in."

"Winston-Day puts her in the ground tomorrow," Quinn said. "The tail is going to stick until she's in the potter's cemetery."

"We scope him out, and I can harass him a little. Got it."

"You've got no legal grounds," Quinn said. "You nab him, you'll get nothing out of him, other than blowing the fact that we know there's someone out there looking for a connection to Kristina."

"You've got no legal grounds, he says," Benoit said, smiling. "I never thought I'd see the formidable Curtis Quinn writing on a legal pad with shitty eyesight and lecturing me on legal grounds. I wish I could have met this Kristina."

"I need to do this clean, Scott," Quinn said. "I need to do it straight." He rolled up his sleeve and showed Benoit his griffin tattoo. "The griffin is loyal to one partner for life. If one dies, the other remains loyal and committed forever."

"Sounds a lot like real marriage, only shittier," Benoit said.

"I promised her I wouldn't be what I used to be," Quinn said. "I need you to help me keep that promise."

"How?"

"I need you to be the guy faking tears by her grave site tomorrow," Quinn said.

"You want me to be bait?"

"No, I want you to be the cop with a golden heart who didn't want that poor girl buried alone."

Benoit shifted in his chair. He tapped his mug. He looked out the window, sighed, shook his head.

Quinn let him squirm, saying nothing. Waiting.

"This, whatever this is—this settles it," Benoit said. "I'll see this to the end, but when Jane Doe fades away into a zero-lead cold case, or we chase down every last thread we can muster, I'm done for good with you, Curtis. You got that? I owe you nothing else."

Benoit just stared into his mug, which was nearly empty, leaving a sugary sludge lingering at the bottom. When he finally looked up, Quinn nodded.

"It's not that I'm not grateful for what you did, but if I'm gonna be anything other than what I am right now, that future can't have you in it," Benoit said. "Not even your shadow. You swear to me, I walk away clean after this. You give me your famous and unbreakable word."

"I didn't pull your bleeding ass out of a hailstorm of bullets just to make you owe me for the rest of your life," Quinn said. "You paid that debt already. You've been a friend."

A freckled waiter offered them refills. Quinn took his to the brim, but Benoit waved him off.

"That's what has to stop," Benoit said.

Quinn stood up and threw a twenty on the table. As he turned to leave, Benoit grabbed his arm.

"What if it's someone tying up loose ends?" Benoit said. "Someone watching me through a scope, waiting for a clean shot?"

"Then I'll save your life a second time," Quinn said. "And you have my famous and unbreakable word on that."

Beth sat in Galen's old Ford, watching the sun burn down to embers and fall behind the trees. Summer was all but over, but the humidity stayed behind, giving Beth a bib of sweat that matched Galen's.

They watched the Kinoka blacktop. The fields, the cover, and its remote location made it a ripe spot for unapproved escape attempts.

Each night, Beth and Galen dragged stop sticks over a different part of the blacktop. Beth knew them from the movies, when cops laid them out to puncture the tires of a fugitive's vehicle. The strip they used was spray-painted black, masking its location on the blacktop. Headlights would never pick them up—not until it was too late.

They stared at the inert darkness for hours. Crickets strummed along in the distance, giving the night a pulse.

"You're quiet tonight," Galen said.

Beth wasn't asleep, but her mind was somewhere out there in the muddy fields by Kinoka Road. She imagined holding Trent's hand, running away from Harlow forever.

"I'm always quiet," Beth said. She wasn't being a smartass—it was the truth. She obeyed Galen's commands and never bothered him with plain talk. Galen was a scout, and scouts caught those who ran. The man wasn't her friend.

"There's different kinds of quiet," Galen said. "Your kind is usually the ain't got nothing to say type. Tonight, you got things on your mind."

Beth stared out the window. Corn stalks swayed, their leaves brushing, a sandpaper sound.

"You're thinking about running," Galen said. "But who wouldn't think about running?"

"What do you want me to say?" Beth asked.

"Not a damn thing," Galen said. "To me or anyone else. You tell your pops?"

"I don't make it a point to give him a detailed inventory of what I'm feeling or wondering," Beth said.

"He's a hard man," Galen said.

"Hard isn't the word. He's just kind of there. He feels around the edges of every conversation."

"Oh, hard's the word," Galen said. "He don't have to scream at you or whip you to be hard."

"He won't talk to me," she said. "He won't answer me straight, not ever."

"You don't want it straight."

"You sound like him now."

"He's got good reason not to tell you."

"What's that?"

"He loves you," Galen said.

She returned her attention to the stillness of the night. All this time she hated the outpost because it was so boring, but now she was equally bored and losing her premium sleep hours on top of it. The passage of time was measured by each dropping degree. The humidity lifted. The crickets grew tired, their cries fading away until a brutal silence settled in like a fog.

Beth dozed off. She wasn't supposed to—sleep deprivation was part of the apprenticeship—but Galen never reprimanded her for dozing off.

Then, the Ford's engine exploded to life, jarring her awake. She tried to blink away the dullness as Galen slammed the accelerator. The Ford blasted across the blacktop, ramming into the soybean fields. Beth saw the headlights of a crippled vehicle on Kinoka; its tires chewed up by the stop sticks.

"Get that spotlight, Beth," Galen said, both hands locked on the wheel, his eyes wide and alive. "He's running for the northern tree line."

The truck bounced, chewing through the field. Beth clicked on the spotlight. A beam unspooled across the green sea of soybeans. She saw white legs churning, wearing Nike shoes blackened with mud. Beth adjusted to the rhythm of the truck's movement, centering the spotlight.

She saw a boy no older than herself dashing for the woods.

CHAPTER 5

Quinn spent the afternoon scouting the Mount Lebanon Cemetery. Winston had agreed to bury Kristina at 3:00 p.m. sharp. He even let Quinn pick the location in the potter's ground, so he chose a spot with clear sightlines from the woods nearby.

Confident in his cover, he pulled out his binoculars and waited.

The Winston-Day hearse showed up right on time. The casket was polished cherry wood, engulfed in a spray of red roses.

Benoit pulled up behind the hearse.

Moments later, a Toyota Camry passed the potter's ground.

Quinn watched as it parked among the headstones down the street. The man who emerged had gray hair clinging to the sides of his freckled, balding skull. He wore a beat-up leather jacket and carried a bouquet of roses. He rested them in front of a random gravestone. Then he knelt, feigning prayer as he watched Kristina's burial.

Benoit stood before Kristina's grave, his hands clasped, his head bowed. He played the part, and had the Camry-man's attention.

That was the only opening Quinn needed. He charted a course

that allowed him to stay among the cover of brush and gentle hills as he tried to flank the mysterious mourner.

Quinn gassed himself making the run, his out-of-shape lungs betraying him. He pushed through the burn and emerged at the foot of a hill near the Camry.

The mourner raised a camera. He twisted the lens, focusing on Benoit.

Quinn yanked down the ski mask he had perched on the crown of his head. Then he made his move, opting for silence over speed, closing ground as he drew his gun. While the mourner was clicking off pictures, Quinn tapped the back of his head with the muzzle of his pistol.

"On your knees. Now."

The man remained calm, setting the camera down, raising his hands.

"I said, on your knees."

The bald man got on the ground, one knee at a time, his joints clogged with noisy arthritis. He put his hands on the back of his head.

"I didn't hear you coming. That's impressive," the bald man said.

"Your wallet. Which pocket?" Quinn asked.

"Someone's going to see us."

"You're on your knees grieving. Not unusual."

"With a tall guy wearing a mask standing behind him?"

That one froze Quinn—the guy hadn't looked behind him. Not once. How could the bald man know how big he was or that he was wearing a mask?

Muffled voice, Quinn thought. *The angle of the gun tapping the back of his head.*

"Wallet. Now."

"I do not negotiate with terrorists," he answered, dripping sarcasm.

"You know the best place to hide a body?" Quinn asked. "On top of another fucking body."

"You would have shot me already if you were gonna," he said. "But I'll play along. The wallet is in my back right pocket."

Quinn didn't like how calm the man sounded. *Shoot him*, he thought. *Shoot him now.* He shook it off.

"Take it out," Quinn said. "Slowly. Hold it behind you."

The man obeyed. Quinn grabbed it, letting gravity flip the bifold open as he kept the gun trained on his target.

"You armed?" Quinn asked.

"Does a bear shit in the woods?"

"Dump whatever you're packing, and be slow about it," Quinn said.

The man produced a pistol and dropped it behind him. Quinn picked it up—a Glock 26 subcompact. Nothing special there. He dropped the clip and threw the gun away. It smacked against a distant headstone.

"Jewelry, cell phone. Place it all behind you."

"Do I have to take off my watch?" the man asked. "My wife gave it to me. This isn't a real robbery. I know that much. So maybe just let me keep it on."

"If this isn't a robbery, why do I have a gun pointed at your head?"

"I'm following a dead Jane Doe," he said. "You want to know if I know anything about her. I don't."

"What Jane Doe?" Quinn asked, trying his best to keep up the ruse.

"Check the wallet," he said. "Check it close. Empty it if you have to."

Quinn obliged. Ben Cartwright, forty-eight years old. Licensed Illinois driver who lived on Worrell Street in Harlow, Illinois. Credit cards matched the name, making it more likely it wasn't a fake ID. Then he found what Ben wanted him to find—a private investigator's license.

"You got the wallet, scary robber man," Cartwright said. "Run away now. Enjoy the forty bucks."

"Who hired you?" Quinn asked.

Cartwright chuckled. "Can I get up now? I got bad knees."

"You move, you bleed. Who hired you?"

"No one," he said. "Case like this? You crack it or get a lead, you get on the news. You earn business, which is hard to come by. I'm small town, small time. I have to commute to chew on a case. Clients aren't exactly beating down the door."

If the guy was playing him, he was laying down the smoke nice and thick.

"You know, for a stickup man, you ask a lot of interesting fucking questions."

"Wasn't too long ago that one would earn you a right cross, just as an appetizer," Quinn said.

"Then I'm glad it's not a long time ago," Cartwright said. "Maybe we can work something out. Sounds like we both want the same thing."

"We don't want the same thing," Quinn said. "My patience might have evolved enough to save your jaw, but I didn't get dumber."

"Well, if you're so smart, what do you make of the guy bawling over a Jane Doe's unmarked grave?"

"You tell me," Quinn said.

"He's a cop," Cartwright said.

"Bullshit," Quinn said, inviting Cartwright to show off his logic.

"Bet me," Cartwright said. "He's not on the case, but he's a cop. You can always tell. They wear the job on their shoulders, you know? A heavy, invisible thing around their necks."

"So he's gnawing around the edges of a case that was on the news, just like you," Quinn said. "Big fuckin' deal."

"Don't make sense to me," Cartwright said. "He's not here because he wanted to be here. He ain't crying. To me, he looks scared shitless."

"You're done with this case, Mr. Cartwright," Quinn said. "You go home to Harlow, and stay home. When you wake up in the morning, kiss your wife. Count your blessings."

Cartwright laughed. "If only you met my wife."

"Fuck with me, and I just might," Quinn said. "Get out of here, and stay gone."

"I can handle that, amigo."

"Car keys," Quinn said.

"In the ignition."

Quinn yanked them out, keeping his barrel aimed at Cartwright. He launched the keys into the graveyard.

Quinn started to back away.

"Thank you," Cartwright said. "I think this was mercy, wasn't it? Been a while. Hard to tell. But if it is, I thank you."

Quinn knew he should leave it there, but he couldn't resist. The feeling was so strong, he had to give it a voice.

"Do you know who she is?" Quinn said.

"No sir," Cartwright said, without hesitation.

"You may not be shit for a private detective," Quinn said, "but you're a damn good liar."

"And you're not," Cartwright said. "You don't know who she is, but you wish you did. The fact that you don't is another one of those rare little mercies."

Kill him now. His finger pressed against the smooth metal of the trigger, trembling in withdrawal. *You'll regret it if you don't.*

However, Quinn knew a foot soldier when he saw one. Kill one, and two more pop up. There was always someone like Nico Coletti at the top, smiling as the puppets bloodied each other. Whoever this man's Nico was, Quinn intended to find him.

"If I ever see you again, I will not hesitate," Quinn said.

"I don't believe you," Cartwright said. "They say it's two pounds of pressure to pull that trigger, but for you? It's in the megatons now, the weight of everything you ever did."

"You say that like a man who's done some shit."

"Ain't we all, amigo. Ain't we all. We done here?"

Quinn wasn't going to get the last word with him, and the bastard was right—he wasn't going to shoot him. He lowered the weapon and vanished into the woods.

From there, he watched as Benoit headed back to his car. Kristina's casket disappeared into the ground.

Cartwright was still on his knees, paying no attention to Kristina's grave anymore, as if worshipping something that only he could see.

Galen's Ford fishtailed in the mud, stalling, yet the bursts of acceleration were enough to gain ground on the fleeing boy, who was sprinting for the woods beyond the field. He was close to the thick cover of brush, beyond the reach of spotlights and trucks.

Beth steadied the beam, illuminating the boy as he dove into the brush.

"He got away," Beth said.

Galen ignored her, bringing the Ford to a gentle stop. He cut the ignition.

With the engine quiet, Beth heard the boy shredding his own vocal cords with shrieks of pure agony.

"Stay behind me," Galen said, grabbing a flashlight, a long one, made heavy from a sleeve of batteries tucked in an aluminum tube, the kind of flashlight security guards liked because it could bludgeon as well as illuminate. He waded into the brush. Beth trailed close behind as his flashlight beam settled on the boy. She recognized him. Shaun Murray, a classmate and basketball player. She'd always liked Shaun, but for the past year or so, he'd turned mean, picking on freshmen. His favorite move was slapping textbooks out of their hands between classes. No one fought back. He was tall, strong, quick to anger. Beth steered clear of him.

Now, here he was, whimpering in the dark, his eyes wet and blue in the flashlight's glow.

He was caught in a nest of razor wire. Blood streamed from deep gashes in his arms, looking purple in the flashlight's jaundiced eye. A flap of skin below his eye has been slashed loose, and it flapped as he screamed, like the curtain of a breezy window. Dark blooms spread across his jeans where the razors bit through the denim.

"Please," he said, his voice turned rusty from the screams.

Please what? Please help? Please kill me? She thought of a fly thrashing in a web, reaching a point of exhausted resignation as the spider pranced over to feed.

"Beth, is that you?"

Beth said nothing.

"Please," he begged. "Don't let them get me."

Galen held out his arm, holding Beth back. He turned around to leave the thicket, and Beth followed him.

"What do we do?" Beth whispered.

He ran his fingers through his sweat-greased hair. She didn't like that Galen looked panicked. "We're scouts. We got him. Our job stops here." He paced, thinking. "That's Cooper Murray's grandson?"

"You know it is," Beth said. Cooper Murray was a Harlow relic, an old and quiet man. He owned much of the farm acreage on the edges of Harlow. His two grandsons lived with him ever since their parents died in a tragic dig site accident. Beth believed it at the time—before she turned sixteen and learned the truth behind the rules of Harlow.

Galen paced. Then he grabbed the handheld radio from his belt. Before he keyed it, he put his hand on Beth's shoulder.

"I'm going to call this in," he said. "I want you to take the truck. Go get Cooper Murray. Don't call, don't ask—*demand* he come back here with you. That'll be enough duty for you tonight, I think. You bring him here, maybe they'll let you go on home."

"They?" Beth asked.

"The Sheriff," Galen said. "And whoever he brings with him."

Quinn waited for Benoit in yet another diner. Always a different diner, always attached to a truck fueling station off of I-64. Southern Illinois truck stops were miniature, bustling cities, their citizens temporary. They saw and remembered nothing, hurrying along to someplace else.

Benoit showed up at 2:00 a.m., after his shift.

"Harlow, Illinois," Quinn said, squinting at his legal pad. "An old mining town. Mostly farmers now. Small. The new highway completely bypassed it, yet it's still around. There isn't another town of substance within ten miles in any direction."

"Throw a dart at a map of Southern Illinois, and you'll hit a hell-hole like that," Benoit said.

"Kristina's mother was dead, but she always spoke as if her father was still alive," Quinn said. "Her picture was on the news. Why didn't he come forward?"

"Could be out of state," Benoit said. "National media didn't take this one up."

"She talked about her father's willow trees down by his pond. That's as rural as it gets. You don't have that in a subdivision or a city."

"You're reaching," Benoit said.

"What kind of P.I. sets up shop in a town like Harlow?" Quinn asked. "There's no business. No clients. I looked him up—nothing in the yellow pages."

"If he's good, word of mouth can do wonders."

Quinn stared at his plate, refusing to dig into his cooling hash browns. "Harlow's the thing that doesn't make sense," he said. "Who the fuck is he working for when he lives in a down-home shithole like that?" He leaned closer. "The town is our best lead."

Benoit pinched the bridge of his nose. The fatigue of a long shift pooled in the darkness underneath his eyes.

"You want me to shake down a town with like four people in it?"

"Six hundred, as of the last census," Quinn said. "I got you a lead. Now, do your job."

Benoit considered it over a long sip of coffee.

"I'll give it one day," Benoit answered. "I'll show her picture around. If something smells, I'll make a few calls and drag this weirdo Cartwright to the station myself."

"Scott," Quinn said, one of the rare times he called him by his first name. "The P.I. was good. He beat me this round—sniffed out my robbery-hoodlum routine, and cracked it just as fast. Whatever taste we got here, I didn't take it. He gave it to us."

"He that good?" Benoit said. "Or you just that rusty?"

"Don't get sloppy on this," Quinn said. "You snoop around, you bring someone along. Take precautions. At least tell someone you trust where you're going and why."

"Okay then," Benoit said. "I'll see if any of my overworked brothers in blue want to drive two hours into the armpit of Illinois to sweat out rednecks door to door. I'm sure they'll leap at the opportunity."

He pushed his unfinished mug of coffee to the center of the table and left the booth.

As he grabbed his jacket, Quinn reached out and snatched his forearm.

"Be careful," Quinn said. "But be thorough. Make the arrest and make it stick. Do that, and I'm just a bad memory."

"You've always been a bad memory," Benoit said. "Besides, why would I worry? You promised to watch my back, remember?"

Quinn let him go. Benoit tossed a twenty on the table and winked at him before strolling out of the diner.

Quinn ate cold hash browns as Benoit got in his car, another weary and secret traveler leaving the truck stop's fluorescent shadow.

You warned him, he thought. *It's on him now. He's sick of being the bawling kid in a foreign jungle all those years ago; tired of feeling like he owes me. He'll make the smart play.*

The thing was, Quinn didn't have to warn him. The old Quinn wouldn't have, despite their long allegiance. The old Quinn didn't have to squint to see his own handwriting. He wouldn't have left the fate of his wife's killer in the hands of the police. The clever P.I. wouldn't have survived.

Of all the people Quinn had killed, the person he used to be was the toughest target. That man would never die, but he'd atrophied to the point of uselessness.

The thought saddened him. He shook it off and touched his griffin tattoo, remembering Kristina. Even after her death, he yearned to feel worthy of her love.

He never deserved her. He never would. Yet, he would never stop trying.

CHAPTER 6

B eth drove through the heart of Harlow, following the old highway. They called it the superslab nowadays, a concrete monument to Harlow's past.

Beth's father always shared stories about what Harlow used to be, stories that were passed down by his father—a grandfather she had never met.

The town once thrived, its economy built on mining jobs. The highway cut through the center of town, the traffic slowed by stoplights. Cars pulled over to visit the shops, or eat at the restaurants, or fuel up at the full-service station on the edge of town. The Harlow she knew was a ghost of the one from those stories. Plywood covered the old shop windows on Main Street. Foundations tilted from mine subsidence. The gas station was an outpost now, the fuel islands dry, the garage bays empty. The highway was in pieces, the widening joints patched up with gravel.

She followed the superslab. A few miles away from Main Street, she turned off on Rural Route 400, but everyone in Harlow knew it as Murray Road.

Stars clawed through the clouds and threw a murky light on the Murray farmhouse. The porch light popped on as Beth parked the

Ford. By the time she got to the front steps, Cooper was outside, fully dressed, his hands stuffed into his jean pockets. The man's face was a craggy map of the things he'd seen. He didn't look surprised or worried; he looked expectant.

"What side of town?" Cooper asked.

"Kinoka blacktop," Beth said.

Cooper nodded. He walked down the stairs, heading for the Ford.

"Come on, then," Cooper said.

They got in the truck. Cooper stared at the windshield. Beth hoped Galen was right, and the Sheriff would let her go home, that this would be the end of her lesson for the night.

"Whose truck is this?" Cooper asked.

"Galen Mettis's," Beth answered.

"Mettis, eh?" he said. "I ain't heard that name for a long stretch."

Once they got to the Kinoka blacktop, Beth saw the flashing light bar in the distance. Sheriff Vance had arrived.

"Listen to me, Beth," Cooper said. "They're gonna make you watch. You're not eighteen yet, but this will teach you everything you need to know about Harlow."

"Galen says the Sheriff will let me go home."

"Galen ain't the Sheriff, he ain't a High Servant, and he damn sure ain't the Mayor. He's a goddam fool, and you're a fool if you believe him."

Mayor. As children, the name was synonymous with the boogey-man. *The Mayor's gonna get you*, they'd scream at each other, playing tag. You never really shook childhood fear, no matter how irrational. Fear never grew up, always petulant, clinging to your leg, begging you to listen. In Harlow, it whispered *Mayor*.

They got closer. Cooper turned into a ball of steel wire, every muscle and tendon clenched. He knew all of Harlow's secrets, but the stitches sealing those days away were breaking as he braced himself for what was yet to come.

Beth parked behind the Sheriff's black Tahoe. The flickering light bar bathed three men in a kaleidoscope strobe—Sheriff Vance, Morgan Albers, and Jason Vowell.

She knew that Morgan was a High Servant but never suspected Jason had such standing. She'd seen him at the diner before and sometimes at the basketball games. He was a clumsy giant who always wore trucker caps. His boy, Doug Albers, was as big as his old man was, a lumbering oaf with a nice touch on his hook shot. Must have gotten that sliver of grace from his mother.

"Coop," the Sheriff said, tipping his cap, unable to conceal his smirk. His eyebrows looked like fat caterpillars, his sideburns a nest of steel wool. Cooper ignored him, walking to the edge of the brush.

"Hold on there, Coop," Morgan said, stepping up to him. Morgan was the tallest man there, his face slathered in freckles and sunburn. He grabbed Cooper's arm.

"Let him see," Vance said.

Cooper saw. Shaun was whimpering as Cooper knelt beside him. He whispered to him in low tones Beth couldn't hear over the idling Tahoe.

"Where's Galen?" Beth asked.

"He's a scout. He's got no place here," Vance said.

"Does that mean I can go home? I'll drop off Galen's truck. Just tell me where."

"You're not a scout," Vance said. "You're an apprentice. Do more listening than talking, and I'll give your buddy Galen a nice report on you. That's what you want, right? To be picked? To be a scout?"

"A fucking Jarvis scout," Jason said, laughing.

"What if a Jarvis told you to shut up?" Beth said. "Would you laugh then?"

"I guess that depends," he said, stepping closer. "Is a Jarvis telling me to shut up?"

"Sure ain't her sister telling you," Vance said. "She's not saying much to anyone these days."

Their laughter turned acidic in her ears, and the only sound that cut through it was Cooper.

"Do what they say," he said. "That means watch if you got to. Understand?" The old man's voice and kind eyes calmed her.

"That's right, Beth," Morgan said. "Listen to the Great Survivor."

Cooper glared at Sheriff Vance. "So what's it gonna be, then?"

Vance nodded to Morgan, who reached into the back of the Tahoe. He brought out a bullwhip.

"We ain't done lashes in years," Cooper said.

"You're the Great Survivor," Vance said. "You're grandfathered in. Now, hold up your right hand."

Cooper obeyed. Vance took his pocketknife and plunged it into the center of Cooper's palm. Blood trickled between the old man's fingers as Vance lengthened the gash. Then, Morgan held out the whip's handle. Cooper seized it with his wounded hand.

"How many?" Cooper asked.

"All of them," Vance said.

"I can't."

"You will," Vance said. "You got another grandson who was smart enough to not run. He's asleep, right? Be a shame to wake him up the hard way."

Blood dripped off the whip's shaft. Again, Shaun moaned.

"Shaun's nothing but scraps now, anyhow," Vance continued. "This isn't a punishment; it's the Mayor's mercy."

As Cooper walked into the brush, Beth looked down at her muddy sneakers.

"Eyes up," Vance said. "Follow him. Your job tonight is to watch."

She walked into the brush as the Sheriff lingered behind her. She saw Cooper's hand lift up, but didn't intend to watch the whipping. She closed her eyes. The men didn't notice; they were too busy catching the show themselves.

She heard leather bite flesh, snapping it apart, fueling Shaun's screams. She heard Cooper's anguished grunts as he mustered the strength to bring down the whip again and again. The pauses between lashes lengthened. Shaun begged for his grandfather to kill him as Cooper struggled to finish the job. That was the purpose of the cut—Cooper couldn't strike Shaun as hard or as fast with his damaged palm.

Shaun finally stopped crying. The silence felt like mercy, but the leather cracked against flesh again. And again. And again. Cooper bawled, a grown man melting into the anguished cries of the little boy he used to be, and Beth had to bite her cheek to prevent herself from crying along with him. She couldn't let them see her crack— she didn't know if there would be consequences.

Cooper, exhausted and bereft, panting, striking his grandson's dead body to assure the boy was dead.

When the whip fell silent, she heard the mocking applause of the men behind her.

Cooper threw down the whip. "He's beyond you now. Even the Mayor can't touch him. Bastards."

"The Mayor's mercy, indeed," Sheriff Vance said. "Freedom for the boy; a gift from the hands of his own kin."

Against the cinched-down dark of her closed eyes, Beth envisioned her father at the kitchen table, the stitches etched in the crease of his palm.

To escape the memory, she had no choice but to open her eyes.

CHAPTER 7

Q uinn waited for days, watching the news, hoping for
updates that would hint at a break in the case. So far,
nothing. No new leads or developments. The Jane Doe
case had already faded away from the media cycle.

Three days after his last meeting with Benoit, a news chyron
caught his eye—*County Police Searching for Missing Officer.*

Quinn wasn't surprised to see Scott Benoit's picture.

At the end of the report, the anchor gave out a tipline for any
information involving Detective Benoit's disappearance.

Quinn drove to East St. Louis and selected a pay phone on the
seediest corner he could find. All he had to do was give them the
Harlow tip. Cops protected their own, so the move was simple—
kick that beehive of pissed-off cops and set them loose on Harlow.

He dialed the tipline. The phone rang.

He wondered how many cop-haters were giving them shitty
information. Tiplines were a treasure trove of false leads.

Another ring.

And what if they did pluck Harlow out of the haystack of leads to
investigate? They send out, what—two cops? To ask around? Just

like Benoit had asked around? Then the citizens give them a polite "I don't know, I haven't seen him" over and over again, in lockstep.

He could give them Cartwright's name and description, but he was confident the old P.I. would navigate mild questioning with ease.

The line clicked to life. "St. Louis Regional Crimestoppers," a female voice said. She wasn't even a cop. He had to convince the neighborhood fucking watch to get a tactical team into a speck of a town two hours east.

"Crimestoppers," she repeated.

Whoever killed Kristina was getting away with it. Was he prepared to abandon her, if only to preserve the man she knew him to be?

"Hello?" she said.

Rigidity was the problem. Small towns like Harlow were no different than the Coletti crime family. They tensed up against outsiders, repelled everyone who couldn't be trusted until they could prove otherwise. So what was the answer to rigidity?

"This is an anonymous line," she said. "You can talk to us."

Kristina had already given him the answer. *Water.*

Quinn slammed the phone into the cradle, ringing the bell in the heart of the phone's chassis.

"Put water in a cup, it becomes the cup," Kristina had said, a nugget of Bruce Lee wisdom she loved to recite when he grew angry or frustrated. "It's not rigid. It lets the outward things disclose themselves."

Water could flow, or it could crash. He couldn't crash against Harlow, but what if he became one of its own?

HARLOW

CHAPTER 8

S haun Murray's official cause of death was called a farming accident. He was careless and got caught up in a PTO
shaft, bleeding out before he could call for help.

The lie was for the children. Wasn't long ago when she was one
of them, a freshman girl with friends and crushes, with dreams of
success and family beyond Harlow. Maybe they actually believed
it, as Beth once believed her sister had died in a car accident.

Shaun's absence wasn't noticeable in her classes. No one
mourned. The teachers said nothing. Superintendent Ronato
made no announcement. On the basketball scoreboard, Shaun's
name and number were gone.

Everyone conspired to make his death feel like a disappearance.
They wanted to forget him, but they had nothing to forget. Not
like her. She saw his dead body, shredded by razor wire and the
repeated stings of a bullwhip.

The sight of his corpse visited every time she closed her eyes. In
her sleep, it came alive, the eyes opening, white and alive, glistening
in the mess of his shredded and blood-soaked face.

"Do you still want to run?" he asked, his mouth creasing into a
smile. "Come on then," he said, and reached out to her, ripping

his chewed-up arm from the razor wire, leaving chunks of flesh behind. He reached out, his forearm shorn to the bone, drapes of skin shaking as he waited for her touch.

She woke up in Galen's Ford, lacking an answer.

After catching her breath, she checked the time. Her shift was almost over. The cool morning mist of early October rolled over the fields.

"Thanks for letting me sleep," she said.

"Don't seem like much of a favor," Galen said. "You're squirming around over there like something's digesting you."

Beth cranked her window down, letting a gust of chilly air swirl through the cabin. Her forehead felt clammy with sweat.

"That thing, a few weeks back," Galen said. "I shouldn't have left. I'd earned the right to not see that, and I took it. I didn't imagine they'd make you watch."

"What if we hadn't caught Shaun?" Beth asked.

"We'd have been punished," Galen said. "And if he'd gotten away, he wouldn't have stayed gone for long. They would've sent a Ranger. Special kind of High Servant."

She'd heard whispers about High Servants, but never a Ranger. Must have been a Ranger who finally found Kate and brought her home to die.

"I saw a cut on my father's hand," Beth said. "I haven't asked him about it. I think I'm afraid to."

"Yeah, well," Galen said, trailing off, looking out the window. No answers lurked there. Since Shaun died, Galen was chattier during their shifts, as if the silence could bite them both. Like most farming types, he loved to talk about the weather.

October's real sting was coming soon, and once the first frost arrived, the Harvest Ceremony was never far behind. As a child, she'd looked forward to the festivities—waking up early, gathering with her friends in the school classrooms they decorated for the occasion. They watched movies with the volume turned way up, made turkeys out of paper plates to hang in the fridge for Thanksgiving, and with enough sun, they'd go outside and enjoy the playground without the threat of the class bell to prematurely end their time at play.

As a teenager, the edges of the truth began to reveal itself—the true heart of the Harvest Ceremony took place in the locked-down gymnasium, during rituals where children were not welcome. At sixteen, apprenticeships began. At eighteen, you attended your first Harvest, and learned if your apprenticeship earned you a job and the status that came with it. Only the best and most trusted became High Servants. Those who failed would work the dig sites forever, or worse, become Low Servants, a fate she didn't understand, but feared.

"I got you a couple nights off," Galen said. "Your birthday's in two days, right?"

Beth nodded.

"Open the glove box," Galen said.

Beth popped it open as Galen clicked on the dome light. She reached inside, finding the smooth plastic necks of tiny liquor bottles.

"You're thinking of the wrong birthday," Beth said.

"Towns like this, you drive at ten, fuck at thirteen, and drink when your parents ain't lookin,'" Galen said. "Besides, they're not all for you. This is a toast."

Beth emptied out the glovebox. Six bottles, all whiskey.

Galen grabbed one and picked the plastic seal off the neck. "Well?" He raised his bottle. Beth cracked hers open and held it up.

"We got to toast first," Galen said. "It's your birthday. Toast to something."

"I don't think I've ever proposed a toast," Beth said.

"Pretend you're at a wishing well," Galen said.

"To Trent," she said.

Galen nodded, cracking a smirk. "To Trent, then." He slammed the whiskey.

Beth struggled with her bottle, getting two sips down, then choking on the rest.

Galen laughed. "All the way back, or it don't count!" he said as dribbles of whiskey ran down Beth's chin. Her eyes watered and the final swallow made her grimace.

Galen opened two more.

"I can't," Beth said.

"Bullshit," Galen said. "You shouldn't, sure. But can't? Come on now. Be polite. My turn to toast."

Beth hesitated, then gave in and grabbed the bottle.

"Happy birthday, kid," Galen said.

Beth thought she was going to puke on this one, leaning out of the open window and gagging, but never quite letting it go. She held it down.

"You forgot to toast," Beth said.

"I guess here's to winning one for the good guys."

"Winning what?" Beth asked.

"The games that bad men play and always win."

"But they don't always win," Beth said.

"Yeah, they do," Galen said.

"I don't believe that," Beth said.

"Truth could give a fuck less about your consent."

"What I saw with Cooper, with Shaun—you call that a game men play?" she asked.

"No," Galen said. "Neither would you. Neither would Cooper, or Shaun. That's why we sure as fuck ain't ever winning."

"I guess we'll see," Beth said.

"You will," Galen said. "I've already seen. Seen my fill, at that."

He turned off the dome light to preserve the Ford's battery. Beth sat in the darkness, the birthday celebration over.

She ran her fingers over the ridges of one of the empty bottles. She wondered how often Galen got drunk, hoping to forget, finding nothing but a hangover and the same barren truth.

Maybe Galen was right. Everything's a game, a matter of managing the stakes, the odds, your investment of skin.

Care for nothing, love nothing, feel nothing, and you can never lose, she thought. *You become invulnerable. You become more of a thing than a person.*

Maybe that's how you become the Mayor.

In the mornings, Beth wore a hoodie and could see her breath. By sixth hour English class, the hoodie was stuffed in her locker because the coat hooks along the hallway were full of discarded hoodies, jackets, and sweaters by then. The windows were open, the ceiling fans chasing away the afternoon humidity. This was October in Southern Illinois, either too confused to decide what it wanted to be, or a trickster amusing itself. In other words, perfect Harlow weather as Beth's first Harvest Ceremony loomed.

She tried to stay awake during Ms. Diesen's sentence diagramming. Fatigue accrued with each night of shortened sleep, a residue that felt more permanent each day. As Ms. Diesen plucked an adverb from "The girl awkwardly ran to the market," Beth noticed Chrissa Collins staring at her. She had fine blonde hair that broke easily, and a ring of crimson puffiness around her blue eyes—from sleeplessness or sorrow, or a portion of both. Her mouth was a tight slit, and she was unblinking, her forehead scrunched in an angry glare.

Beth drifted away to another half-dreamt thought before she could connect Chrissa's gaze to the reasons behind it.

The bell rang. Beth's legs felt heavy, as they always did during the post-lunch afternoon slump. She shuffled out of class, promising herself an after-school nap. In the hallway, she reached out to open her locker when a small hand palmed the back of her head and shoved it forward. Her forehead slammed into the metal, turning her once-heavy legs to gelatin as she collapsed. On the way down, she thought herself lucky that her nose didn't hit the grates of the locker first.

"Fucking bitch!" She recognized Chrissa's voice. As Beth rolled over, Chrissa's K-Swiss sneakers bit into her ribcage. Beth crashed into the lower bank of lockers. "You might as well have killed him yourself," Chrissa screamed.

Beth's concussed mind assembled her motive—Chrissa had dated Shaun, and the lies around his death had finally crumbled in the rumor mill of kids older than sixteen.

"I'm sorry," Beth said, her breath choked by the tightness spreading in her bruised ribs. She tried to get to her feet, anticipating another blow, thinking she probably deserved it.

"She was doing her job." A booming male voice—Doug Albers. Morgan's son was a skinny tower of joints topped with a tanned, oddly handsome face. Beth didn't think him much to look at, but he'd dodged the affliction of teenage acne and carried himself with the pitiful swagger that pitiful girls always fell for. Back when she and her friends fantasized about such trivial things as boys worthy of dancing with at the junior high Halloween Hootenanny, many of them had a sketchbook with their names, a plus sign, and Doug Albers as the second part of their fantasy equation.

His voice alone kept Chrissa at bay. Everyone his age now knew he was the son of a High Servant. Beth made it to her feet. With the surprise worn off, she was no worse for wear—Chrissa was tiny, the girl at the top of the cheerleader pyramid, easy to toss and catch, not much mass behind her shoves and kicks.

"You okay?" Doug asked.

Beth wanted to cry, or go to sleep, or die, or eat a sack of candy. She thought of the Pearl Jam song "Better Man," and she was dreaming Doug Albers in color. She said nothing.

The crowd of high schoolers that had gathered began to disperse. Teachers hovered in their classroom doorways, saying nothing. They never did. This wasn't like *The Breakfast Club* or *Saved by the Bell*—in Harlow, the high schoolers policed themselves, the authority of the town and their parents respected and trumping any authority from the lowly faculty members. No one wanted a teaching job assignment. Her fifth-grade teacher, Miss Vinson, took the job from a dig site and by the end of the year she had transferred back to a dig site. Some folks preferred swinging a pick in the heat to dealing with kids all day.

As the small crowd parted, Trent remained. She brushed past Doug, ignoring his question, and took her boyfriend's hand, grateful for it. She turned and saw that Doug's face had changed from a flirtatious chivalry to the same glare that Chrissa had shot her in class.

"I'm with you, girl," Trent said. "I got you."

He was, and always would be. As long as she'd have him. And she hated herself for it, because she didn't know if it was love, or high schoolers not knowing any better, just playing pretend like the TV kids who showed them how the normal world might work. Or maybe he was just too pathetic to survive Harlow alone, and clung to her accordingly. Maybe it was her clinging to him.

"I got you," he repeated, and put his arm around her.

"I know," she answered. With her eyes closed, she saw Shaun reaching, his fingers so close to hers—she was reaching back. She opened her eyes and shrugged Trent off of her.

"I'm fine," she said, touching her forehead. "Just a bump." She forced a smile.

"Let me walk you to class," he said.

She shook her head. "I said I'm fine." The wounded look on his face was heartbreaking and disgusting at the same time. "I'll see you after school, okay?"

He nodded and left her alone in the hallway. She waited for the bell to ring so she'd have the restroom to herself. Once there, she locked herself in a stall, and cried softly into her palms.

"I'm so sorry," she whispered—to Shaun, to Cooper, to Chrissa. "I'm so, so sorry," to Trent, to her father, to her once-lost and now-dead sister, to the girl she could have been anywhere else— anywhere else in the whole damn world but here.

Despite the dull headache lingering just behind her eyes and the crushing fatigue, Beth opted to walk home. She loved taking long walks, especially at the beginning of fall when leaves rained all along her route home. She especially loved the oversized maple leaves in Donald Harmon's yard, the way they rode the wind, drafting up and then drifting down, big shavings of gold and red defying gravity. Sometimes she could reach out and catch them; sometimes a breeze would yank them away from her fingertips. The rattling leaves offered a meditative white noise, a soundtrack to her walks that allowed her to think.

Trent often walked her home, a dutiful staple of his afternoon routine, even though the walk took him a mile and a half from his own front door.

"You could have napped on the bus," he said.

"Chrissa rides the bus," Beth answered.

"So? I think you could take her." Typical Trent, trying to lighten the mood, joking his way out of anything heavy or real.

"She's right, you know," she said. "It's my fault."

"You're a scout," he said. "You can't apologize for doing your job."

"The job is the problem," she said. "You don't even know what they did to him. How he died."

They didn't talk for a long time, not until they crossed the Kinoka blacktop and transitioned from walking road shoulders to sidewalks in the heart of town.

"For your birthday, I was thinking I'd take you out for pizza or something," Trent said. "Has to beat those turkey sandwiches, am I right?"

He spoke as if a few minutes of silence could wash away what had happened, what had been done to her, what she had done to Shaun. She couldn't tell if it was Trent's strength, or his weakness.

"Take me out?" Beth asked. "You're kidding, right?"

"You'll get a few hours of passage for your eighteenth birthday," Trent said. "It's what my Dad says, anyway."

"I don't want to spend my birthday thinking about how I'll get dragged back here to be executed if we're late coming back to Harlow," she said.

"How about dinner at my place, then? I won't cook—I wouldn't put you through that—but I'll help my mother, and I know you love her meatloaf."

"Can we just not?" she said.

"Not what? Not go out?"

"Not talk about my birthday," she said.

"We'll make it through all this," he said. "We'll make it through the Harvest Ceremony. You'll make scout. Maybe even be a High Servant someday, the first one in your family."

"A Jarvis will never be a High Servant," she said. "And being a High Servant isn't my idea of success."

"It isn't for me, either," he said. "Family is what we have. You've got your dad; I have my parents. We can build a new family ourselves if we do this right. That's enough for me. That's a good life, no matter where you live."

"We could run," she said.

Trent squeezed her hand tight enough to hurt. Beth couldn't tell if it was out of fear, or anger.

"I've thought about that, too," Trent said. "Every kid does, once we learn the Mayor's real. I think that's why they tell us when we turn sixteen—to see who runs. To only bring the ones who are loyal to the Harvest." He stopped and looked her in the eyes. "Running never works. Only dummies like Shaun Murray run."

Beth yanked her hand away from him.

"I'm sorry," he whispered.

"No, I'm sorry," she said. "I shouldn't have said that."

"We wait here," he said. "In Harlow. We wait and live our lives, and maybe the Griffin will come."

"Honestly, forget the Griffin," Beth said. "If you think some magical Griffin is going to show up and destroy the Mayor, you're the dummy. At least Shaun was brave enough to stare down the truth."

"The Griffin will come," Trent said. "Someday. If he doesn't come to free us, maybe he'll come years from now and free our children."

"You're the child," she snapped, shaking her head. "Only children believe in fairy tales."

"You don't know the Griffin is a fairy tale," he said.

"Maybe we're the fairy tale," she said. "Me and you. Something from a storybook, something too perfect to survive in real life."

He looked her in the eyes, his cheeks ruddy from the whip of the breeze, his gaze soft and wounded. She pitied him— still just a boy. She knew enough of Harlow to know it would break him if he stayed. She saw him becoming a High Servant, loyal and unwavering, all to protect his hands from the dirt of the dig sites and to protect Beth from herself. Maybe she didn't love him, but maybe she could someday.

He stayed quiet for the rest of the walk. Once they came upon the maple trees, she felt better, her lungs filling with the smoky yet refreshing smell of fall. She held his hand again, hoping to take the sting out of all the ways she had wounded him. When they reached her front door, she hugged him.

"I don't want to leave you," she said. "But I need to be honest with you. I don't know if I can ever be happy in Harlow."

"Just remember, happiness isn't something you go out and find," he said. "Happiness is something you take with you."

...

When Beth went inside, Marcus was sitting at the kitchen table wearing a collared flannel shirt, his hair slicked back. Usually, the kitchen smelled of smoke and grease from his unskilled cooking. Tonight, his aftershave filled the air, smelling like freshly chopped wood.

"That old microwave finally break?" Beth said.

"It's your birthday tomorrow," Marcus said. "I figured we'd do something tonight since you'll want to spend your actual birthday with Trent. Right?"

"I guess so," she said.

"Okay then." He scooped up his keys, and they headed for the truck—a sturdy Ford F-150 that he always kept immaculate.

They backed out of the driveway, and Marcus turned the radio off.

"I figured we'd hit up the mini-golf joint. I'll feel better about buying your food if I embarrass you at putt-putt first."

"You wish," Beth said.

On their way out of town, Marcus stopped at the southern outpost. Beth stayed in the truck, but peeked inside and saw Doug Albers working the book. She sunk into the bench of the truck seat so he wouldn't see her in the cab.

Marcus was only gone a few minutes. She knew the drill—the request, the phone call, the approval, the signatures. He got back behind the wheel, their passage approved.

They drove for a half hour to a rundown mini-golf place called Shotz! in the closest real town, Vandalia. Teenage clerks sold overpriced ice cream in cheap, brittle waffle cones. The balls were all scuffed up, the water traps were dry, and the green carpet was worn down to the black mesh in all the high-traffic areas. Beth banked shots off of rails and bricks. She navigated PVC pipe funnels, and landed a hole-in-one through a broken windmill. When it was over, Beth won by three strokes, and Marcus handed her the scorecard.

"Frame that one, kid," he said.

They went to Pizza Hut, and when Beth smelled the baking cheese, her mouth watered. Marcus ordered a pitcher of Bud Light, which he drank by himself while they waited for a pepperoni pizza. The pitcher was gone before the pizza arrived, but when it did, they ate every bite.

"I hope you don't resent me for not doing this more often," Marcus said.

"It's fine," Beth said.

"How many times have we gone here? Jesus. Probably less than ten." He drank the final warm inch of beer in his smudged-up glass. "Shaun Murray. They made you watch?"

Beth froze.

"You didn't think I knew?" Marcus said. He squeezed his scarred right hand into a fist, then released the tension.

"Just like you don't think I know what that cut is from," Beth said.

"That memory is mine to bear," Marcus said.

"Better to hear it from you than someone else."

"I'll take my chances." He paid the check.

When they were back in the truck, Beth waited for her father to continue the conversation. He didn't. They left Vandalia without a word, but Beth wasn't going to let it go. Not this time.

"Mom ran," she said. "Kate ran. What about you, Dad? What keeps you in Harlow?"

"Caged birds, the both of them. First opportunity to fly, they can't help themselves."

"You didn't answer me."

"Defiance is easy," he said. "Ain't nothing special about being petulant."

Vandalia shrunk behind them. The highway degraded in quality as they neared Harlow. Soon, they were on the familiar, craggy blacktop that cut through the heart of town. Marcus signed back in at the outpost.

When they got home, Beth intended to go to bed early, even though she knew she wouldn't sleep. "Thanks for tonight," she said, and headed for her bedroom.

"Stay, Beth," he said. He pulled out a chair at the kitchen table. "Sit."

Marcus went to the fridge and withdrew two Budweisers, opening one and placing it in front of his daughter. The silver tab poked up from the top of the can, and a tiny head of foam frothed out of the hole. Marcus popped his own can with an aggressive pull that sounded like a clap of thunder.

Beth sat down.

Marcus opened a kitchen drawer and brought out a felt case, the kind that might hold a ring, a coin, or some collectible. He placed it in front of her. Dust clung to the red felt. He didn't usually store it in the drawer; he'd gotten it from some other hiding spot, readying it for this occasion, whatever it was. She split it open, and inside was a silver coin.

"That's a peace dollar," Marcus said. "Your great-grandfather was a coin collector. That's one of his favorites. Nineteen-thirty-five, last year of the peace dollar. He used to give them out to grandkids for birthdays. He left my dad a whole set before he died, which became my set."

Beth examined the coin. The *Miss Liberty* on the front of the coin was set between the words *In God We Trvst*.

"Trust is spelled wrong."

"They were all minted like that," he said. "It's not worth much. I just wanted to give you something for your birthday. A little piece of family history."

Marcus took a long drink of Budweiser, the gulping audible in the silence of the kitchen. He put down the can and let out a long, deep breath.

"Beth, listen to me close," he said. "You keep that coin on you at all times. You hear me? Keep it and don't tell anyone about it. Don't show it to a single soul."

On the back of the coin, Beth saw an eagle perched on a rock, with *E Pluribus Unum* printed underneath.

"Your grandfather didn't give this to you," Beth said. "Did he?"

"One story's as good as another," Marcus said. "Just keep it on you."

"Why?"

"Because you may need it," Marcus said. "Because we both know that you don't intend on staying around for Harvest. Do you?"

She couldn't answer. Marcus drank again. After the silence lengthened between them, she said, "You really believe I can have a good life here?"

"Like I said, one story's as good as another."

Beth pushed the untouched beer away and stood up. "Good night, Dad."

"Sit the fuck down," he said. He never swore at her. He never flashed anger. Hell, Marcus Jarvis rarely flashed any emotion at all. She obeyed.

"You come from a family of traitors," Marcus said, staring into the top of his Budweiser. "Our family tried to destroy the Mayor and paid the price. He won. He always wins. My father, your grandfather, he tried something different. He created something the Mayor couldn't destroy."

"The Griffin," Beth whispered.

Marcus nodded. "You can't destroy what doesn't exist," he said. "And when a lie gives people hope, hope itself becomes indestructible. But that wasn't good enough for your sister."

Beth grabbed the sweating can, an offering from her father. A sign that it wasn't age or the Harvest Ceremony that made her an adult, but the strength to carry her family's legacy.

She drank deeply as her father continued the story.

CHAPTER 9

B eth spent the next morning at school in a sleep-deprived trance. After two hours of talking to her father, she caught up to Galen for her scouting shift. Sleep came late—was 3:00 a.m. late or early?—and didn't stay for long.

She rummaged through her locker for a textbook that was already in her bookbag. She chuckled at the drowsy error, sensing someone behind her—not Chrissa. She didn't ride the bus that morning. Beth wondered if assaulting a scout was punishable in Harlow, but she didn't let herself wonder for long, otherwise she'd end up back in the bush of razor wire with Shaun Murray reaching for her.

Thinking it was Trent, she turned around, wearing a tired smile.

Doug Albers smiled back. He leaned in and touched her waist.

"I tried to help you yesterday," he said. "I was thinking it was a kiss-worthy thing I did there, sticking up for you. But I didn't even get a smile. You walked off with Midget Boy. That shit ain't right."

"Doug, I'm not in the mood. Okay? Just go to class."

"Bell ain't rung yet," he said.

"Half the girls here are bickering to get your class ring hanging around their necks. Just take your pick and leave me alone."

"You're my pick."

"I'm taken," she said.

He yanked her closer, his meaty palm eclipsing the entire blade of her slender hip. He was country-strong, and his breath smelled like a pile of leaves left out in the rain.

"I decided I'm not going to let Trent have you without putting up a fight," he whispered.

She smiled, feigning delight, standing on her tiptoes to whisper into his ear. "You aren't the only one who can put up a fight."

She kneed him, aiming for the groin, but the point of her knee drove into the inside of his thigh instead. He didn't even flinch.

"My father's a High Servant," he said. "Best be careful about who you attack, and think a little harder about who you choose to fuck."

"With romance like that, I know who I'm *not* choosing," Beth said. She tried to brush past him. He grabbed her arm.

"My old man says not to bother with you. Says Trent's probably got you loosened up already. I got my doubts. He's not man enough to go all the way with you."

"You want it tight? Squeeze your tiny mushroom a little harder." She moved to slap him with her free hand, dropping her book bag. He caught her arm and shoved her away. She crashed into the locker and fell on her rump.

"Everyone knows you're gonna run," Doug said. "Trent'll run with you. He'll get made low, just like you. I'll be the one who picks you up, and when I reach out, you'll take my hand. You won't have any other choice."

He reached out, offering his hand to help her up. Students gathered in the hallway, watching. One of them was Trent, his face tightened by rage, blushing with shame. No one would dare act against a High Servant's son. Otherwise, they'd be the ones not on the bus the next morning.

She ignored his hand and got to her feet alone. "You're nothing without your daddy," she said. "*Boy*."

That one hit a nerve—Doug cocked an open hand to slap her. But before he could strike, a mop head splashed against his sneakers.

He froze, surprised that anyone would interrupt him. Yet there was the new janitor, Mr. Silver, the big guy with the burn scars. He was a giant, at least six inches taller than even Doug, his arms the size of a cheerleader's waist. His face looked like leather, tanned and wrinkled on one side, gnarled with scar tissue on the other.

The janitor stared at him. Doug stared back. The janitor's eyes glanced down at the head of the mop, his eyebrows arching in a nonchalant *let me do my fucking job* look.

"You need to clean this part of the tile right this second?" Doug said.

The janitor didn't budge. Or speak. The standoff continued.

Doug stepped away, but not before spiking Beth with one last, fearsome glare. Once he vacated the spot, the janitor pushed his mop forward and started swirling it around the tile.

"Thanks," Beth said. The janitor didn't even look up. "Mr. Silver, right?"

"I'm just mopping, kid," he said, a mild growl lingering in the back of his voice.

"Plenty of hallway to mop, sir," Beth said. "I know what you did, and I appreciate it."

"Listen—" The janitor looked up from his mopping and froze mid-sentence, staring intently. It creeped Beth out.

"What's your name?" he asked.

"Beth Jarvis," she said. "Is there a problem?"

The janitor said nothing and continued mopping. The bell rang, and everyone scurried to class. Trent stayed behind. He wouldn't risk fighting Doug, but she was worth a tardy. How romantic.

"Are you okay?" he asked.

She nodded. Upset, but calm.

"You cool to go to class?"

Again, she nodded.

"I guess I'm just the biggest troublemaker in school," she said.

He smiled. She walked away, eager to get to class, promising herself a nap—at least until Mr. Campbell decided to prod her awake between equations.

"Beth!"

She turned around. Trent was alone in the hallway, resolute. He nodded once. Not just any nod, but a commitment. If she ran, she wouldn't have to run alone.

She nodded back, her mind made up, all the way, for the first time. Happiness in Harlow was as mythical as the Griffin, and she'd rather die a traitor than live in fear.

Even though she was grateful for him, she now had two lives to consider. She made a fist, imagining blood dripping from her palm as she held the hilt of a bullwhip. She heard Trent begging her to kill him, telling her it wasn't her fault, they were making her do it, that he forgave her.

She had to succeed where her sister had failed. She had to escape Harlow and forget about its prisoners, forget about her family—she had to forget about the Griffin.

Beth watched as Trent disappeared up the stairs. Both of them were working on their second tardy in two days. Mr. Silver looked up from his mopping again, a hulking man hunched over a mop with a too-short handle, with scars and a mean face that made it seem as if he'd jumped off the screen of some old slasher movie.

Still, she found herself waving at him, another thank-you he didn't want to accept. He ripped his gaze away, back to the floor, the job at hand. She had seen something he didn't want her to see in him.

Maybe even something that he didn't know was there all along.

When Quinn had interviewed for the janitorial job, he stuck to his background notes. He was now Mike Silver, a downtrodden and divorced father of three. The mother had sole custody of the kids and lived hours away. Since he rarely saw the kids, sending his child support checks on time was the next-best thing he could do.

The principal, Dan Wilson, offered him the job on the spot.

After the interview, Quinn drove through Harlow, getting a sense of the town for the first time. He saw derelict buildings, their walls shadowed where signs used to hang. Slabs of sidewalk heaved up, creating thick ledges where dandelions grew.

In the residential areas, the lawns were neat and green. Houses had clean siding and colored shutters. Driveways held Fords and Chevys, many of them backed up to trailers that held ATVs and lawn tractors.He found an American Legion, that small-town staple where husbands drank and wives served sloppy joes during weekend fundraisers.

He looked for houses for sale or rent, finding none. Eventually, he found an orange-and-black sign with FOR RENT drawn in Sharpie, with an arrow pointing to the end of a dead-end road.

He pulled up to an old house made from white ceramic blocks. It looked like a White Castle restaurant, only older and dirtier. Patches of paint hung off of the bay window's frame, like curls of burned flesh.

The house looked to have a half-acre yard and plenty of privacy. Quinn got out of his Camry. He still had the signed title stuffed in the glovebox from the all-cash deal he'd pulled for it two days ago.

A woman opened the front door. She was tall and thin, a touch under forty, if he had to guess, with eyes that were a severe shade of blue.

"You must be the new janitor," she said.

"Word travels fast," he said.

"Did you expect anything less in a town like this? Sarah."

He shook her hand and got a finger-crunching grip. She must be a farm girl. She wore jeans and a white sweatshirt with a hood that flapped as the unbroken wind ripped off of the surrounding bean fields.

"Any other rumors floating about?" he asked.

"Well, it's a fact you're the janitor, right?"

"I guess. Got offered the job—oh, twenty minutes ago."

"You wouldn't be driving around town looking at rental houses if you didn't get the job. Am I right?"

"That's right."

"So it's a fact, not a rumor. We don't deal with rumors here, despite what you may think of small towns' thirst for gossip."

"If you say so, ma'am," Quinn said.

"Well, ma'am says to come on in for some coffee and a tour. Certainly, they're not putting you to work right away."

He accepted the invitation. The house had hardwood floors, gouged, old, and real. The walls had cracks and dimples. The windows were bare, no drapes or blinds.

She took him to the kitchen, and the only thing on the countertop was a bubbling coffee maker.

"Caught me cleaning the place," she said. She poured two cups, handing him one without asking if he took cream or sugar. "Don't take this the wrong way, but it looks to me like custodial work is beneath you," she added.

"Honest work isn't beneath anyone," he said.

"Kids?"

"Three, but they're with their mom right now."

"Only two bedrooms here."

"That's one more than I need," he said. "I'm divorced. I'm behind on child support, and now I'm an hour farther than I used to be because I have to go where the work is."

"The pervert we have in the Oval Office seems a little too concerned with interns as opposed to helping prop up common folks like us," she said. "Sorry. I don't mean to get political."

"Small towns in these parts may not thirst for gossip, but I'm glad to see they still thirst for the blood of Democrats, and they vote just as red."

"Amen. So, once that garnishment hits your check, you got enough left for four hundred a month?"

"This is some tenant interview you're pulling off."

"The walls are concrete," she said. "The floor's already fucked.

What could you possibly do to the place? Unless you're an earthquake, I'm not concerned."

"Fair enough. Deposit?"

"I live down the street, and I live alone. The neighbors in this part of town are old or senile or both. You'll earn your deposit when a heavy thing needs lifting, or a chore needs doing. You look like a man who can lift things."

She smiled, not even bothering to disguise her intent to flirt.

"It's a good thing this town only deals in facts," he said. "I'd hate for any gossip to pop up about the new guy and his landlord."

"I wouldn't worry about that," she said. "Everyone already knows I'm fucking the Sheriff."

"Well, then," he said, punctuated by a sip of coffee.

"I'm only conservative at the ballot box," she said through a grin.

He opened the pantry door, the wood swollen with rot, making it stick in the frame.

"This place is just my style," he said. "Broken, but still standing. When can I move in?"

"Now," she said. "Saves me from scrubbing that godawful linoleum again. She's all yours. Rent's due on the—what day is this? Let's say the tenth of each month."

She flipped a key at him.

"No paperwork? Lease agreement?"

"This ain't a paperwork kind of town," she said. "You never gave me your name."

"Mike Silver."

"Well, Mike, I wish you luck, and nice to meet you."

She headed for the door.

"Wait, Sarah—where can a guy get breakfast around here? You know, where the locals shoot the shit and whatnot?"

"Joyce's Cafe, on Main Street," she said. "Look through the windows of those beat-up buildings until you see one that has a waitress bustling behind it."

She left him to get settled in. He stood at the bay window and looked at the fields full of brown crops, ready to harvest. He heard nothing but the rattle of his air conditioner, and the coffee tasted like shit.

This is the world you deserve, he thought.

Once, long ago, he could step outside and smell exhaust and asphalt. The city. Silence was as impossible as darkness. He'd walked in the mouth of a living thing that could close its jaws at any moment. You could taste the friction. The tension was everywhere, each day a chance to feast on it, to survive, to prove something.

Now, he was in Harlow, a place that smelled like cow shit and truck exhaust. A witness protection kind of town, where cowards and snitches ate a life sentence of boredom.

Harlow was the kind of place he'd always hated, which made it the grave he deserved.

But Kristina didn't deserve it. Neither did Benoit.

Someone in Harlow knew the truth, and this town was too small to hide its secrets forever.

Quinn put on his best redneck worker costume for a day of mopping floors and dodging kids—jeans, a Carhartt T-shirt, beat-up work boots. As a finishing touch, he looped a Leatherman multitool into his belt.

In the darkness of early morning, picking out Joyce's Cafe was easy—it was the only storefront window with lights on. Muddy farm trucks aligned in the single parking row out front.

As Quinn got out of his car, he heard a soft *pop* and a low rumble—the reverberation of a distant explosion. He had no idea where it came from, so he made the appropriate mental note, and went inside.

The cafe was bursting with energy. Hearty laughter mixed with the clink of spoons on mugs. Forks smacked against porcelain, chopping up fried eggs and hashed browns. He smelled coffee and gravy and deodorant.

"No tables, hon, but you can sit at the counter if you like," a waitress said. No name tags, no uniforms. She wore jeans and a T-shirt, her flesh too tan, covered with moles and wrinkles.

He sat down at the counter next to a middle-aged loner.

"Happening place, being so early," Quinn said. The man ignored him. He was pushing sixty, with tight-cropped silver hair. He hunched over his coffee like a caveman over a fire.

"I'm Mike Silver. I just moved here," Quinn said.

"Lucky you," the man said.

"I'll say. Tough to find work out there nowadays."

The man laid three dollars on the counter, got up, and left. A waitress passed by, picked up the money, and said to Quinn, "Can I getcha something?"

"Farmer's omelet," he said. "Seems like a favorite. All these guys farmers?"

"Some, but they're too busy with harvest to eat a decent meal this time of year. Most here are working the dig sites."

He remembered reading about an oil pipeline project, one that skirted Harlow, but wasn't inside the city limits. According to his research, that project ended years ago. Yet he'd heard an explosion of some sort no less than ten minutes ago.

"What kind of digging?" he asked, trying his best to make it sound like polite small talk.

"I don't know the specifics," she said.

"Is it related to that explosion I heard a few minutes ago?"

"You hear those from time to time," she said. "Someone should have warned you at least. Part of the work at the dig sites, I'm told. Hope you didn't piss yourself."

"I never leave the house without my Depends," he said. "I suppose I'm lucky. Digging's hard work, and I have a bad back."

"Preach," she said. "The crews leave at breakfast time, clean and loaded with caffeine, and they come in at lunchtime dirty, hungry, and a lot less spirited. Lots of digging, looks like. Hash browns with that?"

"Of course." He tried to wedge in another question, but she was gone, turning in the ticket at the kitchen window.

He ate alone. That first day, no one talked to him, and he felt their eyes as they sized him up. He tried his best to smile a lot, kept his waitress banter good-natured, and left a big tip.

On his way out the door, he noticed a man wearing a police uniform and a badge in the corner booth. He hooked his coffee mug with his index finger, flanked by deputies in much shoddier uniforms. A couple good old boys in sweat-crusted hats sat with him.

The Sheriff made no effort to conceal a long, hard stare. *If Sarah's with this crotchety fuck, she's lowering her standards*, Quinn thought. The Sheriff looked too old for a woman like Sarah, and dripped a disconcerting arrogance that went beyond carrying a gun and badge. Quinn gave his best good morning nod and received nothing in return.

Quinn chalked it up to the instinctive ire he drew from cops no matter where he went. He and the police were like cats and dogs, instinctively conscious of the presence of the other, carefully observing, waiting for the inevitable confrontation.

...

The first day of school was teachers-only. Quinn got a morning greeting from Principal Wilson, who introduced him to Superintendent Ronato.

Ronato was imposing, just an inch or two shorter than Quinn. He challenged every stitch of his suit, a thick build buried under a sport coat. He had black hair, dark eyes, and olive skin. The last thing Quinn had expected to find in Harlow was a Latino in a position of authority, with what was likely the highest paying job in town.

Their handshake could have been like two bucks cracking antlers over a doe in heat, but Quinn let Ronato's grip overwhelm his own.

"We've had trouble keeping things tidy around here," Ronato said, no hint of an accent. "Glad to finally have you aboard."

They walked the main hallway, the clop of Ronato's dress shoes echoing off of the lockers. The combination locks were all black, making it feel like dozens of tiny eyes were watching them.

"Didn't think I'd meet the super," Quinn said. "How many schools in the district?"

"One," Ronato said. "We're our own school district."

"Small town like this makes enough off taxes to run a whole district?"

"I figured you'd be asking where the mops were stored," Ronato said. "But I like the curiosity."

He stopped walking, considering his answer. "We have bountiful farms here," he said at last. "While the mines have run dry, a crude oil pipeline cuts through Harlow territory, on the very edge of town. The company disputed our claim to that particular land, but let's just say the settlement of that dispute fills the town coffers quite nicely."

"And you've got another pipeline coming through, I take it."

"Pardon me?"

"The diner. The waitress was talking about a dig going on. Local jobs."

"I'm afraid she's underestimated the complicated nature of that project," Ronato said. "But that's a conversation for another day. How about we get you to work?"

"Sure thing, boss," Quinn said. "Sorry. Sometimes I'm a motormouth."

"You wouldn't be the only one in Harlow," Ronato said, finally smiling.

For some reason, the superintendent himself showed him through the paces of his workday. He toured the whole school with him, showing him each classroom. He pointed out the brown places in the ceiling tiles where they had the occasional leak during hard rain. He showed off the massive gymnasium, one far larger and newer than Quinn expected, considering the rest of the school's weathered condition.

"The Harlow Orphans," Quinn said. "Haven't heard that one before."

"If you think that's weird, we play the C-Town Wooden Shoes in conference," Ronato said. "I suppose the schools around here aren't lacking for imagination."

The boiler room was beneath the stage of the gym, packed with dirt and grime and cobwebs, lit by a single, naked bulb.

They didn't stay there long, but Quinn noticed an undersized, decrepit door in the corner. The brass of the doorknob and dead-bolt glinted in the sallow light. They looked brand new.

When the tour concluded, Ronato took him to the janitor's room and gave him a keyring to the school.

"It's hard work," Ronato said. "Not to alarm you, but we've had difficulty keeping the position filled."

"I can't promise I'll retire here, but I can promise you that no day's work is too hard for me."

"Good to hear," Ronato said. They shook hands again, and Ronato wished him luck.

With Ronato gone to his office, and no students, Quinn tried to enjoy the meditative quality of cleaning in silence. Not everything could be recon—sometimes you just had to mop the fucking floor.

CHAPTER 10

Quinn's first month in Harlow yielded nothing but the boring routine of a working-class janitor. Same routes to and from work. Same mopping routes through the school. Same seat at Joyce's for his morning breakfast, where he settled in at his countertop seat. Shirley was his chatty waitress's name, and she was in the habit of pouring him a black coffee before he even sat down.

Lately, he'd started hearing the cafe regulars talking about a harvest ceremony. Most farming towns had some sort of harvest celebration or fall festival, so he didn't think much of it. Yet, he saw no sign of this annual party anywhere in Harlow. No flyers on the bulletin board at Joyce's, no signs, no dates or times floating around.

He was hoping for a beer garden at the harvest celebration. Even though he hadn't touched a drink in ten years, he could nurse one while the locals got wasted, fit the good-old-boy profile and let the booze loosen them up. The only other place in Harlow to get a beer was the American Legion. He'd tried to visit after work one evening, but he didn't have a membership card to key the door. He tried to buzz in, but a curt voice denied him entry when he couldn't name a sponsor.

The cafe remained his best shot to create trust and eavesdrop.

As usual, the loner guy was already in Joyce's, sitting next to him. Quinn had yet to get his name and wasn't bold enough to ask around about him—at least not yet. As Quinn took off his jacket and hung it on the back of his chair, a hand grabbed his arm.

"Hey, Mike."

Quinn turned around, fighting the reflex to break every finger of the hand that grabbed him. The Sheriff was the culprit, his chest puffed out by the Kevlar underneath his uniform.

"Come on over and sit with us this morning," he said.

"Sorry sir, have we met?" Quinn asked, his acting horrible, cracked by his inherent hatred for cops. Especially this one, wearing Kevlar in a town where you're more likely to get hit by a fucking meteor than get shot at by an actual perp.

"Wendell Vance," he said.

"Sheriff, I presume?"

"Sharp as a tack, this one," he said. "Just come on over."

"Are you asking me, or telling me?"

"Just asking, all polite-like," Vance said. "Trying to save you some embarrassment."

"I don't follow," Quinn said.

"There's a reason this seat you like so much is usually empty."

Quinn followed the Sheriff's eyes to the loner, who hunched over his coffee. The guy never talked to Quinn, no matter how hard he tried to chat him up each morning. He was impenetrable, so Quinn had given up, thinking he was an icy asshole. Now, he felt almost sorry for him.

"I appreciate it," Quinn said, trying to smile. Now wasn't the time to make a stand or take the Sheriff down a notch. He needed trust, he needed information. The days of being a hammer were over. Be a scalpel, and be patient as you make the cut.

He followed Vance to the corner booth, where he met Morgan

Albers and Jason Vowell. They looked like the kind of guys that smelled like grease five minutes after taking a shower.

"That there's Marcus Jarvis you're sitting next to each day," Vance said. "It's not a good look for you, being by him and all."

"I don't know him," Quinn said.

"He's low," Morgan said.

"By that, he means he's scum," Vance added. "Scum that the law didn't touch, so we here punish him in our own little way. May be that he didn't go to jail for what he done, but that don't mean he can't be punished."

"So you just ostracize him?" Quinn said.

"That's a big word for a janitor," Jason said.

"We don't want no part of no chomos," Vance said.

Chomos—prison slang for child molesters. Still, Quinn tried his best to look confused.

"Child molesters," Morgan added.

"I've got no love lost for child molesters," Quinn said. "But sitting by one don't mean you contract it. Especially when you don't even know the guy or his past."

"True, but now you know."

Shirley came over and filled up their coffee mugs. She looked wrinkled enough to be forty, but fit enough to be twenty-five. She wore jeans that were too tight and a top that was too low, and she knew it. When she got in range, Vance smacked her ass as she filled up Quinn's cup.

Quinn thanked her for the refill as she leaned closer to Vance and kissed him on the cheek. "You be safe today, baby," she said.

She wore a wedding ring spiked with an oversized diamond. Two karats, minimum. Maybe the dig sites were secret diamond mines—he'd been around a lot of Italian mobster types that loved to wear gaudy jewelry, but he had never seen a stone that big. Vance pulled her closer, kissing her on the lips, and Quinn noticed the gold wedding band on the Sheriff's ring finger. Shirley went back to her rounds.

"Mrs. Vance, I presume?" Quinn asked.

"Proud to say it," the Sheriff answered.

Would you be proud to admit you're fucking my landlord?

"Anyhow, what makes it worse is that it was his daughter," Vance said. "She was sixteen or so when she came out and told everyone about what he done. The only reason he didn't get convicted is because once he got charged, she ran away."

Quinn almost choked on his coffee. He pretended as if it were too hot, blowing the steam away from the rim of the mug.

"She ever come back?" Quinn asked.

Jason and Morgan both looked at Vance, deferring to him.

"I hear she settled down somewhere up north," he said. "It's her life. She wants him walking free, that's on her."

Could it possibly be Kristina they were talking about? But she loved her father—that much came through in the rare times she spoke of him. Yet she always had a layer of disappointment in her voice, even if her words were affectionate.

More likely, these inbred fucks cooked up a lie, and it was more about Marcus Jarvis than some girl, whether that girl was Kristina or not. Marcus was the man he most needed to talk to now.

"Thanks for the coffee," Quinn said, getting up. "And the company."

He picked up his mug. Vance grabbed his wrist. "You haven't had breakfast yet."

"I intend to eat over there," Quinn said. "I can get my food about ten steps faster from the counter."

"You'd rather sit by a chomo than the Sheriff and his deputies?" Jason said.

"He's not a molester," Quinn said. "At least not according to the courts of the great state of Illinois."

Quinn wrenched his wrist away.

"He's a molester," Vance said. "Pure and simple. You go on, rub elbows with him. Rub dicks if you like, but I doubt yours is hairless enough for his taste."

Quinn leaned in, making sure to whisper. "Allegedly," he said, then returned to his original seat.

"Marcus Jarvis?" he said to the loner. "Pleased to meet you." He held out his hand, side-eyeing the rest of the diner.

Marcus kept staring into his mug.

"There's nothing in Harlow for you," Marcus whispered, refusing to look up.

"A job and a paycheck is something," Quinn said, in full Mike Silver mode. Then he leaned closer. "You didn't do shit to your daughter. I know bullshit when I hear it. But she ran away—that part is true. Isn't it?"

Marcus stood up and fished out his wallet. "Gone is gone," he said, placing a crisp twenty on the counter. He turned to Quinn, looking him in the eyes for the first time. "And dead is dead."

CHAPTER 11

Quinn tried to sneak in a quick mop of the school's main hallway before lunchtime. The bell rang, and the hallway flooded with kids before he could finish. The students steered clear of him as he mopped, leaving gleaming tile in his wake.

Then he saw the Albers kid towering over a girl at her locker. A circle of students formed, watching. He recognized the girl—Beth. She always ate lunch with that mealy little Trent kid, who trailed her around the school like a lost puppy.

Albers put his hands on Beth. She fought back. He came at her even harder. No one moved a muscle, not even Trent, who must have kissed her on the cheek fifty times a day. Everyone watched, saying nothing. Doing nothing.

Quinn hadn't been around a high school in a long time, so he wasn't exactly qualified to identify normal high school behavior. But this? A high school cutie was getting manhandled by an oversized redneck, and no one, not even her boyfriend, dared to even say "stop."

So Quinn mopped a little faster, smacking his mop into the feet of Doug Albers.

The boy stared him down. Zero fear. Quinn didn't like that look. Still, he'd broken up the fight, and Doug slithered away.

When the crowd dispersed and returned to class, he got a close look at Beth's face for the first time. He saw the familiar way her blue eyes were set, the slender cut of her nose and cheekbones. Kristina's face, only younger, with a few more makeup-caked pimples and shorter hair. He leaned on the mop handle, the residue of grief that lingered in his system scraped free by the truth—this was her sister. Marcus Jarvis was her father.

And someone in Harlow had maimed her, killed her. That same someone likely put Scott Benoit in a hole in the woods—and would do the same to him if he made the wrong move.

He had the leads he needed, but Marcus Jarvis was a broken man, watched closely by the Sheriff and who knows who else. Beth was just a kid, and he didn't want to endanger her, not after what they did to her sister.

Crying in the hallway wouldn't draw the right kind of attention. God, how he missed her, and he had yet to grieve her, had yet to cry, even after seeing what they did to her. Anger had a way of burning up any emotion that wasn't useful. He lived with a skin of gasoline floating on top of his every thought, but had forgotten how to ignite it on demand.

Maybe you didn't love her, he thought. Quinn was not a romantic. He always thought that love was a fallacy of logic, the way humans attach reason to something that happens randomly. Brain chemicals fire so that the species continues to fuck its way to the next generation; we attach ideas of romance and monogamy to it, trying to neaten and explain away something primal. Did he love Kristina, or just the idea of her? The version of her that he had created in his head? Isn't that the only way a person can exist to someone else? Relationships only fell apart when ideas changed, not people. People never changed—but they could sure pretend to be someone else for a long time, and believe it.

The kids scurried away, trying to beat the bell. Beth looked back at him and waved, and the tears almost came. Fuck it, let them. No one else was in the hallway. He mopped. He invited his tears to fall from his eyes and mix in with the wet, soapy glaze he was spreading along the murky tile.

None came. They never came, and perhaps never would.

He spent the next period mopping the hallways, and when he finished, he headed for the janitorial closet to switch over to spray cleaner and rags so he could clean the boys' locker room. He passed the boiler room and glanced inside—that tiny door in the corner, the one with the shiny locks, looked ready for him.

"Fuck it," he whispered. "I'm on a roll."

He entered the boiler room and laid out his lunch on a dusty worktable, providing a cover story if someone walked in. Then he stooped under the ductwork to take a look at the peculiar, under-sized door.

He started trying his keys on the deadbolt, one at a time. None of them worked, which delighted him. If he wasn't supposed to unlock the door, whatever was behind it took on a far greater interest.

He always carried a pair of bobby pins in his pocket during his shifts. He bent one into an L-shape, doubling the tines of the pin to make it short and thick—a makeshift tension wrench. Picking the deadbolt took longer than usual, but it was a skill of feel, and those are the ones that are hard to forget.

The lock released. He opened the door and saw nothing but darkness beyond the threshold. He drew a tactical flashlight from his belt and clicked it on, illuminating a set of wooden steps. They descended beyond the beam of the light.

Quinn tested his weight on the first wooden plank. The creak echoed. Cold, dank air from the opening spilled into the boiler room.

He was careful, feeling out each step, cautious for signs of buckling under his enormous weight. They held. He kept descending.

Finally, the flashlight beam terminated on a muddy floor. The temperature had dropped by twenty degrees this far down. He arrived at ground level, flanked by walls of stone and dirt, as black as rot.

Ahead, wooden ties framed out the ceiling and sidewalls. Dripping water echoed. Harlow was an old mining town, and this was likely an access tunnel. The moist earth sucked at the soles of his boots as he walked, and soon, he saw a splinter of light. The tunnel terminated somewhere outside, near the woods to the east of the school.

He didn't have time to walk the whole tunnel, or explore any areas where it may have branched off. He made his way back up the stairs, still distrustful of the weathered boards.

As he neared the doorway, he heard the echo of footsteps in the gymnasium. He didn't panic, gently closing and locking the tunnel door behind him.

He pushed his bucket into the hallway and started mopping the hall near the janitorial closet to give himself cover.

The footsteps were closer than ever. He pretended not to notice, acting focused on his work.

"Mike?" Ronato said. Quinn acted startled, playfully grabbing his chest.

"About gave me a heart attack there, boss."

"Did we have a situation today?"

"If you mean a dirty floor, yeah, we had a hell of a situation," he said. He kept mopping.

Ronato touched the handle, stopping him.

"I mean about Beth Jarvis and Doug Albers."

"That? Not much of a situation, as you put it. Just kids being kids."

"Doug says you threatened him."

"Never said a word," Quinn said.

"There are different ways to threaten people," Ronato said. "Kids are sensitive. And let's face it—you're an intimidating guy."

"Whatever you say, boss," Quinn said.

"I agree; it's nothing major," Ronato said. "But I want you to report those types of incidents to me or Principal Wilson instead of mopping into the line of fire. Deal?"

"Sure thing," Quinn said.

"You're awfully dedicated to the cleanliness of the school, Mike. I'm glad we hired you."

"Thanks," he said. "Cleanliness next to godliness and all that."

"Next to godliness," Ronato said, smiling. "I like that."

He left Quinn to finish his shift, and the word godliness hung in the air, as heavy as the scent of the pine soap drying on the floor. Harlow had no churches. Not even empty ones. Rural towns typically had more churches than traffic lights or gas stations; a big Catholic Church and then a couple offshoots that looked like community centers instead of cathedrals—a Lutheran one here, a Methodist one there. In southern Illinois, he'd even seen a few Pentecostal ones to help complete the collection.

But not Harlow. Not one church. *Maybe one*, he thought, thinking of the mining tunnel. The digging. The explosions. An entire town sinking deeper with each passing day.

Quinn was ready to ride it all the way down to the fires of hell itself. He had survived fires before. Fire was home, and maybe a little brimstone was just the spark he needed.

On the drive home, Quinn noticed one of the nicer houses with its front porch completely removed. Work trucks surrounded the property line, and a concrete truck was backed up to the side of the house.

The foundation was failing, needing significant repair before the porch could be rebuilt. Mine subsidence, he thought. Fresh from visiting the darkness branching off from the school's boiler room, the subsidence was more obvious throughout the rest of town. Houses looked askew, one corner sinking deeper than the other. Subtle, but consistent with most homes in the center of Harlow.

The farmhouses on the hills at the edges of town likely didn't suffer from such issues.

Quinn was so wrapped up checking house foundations that he almost didn't notice Sarah bent over in her yard, inspecting the deck of her rusted-out riding mower. He pulled into his driveway, got out, and started walking to Sarah's house. He touched the griffin tattoo. He kept his tattoos concealed with the thermal sleeves he wore under his work shirt, but touching the griffin reminded him that he was here for justice, not to flirt with the sexy neighbor covered in grease and sweat.

"You're not cashing in on the whole favors-as-deposit thing," he said, startling her. She stood up, her face shining with sweat in defiance of the forty-nine-degree temperature.

"I said I'd ask for help lifting stuff, not fixing stuff," she said. "That's my department."

He believed her—her hands were dirty, and she didn't wear gloves.

"You want me to take a look?"

"Nah," she said. "Belt's cooked, and I was mowing more out of boredom anyway. Grass is about done for the year. Hard to believe it was eighty degrees just three days ago, but the heat is gone for good now, I think. How's the house?"

"House is fine," he said. "The people are peculiar. I know there's something to be said for not coming across as nosy, but people barely look at me."

"Now that's a lie," she said. "Wendell invited you to his table this morning."

"Word continues to travel fast around here," he said. "I bet that waitress wife of his would love to serve you a fork in a delicate place."

"Maybe so," Sarah said. "I wouldn't know. She accepts the reality of the situation."

"And what is that reality?"

"One I doubt you would accept or understand," she said.

"Let me ask you something, Sarah—is this thing consensual? Or are you letting a badge and a gun back you into a corner?"

"Let me ask you," she said. "Which answer would you be okay with?"

He said nothing.

"Because you don't care," she said. "Neither answer leads where you want it to."

"If it's a no, I can help you," he said. "I have no standing to lose around here. I can make him stop."

"And if it's a yes, if I care about him, that means the possibility of me fucking you is out of the question."

She turned around and peered at the deck of her mower again.

"You're wrong," he said. She ignored him. "Maybe I'll ask the Sheriff. See what he says."

"Is that why you're in Harlow?" she asked, tossing her wrench down in frustration. "To pick a fight? I hope it's that simple—that you're a violent, small-minded man. People need to figure out why you're here before they'll trust you. Some people think you're a dumb, harmless janitor. Others see the scars, the way you hide what are obviously tattoos, and wonder about you. Some of them wonder pretty loud."

"Where do you stand?"

"You said you had kids?"

He nodded.

"Don't bring them here," she said. "I'm scared for them."

"You have to tell me why."

"You first," she said. "Why Harlow?"

"I need the work," he said. "If I find a better job, I'm moving on."

"You're a liar," she said. "I said your kids would be in danger here, just to see a flash of primal fear in your eyes. Nothing. You don't have any kids."

Sarah wrenched her mower away, and he stood there, the darkness coming early, undeterred by shoving the clocks back for daylight savings, and only the crunch of gravel ended his drifting thoughts.

A police cruiser pulled up in the driveway. Sheriff Vance and Morgan Albers emerged, the Sheriff in full uniform and Morgan with a deputy's badge pinned to the strap of his overalls.

Vance had the coiled look of a cop in heat, his palm resting on the heel of his service weapon.

CHAPTER 12

A fter the run-in with Doug Albers, Beth wanted nothing more than to cancel her evening with Trent and sleep for about twenty hours. But the decision to run meant keeping up appearances, and there were worse things in the world to endure than getting a dose of Jessica Keller's delightful meatloaf.

When she saw the food, she was happy she'd kept the plans intact. After years of punching holes in cellophane to prepare dinner, a home-cooked meal took on the aura of a regal feast. The Kellers used actual plates. Bowls and trays of food adorned the table. The gravy container looked like a boat, and Beth was delighted to learn it was actually called a boat.

Trent's father, Chris, sat right across from her, cutting his meatloaf with a delicate patience. They all ate in relative silence, except for the clank of silverware. Jessica stopped eating twice to reload Chris's mashed potatoes and meatloaf. He never even asked for seconds. Beth chalked it up to the intimate telepathy that develops after twenty years of marriage.

When Chris was done, he placed his napkin on the plate and smiled at Beth. She took it as a cue to finish up so they could talk.

Jessica cleared the table and poured her husband a glass of red wine.

"You two have been together, what—almost a year?" Chris said.

Beth nodded.

"Time is relative, and that's an eternity to a teenager," he added. He leaned a little closer. "I don't dislike you, Beth."

The comment exhausted her more than it offended her—she wasn't even eighteen and already tired of juggling the opinions of men.

"Thank you, I guess." she said, smiling through the disgust, but leaving just enough in the tone of her voice.

Trent stared at the table, head down, deferring to his father, intent on letting a man push her around for the second time in one day.

"Context, Beth," Chris said. "You haven't experienced your first Harvest, and neither of you have taken the Oath."

"I don't know what that has to do with anything," she said. "I wish someone would tell me."

"Men want things," Chris said. "A wife. A family. My son wants those things with you. How do you feel about that?"

"Dad, come on," Trent said. Chris's glare withered him, and he spoke no more.

"Someday," Beth said.

"A fine answer," Chris said. "Trent's a good match for you. He has a little dash of defiance to him, although you wouldn't know it. Come to think of it, I think that's why you two get along."

"I know enough about my family to know what you're getting at," Beth said.

"And I know what happened today at school," Chris said. "I know what Doug Albers said to you. I also know that Morgan Albers is a pillar of the community, one of its hardest workers, from pipeline to deputy. A High Servant. I know him well."

Trent tried to hold her hand under the table. She yanked it away, but not to be cruel. She didn't want him to feel the tension of her fingers curling into his palm as a fist began to form.

"I know him well enough that I can call him and ask him to talk to his son—to deliver the message to young Doug that I truly believe Beth Jarvis can set right the legacy of her family. To tell him that Trent's relationship with you has my blessing."

Beth then realized what she was up against. Chris feared she was going to run, but more than that, he feared that Trent would go with her. Chris was offering safety in Harlow, with Trent, if she stayed.

"I need you to swear to me, Beth," Chris said. "Families put roots down and stick together, so promise me that Harlow is your home. Commit to those roots, make that your future, and Trent will have my blessing to be a part of it, and no one else will bother you."

Beth didn't answer.

"You'll be a scout," Chris said. "That's a good living in a good place. Look around you. Everyone seems pretty happy, no?"

Chris finished his wine, as if knocking back the last inch of the glass were a masculine statement. "If you don't have anything else to say nor a promise to give, you're both excused."

Beth got up from the table. Trent followed her.

"Don't leave," he whispered.

The disappointment radiated from her face with enough heat to bend her vision.

"I know, I know," he said. "I know you want to go home, but walk with me first?"

"Hey Mike," the Sheriff said, feigning a folksy tone, unable to contain the glee that leaked from every word. "I think we need to have us a little talk."

They approached. Morgan had his baton drawn and extended.

Right now, Quinn could have them. He could burst forth and close the gap before the Sheriff could pull his service weapon. Morgan was the big one. He could kick the fucker's fat-encrusted knee and have that baton wrested from him before he even hit the ground. The gun would be his. Four gunshots—a double-tap for each man—and both of them would be bleeding in the driveway, all in about six seconds.

But what then? He'd be done in Harlow. He'd have to leave the town and all its secrets, all because he shamefully relapsed, trying to play pretend with a version of himself that lacked the decisive quickness and brutality such murder would require.

"You two seem more hellbent on walking than talking," Quinn said.

"See, Sheriff?" Morgan said. "Told you he'd be a feisty one."

They crept closer. Morgan was itching for an excuse to swing the club. Vance was more composed, his hand relaxed on the butt of his pistol.

"I'll go quietly, and we'll have a talk," Quinn said. "I'll ride in the back. You won't get any blowback from me all the way to wherever you want to have us a fruitful discussion. But you're not cuffing me."

Morgan glanced at the Sheriff, just begging for the green light. Vance looked at Quinn and nodded in the direction of the police car.

Quinn headed for the cruiser, smoothing out any sudden movements or jerkiness from his gait. When he grabbed the handle of the back door, he heard the baton whistling through the air. He tried to duck, but didn't get down all the way, and it smashed him in the skull, dropping him to his knees. He recoiled, his balance disabled, as they shoved him down to cuff him. He could taste the dust in the gravel as they snapped the clasps shut.

Morgan dragged him to his knees, and he saw Sarah kissing Sheriff Vance, her palms on his cheeks. A deep kiss, the kind that makes a point. She opened her eyes in the middle of it and looked at Quinn. He spit out blood, and Morgan hit him again, this time in the trapezius, sending a bolt of pain down his arm.

The end of a long and legendary career would happen like this— his reflexes muddy, his mind dull, getting stuffed into a car by evil Andy Griffith and his fat sidekick in backwater USA.

Quinn felt the door slam shut and saw the Sheriff's confident, gum-chomping grin in the rearview mirror.

"Yes sir, you were right," the Sheriff said. "Maybe we're just making that shit up about Marcus Jarvis. I'll shake his hand and apologize myself—once you confess."

"To what?" Quinn muttered.

"You're the man who harbored Kate Jarvis."

Was that Kristina? Her real name, whispered not by her lips, but by this greasy cop? He tried to talk. The words came out thick and slow, but he wrapped his voice around them. Only one came out in full coherence: "Lawyer."

"Ain't no lawyers here, boy," Morgan said, laughing.

"No extradition," Vance added. "No tricks, no loopholes, no bullshit. No law but what the Mayor himself set down long ago. He and he alone will decide if your punishment is right and true."

The swelling in Quinn's head spread to his right eye. The trauma was impressive and complete, and he was afraid he might have a cranial fracture, causing blood to pool underneath the firm plate of his skull.

Maybe the fuse was lit on his imminent death—and maybe that was a blessing in disguise.

Harlow's residential streets were tar-and-chip roads with intersections that had yield signs hanging on wind-bent posts. Tears of rust streaked the reflective white bands. Everyone ignored them—two cars at an intersection was about as common as solstice. Beth and Trent walked along the shoulder of the road, and Beth kept her hands stuffed in her pockets, knowing that if she didn't, Trent would try to hold one of them, as he often did when they walked to the park.

Most towns established parks in or near the center—a big, green stamp in the concrete meshwork of city streets—but Harlow Village Park felt like an afterthought, built late and neglected ever since.

The park was shaded by oaks, their leaves stripped down by the bite of fall. The breeze rattled the swings, making the rusted chains groan. The basketball hoops leaned from wind and neglect, their rims netless, with rivulets of weeds entrenched in the cracks of the blacktop.

He took her to the bleachers by the baseball diamond. The outfield hadn't been mowed since Little League ended in early August. Faded signs from businesses long-since gone hung crookedly on the saggy chain-link fence in the outfield.

"Don't you wish we were kids again sometimes?" Trent said. "Running the bases the wrong way after hitting a tee-ball dribbler? Worried about nothing but what flavor snow cone we'd get from the concession stand?"

When she was in tee-ball, her mother and sister were alive. Her father laughed all the time and drove a crash-up derby car during SummerFest, and always won. Plus, she was the fastest kid on the team. Coach Parmalee had nicknamed her "Flash," and she adored having a nickname, a gimmick. She wondered what happened to him—he wasn't in Harlow anymore. She wasn't a kid any longer, and doubted very much her beloved coach was still alive. He was dead. Like her mother. Like her sister.

"Being kids again wouldn't save us," she said.

"Maybe I can," he said. "But not here. The thing is, Beth—I can't protect you if we stay in Harlow."

"No kidding?" she said. Her dismissive tone hit him hard. He looked away, through the links of the fence just behind home plate, likely wishing himself back into the dugouts on a hot day, far away from what he needed to tell her.

"The role of 'father' is a granted position in Harlow," he said. "If we stayed, hoping we could be together, we'd have to get permission from the Mayor to have children."

"How do you know?" Beth asked.

"And to get married, both fathers have to agree."

"Trent," Beth said, trying to recenter his attention. "How do you know all this?"

"I know more than my father thinks," Trent said. "He's playing along, trying to make sure we don't run. To protect me, more than anything. But I know that we can never be together in Harlow. Not the way I want us to be. Not ever."

"Because of my family," she said. "Right?"

"Your father is low," Trent said.

"Low?"

"The opposite of a High Servant. He was made low, and is to this day a low man. He's got no right or station here. So, he can't give permission for you to marry me. The only other option for us would be to try and stay together in secret. But without a husband, without permission—if you got pregnant, do you know what happens?"

"A death for a life," she said. "They'd make you choose between me and the child."

"Now it's my turn to ask. How did you know that?"

"An educated guess," she said. "Just seems like the way things would work around here."

"Your father is low. Your future is sealed. So is mine—because I love you."

A vacant swing swayed in the wind, the hinges crying out, its joints rusty. Beth turned away from him. "You don't love me. You may believe you do, but you don't. You're with me because I'm a Jarvis, and Jarvises always run."

"And you're with me because you don't want to run alone," Trent said. "Falling for you was self-destructive. My father's words. He was sure you'd try to run."

"I don't care to be a weapon you use to battle your daddy issues," she said.

"I didn't expect to love you, or to risk my life to try and be with you, but here we are."

He closed his eyes. His chin quivered as he tried his best to stomp away with urge to cry. Harlow was a town of cowards posing as tough and filthy men, but Trent was real and vulnerable.

She hugged him. "Here we are," she said.

They held each other. The streetlight in the park clicked on, casting them in a flickering yellow as it hummed over the wind. This time of year, the dark didn't stay away for long.

The Harlow City Hall was nothing more than a modular home set on a gravel lot. Sheriff Vance dragged Quinn inside and stuffed him into the unisex bathroom behind the administrative area.

The restroom was clean but small. Quinn looked in the mirror and saw a lump the size of a golf ball on the side of his head, pushing out the thinning hair that had turned even grayer since he came to Harlow.

To his surprise, he felt Vance working his wrists, and felt the cuffs fall away.

"Clean yourself up," he said, handing him a roll of paper towels. "Morgan, make up an ice pack."

As Morgan scurried away, Quinn caught the Sheriff's eye in the mirror.

"Don't go fuckin' around and wasting all this hospitality," Vance said. "Look presentable, is all I'm asking."

"I'd already look presentable if your man didn't club me for no good reason."

"You look like a somebitch who's done a lot of shit to a lot of people for no good reason," Vance said. "Look me in the eye and tell me you didn't deserve it."

Quinn reached down and turned on the faucet.

"That's what I thought," Vance said. "You got ten minutes."

Vance closed the door.

Quinn took a deep breath, trying to stem the tides of nauseating dizziness that rose with each throb of the lump on his head. He savored the cold water on his face.

He breathed. Three seconds in, hold four, exhale for a five-count. He wanted calmness, control. He wanted presence. Whatever happened, he needed to be clear and decisive. He needed to respond, not react.

He surveyed the damage from the club's blow. A knot, sure, but no broken skin, no bleeding. Soreness and a killer headache had arrived and would likely stay a few days, but his pupils were healthy and moved with the light. No concussion. No brain bleed. He had a thick skull and a strong neck, and it wasn't the first time they'd saved him from crippling damage.

The Sheriff knocked on the door, jolting him out of his meditation. He exited, taking careful pains to look off-kilter, to make them feel comfortable about his dampened ability to threaten them.

If it came to it, he'd kill them both. He'd take two lives—one for Scott Benoit, and one for Kristina, a girl known in Harlow as Kate Jarvis.

If you kill them, they win, he thought. *You might as well go home and open up the bottle. Get a nice drunk on. Remember how that used to feel? How long has it been? Kristina's not watching, remember? Gone is gone. You might as well complete the transformation. Then go knock on your old boss's door. Nico would be so, so happy to see you after all these years. That's as good a suicide as any.*

They ushered him into a dull conference room—beige walls, white tile, a cheap desk, a few chairs.

Vance pulled out one of the chairs at the head of the conference table. "Sit," he commanded. Morgan continued to hover behind the Sheriff, baton at the ready.

Quinn obeyed. But first, he took off his jacket and rolled up his sleeves. He wanted to unleash his scars and tattoos. He wanted them to see the hieroglyphics of his history.

"You're being a good little boy so far," Vance said. "Now, if I hear any sort of ruckus, if I have to come in here for any reason, you can count on having a bullet wound to clean up next."

He exited the office, leaving Quinn alone in the room. He looked around. No two-way mirrors. No cameras or other remote surveillance devices. He rested his hands on the table—a fake walnut surface, slick, smelling faintly of lemon furniture polish.

Eventually, the door opened. Ben Cartwright entered the room. He sat at the opposite end of the table.

"Hello, amigo," he said.

CHAPTER 13

As Cartwright sat down, he studied Quinn's face during a long, cool silence. Finally, he spoke: "I thought you said if you saw me again, you wouldn't hesitate."

Play dumb, Quinn thought. *He's never seen your face.* Would it matter? Cartwright could easily that he was every bit of six-foot-seven, and the moment Quinn spoke, he would have trouble masking the recognizable baritone of his voice—and Harlow didn't seem like the kind of town that cared about things such as evidence or due process.

Still, he tried. "I don't know what the fuck you're talking about, old man," Quinn said.

"There's my little stick-up artist," Cartwright said. He stood up. The interrogation was already over.

"That's all you came to say?" Quinn asked.

"I didn't come to say jack shit," Cartwright said. "I came to see you with my own two eyes—and to hear your voice. You're the one. Not the cop."

The cop—Scott Benoit. Kristina was dead. Even when she was alive, she was Kate Jarvis, and belonged to Harlow. Maybe she was never his to lose, but it didn't matter anymore. Gone was gone. But maybe Benoit wasn't gone. Maybe he could square up the ledger with an old friend.

"Did you kill him?" Quinn asked. No use keeping up the ruse. From one professional to another, all he could do was tip his cap and skip right to the point.

"I bet he wishes we had by now."

Quinn twitched, but caught himself. He breathed away his quickening pulse.

"The facade continues to crumble," Cartwright said. "You know, for a while there, I thought it was Detective Benoit that Kate had shacked up with. Good on you for keeping me twisted up on this so long."

Quinn stood up—a long, slow unraveling of his massive frame.

"You haven't been twisted yet," Quinn said.

"I can tell it's been a while since you lit up that mean streak of yours," Cartwright said. "It's like clothes that don't fit anymore. Best sit down before you make a mistake you'll regret."

Quinn didn't sit, instead resting his hands on the table, palms down, turning his forearms into veined pillars.

"Your friend confesses once a day now," Cartwright said. "Every time we go down there, he's begging us to believe him. Says he was working for a man named Curtis Quinn."

Cartwright placed his own hands on the table, leaning forward, doing his best to offer the temptation of his frail, elderly jaw. Quinn figured him for sixty-five years old or so, with a body that had deteriorated far quicker than his mind—a shining scalp pocked with liver spots, loose flesh dangling underneath his chin, deep creases in his forehead and around his eyes. A face like a baseball mitt left outside all summer.

"I did a little digging on that Mr. Quinn," Cartwright continued. "Nasty fella. Turns out he had a boss of his own—Nico Coletti. Mr. Quinn stuffed a lot of body bags for his employer, carved out a bit of a legend for himself. Nico didn't like that, did he? People more scared of his henchman than himself? However you slipped him, I bet you got those burns on the way out."

Quinn felt like he could push all the way through the table. He wanted to shatter the fake wood, then pick up a sharp piece and shove it right into Cartwright's guts. The fantasy was so intense, he could sense the familiar heat and acrid stench that always came out of abdominal wounds. He fought the craving.

"You're a killer," Cartwright said. "And the wicked get punished around here, Mr. Quinn."

The dam was about to burst. Quinn visualized it, how he'd dive over the table and smash the gloating P.I.'s face into the back of his skull. No use questioning him about Benoit. The man would never talk. Better to kill the real threat and take his chances with the Sheriff and his redneck deputies.

Then the look on Cartwright's face changed, hardening with shock. He leaned away from the table, his eyes wide and unblinking, his mouth agape.

A knock came at the door. "Everything copacetic in there?" the Sheriff hollered.

"Roll down your sleeves and put your jacket on," Cartwright whispered. Another knock. "The griffin tattoo," Cartwright continued. "Cover it. Sleeves down, jacket on, and don't take it off."

Quinn had no reason to suspect Cartwright's sudden reaction wasn't genuine, and didn't have time to figure out the possible motives, so he snatched his jacket off of the back of the chair and hoisted it on.

"We're done in here," Cartwright yelled, never taking his eyes off of Quinn. The Sheriff entered. Morgan loomed behind him, wild-eyed, hungry for brutality. Both had their batons extended.

"Let him go," Cartwright said.

"What the fuck is this, Ben?" Vance asked. "Let him go? You serious?"

"It's not him," Cartwright said. "You dragged him in here for nothing."

"That's on you then, you dumb somebitch," Morgan said. "Some Ranger you are."

"Maybe," Cartwright said. "I made a mistake. It's not him."

Vance slammed his baton shut and clipped it back into his belt. "You sure?"

Cartwright nodded.

"I have to send word to Ortega," Vance said.

"So be it," Cartwright said.

"Wait here." The Sheriff left, and Morgan followed.

"Keep up appearances," Cartwright said. "You're Mike Silver, janitor. Nothing more, nothing less. Do that, and you'll survive the night."

"What's with the sudden change of heart?" Quinn asked.

"I told you I wasn't used to mercy," Cartwright said. "I'm paying you back. Don't waste it. Just remember—Mike Silver. No matter how deep Ortega digs, no matter how much he seems to know. Got it?"

"Who in the actual fuck is Ortega?"

"He's the right hand of the Mayor, and he's dangerous. More dangerous than even a man like you can imagine."

"Convince me."

"If I told you everything there is to know about Ortega, about Ronato, about the Mayor—you'd think I was insane."

"It's insane that my tattoo spooked you."

"I wasn't spooked. I just never thought I'd live to see him, let alone meet him."

"Who?"

"The Griffin," Cartwright said. "Show no one that tattoo. Not until you know what it means around here."

"Give me the short version."

"Hope is the short version," Cartwright said. "She marked you."

"Kristina," Quinn said, then corrected himself, adding, "Kate Jarvis. Who killed her?"

"It all comes back to the Mayor, one way or another," Cartwright said. "Everything around here does."

"Then I can't wait to meet him," Quinn said.

"You won't get your chance unless you survive Ortega. He's going to test you. The Mayor trusts me, but Ortega doesn't."

Quinn scrutinized Cartwright's every tic, every gesture, every flicker of his eyes, looking for signs of lying, finding none.

The door opened. The Sheriff walked in and slammed a laminated card on the table. "That'll get you into the Legion," he said. "Ortega says if Ben here has you cleared, you're not being questioned anymore. You're an innocent man. Still, he insists you join him for a drink."

He pushed it across the table. Quinn picked up the card. It said *Guest Pass*, with a Legion Auxiliary star emblazoned in the center.

"Right now, in fact," Vance added. "I'll take you right over."

Quinn tapped the card on the table. The yellow paper stock was creased in the corners where the laminate was coming apart.

"Finally, a chance to get a beer around here," he said.

When Quinn had walked into city hall, he didn't think he'd be leaving as a free or a living man, yet here he was, following Sheriff Vance out of custody and into the clear, dark night.

The good luck of bad men, he thought. He used to joke with Kristina—*Kate, damn it*—that the good luck of bad men is what kept him alive, what caused her to love him. And here he was, still alive, and she was dead. Luck was a lot like love, though—you see what you want to see, and nothing else.

He rode in the back seat of the police cruiser, headed for the Legion and a meeting with Ortega, another chance to see just how far his good fortune could stretch before it finally broke.

After dinner with the Kellers, Beth had one more scouting shift before she got the birthday break that Galen had promised her.

The first order of business, as it was most evenings, was to set out the stop sticks.

They planted the spiked strips close to the eastern edge of the cut-down cornfield, about two hundred yards away from where they'd set them down the night before, always varying the placement.

After that, they walked the tree line. Winter was looming, and they had to make sure that the hidden coils of razor wire were sharp, tight, and uninterrupted.

"In the spring, we get a garden sprayer, hit them with a silicone solution," Galen said. "It prevents rust and keeps the bite sharp. We haven't had to replace much. At least not since I've been around."

Beth followed him, their flashlight beams moving in a constant rhythm.

After they'd knocked out a half mile of tree line inspection, they came across an area thinned of razor wire.

"Bingo," Galen said. They crept closer. The trunk of a young oak had digested most of the wire as it grew. Rust grew around the wire poking out of the tree. Galen waded closer and took out his multi-tool, grasping the wire with the jaws of his pliers. With one tug, the wire snapped.

"Well, this won't do," Galen said. "Not at all."

They walked back to the truck, flashlights off, conserving the charge. A roll of razor wire was in the back of the Ford, along with work gloves that went up past the elbow, specifically made for handling the wire safely. Galen had wire cutters and pliers, along with metal twists so he could braid the wire into the existing border.

They cut across the field onto the blacktop, wanting to take easier terrain to make the long walk back to the truck.

"You still wanting to run away?" Galen asked.

The road soaked up the clop of their boots, the tar softened by the full sun of an otherwise cool day. Beth didn't answer.

"Look, you do what you gotta do," Galen said. "But if you stay and I got a say in it, which I do, you ain't gonna be no coiner like your daddy."

Beth unpacked that sentence in silence. She felt her father's silver dollar in the front pocket of her jeans, its ancient edges digging into her hip flexor with each step.

"Low men get coins," Beth said. "Silver dollars."

"Your old man finally coughing up some information?" Galen

said. "I don't blame him. Shut your ass up, and all. With all the questions you're like a baby bird, maw open, always hungry." He tried to bury it with humor, but Beth wouldn't let it go.

"I know he's low, but I can't figure out what the coin means. The word 'trust' is spelled wrong, but other than that, it's just a coin."

"The coin is a low man's life," Galen said. "Produce it at Harvest, you live another year. If you lose it, you die."

"That's pointless," Beth said. Yet her father's coin was in her pocket. If what Galen said was true, Marcus had sentenced himself to death for that secret coin.

"Did your daddy give you his coin?" Galen said. "Is that what this is?"

"I just want to understand."

"You'll change your mind once you do," he said.

Galen had a way of killing conversations with a sliver of a joke, and then a crushing boulder of silence. Beth had no choice but to absorb it, thinking through it all as they got to the truck.

Beth was ready to let it go—she knew pressing Galen was pointless. Then, Galen hesitated before opening the tailgate. "I think we need to take ten," he said, and trudged to the driver's side door, hoisting himself inside. Beth slid into the other side of the cab, and Galen tweaked the radio.

The volume was so low it was little more than white noise, but Beth caught the twang and rhythm of a country song, sensing the timbre of a deep voice without being able to make out the words. Galen tapped the steering wheel with all his fingers, matching the beat. Eventually, it sounded like a maddening war drum, blotting out the faint music.

"Those coins are the most valuable currency in Harlow," Galen said. "If you bring one to Harvest, you'll curry favor with the Mayor. But the only way to get one is by taking it from the low servants. You're not allowed to kill them for it, and you can't invade their property—but you can hurt them. You see them in the street, you beat them, you take it. If they don't carry it, that's an executable offense."

Another form of complicated torture—ostracized within Harlow's borders. Yet her father had left the house, time and time again, and Beth never detected any danger. No one tried to assault him and take the coin. She used to think it was because her father was cold and antisocial, but now she understood.

"Your daddy's lost it twice before—and both those men paid the price," Galen said. "That Marcus Jarvis is one cold-blooded motherfucker, let me tell you. Hell, you were shitting your OshKoshes when all that went down."

A new image of her father was forming, ripping away the scabs of that old coward she thought she knew. "Harlow made him the way he is," she said. "The Mayor. The fucking Mayor and his stupid coins and whips and ceremonies." She stared out the window, refusing to let Galen see the shine of tears pooling in her eyes, but the sorrow sounded off in her breath.

"Beth," Galen said, drawing it out with that country tone, slathering the reassurance onto each syllable, "people hate your family because they have to, but your name means something. Even the Mayor can't change that or kill that."

Beth turned to him, fat droplets forming in her eyes. She slung them away with a hard shake of her head, casting them onto the dashboard, refusing them.

Galen leaned over, putting his arm around her. Beth took it further and hugged him, hard, and with her face smashed into the dusty leather of Galen's jacket, she let it all go—all the fear, the love, the pain, the doubt. The lack of sleep had stripped her down to bare wire. She was up past midnight yet again, another maddening day fueled by three hours of nightmare-addled sleep looming before her, all part of the testing grounds she had to endure before Harvest.

"I did wrong by the Mayor, once," Galen said. "I ain't no real scout. I ain't built for this. I ain't built for what I got to do." He seemed to be battling with himself, smashing through the inner voice that was urging him not to say another word.

"I'm supposed to lure you into running," he admitted. "I'm supposed to earn your trust and then let you see where to slip through the cracks, to tell you how to do it. Build your confidence up. Make sure you make the move that everyone thinks you're going to make. That's why you're a scout. Hell, that's why *I'm* a scout."

He smoothed his sweaty hair back. He took a loud, long breath, and then turned on the dome light.

"A trap," she said.

"Not for you, understand?" he said. "For your family's name. To keep it meaning what it means."

"What if I don't run?" Beth asked.

"Then I failed at the job that spared me my life, and I've seen enough Harvests to know that failing the Mayor will be the last thing I ever do."

Beth could see him in the dashboard lights, his face vivid and intense. "But you're gonna run. You hear? I'll make sure you slip out clean."

"They'll kill you if I escape," she said.

"They'll kill me if you don't try," he said. "But you promise me something, Beth. There's good people here. Come back and fight one day, and you may be surprised just how many folks would gladly lend a hand. Get help if you need it, but you come back here and you break that son of a bitch, you understand me?"

"The Griffin," Beth said. Kate had left to bring the Griffin back. She failed.

Jarvises ran. Jarvises were traitors. They always failed. That was one thing she could change if she got away.

"The Griffin," he echoed. "Now that would be a hell of a thing."

Galen held out his hand. "This here's a Harlow contract if there ever was one," he said. "You shake my hand, I'll get you out. But if you get out, you come back. I don't intend on dying for nothin'."

Beth shook his hand.

"Now listen to me close, do as I say, and don't make me repeat myself," Galen said.

The American Legion sat on a corner lot at the edge of Harlow. The windows were completely covered in plywood and two-by-fours, as if the building were prepped for some massive storm that never came.

Quinn got out of the police cruiser, walking by what looked like an old fueling island. The pumps had been yanked out long ago, leaving square scars in the concrete. A muted *pop* sounded in the distance, and Quinn flinched. Another explosion at one of the dig sites he had yet to investigate.

The cruiser idled, waiting for him to enter. The Legion's door had a silver keycard slot. He punched in the guest pass, and the slot swallowed half the card. When he pulled it out, the barcode did its job, and the doorknob gave off an audible click.

Quinn stepped inside as the cruiser zoomed off. The smell of booze and body odor was overwhelming. The customer area of the old gas station had been converted into a makeshift bar—the countertop had crude beer taps that poked out of sloppy holes cut in the Formica. An old man stood behind the bar, looking annoyed that he had another customer to serve.

Not that the place was crowded. A chunky farmer sat at one of the stools near the bar. Another man sat in a booth by the boarded windows. He wore a dress shirt with his sleeves rolled up, his forearms thick and muscular. His meaty biceps were sliced in half by the border of a farmer's tan. Three shots of whiskey rested next to his left hand as he read a newspaper.

Ortega. He was a tall man, that much was clear even when he was sitting, and he had the olive skin shared by only one other man in town—Ronato. Brothers, perhaps.

Quinn walked up to the countertop—he couldn't quite bring himself to call it a bar. The old man had a mix of gray and black hair, sticky with sweat, matted against his forehead. Quinn could tell that the guy wiped his brow left to right by the way the hair laid in that direction.

"Who the fuck is this?" the old man asked, looking past Quinn to Ortega.

"Easy, Rich," Ortega said. "He doesn't mean you any harm. That right, Mr. Silver?"

Ortega was neatly folding the paper back into its original shape, preparing the booth for a guest.

"Hope you like Budweiser," Rich said. "It's all we've got."

"You got Coke instead?" Quinn said, taking out his wallet. Rich stared at him.

"The members here don't pay for drinks," Ortega said. "Have all the Coke you can drink, my friend."

"I'm not your fucking friend," Quinn said. "I don't know who you are, but the Sheriff seems to answer to you, so you want to answer for this knot on the side of my head?"

"Nothing a little Tylenol can't fix," Ortega said.

Quinn took a deep breath. He could taste the anger rising like bile, acidic and involuntary. At least it was somewhat useful right now—confused, innocent Mike Silver would definitely have some real anger. He tried chasing away his headache with the sugary kick of Coke as he sat down across from Ortega.

"So, Mike, did you aspire to the heights of the custodial profession your whole life?" Ortega said.

"I was just looking for work," Quinn said. "I can look somewhere else, though. Somewhere where the new guys don't get thumped in the fucking head."

Ortega knocked back one of his whiskeys. "We can play that game if you like," Ortega said. "Too many times, people think what we do is what we really are, but we do these things—mopping, pouring drinks, digging holes—in the view of other people. But when no one's looking? That's when we can be ourselves."

"Well, at least you're not the world's only non-philosophical drunk," Quinn said.

"Finally, some interesting company," Ortega said. "You know, Mike, I appreciate what you're trying to do. The small talk and all. So stay, and keep it up a while. Let's have our laughs and our drinks while we can."

Quinn heard the click and snap of the door opening, and this time, Marcus Jarvis entered.

"Hell, we're going extra low tonight!" the farmer in the corner exclaimed. When Marcus was within range, the farmer shoved his shoulder. Marcus braced himself enough not to stumble, then steadied himself and kept walking.

"None of that juvenile shit tonight!" Ortega shouted. "We have a guest. Let's not have him thinking Harlow is full of heathens."

Marcus walked behind the bar, never once making eye contact. Old Rich handed him a towel, signed a logbook, and left the bar. Marcus wasn't there for a drink; this was a shift change.

"Do you know that man?" Ortega asked.

"No," Quinn said.

"You lie," Ortega said. "The Sheriff told you who he was and what he'd done."

"Knowing a name and knowing a man are two different things, and I don't give a fuck what that asshole Sheriff says. I been around enough awful people in my life to know that Jarvis fellow didn't do a damn thing to his daughter."

"I know," Ortega said. "I was there. I was the first to greet Kate when we brought her back to Harlow. We called it the Homecoming."

So here it was. Ortega was laying the bait down, giving him a taste of the truth. The tale of Kate's death would enrage Curtis Quinn, but Mike Silver, janitor, would get scared and want to go home. The thing was, Mike Silver, janitor, didn't look scared—he looked pissed.

"You can go home if you like, janitor," Ortega said. "And if you like, Mr. Silver, you can pack your bags and leave town with a month of severance pay in your pocket. Pick it up from Mr. Ronato in the morning on your way out. Or," he said, drinking a shot to give that offer enough time to settle in, "you can keep your job, Mr.

Curtis Quinn. You can continue the ruse and stick around until we have our big harvest celebration. I think I'll see you there, because I know you don't care about your janitorial paycheck, just like you know that I'm not another barfly laborer in another small town."

Ortega took the final shot of whiskey. "You can go now," he said. "I'll see you soon."

"What makes you so fucking sure?" Quinn said.

"Because you won't leave Harlow until you know the truth. All of it," Ortega said. "Even if it kills you."

Quinn left the Legion, and with no car, he was in for a long, cold walk back to his house. That is, if he was intent on staying a step behind the string-pullers in Harlow, like Sheriff Vance, Ortega, and Superintendent Ronato. He needed information more than sleep.

He spotted a Ford F-150 that wasn't there when Vance dropped him off. The door was unlocked. *Score one for small-town America,* Quinn thought as he rooted through the glove box. He found the registration with Marcus's address—506 Dollar Street. The street name sounded familiar, and the cross-street wasn't far from his own house.

Quinn started walking, sticking to the darkest side of the roads, where the street lights were the weakest. He planned to bail into the darkness if he saw any headlights, but the entire walk was traffic-free. The town didn't just sleep at night—it died.

The intersection of Dollar and Vine streets was exactly where he remembered. Time had atrophied some of his muscle and his instincts, had settled into some of his joints and dulled his eyesight, but it had yet to erode his memory, at least.

Marcus's house was a squat, symmetrical modular home at the end Dollar Street's cul-de-sac. The back doorsteps were the stand-alone kind you buy in hardware stores, anchored by cinder blocks. Wet blades of overgrown grass licked his ankles, and would likely be frosted by morning. He moved toward the back of a rickety tin shed. A motion light ticked on, flooding the backyard in white light. He crouched behind the shed wall and peeked around, trying to detect movement in the house. If Beth wasn't home, he had already decided he was going in to have a look.

As he surveyed the yard, he noticed something curious below the oak—two slabs of rock sticking out of the ground. Gravestones, he was sure of it. The motion light switched off. Quinn made a soft, creeping run for the tree, the fallen oak leaves crunching underfoot. The movement refreshed the motion light, but any number of innocent things could kick on a motion light in southern Illinois, especially near a cornfield, where deer and coyotes might be making their evening rounds.

He knelt by the trunk of the oak, cocooned in its shadowy embrace. The headstones were thin chunks of rough-cut granite. The floodlight allowed him to read them clearly, the faint letters etched by hand:

CHRISTINA M. JARVIS
1945 – 1989

KATELIN M. JARVIS
1979 – 1999

No sappy words of remembrance. Quinn liked the elegant simplicity. Kate's life defied the simplicity and summary of an epitaph.

He placed his hand on Kate's gravestone. *Not a grave*, he thought. *A monument.* Her body was in the dirt of a potter's field.

Throughout all the time they were together, for each alias she had to take, she'd pick some form of Christina as her first or middle name. He'd assumed it was her real first name, at least, but he'd been wrong; she had taken the name of her mother.

He knelt by her monument until his kneecaps were soaked with dew. The floodlight was long dead behind him.

He felt the curve of her name against his palm, a secret Braille that woke up a thousand memories, each of them blotting out the savagery inside of him that craved to unleash itself.

If only he could ask her permission—but this was just a rock. Gone was gone.

He let his hand slide off of the monument and read her name, her true name, one more time. Then, he went inside and waited for Marcus, her father—a father who had failed her.

...

Quinn sat in the dark at Marcus's kitchen table, waiting for him. Marcus returned at two-thirty in the morning, and when he turned on the kitchen light, he showed no surprise. No fear. Quinn didn't like that.

"Coffee?" Marcus asked.

Quinn nodded. He watched Marcus work the coffeemaker, reaching behind it, coming away with a hidden .38.

He turned, aimed, and squeezed off three rounds before he realized the gun was empty.

Quinn opened his fist, and the bullets rolled across the table.

"This ain't my first rodeo," he said. Marcus had already surprised him. No threats, no negotiating. No hesitation. He'd squeezed the trigger, intent on killing him. In Harlow, he always felt behind the learning curve—a problem he aimed to fix.

"Make the coffee," Quinn said. Marcus got to work.

"It's two-thirty in the morning, and your teenage daughter isn't home."

"She's working."

"She's got school in a few hours."

"I thought you were a janitor, not a truancy officer," Marcus said. "That what you came for? To look in on Beth?"

"I've had a long night," Quinn said. "I'm gonna lay down how I figure it, and you're gonna fill in the blanks."

"What makes you think I have any interest in helping you?"

"I'm your son-in-law," Quinn said. "I figure it's a courtesy among family."

"Kate wasn't dumb enough to get married."

"Our relationship didn't require government intervention," Quinn said.

The coffee brewed. Marcus stood at the counter and waited.

"Ten years back, Kate skips town," Quinn said. "She's running from something, so she latches on to me. Not because of my dashing good looks, either—I don't try to *not* look like the baddest motherfucker in the room. That's what she needed, and the only thing we had in common was a need to run away, to stay on the move. Necessity turned into affection, which turned into love."

"Love?" Marcus knew he was pressing a hot button. He pressed it anyway.

"For me, at least," Quinn said. "She said she loved me. I believed it, and I'm good at spotting liars. Used to be, anyway." He shrugged, then continued. "Ortega runs this place with his brother, Ronato. One of them is the Mayor of Harlow. They don't like when people leave Harlow. Why? No idea, but they don't. So when someone gets away, they send the slick P.I., Ben Cartwright, on the trail. They call him the Ranger. He's the one who ends up cracking Kate's location. They jump her, bring her back here. If they buried her body in a cornfield, that would be the end of it. But they don't. They mutilate her. Cut off her hands—no prints. Take out her teeth—no dental records. They throw her in a ditch. A taunt. A dare. She's a Jane Doe. No one claims the body, even though a town with six hundred people knows her picture on the television. No one, including her own father."

Quinn thought he'd found his own hot button, but saw no tightness in Marcus's face. Not a trace of anger or regret. A man who was dead inside, or had crafted a perfect mask.

"She's bait," Quinn said. "Bait for me. They want to know who she's been running with. Who's been protecting her. They're looking for me, but I stay one step removed. They get Scott Benoit instead—the cop. Then I circle around and find Harlow, instead of the other way around."

"The only thing that can save your friend is death," Marcus said.

"A guy like me never truly has friends," Quinn said. "But I've got questions. They keep stacking up, ever since I got here. Shit blowing up in the distance for no reason, remodeled houses tilting from mine subsidence, people acting the exact opposite way I expect small-town assholes to act. Those are the little things. But you've been turned into the scourge of the town. The Sheriff and Cartwright were gonna execute me tonight until Cartwright saw my griffin tattoo. The Legion is a converted gas station where an oversized Mexican holds court."

"I don't hear a question in there," Marcus said. The coffee was done. He poured.

"I'll start with this one—why would you shoot me, but not the men who killed your daughter?"

He passed along Quinn's mug. "I killed Kate," he said. He gestured to the chair across from Quinn, asking permission to sit.

Quinn nodded.

"Now that I've admitted guilt, take your vengeance on me, and leave Harlow. That's what you came for, isn't it?"

"I've been toyed with enough tonight," Quinn said. "When people toy with you, it's either because they're stupid, or because they have you right where they want you."

"They don't have you where they want you," Marcus said. "Not yet, anyway. They want you to be someone you're not—*something* you're not."

"The Griffin," Quinn said.

He thought of Kate tracing the flesh on the inside of his forearm. *Tattoos*, she'd said. *We don't need wedding rings. You can take them off. But griffins—a griffin remains loyal for life, even after the death of his mate.*

Quinn turned his arm, showing Marcus the tattoo.

"That's why I pulled the trigger," Marcus said. "To kill you and bury you in a cornfield is to keep the Griffin alive, but if you let them make you the Griffin and execute you in public? You can't let that happen. That's why Kate changed her mind. She marked you as a savior, then kept you away. The Griffin is invulnerable if it doesn't truly exist."

Marcus leaned across the table. "Harlow is a town of superstitions and legends, filled with things you wouldn't understand or believe. If you go, they'll let you leave. You're of no use to them if you refuse to fight."

"Maybe it's high time someone fought around here," Quinn said.

"With what? You think punches and bullets and a mean streak are worth anything around here? If you fight, you'll fail. She marked you, but didn't send you because she knew you'd fail. So if you want to honor Kate, you'll leave, and you won't look back."

Quinn didn't understand Harlow, and you couldn't fight or defeat what you didn't understand. Once, a gap in knowledge got him scarred and almost killed. He knew Nico had grown jealous of his reputation. He ignored his gut, ignored the knowledge gap. To do that again would be suicide. Death he could handle, but failure? Failing Kate?

He couldn't stay in Harlow, not without being *that guy*. She didn't want that for him. He'd violate Kate's wishes in more ways than one. He had to leave. He had to let it all go.

"I'll go," Quinn said. "But first, you have to tell me…what did they do to her?"

"Never," Marcus said. "Whatever self-control you think you have would crumble if you knew the whole truth. I killed her with my own hand. That is all the truth you need to know."

"A mercy," Quinn whispered.

Marcus broke eye contact, looking down at his hands. He made a fist, then released it. Quinn saw a diagonal scar across his palm.

"My duty," Marcus said. "My punishment."

CHAPTER 14

D espite the lack of sleep from her scouting shift, Beth
stayed awake in classes, even if she was constantly distracted by fantasies of a life outside of Harlow.

She'd find a small apartment in a big city. She'd throw herself
into learning something complicated at a modest college, something like engineering or biology. She'd wait tables and live broke,
but she'd walk the streets late at night just to see how a real place
never went dormant, that she was a cell in a living, thriving organ-
ism that didn't have the cancer of Harlow's dark mysteries and
oppressive traditions.

And yet, the voice in her head began, over and over again, rebuk-
ing her thoughts at every turn.

You'll live in fear.

I already do.

You'll be stuck with Trent.

Maybe. We can't tell how we feel until we're somewhere else.

You'll leave your father behind to die alone.

That one gave her pause—the real barrier to running. She
wasn't just running away from Harlow anymore. She was running

away from her family and the good people that remained trapped. People like Galen, giving off the appearance of subjugation, toiling away in misery and constant danger.

The Jarvises had a legacy—secrets of Harlow no one else knew, the truth behind the myth of the Griffin. Kate had run away to try and fulfill the Jarvis legacy, to turn myths into realities, but Beth was just running away from all of it, legacy included.

Her family's reputation didn't sway her decision to run—but it might. She was clear and decisive and had a few days off for her birthday, so she wouldn't be caught late on her shifts. If she was going to run, sooner was better.

The school day ended, and she began stuffing her books in her locker, waiting for Trent. She would tell him during their walk home. As she waited, she noticed the janitor mopping along, sporting bags under his eyes and a massive lump on the side of his head. He looked at her, and she nodded hello. He looked away.

She spotted Trent, carefully sidestepping the freshly mopped areas as he navigated the hallway. He kissed her cheek when he reached her.

"Tonight," she whispered.

They walked home together, and she told him the plan. She mentioned nothing of her promise to Galen, or his role in leaving her a gap to escape. Trent would believe she could create a gap like that herself, since she was a scout.

"My brilliant girlfriend," he said.

"How ready are you?" she said.

"I'm ready," he said. "But I hope Plan A works."

Plan A was of her own design. Leave in the early evening, sign out at an outpost for an ice cream date, and never return. Galen had nothing to do with that one, but it was too simple and risk-free to not try. She chalked it up to him not being able to see the forest for the trees. Harlow could narrow one's view of the world.

"We'll take your Jeep," she said.

Plan B was equally simple, yet far more dangerous. Go at night.

Dodge the stop stick drops, take the Jeep across the field to the gap in the fencing. Arrange loose brush over the Jeep to make it hard to spot and slip through the fencing to freedom.

Harlow was rural and had plenty of other border opportunities, but she didn't know what scouts worked them, what traps were set, or how they were surveyed, if at all. Fear was always Harlow's most effective fencing material.

"I'll pick you up at five," Trent said.

"It's a date," she said, smiling, winking at him. Now was the time to flirt, to seal the deal. More than ever, she didn't want to run alone. Perhaps she couldn't run alone. To cross that fence line, she needed a hand to hold.

Beth hurried home, expecting to see her father. Escaping in secret wasn't the kind of trip you packed a suitcase for, so all Beth had left to do was say goodbye.

Marcus was standing in the kitchen, watching a frozen lasagna spin in the microwave. He looked as tired as Mr. Silver. She knew he'd had a shift at the Legion, but it had never affected him in the past. She couldn't allow pity for him to sway her. Marcus Jarvis had cast his lot in life.

"We need to talk," Beth said.

"I work the Legion again tonight," Marcus said. "You got until the microwave beeps, then I have to wolf down some food and get the hell out of here."

"I'm leaving tonight," Beth said.

"I thought you knew better," Marcus said, still hypnotized by the spinning lasagna.

"I'm trying to tell you goodbye, Dad."

"It's gonna be the wrong kind of goodbye," Marcus answered.

"Don't worry," she said. "I've got a plan."

"What is this brilliant plan of yours?"

"I can't say. I don't want you trying to stop me."

"Galen give you the lay of the land?"

Beth said nothing.

"I'd lie and say you can't trust him—but you can. He's old Harlow, and no friend of the Mayor. Known him a long time, but I have to say, I ain't talked to him in a good stretch. Not since they made him a night owl. You have to be careful, all the same. Maybe you'll make it out, but that boyfriend of yours is going to miss you."

"No, he won't."

Marcus finally stepped away from the microwave. They stood near the dining room table, face to face.

"Can you trust him?"

"With my life," she said. *It's his father I'm worried about.* She thought better of mentioning Chris Keller out loud.

"Then that's what you'll give," he said, and returned to his lasagna.

Beth felt for the coin in the pocket of her jeans. She put it on the kitchen table, making sure the edge snapped against the laminate wood.

The coin rested face-up, with the misspelled *trust* etched in silver.

"Take it with you," Marcus said.

"I know what this coin means now," Beth said. "No thanks to you. I won't have your death on my conscience."

"You fucking take it," Marcus said. "If you leave it here, I swear I'll toss it into the cornfield."

"That's your choice," Beth said.

"You think there's some great life out there for you?" Marcus said. "A life on the run is no life, Beth."

"You call this a life?"

"I've loved," he said. "I've had children. I've enjoyed happiness and nights where I can sleep without nightmares. A better life than most, and that includes many folks who live outside these borders."

"Sometimes I think you're the bravest man I know," Beth said. "Staying here isn't easy. But you know what? Maybe I'm giving you too much credit. Maybe you're a coward."

"You'll believe I'm a coward until the day that you don't," Marcus said. "You don't intend on being around here to see it. So go."

"That's your idea of goodbye?"

"I've lived in Harlow my entire life," Marcus said. "I heard the same shit from your mom, and your sister, and now you. I saw them go and saw them brought back. I know how the Mayor operates, and I don't believe for one second I'm seeing you for the last time." Marcus reached out and scooped up the coin. He held it out to Beth, pinching the edge, offering it to her. The coin quivered as Marcus's hand shook, the silver catching the fluorescent kitchen lights. "Goodbye, and I mean it," he said, his voice wobbling. "I hope above all hope that I never see you again."

Her father, as he usually did, had the last word. Beth lingered, searching her mind for fitting last words, finding nothing.

Beth took the coin, and then she was gone.

Quinn had returned home from Marcus's house at three-thirty in the morning. By then, the headache was thunderous, and his feet ached from walking all over town.

He took four ibuprofen and chased the pills with two bottles of water, then took a hot shower. By the time he was done, he was due at work in less than two hours. If he called in sick or didn't show up, he'd raise suspicion. Even if Ortega and the men who ruled Harlow intended to let him leave, Quinn still wanted a lengthy head start before they noticed he was gone.

That meant business as usual, and that started with a pre-dawn breakfast at the diner.

He ate his omelet with ravenous intent. The carbs from the hash browns dulled his headache, and he felt almost normal. Exhaustion didn't set in until the afternoon. Still, he pushed through.

When the day was over, he sat in his car, wondering if he'd stay awake for the three-minute drive back to his house. Stalk dust floated in the air, the fallout of harvest season, covering his windshield in a brown film. He ran his wipers with a few squirts of washer fluid.

In the distance, he saw a dip in the tree line. Illinois was famously flat, but Harlow's topography was one of hills and bottoms that were always covered with an old, black film from the flooding of the Kaskaskia River, which snaked around the southern border of the town.

The dip wasn't uncommon, but he kept thinking of the mineshaft that connected to the school's boiler room. The true entrance to that mine was out in those woods somewhere. The gym was new, an add-on to the old school. Someone built it despite of the old mines, letting the boiler room tap right into one of the main tunnels. Why?

He had run out of time to find out, so he headed home, the sky turning black early and fast.

When he pulled into the driveway, Sarah was sitting on his porch. She had a dour pose, head down, staring into her empty lap. Even the slam of the truck door didn't immediately attract her attention.

For a moment, he thought she was dead, right there on his porch. Wouldn't the Sheriff love that? Then she looked up, slowly, her skin ashen in the newborn dark.

"The Harvest Ceremony is tomorrow," she said. "We are to send word to all we know."

He put his lunch cooler down on the rail of the porch, thinking over the consequences. He hadn't seen any Ferris wheels getting set up in the city park, no beer garden trailers pulling in. No flyers. No rednecks wrenching their derby cars in dusty driveways, the town covered in the big yellow eyes of garage doors at night.

"Harvest is at dawn," she added. "It's a different day every year, but it's always in October. It's a bit earlier than usual."

Because I'm here, he thought.

"I may be telling you shit you already know, but the Sheriff answers to a man named Ortega," he said. "This Ortega admitted to doing things to Marcus Jarvis's daughter."

"And you didn't bite," she said. "Good for you."

"Everyone keeps assuming I'm not telling the truth," he said.

"Are you?" she said.

"I know one truth," he said. "I took the wrong job in the wrong fucking town."

"If that's true," she said, "I'm assuming you'll leave tonight. There's nothing for you here, and your presence at harvest is only required if you want to remain in Harlow and become a true citizen."

"If I got nothing to hide," he said, "then why the fuck would I run away?"

"I know men like you. You're a man who runs."

She headed for the steps. He stared her down, leaving her little space to brush past him. When she reached him, her hand found his ribcage and lingered there. She looked up at him, her eyes wet in the moonlight.

"My relationship with Sheriff Vance is not consensual," she said. "Ask me to go inside with you. Please. If you're going to leave me behind, leave me something to remember."

She was on her toes, her neck stretched, inviting him to kiss her. Her slender fingers crept up, lighting the tissue of his ribs on fire, sending a familiar heat into his spine.

"Goodbye, Sarah," he said, breaking away from the contact, walking into the house without looking back.

Once the door was closed, he stood there, his back against it, taking three long breaths. He heard her footsteps moving down the porch steps and into the driveway. He moved through the house without turning on the lights, going to the kitchen, drinking a glass of water under the green hue of the oven's clock.

He hovered over the sink. If Wendell Vance knocked on his door that moment, he wouldn't be able to control himself—and control was what he needed to find.

Calmness eluded him, replaced with thoughts of the mineshaft. He closed his eyes, and the stagnant air was in his nose again as he put himself there. He felt the cold but humid drafts licking his flesh. He was inside a tunnel that ate light and swallowed sound. A secret place. A tomb.

"A prison," he said, opening his eyes. Cartwright had spoken as if Scott Benoit were still alive, sure, but he also hinted at his location: *Every time we go down there, he's begging us to believe him*, he'd said.

Down there. He could have been referring to any basement or cellar, but that was too normal for Harlow. Using the dank mining tunnel as a medieval holding chamber felt not just possible, but likely.

He could have left Scott Benoit in the muck thirty years ago. Was Harvest much different than the Tết holiday, anyhow? Harlow was a foreign land with customs he didn't understand. Back in '68, he and Benoit didn't know any better, but now? All he had to do was drive away and admit defeat, something an entire country was too proud to do when it mattered.

Quinn chugged a half-pot of coffee, then laid down and set a timer for twenty minutes. He'd get the benefit of a power nap, and the caffeine would kick in as he woke up, giving him the fuel he'd need to get out of town.

He did not intend to leave Harlow alone.

Trent's Jeep Wrangler bounced along, the shell of the cabin rickety against the vehicle's joints, but Beth liked knowing they had an off-road beast that could tear through almost any terrain. He drove them to the southern outpost, where Beth used to manage the permission ledger. She knew the protocol and volunteered to sign them out.

Torre Nance was tending book. He had the unfortunate trifecta of glasses, freckles, and acne. Like most high schoolers, she knew him, but as people turned sixteen and were told the Way Things Were, cliques tended to fracture. The first test of Harlow loyalty— or servitude—was to not tell anyone under the age of sixteen the truth about Harlow.

Torre slid the ledger to Beth but looked unsure of himself, perhaps even nervous. Beth figured he was new, which was a lucky

break on a night when she needed every advantage. Beth logged
the departure information—*ice cream, Vandalia, one hour*—and passed
the book along.

"You're an apprentice scout, right?" Torre asked.

"Started in your chair, in fact," she said, managing to sound
conversational.

"Cool," Torre said. He froze, seeming unsure.

"Call it in," Beth said, her tone gentle. "The number's taped to
the base of the phone."

"Yeah," Torre said. "That's right."

He grabbed the old rotary phone and started twirling the numbers. Beth looked out the window—Trent was staring into the center of the Jeep's steering wheel, afraid to look.

"Beth Jarvis," Torre said. "And, um, Trent Keller. Ice cream.
One hour."

Granted, Beth thought. She didn't know whose voice was on the
other line, but she knew the word she wanted to hear was *granted*.

"Uh, okay. I will," Torre said. He hung up the phone. "Denied."

"What?"

"He says that word hasn't reached us yet. A curfew is in effect
for 8:00 p.m."

"Why?" Beth asked.

"Harvest," Torre said, looking as if he couldn't decide if he
wanted to pass out or puke. "Word has been sent. Harvest is tomorrow at dawn."

Torre scribbled in the book, logging the denial of their request,
his hands shaking.

"It's okay," Beth said. "It's all going to be okay. You did your
job."

As she returned to the Jeep, Trent looked handsome in his dis-
traught glory. Her path into the center of his heart was effortless,
achieved with a touch, a laugh, a mere second swimming in his
eyes.

She'd gotten him into this. She would get him out.

"Harvest is at dawn," she told him. "I don't intend for us to see it."

"We'll be gone by then," he said. "Or dead. Whatever works, am I right?"

She smiled, then burst out laughing. He laughed with her. Why not? When death smiles, smile back, and all that.

She put her hand over his. *This is why we need each other*, she thought. Like two people carrying something heavy, you never knew the truth of the burden unless you were alone. The fear, the risk—they could lift it as long as they were doing it together.

"Drive," she said.

Quinn only knew one way into the tunnels. He couldn't risk opening up the school after-hours to get through the boiler room doorway. However, that tunnel terminated in the woods. He had glimpsed the spark of light when he was below, so he drove past the school on the Kinoka blacktop, looking for the telltale dip in the woods.

He promised that he'd abort this mission at the first sign of trouble. Benoit was worthy of the attempt, but he wasn't worth dying for.

A dusty path carved through the cornfield that tucked into the dented tree line. A worn path to nowhere in particular was another sign the tunnel held secrets.

He cut his lights and turned down the path. The moonlight offered plenty of guidance as he navigated the neglected road. The tire channels were carved so deep that the path's middle hump occasionally scraped the Camry's undercarriage.

He made it to the end of the field unscathed and guided the Camry into the thick brush of the tree line.

The rear part of the car was still visible to any hillbilly out spotlighting deer, or a passing car with a keen eye. He started tearing off chunks of branches and brush, stacking it up behind the car—not so much to conceal it, but to blunt the telltale reflective surfaces of the taillights.

When he reached for the last piece, his hand came back bloody. A ragged cut was dripping blood in the upper part of his palm. He clicked on his tactical flashlight to investigate, and the beam caught a glimmer of steel—razor wire hidden in the trees.

He walked the tree line for thirty yards, tracking the metallic braids all the way. He figured the mine shaft terminated a quarter mile west, and kept walking. As he got closer, he saw the school's bus barn roof in the distance, the pole light reflecting off of its white, metallic flesh. The brick facade of the school was just beyond the barn.

So, the old mining tunnel *was* close. The razor wire turned off into the woods, away from his destination.

He kept exploring and arrived at a steep hill. Mature trees jutted from the slope—this was the draw that put a slope in the tree line. The tunnel had to be nearby. He navigated to the base of the hill, his boots finding the crunch of river rock in an old, dry creek bed.

He walked the creek until he found the tunnel. The entrance was an open gash at the foot of the hill, framed with large blocks of rip-rap held in place by wooden ties. He shined the beam inside, and the tunnel swallowed the light.

Quinn went inside.

With Trent behind the wheel, Beth was sure they'd make it. He was nerdy, his jump shot sucked, and he was always too shy to try and kiss her first, but he drove that Jeep Wrangler with a heavy foot and a disdain for pavement. He always took her mudding after fresh rains, and veered into snowdrifts during the coldest winters. She had actually forgotten that the Jeep was red, since the paint was always covered with scabs of dried mud.

He turned onto the Kinoka blacktop. Trent slammed the accelerator, and they passed the high school. Under the windows-open whir of high speeds, he screamed—a primal sound filled with excitement and relief. The school's lit-up reader board started to fade behind them. She watched the road in the white, reaching glow of the high beams.

Miles passed. She watched them tick away. "Slow down," she said. She saw the stop sticks—Galen had kept his promise. The spiked strip had a reflector pinned to its base, so that wary eyes could see it if they were looking hard enough.

"Stop," she said, hopping out of the Jeep. She looked around, wondering if she would find Galen's Ford. No sign.

Beth dragged the stop sticks away, then sprinted back into the Jeep.

Trent hammered the gas. With the stop sticks marked and Galen's pledge to let them escape, no other obstacle remained.

The tension in her clenched hands drained. She eased back as Trent reached eighty miles per hour. She then saw what looked like a snake draped across the road, a glint of red on its back. She recognized this second, unexpected set of stop sticks too late for them to bring the Jeep to a safe standstill.

"Stop!" she screamed. Trent slammed the brakes, but was going to slide right over the stop sticks and blow out the tires. She reached over, pushing the steering wheel, dodging the sticks, sending them bumper-first into the ditch. They ramped into the air at high speed, the Jeep tilting. Upon landing, the seat belts snapped tight against their collarbones and the Jeep wobbled, but the rugged ride maintained its footing. Trent regained control, but they were in the wet field now. The tires spat mud as they battled for traction.

"What the hell was that?"

"Stop sticks," she said. "Another strip."

"I thought you said—"

"I know what I said. We missed them, though. Get moving. Go around."

The mud worsened, even though she could recall no recent rainfall. A few lingering pockets of deep wetness wasn't uncommon out here by the river. The tree line beyond the field was the Hardwood Bottoms, where most of the trees had permanent brown rings on their trunks—choke marks from floodwater.

The Jeep fishtailed as Trent navigated the mud.

"This shit's thick," he said.

"Get us back to the road," she said.

"I'm trying," he said, the wheel gliding and twirling in his hands as he battled to maintain traction. The engine whined high and hard. They finally hit a dry patch, and the tires bit, lurching them forward. They headed back toward the road, well past the stop sticks, ready to put the unplanned detour behind them.

As they approached the blacktop, the Jeep bogged down in another patch of mud.

They irrigated the field, she thought. *Fresh mud, no rains. They're always muddy, but never like this.*

"Come on, Trent," she said, faking calmness. "Come on. You can do it."

The Jeep fought the suction of the mud. The headlights lit up the smooth darkness of the blacktop. Then, the front of the Jeep dove down, tilting almost vertical, and she saw a dark, wet bloom smearing across the windshield.

They had plunged head-first into a sinkhole.

Trent took her hand. "Out the back. Go."

They climbed into the back seat, gravity working against them as they scrambled to the rear hatch. He boosted her out first and heard her plop onto the muddy field. Once she was clear, he scaled the cargo area and joined her.

Half the Jeep protruded from the sinkhole, its face speared into the ground. The earth continued digesting Trent's beloved ride, one slow inch at a time.

"We have to go back now," he said. "We have to beg forgiveness."

"We're already gone," she said.

Beth's right arm dangled at her side as she moved.

"What happened?"

"My collarbone," she said.

"Is it broken?" he asked.

"I don't know," she said, and she lifted her arm, testing it. "But I'm okay. It's not grinding. Let's move."

Beth saw headlights on Kinoka Road. She remembered the rusty gap in the fence, their best chance of escaping on foot. Galen said he'd wait to repair it, just in case—a gap for her to slip through. Clear that, and they could use the cover of the Hardwood Bottoms to escape on foot. The looming expanse of the forest looked so close, but as they ran, it felt like they weren't gaining ground.

The headlights came for them, hungry in the night. A spotlight circulated a cone of light through the field, searching.

Beth led them to the gap in the barrier, marked by the massive oak tree. They'd beat the pursuing vehicle to the gap in the fence. They would make it. For at least a little while.

But once they got there, she saw that the wounded fence was repaired—fresh coils of razor wire glittered in the moonlight, their teeth dripping with fresh oil, salivating.

"You said…" Trent began, not finishing.

"I know," she answered. "I'm sorry."

"What do we do now?" he asked.

The headlights curled in the night as the vehicle took the dry path to the fence line. The trap was set, all this time, and she'd dragged herself and an innocent boy right into it.

"What do we do?" he repeated.

She didn't know. All she knew was that they had nowhere left to run.

CHAPTER 15

W ithin ten paces of entering the mining tunnel, the air grew cold and heavy. The opening behind Quinn already looked a thousand miles away. He clicked on his flashlight, and the opening to his left startled him—a black hole in the wall, inviting him to step inside. He shined the light and saw wooden steps descending into total darkness.

As long as the opening was visible, he had enough orientation to escape. He opted to walk further along the main tunnel, toward the school. Another ten paces, and he saw another opening, this one less polished. No stairs. Only darkness. The hole's border was messy and uneven, looking as if it were dug by hand. He'd have to duck to step into it, and if he did, how far would he fall? What was down there?

As he turned away, he sensed a presence in the tunnel. The flashlight revealed nothing, so he turned it off and remained still, listening. In tunnels and caves, a whisper can rise from a thousand feet down, full-throated, if the acoustics were right.

Quinn heard a subtle rise and fall of white noise. Breath. He swallowed. The sound crunched in his eardrums, and he thought he was hearing his own breathing, so he held it.

The breathing was distant and faint, but he still heard it. Someone was in the tunnels. He thought of screaming for Benoit. If it were him, imprisoned somewhere in the darkness, he could lead Quinn to his location.

But if it wasn't?

Quinn turned around. To search for Benoit was to get lost in the dark with an unknown enemy. Unacceptable. Benoit would push on, powered by an illogical sense of duty. He was once shot and bleeding in the mud, a failed soldier, and that failure had followed the man ever since, all the way to the rank of detective.

Quinn had played the role of dutiful soldier, risking his life for a comrade, and only once they were again stateside, ready to go their separate ways, the truth of the war clarifying outside of the haze of rain and gunfire, did he realize that he was a tool. A sharp one, brainwashed to sacrifice for God and country and his fellow man. He didn't believe in any of them. His duty was fulfilled, so he walked a different path, ending up as a tool again, but of men that he understood, men who were honest in their evil intentions.

He turned back, refusing to go any deeper. He crept towards the entrance, feeling as if a stranger's hand could fall on his shoulder at any moment.

Who, or what, would that hand belong to?

As he approached the mouth of the tunnel, he ran. Returning to the moonlight after the darkness of the mines, he could see every detail of the woods and creek bed around him, but all he could stare at was that eye of darkness cut into the hillside, expecting something or someone to emerge. He backed away slowly, watching, waiting. His thunderclap pulse finally eased, and he laughed at himself.

Not as fearless as you used to be, old man, he thought.

Time to leave Harlow. He had at least warned Benoit, and the arrogant asshole ignored it. Whatever happened to him now was as much his fault as Quinn's.

The best Quinn could do was drop a few compelling tips and get Harlow crawling with cops. Ortega, Ronato, and Vance would shit themselves when the calvary showed up, knew about the tunnel, and decided to have a peek.

The people of Harlow were waiting on a mythical Griffin, but a couple SWAT vans full of pissed-off cops would have to be a sufficient consolation prize.

Satisfied with his plan, Quinn headed back to his hidden Camry.

As he walked through the woods, he heard the distant, high whine of an engine. He sprinted up the draw and saw headlights bouncing in the field across the blacktop road. He eased closer, through the cut-down cornfield. The engine churned out RPMs that didn't match the vehicle's speed. *Stuck*, he thought. The headlights fluttered as the vehicle groped for traction.

Another vehicle appeared. Quinn dropped to his stomach, flattening himself against the soil. Broken corn stalks jabbed his ribs. The newly arrived vehicle was a hulking Tahoe with a police light bar, and it veered off-road. The gleaming eye of a spotlight dangled from the passenger window. The Sheriff, of course, and he was searching for whoever was in that desperate car stuck in the mud.

When the Tahoe stopped, Quinn heard doors opening, then slamming shut. He crept closer and recognized Trent and Beth. Inseparable, as usual. He saw three men approaching them, bathed in the headlights—Vance was never without his redneck deputies.

Morgan Albers bashed Beth's hamstring with his baton, collapsing her. Quinn heard the wet thump of the blow and remembered what that particular baton felt like. Trent tried to intervene, but Jason Vowell shoved him in the back. The undersized kid slammed into the mud, face-first.

Sheriff Vance leaned against the hood of the Tahoe, one hand looped in his belt, the other resting on the butt of his service pistol. He laughed.

The muscles in Quinn's jaw hardened into wire. The clenching almost shattered his teeth. He closed his eyes, took a deep breath, and turned around. If he could leave Benoit behind, he could leave a couple of kids to get roughed up for trying to run away. They'd never see him strip the brush off the Camry a half-mile away, and they were too distracted to notice it creeping on the Kinoka blacktop with the headlights off.

Besides, what could he do? Other than get a mouthful of baton? He didn't have a gun. The Albers prick was as big as Quinn, and at least thirty pounds heavier, thanks to his morning loads of biscuits and gravy. Taking him out hand-to-hand would be like chewing gristle, and he had two other men with him—one of them armed.

If he made a move, he'd piss all over a decade of restraint. That same decade had rusted him, blunting his training, his edge. He couldn't fight them, not only because he didn't want to become *that guy*. He couldn't fight them because he would fail.

He walked to his Camry as Morgan Albers dragged Beth into the beam of the headlights. She was screaming, and Trent was begging them not to hurt her. The men laughed at him. Jason kicked the boy in the ribs.

Quinn kept walking. He was a man who ran.

CHAPTER 16

The knurls of fresh wire sparkled in the Tahoe's headlights as it approached.

"Let's go," Trent said. "We have to do something."

"Something like what?" Beth said. "We save our energy now. The running is over."

"Save it for what?"

"To fight," she said. "We fight until they kill us. You understand? We cannot let them take us to Harvest."

Trent ignored her, taking off his coat. He tossed it at the razor wire, a trick he'd no doubt seen in the movies, but it got caught up in the brush instead.

"See if you can get through," he said. "I'll fight them myself. Let you get away."

She shook her head.

"Please," he said. The broken tone of his voice reminded her of Shaun Murray begging for his life, not twenty yards from the spot where they were trapped right now.

She touched his cheek as the headlights carved across them. "All I can do now is to tell you I'm sorry," she said.

She side-eyed the razor wire. All she had to do was reach through the brush and find a sharpened tooth. Run it against her wrists vertically, and she'd fade out before they could capture or hurt her.

The Tahoe doors opened. Beth had seen this unfold once before, and it was the same three men this time—Sheriff Vance, Morgan Albers, and Jason Vowell. They strutted into the light.

"You just like your daddy," Jason said. He snapped open his baton.

Trent sprinted at them. He tried to tackle Sheriff Vance, who sidestepped him. He tottered into Jason, who shoved him down.

Beth turned away from the fence and its promise of a quick death. "No!" she screamed.

Just as she was prepared to join the fight, Morgan cracked the back of her legs with the baton, and she dropped. Her knees must have sunk three inches into the field. Mud squirted up between her fingers as she tried to shove herself back to her feet, her palms slipping in the attempt.

"No sir, she ain't like her daddy," Sheriff Vance said, stepping forward, his thumbs poked into his belt in a posture of pure satisfaction. "That fuckin' coward Marcus never had the balls to run. You're more like Katie."

Morgan dragged her out of the muddy darkness and flung her into the center of the Tahoe's headlight beams. He raised his baton, looking to the Sheriff for permission. "Ladies first?" he asked.

"Nah," the Sheriff answered. "Let the boy see what dating a Jarvis gets you around here."

Morgan smiled. He and Jason stood over Trent, who was by now on all fours, almost to his feet. They rained the batons on him, crunching blows to the backs of his legs, the meat of his shoulders, the soft undercarriage of his trunk. No head shots. No deathblows.

He writhed to escape, covering himself in mud and bruises. He mustered the air to cough out the words "please stop," but was cut off by a blow to his ribcage.

"That's enough," Vance said. "Don't kill the little fucker."

Beth ran to him. Morgan caught a fistful of her trailing hair, yank-ing her back. She thrashed, trying to shake herself loose, throwing her elbows and screaming.

"I'll settle her down," Jason said. He raised the baton, but Sheriff Vance grabbed him by the forearm.

"Morg's got her," Vance said. "We don't want to bruise fruit that sweet now, do we? Just call it in."

"Fuck that," Morgan said. "We have a right to taste this bitch before we turn her over. I'd like to fit in some fun before she ends up my daughter-in-law."

"Damn straight," Jason said to the Sheriff. "Why the fuck we out here if we can't get some spoils?"

"The spoils aren't for you to decide with these two," Vance said. "The Mayor wants them."

That was the end of the discussion. Jason lowered the club and sauntered over to the Tahoe, looking defeated.

Trent tried to get to his feet. "Where you assholes going?" he rasped. "I'm not done with you yet."

The men stared at him, unable to hide their surprise.

"For a pussy-whipped runt, you sure are a tough little son of a bitch," Sheriff Vance said. He approached him, daring Trent to throw a punch, which he did. Vance swayed, dodging it, and planted a fist in the boy's ribcage, dropping him to his knees.

"I'll bet your girl is a fine little piece. A juicy one, I'd reckon, all salty when she's primed up. She juicy, boy?"

"Fuck you," Trent spat.

Vance turned to Beth. "Katie, now, that bitch was juicy," he said. "That sister of yours was sweet as a mouthful of fuckin' blueberries."

"Damn straight," Morgan said.

Trent tried to get back up, but Vance kicked him down. He pressed the sole of his boot on Trent's temple, mashing his skull into the mud. Beth tried to break free. Morgan punched her in the kidney, and she was shocked at how quickly all of the fight was drained out of her, how her body went limp, revolting against her, all so it wouldn't get struck again.

"We all got a piece of little Katie," Vance continued. "The Mayor did her good."

Beth regained control of her body and forced an elbow into Morgan's stomach. She broke free, only to get another baton shot to the back of her legs, the bundle of nerves and tendons just behind her knee. She felt the sting everywhere, even deep in her inner ear, her entire body a tight guitar string had just been plucked.

Vance hovered over her. He spat a tobacco-colored glob into the dirt. "You do got a lot of Kate in you. She fought...until she didn't." He drew handcuffs from his belt.

As he knelt to restrain her, Beth heard the thud of something heavy hitting the ground. The Sheriff turned around, hearing the same noise.

A hulking man emerged from the dark, and a baton whistled through the air, colliding with Vance's nose. A high-pitched click echoed as Vance collapsed, the blood from his shattered nose misting the air as he fell.

The man stepped up to Morgan, both men holding extended batons.

Finally, Beth recognized him—the janitor, Mr. Silver. The headlight beams glinted off the whites of his furious eyes.

"Come on, then," Morgan said.

The janitor didn't hesitate to accept the invitation.

Before he joined the fray, Quinn was sneaking away to his Camry and the promise of putting Harlow and all its mysteries behind him.

Sounds rode the wind across the field. Nothing muted the kicks landing, Beth groaning, the laughter of the Sheriff and his men.

Nothing stopped her name—Kate.

Kate did not belong to him. As much as he'd loved her, as strong as he once was, he could not wrest her from this place. She was a

Harlow girl, and belonged to the Mayor. He took her. He saw her as his right.

He killed her, but not before the men of Harlow took their turn.

She was juicy.

"Don't be that guy," he whispered. The words Kate used to chase away his anger and hate, blunting his violent edge over the years until it was gone.

It was no wonder she wanted the journal hidden—a journal he was sure would have led him to Harlow and revealed its secrets. She'd marked him as the Griffin, then softened him too much to do what needed to be done. Burying it with her was burying *that guy* forever.

He stopped walking.

"What do you want me to do?" he asked. To leave was to forever be the soft man that Kate had loved; to turn around was to die as the heathen she wanted him to leave behind. When she kissed him, she needed the safe haven of a man with a conscience. When she marked him, she wanted a monster who doled out grim but just brutality.

The wind sliced through the dark, holding no answers.

They'd killed her. They'd killed his child. They would kill Beth, and she was the only family that remained, the last thread that connected him to the life and love with Kate he'd never deserved.

If Kate were alive, standing next to him, what would she say? Don't be that guy? Or would she beg him to help?

"Neither," he whispered. "She would run into the fray. She would fight them. She would save Beth herself."

Gone was gone—the Kate in his mind was only a ghost, programmed by his own thoughts and biases.

Ghost though she was, Quinn turned around to follow her.

Jason was closest, his back to the darkness. Quinn was able to choke him out without much effort, thanks to the element of surprise.

He took Jason's baton and bolted at the Sheriff—the only one of them armed with a gun. As Vance turned around, Quinn planted an overhand right on the bridge of his nose. The punch came from his hips, the way he'd drilled the technique in Joe's Gym back when he was ten years old. You never forgot how to ride a bike or knock a motherfucker out, it seemed. Bone and cartilage separated, blood vessels were crushed, and Vance's exhalation of surprise was thick with a mist of blood.

Morgan was the last man standing. The baton dangled at his side.

"Come on, then," Morgan said.

Quinn sprinted at him, throwing the baton he held at Morgan's face. The other man brought his hands up to block it as Quinn launched a toe-first kick into his crotch. A steel toe, at that.

The big man crumbled to his knees, holding his shattered testicles. Quinn picked up the loose baton and took his revenge, clubbing Morgan's orbital bone, feeling the bone splinter like ice on a frozen pond. Morgan started to twitch, and the whites of his eyes turned red as blood leaked into his eye sockets. Quinn didn't have the time to watch him die—the Sheriff groaned, fumbling for his gun.

Quinn had a running start to load up a rib-shattering kick. But as he bent over to disarm the Sheriff, Jason bolted out of the darkness and jumped on his back.

Stupid, stupid, stupid, Quinn thought. He didn't choke him out long enough. He didn't finish with a quick jerk of the redneck's skull, snapping his neck. He was too hungry to get at Vance to be thorough, and *that guy* was above all else patient and thorough.

Quinn tried to stand up with the beefy farmhand locked around his throat. Old, herniated discs bit at his lower back as he tried to shuck his assailant. He fell forward, his core too weak to keep him out of the fatal position of being on the ground with a large man on top of him. Now pinned, he couldn't get his hand between Jason's arm and his throat, as Jason had the leverage position. He wrenched upward, Jason's forearm smashing against his windpipe. The ropy thickness of Quinn's neck muscles prevented his larynx from being smashed, but it only delayed his inevitable failure as his vision sparkled, his oxygen cut off. He faded, and he saw Kate smiling at him, her finger tracing his griffin tattoo, smiling at him on their couch, a curtain of blond hair covering one of her blue eyes.

He stopped fighting. If this was what he would fade into, good. Let it happen.

The vision was interrupted by a muted *pop*. Jason went limp. The arm loosened, and he fell away from Quinn. Oxygen returned, a rush that cleansed the sparks in his eyes and steadied him. He looked over at Jason's limp body and saw his temple leaking blood and smoke.

Beth stood over him, her hands extended, cradling the Sheriff's gun with a steady, two-handed grip. Quinn stood and moved toward her, placing his hand on top of the weapon. She let it go, backing away, not shaken as much by what she had done, but the ease with which she'd accomplished it. He knew the feeling.

"Go," he said.

"You can't stay here," Trent said.

"Watch me."

"You don't know what it's like here," Beth said. "You're an outsider."

"They don't know what I'm like," he said. "They'll wish they never found out. That I can promise you."

He nodded at the Tahoe, urging them to move along.

Trent hopped inside. Beth dug into her jeans and found her father's coin.

"Give this to my dad if you see him," she said. "Marcus Jarvis."

She held it out. Quinn didn't take it.

"I don't intend on seeing him."

She flipped it into the air. Quinn caught it.

"If I take this," he said, "you take this." He handed her the

Sheriff's service weapon, an SIG Sauer M11 semi-automatic pistol. Excellent firearm taste for a redneck sheriff, whom he'd half-expected to carry a revolver modeled after his favorite John Wayne character.

Beth got into the Tahoe as Trent dropped it into gear. She leaned out the window. "Harvest is tomorrow, and all I know is that the Harvest Oath is sealed in blood," she said. "It'll be *your* blood if you're not smart enough to run."

Sheriff Vance groaned again, crawling away in the dark.

"I won't bleed alone," Quinn said.

Quinn circled the injured Sheriff, a scavenger bird ready to dive into the scraps.

"Kate Jarvis. Tell me what happened to her."

Vance finally sat up, resigned to his fate. He touched his shattered nose. "So, you were the one all along." He laughed through the pain. "And Cartwright was wrong. That's a first. He may get it worse than you now. Ortega seemed to know all along it was you. So did the Mayor."

"These sound more like threats than answers," Quinn said. "Let's start with an easy one. If Ortega isn't the Mayor, who is?"

"You'll find out," Vance said. "You won't get away. Neither will those traitor fuckin' kids. I promise you that. No one gets away."

Quinn lined up another kick and teed off on Vance's ribcage. The Sheriff coughed and writhed. Quinn waited for him to catch his breath.

"The cop who came around here asking questions," Quinn said. "Scott Benoit. Where is he?"

"He's in the dark," Vance whispered. "I don't know much about the dark down there. The mines. All that's above my pay grade. But they been saving him for Harvest."

"Where is this Harvest Ceremony?"

"The high school gym," Vance said. "Dawn. Hell, it's right over there. Walking distance. Just a couple hours now. Why don't you go on in? Rescue your friend. Avenge your woman. Perhaps the Mayor will grant you mercy."

"What's his name?"

"Whatever it used to be, that person is dead," Vance said. "There is only the Mayor."

"Last chance," Quinn said. "What did he do to Kate Jarvis?"

"Let's cut the bullshit," Vance said. "I'm already dead, and I know you're gonna make it hurt. So how about you go fuck yourself and get to whatever it is you're going to do."

Quinn snap-kicked him across the face.

"That one's for Kate," Quinn said, then kicked him again, crushing teeth with the full force of his steel-toed boot. "That one's for Sarah."

The Sheriff mumbled out of his bloody mouth. "Maybe she'll move on to you," he muttered. "She's had her eye on you from the start."

A heel-kick drove right through Sheriff Vance's forearm. A splinter of bone punched out of his flesh, and another shriek rode the wind.

"Talk, and I'll make it quick," Quinn said.

Vance held up his shattered arm. His limp hand dangled, separated from the soft tissue that made it work, as if a puppet's strings were cut. "You think torture's going to scare me? Compared to what will happen now, if I live?"

Quinn battled the fire of his awoken back pain to get down on one knee next to Sheriff Vance. He withdrew a boot knife from the holster on his lower leg—a big one as boot knives went, five inches, fixed blade, double-sided. A dagger. One side was serrated, the other sharp enough to split atoms.

"You said you tasted her, right?" He jammed the blade into the left side of the Sheriff's abdomen. "Let's see what the coyotes think of you. You a juicy one, Vance?"

Vance squirmed, trying to get the knife loose, but he was too weak. Quinn pushed him down and began sawing with the blade. After adding a few inches to the gash, he stopped.

"Who killed her?" Quinn asked.

"The parents always do the killing," Vance whispered. "It's the Mayor's will. The parents beg to do it, to put the children out of their misery."

"There was nothing left of her," Quinn said. "If Marcus put her out of her misery, tell me about the misery part."

"If I tell you what the Mayor did," Vance said. "You'll do me worse."

Quinn sawed another inch. Blood ran out of the wound, thick as syrup. "I could cut your throat right now and end this," he said.

"Leave me to die painful, then. Beautiful night. There's still worse ways to go."

Quinn carved even harder. Vance let go of Quinn's wrist. He was already on the verge of death, beyond the pain, staring into the sky. Quinn kept cutting until the blade hit breastbone. The knife split the flesh and fat, leaving the Sheriff's guts glistening in the starlight. They steamed in the chilly air.

"The Mayor will punish you," Vance whispered, a strange smile on his face.

Quinn wiped down the blade and returned it to its holster. He'd need more than a knife to launch an assault on the Harvest Ceremony, and didn't have long to prepare.

He headed for his car. Tiny puffs of frost rose from the Sheriff's mouth as Quinn left him behind—they wouldn't continue for long, but each one would feel like an eternity. As he crossed the blacktop, he heard the yelp of coyotes drawing ever closer.

CHAPTER 17

Quinn headed for the Camry, watching the Kinoka blacktop for signs of new activity. Before long, someone would catch wind of the shitshow at the town's border—the missing Tahoe, two missing kids, a missing Sheriff, two missing deputies.

For now, he was in control, and he was ready to kill them all—Ronato, Ortega, anyone with a pulse who stood beside them. He was already off the wagon—a few more bodies weren't going to make a difference.

But now, the knowledge gap was even wider. He still didn't know anything tangible about the Mayor. He knew that Ortega and Ronato were his enemies, but didn't know who else might be loyalists.

Loyalists. A nasty thought crossed his mind.

He reached into his pocket and took out his key ring. The set Sarah gave him for the rental house had come attached to a thick, leatherette keychain.

Maybe she'll move on to you, the Sheriff had said. *She's had her eye on you from the start.*

Sarah's key chain was a silver disc stitched to a fake leather circle. *Home sweet home* was engraved on the disc in a font he could only describe as country-knitting. He drew his knife and pushed the blade into the stitches, splitting the threads, prying the silver disc loose. A coil of tiny wire connected it to a coin-sized lithium battery.

A tracking device. Too small and weak to follow him much outside of Harlow, but plenty to keep tabs on him around town, and his pattern of activity, if anyone was watching, had been suspicious as hell since he got off work that afternoon. If they weren't on top of him already, they had to be close. He dropped the tracker and sprinted for the Camry.

He yanked open the door, and as the dome light clicked on, the hooks of a Taser burrowed into the flesh of his abdomen. His body clenched as he recognized the man sitting in his car.

Ronato, the superintendent.

"So discourteous, janitor," he said. "Trying to leave without putting in your two weeks' notice. Who would mop the floors in your absence?"

Spotlights emerged from the trees, their beams fragmented by the barren limbs. Footsteps. Murmurs. Hands on his body, turning him over. A knee in his back, cuffs closing around his wrists.

"Be gentle." A woman's voice, oily and confident. Sarah. Far more different than the casual, needy, victim's tone she'd taken with him these past few weeks. She knelt down next to him.

"He's not for you," Ronato said.

"Not yet," she answered. "He will be broken, and I intend to fuck the scraps." She ran her finger along his cheek. "We have to clean that traitor whore's juices off of you first. Kate left a stain on everything she touched."

They dragged him to his feet. He saw the others around them, people he'd seen in the diner, around town, at the school picking up their kids. Some held flashlights, others held guns.

"Dawn will be here soon," Ronato said. "And with it comes Harvest. We are overjoyed to have you atop a growing list of honored guests."

THE MAYOR

CHAPTER 18

T he Kinoka blacktop whirred underneath the Tahoe as Harlow faded behind them. The moon was high and bright, filling the glittering eyes of the deer that gathered in the fields, the raccoons perched in the barren treetops, the opossums tucked away in the grassy ditches—the only living witnesses to their escape.

"Almost to Kinoka," Trent said.

Kinoka was another small town, about nine miles from Harlow, but this one was close to an interstate highway, so it was blessed with a gas station and even a couple of stoplights. They had a sturdy vehicle with a full tank of gas, a head start on anyone who would pursue them, and a lethal weapon she had already used to murder a High Servant rested on her lap.

Still, Beth's entire body was a clenched fist, and she began to realize the tension's permanence—that from this moment on, she had to live as if every stranger was conspiring to catch her and return to her to Harlow. To relax was to become vulnerable again.

She thought of Kate, and finally understood her sister's misery outside of Harlow. All the Jarvis girls had done was trade one brand of fear for another, and the fear's beating heart was the town itself, and nothing would ever end, not ever, until a stake was driven through it. Kate had understood that, and the stake she sharpened was the janitor. Unfortunately, he wasn't sharp enough. Beth knew it. She couldn't allow herself to fantasize about him cleansing the town—Harlow would gobble him up and send its Rangers, but its ghosts would be with her, always.

Trent's face was illuminated with the green light of the digital speedometer. He kept glancing at her, sensing her distance. If he asked if she was okay, she was going to scream.

"Hey," he said. "I need you, okay? You remember that stray cat you adopted? What was her name?"

"Cotton," she said. Cotton wasn't a girl, but she wanted him to be a girl. When her father told her Cotton was a boy, she was young enough to be devastated, but also young enough for her imagination to take over. Even now, knowing better, the cat was a she in all her memories.

"I'm Cotton," he said. "You took me in, you fixed me up, and I'm following you anywhere. With minimal rubbing of my face against your leg."

Cotton was all white with the exception of her pewter-blue paws and face, and when Beth found her, she'd had a wounded shoulder, a dark, red bulls-eye dried up in her white fur. Beth nursed her back to health, fed her, made her a bed in a cardboard box. Each morning she'd wake up and put on a sweatshirt and go outside with an old blanket to sit with Cotton on her back steps, spending a few minutes with her before school started.

The wound was from hawk, her father had said. Hawks were everywhere in Harlow—perched on power lines, surveying from the treetops, gliding with their wings spread over the open fields. He said they mostly blasted off on field mice, but that an ornery one would occasionally go after a small cat or rabbit.

Trent mercifully didn't ask what had happened to the cat. He turned off the blacktop road and joined Highway 51, which bisected the town of Kinoka.

"Don't speed," Beth said.

Trent eased the Tahoe back to thirty-five as they rolled past Kinoka's only gas station.

The fuel islands were empty. No cars parked out front. Beth noticed the clerk behind the glass, his attention buried in the pages of a magazine or newspaper.

As soon as the headlights revealed a speed limit sign with two fives on it, Trent floored the Tahoe. The engine responded, pinning them against their seats.

"Take it easy," Beth said.

The Tahoe shifted again. Trent didn't let up.

"I said slow down!"

"Someone's behind us," Trent said.

Beth glanced in the rearview mirror and saw headlights.

"Where'd they come from?" she asked.

"I don't know."

"No one was at the gas station," she said.

"Scouts," he said. "Someone must have seen us."

"Scouts don't work outside of Harlow," she said. She didn't add anything about High Servants or Rangers.

The cabin of the Tahoe filled with red light, then blue. A police light bar flickered in the mirror. The car behind them was a patrol vehicle.

"Don't stop," Beth said. "If it's a real cop, we can stop where we feel safe and be okay."

"What if we get arrested?"

"Please get us arrested," she said. "Have them take us to a cell with bars and constant surveillance from men who aren't Mayor loyalists."

A new set of headlights emerged in the left lane—another car was trailing the police cruiser.

Before Trent could react, a Chevy Impala decked out with *Kinoka Police* on the door zoomed past them.

"They're going to try and bracket us in," he said. The Impala swerved in front of them, but maintained its speed.

A third cruiser jumped into the left lane and flanked them.

Beth looked out the passenger window. The ditch along the highway was steep, and to drive into it at such a high speed posed a significant fatality risk.

Good, she thought. Then she remembered the gun. She doubted she had enough skill, opportunity, or bullets to blast their way out of the predicament, but there was another way to escape.

No good answers, she thought. *Not ever.*

She had once asked her father what she could do to protect Cotton from the hawk, and he told her there was just no good answer to that question. The hawk had a taste for the cat now, and knew where she lived. It saw too far and flew too high for Cotton to escape its reach. Beth knew the answer now, after she came home one day all those years ago and saw her father out back picking up white pieces of Cotton's remains and putting them in a garbage bag. The answer was to kill the hawk—and if you couldn't, the things you loved were destined for the garbage bag.

"What are you doing?" Trent asked.

She held the gun with both hands, prayer-like, the barrel tilted straight up, at the top of the cabin. A few more degrees, and it would be aimed at the flesh under her jaw.

The cruiser in front of them slammed the brakes. Trent was too distracted to react, watching Beth's dance with the Sheriff's pistol.

They smashed into the cruiser. Beth snapped forward and the gun slipped out of her hands, clinking into the floorboard as the airbags erupted, clobbering Beth as the Tahoe chewed up the smaller car in front of them, the front tires mounting the rear bumper. Another cruiser blasted them from behind, and the Tahoe twisted off the wreckage, landing on its side, falling into the steep ditch. They tumbled to a stop, the cabin a womb of white airbag fabric.

She shifted, searching for the gun. She tried to scream Trent's name, but the accident had punched the air out of her, and she had yet to find it.

The airbags loosened. She saw Trent, his face drenched in blood, eyes closed, his body limp against the ruins of the cockpit. She reached for him, and her throbbing collarbone sent a nuclear wave of pain through her system. A wave of dizziness turned her vision splotchy.

Her door opened with a creak—not her doing. She turned around, and a massive hand wrapped around her upper arm.

"Hello, Beth," Ortega said as he dragged her out of the car.

Ortega and his High Servants drove Beth back to Harlow with a bag over her head and tape over her mouth. They ignored her injuries and didn't bother to wipe off the blood from the accident. She had cuts on her scalp from a shower of broken glass, and a few lacerations on her arms and torso. Her collarbone thundered with pain, but she could move her arm without grinding. Was she lucky to escape the accident so thoroughly unharmed? Or unlucky that she didn't die instantly?

Fucking airbags, she thought.

She tracked her movements by feel and sound, the buzz of blacktop, the crunch of gravel. Car doors slamming. The push bar of a door clicking open. The hinges groaning. Finished concrete squealing against the rubber soles of her sneakers.

Rough hands pressed her onto a bench. The wooden plank bit into her tailbone, and she recognized the feel of it from the locker rooms at school. Handcuffs clicked, the metal snapping against metal as they chained her to the bench.

The locker room door groaned shut. No more footsteps or grunting or good old boy small talk. She was alone. So why didn't she feel alone? She sensed someone. Her breath filled the bag with humidity, and her inhalations got shorter and more anxious.

"Breathe," a familiar voice said, echoing against the lockers. The janitor. They caught him, too.

"Hold your breath in for a four-count," he said. "That's what slows the heart rate."

The trick worked. After she centered herself, she mumbled against the tape to let him know she was gagged.

"My real name is Curtis Quinn," Quinn said. "I was married to your sister. Outside of Harlow, her name was Kristina. Same as your mother."

He took a deep breath of his own. "She knew what I was, the first day she saw me, but she wasn't afraid. She'd seen worse. I know that now. She used to tell me, 'Don't be that guy.' For once in my life, I listened to someone with better judgment than me."

Beth wondered if it was total darkness in the locker room. No light came through the threads of the bag. The only sound was the janitor's voice.

"She made me believe that evil wasn't a permanent condition, that you could find the good in it if you just sifted through it long enough. So I'm not that guy anymore, but that made me weak enough and dumb enough to get us both killed, and I want you to know that I'm sorry."

Quinn said no more, and Beth made no sound. He took the silence as a mild acceptance of his apology—he could tell she was the kind of kid that could never hold a grudge, her heart so big that even Harlow couldn't squeeze it dry. He'd known kids like that, but where he was from, they never lasted long. She lowered her head, groggy from a lack of sleep and the comedown of the adrenaline that had sizzled through her body for the past few hours. The haze of light sleep visited her, but not for long.

The door opened, the lights clicked on, and someone ripped the hood off of her head.

The weak bulbs of the locker room hit her eyes as hard as the July sun at noon. Through her squint, she saw Superintendent Ronato dressed in a sharp, navy-blue suit, holding the hood.

With the hood gone, the musty, familiar scent of the locker room flowed into Beth's nostrils. She saw Curtis Quinn bound at the other end of the bench, his cuffed hands behind him. He looked serene, meditative, perhaps even submissive.

Ronato wasn't alone. High Servants flanked him—men trusted

enough to carry weapons. On his left, she saw an old man, mostly bald, arms folded. He looked bored. She didn't recognize him, and figured him for a Ranger, that rare breed allowed to operate outside of Harlow.

The other man was Pernell Baumgartner, a dig site worker, with a daughter two years younger than Beth—Stephanie. Steph played volleyball, and Beth had seen Pernell at the games.

Pernell yanked the tape from her mouth, then freed her from the handcuffs.

"Show her to her seat," Ronato said.

"So, it's you," Beth said. "You're the Mayor."

"You compliment me," Ronato said. "But no. I humbly speak for him in his absence."

"Is Trent alive?"

"He's alive."

Beth believed him.

"Have you no concern for Galen Mettis?" Ronato said in a mocking tone.

"No," Beth said.

"Do you believe that he betrayed you?"

Beth thought about it a long time. "Sure looks that way," she said, and that was an honest if evasive answer. It sure looked like Galen betrayed her, but Beth still couldn't believe it. They must have tricked him somehow.

"Then I have good news," Ronato said. "Galen is dead. I killed him myself."

Beth looked down at the concrete, hiding her face.

Ronato leaned close to her. "He did not die quickly."

"Neither will you," Quinn said.

"I'm bereft at the loss of your skills around here. The floors were never cleaner," Ronato said. "If only your common sense matched your work ethic." He nodded, and Pernell yanked Beth to her feet. She let Pernell lead her toward the locker room door, into the gymnasium, where the Harvest Ceremony awaited.

As she passed Quinn, she realized that what she'd mistaken for submissiveness was something else. Quinn's massive shoulders retained a coiled tension as he gazed at the floor, not one trace of emotion, staring into a space that only he could see. He was a snake trapped in a basket, but venomous all the same, and hungry to strike.

"If you're sorry, Mr. Quinn, I'll forgive you," Beth said. "But only if you kill the Mayor."

CHAPTER 19

W hen Beth entered the gymnasium, all of Harlow was standing in the bleachers.

No one made a sound. Most of the citizens stood with lowered heads, as if in prayer. Pernell directed Beth to the table set up right over the Harlow Orphans logo at center court.

Beth recognized the rickety legs of the foldout tables she'd seen at school functions, now adorned with a red tablecloth.

Pernell seated Beth at the head of the table. She sat without resistance as Pernell bound her ankles to the legs of the chair. Fortunately, her hands remained free. Glancing around, Beth noticed that she wasn't alone at this featured table, and the faces were familiar: they were all fellow students, all seniors. Each had turned eighteen that year. They, too, had their heads bowed in silent prayer.

Trent wasn't at the table. She thought of her father's palm, the deep gash, and wondered if they might force her to whip him to death. She couldn't bear to scan the crowd for her father, to see her failure in his face.

Ronato broke the silence, emerging onto the stage. Temporary steps were set up in front of it, the way they did for graduation or school plays. The stage itself was barren, without set pieces or adornments. Behind him were the painted concrete blocks that made up the walls all over the school, oversized chunks slathered in beige pigment. His dress shoes clacked against the hardwood planks as he paced.

"When you swear an oath to a god, repeating that oath is not for him," Ronato boomed. "The reminder is for you. You have reflected, brothers and sisters. Now, let us refresh our loyalty."

Brad Reynolds was the first man to step forward. He was clean-shaven, the armpits of his blue dress shirt darkened with sweat. The denim of his jeans was a deep blue, the fabric untouched by the rigors of the farm—his "nice jeans." Not two months ago, Beth had watched him seethe at the outpost for not being allowed to leave Harlow, but now at Harvest, he took a slow walk to the front of the stage, climbed the steps, and knelt before Ronato.

Even in the silence of the gym, Beth couldn't make out what Brad was saying. The oath rode a whisper, and when the prayer was over, Ronato offered his hand. Brad kissed it. Then he rose and returned to his seat.

Lacey Reynolds, his wife, was next. She walked to Ronato, knelt, took the Oath, and kissed the superintendent's hand.

When she was done, the man next to her rose, repeating the cycle.

Then another citizen stepped forward to renew the Oath. Then another. And another.

Beth watched as the entire town of Harlow bent the knee, one by one, to a ruler who wasn't even there.

If the Griffin didn't exist, and everyone believed it, maybe the Mayor was built the same way—a boogeyman no one ever saw, a monster used by men like Ronato and Ortega to dominate and torture the town.

Only she had a feeling that the Griffin did exist, that Kate had found him, and that he was chained up in the locker room.

But if the Mayor had his way, the Griffin would not exist much longer.

As Harlow swore their Oaths at the feet of Ronato, Quinn remained in the locker room with Ben Cartwright, who'd stayed behind when Ronato and Pernell took Beth to her seat.

"Here we are again, amigo," Cartwright said. He sat down on the bench, careful to stay out of arm's reach.

Quinn raised his hands, showing him the handcuffs. The chain looped through them rattled and clinked.

"I can't let you go," Cartwright said.

"Then why did you help me wriggle out of that pinch with the Sheriff?"

Cartwright ignored the question. "Kate marked you," he said, tapping his own forearm where he had seen Quinn's tattoo. "But she didn't send you. Two generations of knowledge—her mother's and her own—and she gave none of it to you. Ever wonder why?"

"It's such a lovely place, I don't know why we didn't at least come for the holidays, visit dear old Dad," Quinn said.

"I didn't know guys like you had a sense of humor."

"You don't know guys like me," Quinn said. "You've got sharp wits for an old man in a rural shithole like this, but you wouldn't last with any of the crews I ran with."

"You didn't last, either," Cartwright said. "You were Nico Colletti's man. Wanted in connection with fifteen deaths, guilty of so many more than that, I'm sure. Two of them were minors. Four were women. Skilled thief, but only because you didn't leave witnesses. Your last, biggest score was a thing of beauty—a weapons sale. Criminals never go to the cops, something like that? When that one was over, your own crew went after you on Nico's orders. He betrayed you. A betting man would have put Nico's odds of living through that attempted double-cross quite long, indeed—yet you never went after him. You disappeared."

"You dig this up on account of your fine investigating skills, or you torture it out of Benoit?"

"No torture," Cartwright said. "All it took was asking. He was happy to tell us all about you." He leaned in, a sly look crossing his face. "You really take out seven of the Garza organization's finest enforcers, unarmed, with your dick hanging out when they went after you in a men's room?"

Quinn said nothing.

"Come on. You can tell me. I can believe you pulled it off, but unarmed?"

"Nine of them," Quinn said, raising his hands again. "You going to set me loose on these assholes, or do you still want to play story time?"

"I told you, I can't," he said. "Maybe I could have. Those burn scars? Hell of a tale, that one. They tied you up and set you on fire, the way I hear it. You played dead while the fire ate your flesh, waiting for the ropes to burn. When they did, you got up, still smoldering from third-degree burns, and killed three men. The smoking ghost who rose up that day would have made a fitting Griffin."

Quinn said it aloud before Cartwright could beat him to it: "That man is gone."

"Right on, amigo," Cartwright repeated. "Kate knew it, I imagine. The scars turned numb. You don't remember the fire."

Cartwright saw the truth that Quinn had long known. Time had scraped the worst parts of him away, and he couldn't survive without them.

"A small-town Sheriff with two slow country boys damn near did you in," Cartwright added. "And you're supposed to rise up and destroy the Mayor? Maybe some regular folk will get all excited when they see your tattoo—and they will die. Painfully. But the worst death will be saved for the Griffin legend itself, when you're cut apart, howling, as Harlow watches their flimsy piece of hope bleed and scream on the hardwood."

Cartwright pointed to the wall behind them. Quinn turned and saw the dusty shadow of a Griffin mascot on the brick. How many years ago did they rip it off the wall? How long had Harlow suffered?

"Let me go," Quinn said. "If I die, you can be the first one to say I told you so."

"Harlow has been waiting for the Griffin for many years," Cartwright said, "and it cannot be you."

"It can't be anyone else."

"It has to be someone else," Cartwright said. "Because if I let you go, the Griffin will die."

When Marcus took the Oath, Beth couldn't watch him kneel. Only when he was walking back to his seat did Beth choose to find her father's eyes. Marcus's gaze was hollow, his face blank, devoid of emotion. He sat down and stared into his folded hands.

When the last of Harlow's citizens had knelt, Ronato stepped to the edge of the stage, greeted by pure silence.

"Mayor...receive these Oaths. Hear the humble whispers of your people, and their adoration and loyalty for you, and accept my thanks for the honor of serving you in hearing them."

The gym crowd gave a hushed but audible, "Give thanks."

"And now the Harvest shall truly begin, with those who will finally become men and women," Ronato said. "Those among us who are now strong enough to learn their heritage."

Ronato stepped down from the stage and circled the table on the gym floor.

"There is power in blood," he continued, "and today, that blood is celebrated. Today it is tasted, and as our Harvest begins, the blood thickens into the strongest of bonds."

"There is power in blood!" the people cried.

"But before flesh can be broken, before the celebration of our children's ultimate awakening, we must attend to important matters. We have to lay a feast on the table, and to do that, we must meditate upon those who have sinned. Chief among those sinners is a traitor...do I have to say the name? Must I stain this joyous festival with the name Jarvis?"

The crowd vibrated with disquiet, a collective rumbling. People leaned over to whisper in the ears of others, passing their own judgments.

"Here we have the youngest and only Jarvis child remaining, sweet Beth," Ronato said. "She ran from her duty, betraying all of you. Worse, we discovered the dead bodies of Sheriff Vance, Jason Vowell, and Morgan Albers—the good men who tried to save her from herself."

Ronato positioned himself behind Beth, placing his hands on her shoulders. Beth braced for the worst, but Ronato let go. He continued to pace, the heels of his polished shoes now clapping against the gym floor, a metronome waiting for words to ride its rhythm.

Finally, someone broke the silence, crying out, "Feast her!"

Ronato smiled and clapped emphatically. Other voices joined in. "Feast her!" they screamed, again and again.

"Traitors as low as Beth have always been, and always will be, feasted to the bone. But the Mayor has spoken to me—and while Beth is a traitor, she is not a killer."

If only you knew, she thought.

He walked to the opposite end of the table, staring at Beth from across a sea of red cloth.

"Today, a killer shall confess, and be punished. Today, the Mayor shall hear the Oaths of our young."

He paced for a long beat, working the tides of his speech to stoke the congregation.

"Today, we feast!" he shouted. The crowd cheered in unison. "For an Oath is nothing without blood, and the Mayor has chosen the lowest among us to bind our children to the Mayor's mercy."

A wave of nods rippled through the audience. Ronato took another dramatic pause. "But today, the lowest among us is not from Harlow. He came here, uninvited, and spat upon our way of life."

Beth expected them to drag Quinn out of the locker room. Instead, Ronato surprised her.

"Bring me the cop," he said.

High Servants dragged a man too skinny to be Quinn from the darkness of the hallway. A bag encased his head, and his toes dragged against the hardwood. Pernell was one of the servants attending to him. He yanked away the bag, revealing a man she'd never seen before, his pale face looking sunken and far from the sun, his eyes surrounded by dark rings. His thin, sweat-soaked hair clung to his temples in stringy patches. He moved his mouth as they handled him, making no sound, looking aimless and senile.

High Servants surrounded him. Another group of servants emerged from the dark hallway with a rolling metal post. Beth thought it looked like one of the mobile basketball hoops they brought out for P.E., only modified. The bottom of the post had wheels and a heavy, sand-filled base, but the hoop and backboard were gone, replaced by a metal rod in the shape of an upside-down L.

They looped a rope through the metal arm and started to pull, taking out the slack. The captured man didn't fight as the servants ushered him forward.

Beth finally recognized the makeshift structure: a game hoist, used by hunters to suspend deer when butchering them.

The man started to scream. Beth saw a glint of silver as they worked at his ankles. Not a knife, but something thinner—a heavy needle, thick enough to pull a small cord of rope through a hole in the back of his feet.

Pernell yanked the rope. The cop dangled from the butchering frame, his feet spread into a wishbone position, his body suspended by his Achilles tendons. The High Servants began laying tools out beside him. Ronato extended his hand, and a servant placed the handle of a Kuri machete in his palm. The bent spine of the blade glimmered in the sodium lights of the gym.

The cop screamed again, a guttural, desperate sound, a frequency only reached when the will to live is given a voice. It was a sound she'd heard twice now in the past couple of months—once from Shaun, a boy. But this was a grown man, a cop no less, broken until his only voice was that of suffering. He flailed his arms, trying to swing up to his torso and grasp the rope biting into his Achilles.

"Curtis Quinn," he screamed, over and over again. "He's your man, not me."

Ronato paid him no mind, circling his prey. A servant handed him a whetstone and he began drawing it up the lip of the blade. The grind was slow, methodical, maddening.

Quinn will get his, she thought. *But I'm afraid you won't live to see it.*

The sound of Benoit's torture ran through Quinn like wild electricity. He planted his legs on the ground and tried to squat out of his predicament, hoping to break the bench posts out of the concrete. He trembled with effort, then gave up.

"Let me go," Quinn said. "Do it now. These people want a Griffin? I'll give them what they want, and more."

Cartwright seemed even more calm in the face of Quinn's desperation.

"No," Cartwright said. "If the rage is real, you're an easy target, even sloppier than before. And if the rage is fake, it's useless."

He heard Benoit scream his name.

Quinn closed his eyes. He focused on breathing, hoping to sharpen the only sense that linked him to the gym—sound. He heard Ronato talk over Benoit saying *please* over and over again.

No more words. The screaming stopped. Scott sobbed. Footsteps. Then, Ronato spoke, his sentence punctuated by a scraping noise—stone against metal.

A blade, he thought. *Sharpening a blade.*

Then, Quinn heard the plop of something thick and wet hitting the floor.

Ronato circled, sharpening the machete. Benoit's face reddened, displaced blood pooling in his skull. He cried, a mix of snot and spit dangling from his head in silvery ropes.

"You are not of Harlow," Ronato said. "The Mayor cannot offer you the same mercy as his children."

He knelt down, tilting his head, doing his best to look Benoit in the eyes. He held out the whetstone. A servant took it away.

"The only mercy at your disposal is the fact that you can die but once." Ronato struck with lightning speed, swinging the machete so fast that Beth wasn't even sure if he hit him. She saw the split in the cop's shirt—was Ronato so accurate that he could graze Benoit's skin, cutting only the fabric, but not his flesh?

Then, the slit in the shirt turned red. Guts unraveled from the wound, the intestines rolling down his body.

The base of the hoist thumped against the hardwood as Benoit struggled, but that just emptied the gaping hole in his midsection faster. She thought he looked like a piñata after being well-struck and dropping all its candy at once, and almost laughed. Glistening viscera smacked against the floor.

Soon, Benoit was still. The screaming stopped, his face obscured by the ropes of intestine hanging from his belly.

"Prepare the feast!" Ronato shouted.

Beth saw the teenagers at her table bow their heads in silent prayer. She watched as Pernell worked on Benoit. First, he skinned him using plier-like hide pullers. He threw the skin into a garbage drum set up next to him. Next, he drew an angled blade that curled over two knuckles. A Wyoming knife. Her father owned one, and she had seen him clean a deer before, although he never bothered to teach her. Pernell sliced away tissue and cut ligaments, giving him a clear path to the meat.

As the people prayed, Pernell cut thick steaks from Benoit's decimated body. Each cut was laid on a white plate and placed in front of one of the silent teenagers with assembly-line precision.

How long since she had eaten? The meat looked like venison, lean with a rich, dark red hue. Still, she felt no hunger, and saw none in the eyes of Harlow. She didn't live among secret cannibals, she lived with prisoners forced to take a cruel communion. She was an adult now, and her turn was coming. Soon, a plate would be in front of her, and once they were all properly served and the manners of waiting were satisfied, she was sure that Ronato would command them to eat.

Quinn heard enough to know that Scott Benoit was dead. He heard Ronato speak of a feast, and then he heard the clink of tools and the wet, dank sound of ripping flesh.

He remembered Morgan Albers taunting Beth, telling her that he had tasted Kate.

We all had a taste.

Quinn had assumed that Morgan was referring to rape, but Ronato had mentioned a feast twice during his lunatic sermon, and he'd just heard Benoit being cracked apart and opened up like crab legs. He didn't think anything could be worse than visualizing the woman he loved being gang-raped. Before he'd killed the Sheriff and his men, Quinn had imagined men wearing overalls, their flies unzipped with tiny pink cocks barely peeking from that sea of thermal wool, taking turns with Kate.

Yet now, here he was, imagining her on that hoist, her skin taken off in huge swaths, the meat sliced away with rough blades.

They took her flesh, her meat, her teeth—but left her face. All so they could find him.

"What did they do to her?" Quinn said. "Tell me."

"They called it the Homecoming," Cartwright said. "Only they didn't kill her first, like your friend. Everyone had a bite, all while she was alive. The screams of that girl. My God."

Quinn clenched his teeth hard enough to creak in his mouth.

"She was pregnant," Cartwright said. "You knew that, right?"

Quinn didn't answer.

"The Mayor himself ate the child in front of her. All but the gristle."

Quinn wasn't an easy man to shock, but the image dented his resolve and put a pause in his breath. He centered himself again, his one talent in the most heated moments—staying cool, applying emotions to pragmatic ends.

"You're lying," Quinn said. "Trying to get a rise out of me. Marcus told me himself that he's the one who killed Kate, on the Mayor's command."

"He did," Cartwright said. "They cut his palm and handed him a knife. Gave him the choice of cutting her loose or cutting her throat. Trust me, at that point, there wasn't much left to salvage. He made the right choice."

Quinn looked at Cartwright, suddenly clear-eyed.

"Let me go," he said. The voice felt foreign, as if it emerged from him through its own free will. "Let me go, and maybe I'll let you live."

"Now we're talking," Cartwright said.

CHAPTER 20

Beth's plate arrived. A thick piece of the cop rested on the white porcelain. Blue and red hues glistened in the pool of blood that surrounded the meat, but Beth wouldn't allow herself to gag. She bit down on her cheek instead. Her own blood, she could stomach.

As the other teenagers received their meals, they broke their prayer and ate.

Kids she'd known since kindergarten were gnawing at a piece of human flesh, turning their lips and fingers sticky with blood. Kyle Kehrer, a boy who once passed out at the sight of a bloody nose, had blood all over his maw from pushing his face so deeply into his meal. Gloria Evans, a pretty girl with brown hair who had helped her with math homework in ninth grade, was out of breath from stuffing her face. Eric Bard, a hard-nosed baseball player known for his grit, was crying as he forced down bite after bite. Everyone's hands turned dark as they feasted.

Beth grabbed the rim of her plate and flipped it off the table. The porcelain shattered and the filet stuck to the gym floor.

"Again," Ronato said. Pernell cut the meat, and a servant brought her a fresh plate. This time, she picked up the plate and threw it at Ronato, who ducked, but his face was splattered with stray drops of blood. He didn't even bother wiping them away.

"You will feast," he said.

"Fuck your Oath, fuck this meal, fuck the Mayor, and fuck you," Beth said. The crowd gasped.

Ronato smiled. He nodded in the direction of the far hallway.

Servants dragged Trent from the shadows of the stage, his head bagged, his legs and arms bound. He didn't struggle. They put him in a seat at the table and removed the bag. His brown eyes were rimmed red, his hair glued to his temples with sweat. They had stuffed him in a dress shirt and bandaged his wounds, but dots of blood seeped through the fabric around his ribcage. He was injured and exhausted, but alive.

Duct tape covered his lips. A servant tore it off.

"Our cop friend doesn't seem to suit Beth's mature palate," Ronato said. "Perhaps she needs a different slice of meat."

Trent's father, Chris, sprinted away from his post near the stage. Other servants grabbed him, holding him back as he screamed, "You can't! I'm a High Servant!"

They wrestled him to the ground and tied his wrists as he screamed at Ronato. They duct-taped his mouth, and even then, his cheeks inflated as he screamed against the tape.

"I won't kill your son," Ronato said. He gestured to Pernell, whose Carhartt bibs were covered in blood. "Take one pound from him. No more, no less."

"Stop," Beth whispered.

"Excuse me?" Ronato said.

"I said *stop*."

Ronato gestured for the servants to prepare yet another plate of meat from the cop's carcass.

"I knew you'd change your mind," he said.

"First, I have a confession to make," she said.

His eyebrows arched, and he didn't respond immediately—this, he had not planned for. "Enlighten us," he said at last.

"I saw who killed the Sheriff and his men."

"A Jarvis has finally found her loyalty!" A smattering of laughter.

Her father continued to stare at his hands. He wouldn't look at her.

"Then tell us, who is the criminal who murdered three of our finest men?"

"The Griffin," she said. The tenor changed in the crowd, the tone shifting to whispers and secret chatter. "The Griffin has finally come to bring justice to Harlow."

Ronato's face darkened, a storm front forming behind his eyes.

Marcus looked away from his hands, shaking his head. Only then did Beth realize he was crying.

Ronato held out his hand, and one of the butchers handed him the blood-stained Kuri machete.

Quinn heard Beth standing up to Ronato, and knew that when they brought Trent out, she wouldn't hold up for long. Cartwright stood in the doorway, arms crossed, observing the tiny sliver of the gym he could see through the hallway.

"Let me go, give me that gun of yours, and get the hell out of here," Quinn said. "You can use the tunnel in the boiler room. No one will see you."

"And what would you do with a gun?"

"Bake fucking cupcakes. What do you think? This Ronato guy—even if he isn't the Mayor, he's still something special. Right?"

"He is one of the Mayor's disciples. He serves as his regent in his absence."

"I take him out first," Quinn said. "Flash the tattoo. All hell breaks loose."

"You make it sound so easy," Cartwright said. "You do know if you fail, Kate will have died for nothing?"

"I won't fail," Quinn said. "And I'm done asking."

Cartwright took a buck knife out of the holster on his belt.

"Be still, and I'll let you go," he said.

Quinn obeyed. Cartwright plunged the tip of the knife into the upper fabric of Quinn's work shirt. He sliced enough of a hole to grab the cloth and rip it away, leaving Quinn's tattooed arm exposed.

The Griffin. Their hope was a high school mascot, a lie, some dusty shadows turned into a myth. A mark his wife had put on him, a symbol of loyalty and faithfulness. Or was that a lie, too?

Cartwright uncuffed him and left the gun on the bench. He went to stand in the hallway, watching the ceremony.

Quinn picked up the gun—an XD semiautomatic pistol, a popular and familiar model. The clip was full, and the gun had the oily sheen of being regularly maintained. He hadn't held a gun in a long time, and in his hand was that old feeling of power and lethality, a calming influence. And in the stillness of those mental waters, a single thought boomed in his mind—*run*. Just as Marcus Jarvis had urged him to do.

He could use the tunnel and get away clean. He'd tell the police, even if it meant turning himself in. They would believe him. Fear mixed with truth creates a powerful frequency that cuts through doubt like nothing else.

So why couldn't he turn away from this and head for the boiler room? Why did his hand crave the handle of the gun instead of the knob of the tunnel door?

Because that's Beth's voice out there, Quinn thought. The girl wasn't breaking.

Then she said a word that changed the tenor of the gym. Ronato's smooth demeanor finally cracked. Quinn heard the distinct sound of a palm striking flesh—a vicious slap had interrupted Beth. Still, she kept going. She said the word again.

Griffin.

Beth had said that the Griffin had come, that it had killed the Sheriff and his men. She was ready to suffer to make the town believe. She was brave, like Kate. She was family. If Quinn owed the Jarvis family one thing, it was to make it all real, if only for a few moments, enough time to put Ronato's brains on the wall.

Quinn entered the hallway. Cartwright turned to face him. The look on his face—was that relief? Resignation?

Only then did he notice Cartwright wasn't wearing his watch, the gift from his wife. He wasn't wearing his wedding ring. He'd left it at home. Ben Cartwright was planning to die.

Quinn was sick and tired of trying to figure the motherfucker out. He raised his pistol, mere feet from Cartwright's forehead. The man didn't move. Quinn willed himself to fire, but still, couldn't pull the trigger.

Run. You do not understand this. You will not survive.

He ignored the voice. The gun's nose trembled.

"You see now," Cartwright whispered. "You know what you should do, but here you are. I thank you for doing this. My family thanks you." He waited, silently urging Quinn to fire.

"Don't forget to show them the tattoo," he added. "If you don't, it's all for nothing."

He wasn't the intimidating P.I. anymore. Quinn saw the craggy face of a scared old man who was backpedaling. With each step he took backward, Quinn matched him.

He kept the gun raised, but didn't shoot. Cartwright's job was clear now—to deliver the Griffin in all its rage and glory.

Don't let him win. You can still run, even now.

Cartwright sensed his hesitation. "The Mayor let me take the first bite of her," Cartwright said, his chin quivering. He didn't want to say it, but had to—with Quinn wavering, it was the only way to complete his mission. "I was the one who found her, so he rewarded me. I took it from her left tit. She screamed for you, told me that you would kill me."

Quinn swallowed hard. The gun quivered. He could see into the gym over Cartwright's shoulder. So close now, but Quinn knew he was being baited.

"You're lying," Quinn said.

Cartwright sensed the shift. He looked past the gun, into Quinn's eyes.

"The child was a girl," Cartwright said.

At the ultrasound, the tech was certain their baby was a girl. They picked up pink paint for the nursery on the way home. Quinn painted it himself the next day while Kate rested on the couch, feet-up, touching their child through the skin of her belly—a daughter who was never to know the horrors of Harlow.

"The Mayor—" Cartwright didn't get to finish. Quinn pulled the trigger, sending a cloud of brain and bone into the gym, a grisly heralding of the Griffin's arrival.

Ronato placed the tip of the machete on Trent's shoulder. He skimmed the blade over Trent's shirt, watching Beth as he did it. The blade moved to the skin of Trent's forearm, stopping at his wrist. The sound of the sharpened metal edge kissing flesh was enormous in the silent gym.

"The hand weighs a pound," Ronato said. He waited for Beth to break, but she maintained cool eye contact and fought off the urge to squirm in her chair.

"Tell me again who killed those men," Ronato said.

"The Griffin." Resolute.

Ronato yanked the blade against Trent's wrist, opening up a nasty cut.

"I'll only ask you one more time," Ronato said.

"That won't change the truth," Beth answered.

Ronato walked toward Beth with anger and purpose. She braced herself but refused to close her eyes, even if it meant watching him cut her.

Instead, he slapped her across the face. The open-handed blow knocked Beth's chair to the side, and she fell hard to the floor. She remained bound to the chair, but one of the legs was broken. She had enough slack to bring her ankles to her hands and untie herself. Ronato didn't move to stop her.

"You lie," Ronato said. "I'll make you carve a pound from your precious boyfriend with your own two hands."

"You can't hurt him," Beth said. "His father is a High Servant, and Trent himself is innocent. I forced him to run."

"Another lie."

"Without the Mayor's judgment, you can't harm him any further." She flung aside her ropes.

"I rule through his will and carry out his wishes. My judgment becomes his will. His will fuels my judgment."

"Not this year," Beth said, standing up. Facing him. "The Mayor has returned to Harlow."

Ronato was at a loss for words. She was working him, hoping he'd give up some information, trying to at least embarrass him, but the look on his face all but confirmed the Mayor was somewhere, watching them.

And she finally knew who he was. The thought broke her heart, but she knew she had it right. She also knew she couldn't let it slow her down.

"The Griffin saved me," Beth said, raising her voice. "He will come for all of you. But he only helps those who help themselves."

Ronato grabbed her by the throat, shutting her off in the middle of her rant. She tried to swallow, feeling her larynx struggle to move against his grip. He tossed her aside just before she passed out. She slid across the gym floor, but refused to stay down for long.

"Cut off Trent's hand," Beth said, getting to her feet once more. "Do it. Supersede the Mayor's will. He told you not to harm him. Didn't he?"

Ronato seethed, his every cell wanting to brutalize the defiant brat talking back to him.

"You can't harm me, either," Beth said. "It's more important to see me broken than killed. That about right?"

Ronato struck her across the face again, this time with a closed fist. Beth fell, her mouth full of broken teeth, her jaw throbbing. She spat out chunks of molar mixed with the stringy flesh of her shredded cheek, realizing that her mouth wasn't working quite right, that the jawbone had either broken or come out of its socket.

"Then I suppose I'll just have to break you," Ronato said. He loomed over her, eclipsing the wire-covered lights high above the gym floor. The figure was hypnotizing, swaying in her unmoored vision.

Then, she heard a gunshot.

She thought the sound was a hallucination, but then she saw people reacting to it, their heads turning. Ronato moved away from her, allowing the harsh light back into Beth's aching eyes.

For a moment, she thought it was her father. She wanted it to be him, wanted to believe that this whole time, he was planning on dying to protect her. Maybe he had smuggled in a weapon, just in case they caught her. He would kill Ronato and take his family's mantle—he would tell everyone that he was the Griffin, and the time had come to rise up and take Harlow back for themselves.

But of course it wasn't her father. Quinn had escaped, and when she saw him emerge from the catacombs of the locker room hallway, she knew she'd underestimated the Mayor. Beth had meant to reinforce the power of the Griffin, but all she'd done was refresh everyone's memory before the Mayor finally killed it off for good.

Quinn stepped over the dead body of Ben Cartwright, gun in hand. He was a madman with a lethal weapon who'd just murdered a pillar of the community, but no one screamed or scattered. They were afraid, but not of him.

Ronato smiled, sizing him up. Quinn had seen smiles on enemies before—they symbolized either true confidence or fake confidence, and he found both to be equally fragile in his experience. Neither was bulletproof.

The wood of the gym floor groaned under Ronato's weight. He stripped off his sport coat. He was a huge man, equal in size to Quinn himself, his chest and arms stretching every fiber of his white dress shirt.

"I am going to string you up and cut you open so that you die slowly, choking on the stench of your own guts," Ronato said. "The Mayor will be pleased he won't have to dirty his hands with the likes of you."

Ronato's easy approach filled Quinn with uncertainty. This wasn't mere confidence—this was a man who somehow knew the fight was fixed.

Quinn hesitated no longer. He fired, double-tapping two quick shots into Ronato's chest.

Ronato flinched, clutching at his chest. He stepped back. Quinn waited for him to fall—the XD wasn't a heavy hitter, but it had plenty of stopping power for a man of Ronato's size, and the one skill that hadn't rusted was Quinn's accuracy. The shots landed center-mass.

Yet Ronato recovered and continued pacing toward Quinn.

I must have missed, he thought. But he hadn't—he clearly saw neat, coin-sized holes in Ronato's shirt. Kevlar. *Has to be. That's why the shirt's so snug. That's why he looks so big.* Yet nothing poked from his sleeves or collar.

He concentrated and took a single, deep breath, aiming carefully. Headshots were tougher to accomplish, but there was no Kevlar across the fucker's forehead. Ronato made himself an easy target, walking slowly. Quinn eased the trigger once, then twice. His aim was true. Both shots jammed into Ronato's forehead, and his skull whiplashed backward as it absorbed the impact.

Yet he shook it off and somehow kept walking.

Ronato's eyes were wet and alive. A thin stream of blood began to crawl down the bridge of his nose. Quinn had shot him twice with nine-millimeter rounds, and it only opened up the equivalent of a shaving cut.

With Ronato getting uncomfortably close, Quinn emptied the clip. He started rattling off shots—cheekbone, head, neck. Tiny wounds opened, nicks that barely bled.

By then, Ronato was upon him. He swiped at Quinn's forearms, knocking the empty pistol out of his hand. The blow felt like someone had spiked his forearm with a hammer.

Before Quinn could recover, Ronato's hand was wrapped around his throat. He lifted Quinn into the air. No one had enough strength to lift a grown man with one hand—that was one of those movie tricks Quinn hated because they were so unrealistic.

Ronato flicked him away, sending him airborne, crashing into the base of the stage.

The impact dazed him. He struggled to all fours. His forearm throbbed, but he made it to his feet. Ronato was walking toward him again. He needed a plan—but if guns didn't work, what would?

Quinn started circling the gym, trying to maintain as much distance between himself and Ronato as possible. He studied his surroundings—the crowd was pressed against the back of the gym, because there was no escape. The High Servants watched, holding rifles and pistols. He saw chains tied around the push bars of the exit doors. Big patches of bleachers were barren as the citizens tried to stay out of harm's way.

He thought of simply running, but even if he made it into the abandoned tunnel, it would be suicide—his survival at this point depended on evasion, and the tunnel would turn their fight into a close-quarters massacre he couldn't possibly survive. He checked the ceiling—flimsy drop tiles. Basketball hoops, like in any other gymnasium, were pinned up by chains and bolted to the ceiling frame.

He headed for the vacant corner of the gym near one of the chained-off exit doors. He saw a fire alarm pull, an AED device, and a glassed-in fire axe, all assembled near an array of switches that controlled the lights and the retractable bleachers.

Quinn circled while Ronato stalked him like an unchained beast.

Then, Ronato rushed him again—the bastard was as fast as he was strong. Quinn could only muster a half-step before Ronato closed the gap and crushed him with a short uppercut into his midsection.

The body blow lifted Quinn two feet into the air. He crashed down on his back, and for a moment, he thought he was dying. He clutched at his ribs, trying to breathe, and when the drumbeat of the impact subsided, he sucked in a whooping inhale.

Impossible durability. Impossible speed. Impossible power— Ronato had pulled his punch and still lifted a three-hundred-pound man into the air. He was toying with him, making a show of it.

Quinn slowly recovered. As he got to his feet, he feigned more pain and damage than Ronato had delivered.

"Do none of you want to join your chosen one?" Ronato shouted, turning to the crowd. "Your savior? Your gladiator?"

As Ronato addressed the people of Harlow, Quinn sprinted for the bleachers. He started bounding up the empty planks. The surfaces were precarious, only about twelve inches wide, and one wrong step could send a boot plunging into the crevice between the bleacher seat and the floor. He trusted his balance, however rusty.

Ronato followed, but had to slow down to navigate the bleachers. He looked clumsy, vulnerable for the first time, but he kept his footing. Quinn raised his fists, inviting a fight. Ronato charged him, but on the bleachers, he had to come at a more reasonable speed. The man had no training, no instincts, only his inexplicable empowerments, and he leaned on them like crutches.

Quinn slipped him and drove a foot into Ronato's knee. The blow would have crippled a normal human, but in this case, it felt like stomping a rock. Ronato didn't quite buckle, but it was enough to make him slip between the bleacher gaps at an awkward angle.

Quinn jumped off of the bleachers, taking a precarious ten-foot fall onto the concrete that flanked the bleacher banks. He was right next to the fire control equipment, but that wasn't his first priority. He slammed his palm into the bleacher button instead.

The pneumatic system retracted the telescopic bleachers, sucking them back into the wall with intermittent slams.

The bleachers reached Ronato just as he was about to extricate himself. The metal pinched his leg. He screamed, not in agony, but effort. The underpinnings let loose a metallic cry. Bolts popped. They wouldn't hold him long.

Quinn elbowed the glass and removed the fire axe, then mounted the remaining bleachers, above Ronato. From the top bleacher, Quinn brought the axe down, powering through the handle with his whole body. Ronato moved his hand to protect his head. The blade of the axe smacked against the center of his palm. Instead of lopping half of it clean off, it felt like punching into a thick piece of wood—thick, but penetrable. Durable, but not invincible.

Ronato finally cried out in pain. Blood didn't shoot or gush from his hand—it dribbled with the consistency of molasses.

Quinn was already readying himself for another swing. The next one severed the top half of Ronato's hand, leaving a thumbed stump behind. A third blow landed on his forearm. Finally, Ronato's face twisted in pain and fear. The progress fueled Quinn's efforts. He landed blow after blow, hoping for a clean shot at the bastard's head. Finally, with Ronato's hands and arms hacked apart, he landed a clean blow at the base of Ronato's neck, just above the shoulder girdle.

The blade got stuck in the split collarbone. He tugged it loose and swung again. Ronato struggled, too weak to escape the pinch of the bleachers now, and with thick, gum-like blood coming out of the stumps below his elbows, he had no leverage to swipe at Quinn or push himself out.

Quinn started screaming, needing the extra intensity to fuel the blows. Ronato's bones took multiple shots to finally split apart, and cutting through his flesh had the same consistency as hacking at the trunk of an oak. He pushed past the burning ache in his muscles, ignoring the lactic acid for one more blow. Then another. And another.

Soon, he was spent from the tough work of axe-swinging, but found the strength to bring it down a final time and felt the clean sensation of getting through Ronato's neck. The blade slammed into the bleacher top as Ronato's head fell away and rolled, bouncing onto the gym floor.

The bleacher motor continued to groan, burning up by the time Quinn finally defeated Ronato. His pungent blood stuck to the bleachers like snot. The gym was filled with smoke and the coppery stench of blood and scorched metal.

No one screamed. He didn't hear a sound. The axe trembled in his hands. His body was wrung out, his adrenal glands sucked dry. Spit was pasted in the corners of his lips. He wiped at his mouth with the back of a shaking hand.

Quinn heard the clop of boots echoing through the gym. He turned and saw an enraged Ortega sprinting at him, wild-eyed, building up a superhuman head of steam that Quinn was powerless to stop.

Still, he was hell-bent on going down swinging. He tightened his grip on the axe. Ortega was a blur now.

"Ortega!" someone shouted. The response was immediate. Ortega skidded to a stop, breathing hard—not from exhaustion, but from sheer rage.

The crowd knelt together once more. Ortega joined them, lunging forward to bend the knee.

The source of the command was a tall man emerging from the darkness of the hallway—the same hallway that Quinn had entered from.

The Mayor had finally arrived.

CHAPTER 21

B lood poured from Beth's mouth as she watched Galen
   Mettis enter the gym.
 He's old Harlow, and no friend of the Mayor. Known him a long time, her father had said.

Yet Galen Mettis looked no older than thirty, and this man had just brought Ortega to heel. The whole town was bowing their heads in his presence.

People hate your family because they have to, but your name means something, Galen had said. Of course it did—and that's why the Mayor himself had taken the responsibility of befriending Beth and giving her the confidence to run.

If the real Galen was old Harlow, that meant he was a lot like Cooper Murray—one of those old-timers you heard about, but never saw. Not when you were a teenager worrying about things like boys, grades, and sports, not when you were a sixteen-year-old learning that you can never leave—that Harvest awaits you at eighteen. Not when the old-timers stayed in their farmhouses drinking coffee and waiting for Harlow or themselves to finally die.

The real Galen had been executed. Probably months ago, and no one was told. At least no one the Mayor couldn't trust. Then he took a familiar name, one that Marcus Jarvis would trust whenever Beth brought up her mentor's name in casual conversation.

But this wasn't Galen Mettis. The mentor who had befriended her on those long nights stuck in an old truck was a ruse no longer necessary, killed off for good, and only the Mayor remained—a man she'd grown to trust who was finally ready to crush her family's legacy by slaughtering the Griffin just months after he had eviscerated her sister.

And after the Griffin legend was extinguished for good, the final step would be extinguishing the last of the Jarvis blood from Harlow.

Beth hurt, but she didn't think she'd have to hurt for much longer.

CHAPTER 22

The Mayor walked calmly into the center of the gym as Harlow knelt before him.

The man was thin and lithe, muscle striations rippling in his slender forearms and long neck. His height was enhanced by his dominant posture. Every part of him seemed cut from tanned granite. His presence was tangible, a predatory aura waking that old, reptilian fear that evolution had tried to erase.

"Ronato was strong. You were stronger," he said. Every syllable had the weight of command. "He was vicious...yet you were more vicious. A good day's work for a janitor."

He gently kicked Ronato's severed head as punctuation.

"Well?" the Mayor said. "You've all waited so long for the mighty Griffin. Here he stands, and not one of you will stand with him?"

No one dared to speak, the gym quiet enough to hear the hum of the lights overhead.

"You disappoint me," the Mayor said.

Quinn gripped the axe and started trudging toward the Mayor.

One boy rose from his knees. Quinn recognized him—Eric, a baseball player, a kid who always sidestepped freshly mopped tile instead of dragging his feet through like most of the other little pricks.

"He killed the Sheriff and his deputies," Eric said, his voice echoing in the gym. "He killed Mr. Ronato. He killed a disciple. He can kill the Mayor." He stood at Quinn's side.

The Mayor applauded, mocking him. "Inspired words," he said. "Would no one care to join him?"

A man from the bleachers stood up. The woman beside him— his wife, Quinn presumed—pulled at his arm.

"Daryl, no!"

He tore his arm away and started descending the bleachers. When he reached the bottom, he looked back at his wife. She didn't meet his gaze, staring blankly at the back of the person in front of her. She was going to lose them both, and knew it.

"Cowards!" Daryl scanned the crowd, pleading for others to join him. "You deserve the Mayor. All of you!"

The spectacle gave Quinn time to recover. His breathing returned to normal. His muscles were twitchy and he was dehydrated, but he was forced to work with the tools at his disposal.

He put his final tool to work and raised his arm, turning it, letting everyone see the Griffin tattoo.

No reaction. The tattoo was either too small to see, making it lack the grandiosity he needed, or they simply didn't give a shit. Rebellion was a lovely idea in theory, but not nearly as appealing when a depraved superhuman was waiting for you to reveal yourself as rebel so he could tear you apart.

Suddenly, one of the High Servants raised his gun, pointing it at the back of the Mayor's head. The Mayor sensed it, and smiled. He made no move to evade the shot.

The rifle fired, and the slug chewed into the concrete wall. The Mayor didn't absorb it, he *evaded* it—the bastard was somehow faster than Ronato.

Before the echo of the shot stopped ringing in the gym, the shooter's arm was ripped from his socket. The Mayor flicked it away and punched the offender in the temple. The blow collapsed the man's skull. His ruptured eye spat forth, and compressed brains shot through the hole of his opposite ear.

Another blur of speed as the Mayor crossed the gym, this time, for Daryl. The Mayor twisted Daryl's head from his body. Blood exploded from the stump, two geyser-like bursts before the pressure dissipated and the headless body collapsed.

Next, Eric. The Mayor took his leg and swung him against the brick wall. The boy's skull shattered against the blocks. His mother screamed. The Mayor turned to face her, and the screaming stopped. Her neighbor put a hand on her shoulder, reminding her to kneel. She did, and Quinn heard her muffled sobs in the quiet gym.

Quinn knew he could not defeat him. His every cell screamed at him to die fighting, but the bastard had gone through incredible lengths to set up a dramatic standoff with a worthy Griffin, and Quinn would piss all over his best-laid plans if he simply refused to fight.

He let the axe fall from his hands.

"Fuck this," he said.

"You came all this way for the truth," the Mayor said. "And now you give up?"

"I already know how she died," Quinn said. "So make it quick. Or messy. Or painful. I don't give a fuck."

The Mayor's face twitched ever so slightly.

"Ben left out the best parts," the Mayor said. "Before the feast, we starved her in a dark cellar for weeks." He paced around the table of praying teenagers. "She begged for food. I knew it was mostly for the child. The bonds of family are strong. So for food, water, and vitamins, we made her into a whore. I promised her I'd spare her daughter if she pretended to enjoy it. After that, she began to ask for it. Every High Servant fucked her, Griffin. Almost a hundred men. She was raw by the time I delivered my judgment."

Quinn ran his hand across his forehead, smearing the drops of blood that speckled his face. He was tired, so far from anything that mattered. Going home didn't mean taking one more step—going home meant letting go. He sat down on the gym floor.

"Those who run sometimes lose their legs," the Mayor said. "I made this her father's duty. We cut his palm deeply and handed him a dull blade. It took him the better part of an hour. She would have bled to death, if not for Ortega's skill with a blowtorch."

Quinn laid down, staring up at the ceiling tiles. The caged lights lost their edge, becoming dark in the periphery of his vision.

"We feasted," the Mayor said. "There was no Oath in this flesh, just the celebration that she had returned. We torched the wounds to keep her from bleeding out. She was alive when I took your daughter from her. The last thing she saw was my face, slimy with her fluid, rich with your heir's blood."

Quinn closed his eyes. He heard the Mayor's footsteps near his ear. Harlow's ruler was circling him.

"Extract your proper revenge, Griffin. Fight me, and you'll get the satisfaction of a martyr's death, and the painlessness of a quick one. Neither of which you deserve, but I am merciful."

"I'm not a martyr," Quinn said softly, keeping his eyes shut. "I'm not the Griffin, either. She tricked me into getting this dumb motherfucking tattoo. And fuck these people. They're not victims. They're accomplices."

The Mayor leaned down and scooped up the axe. The tool was every bit of eighteen pounds, but in his powerful hand, it looked as light as a Wiffle ball bat.

"This is the Griffin," the Mayor said, his tone mournful. "He bears the mark, but he's too weak and full of shame to take up his rightful mantle in all its glory."

"Then kill me," Quinn said. "Get it over with. See if they buy the lie. I'm no Griffin. A Griffin is loyal. A Griffin fights."

"If you won't die fighting, die standing," he said, offering his hand. Quinn refused to take it. The Mayor couldn't mask his frustration anymore. He knelt by Quinn and dropped his voice to a nearly imperceptible whisper.

"You see how they bore me," the Mayor whispered. His tone shifted from villain-speak, losing its Shakespearian boom. Quinn sensed a slight drawl. Whoever the Mayor was, he was a performer. He'd created a character and was putting on a show, begging for someone to play along with him.

"Give me this, and you won't feel a thing."

He stood and held out his hand again. Quinn held out his own hand—with his middle finger extended.

The Mayor kicked him in the upper arm. The momentum of the blow rolled him over, and he smashed into the apron of the stage. When he struck the wall, a subtle, metallic sound rippled through the gym.

A coin was rolling on its side across the Orphans logo in the center of the court. It clicked against the rubber sole of a kneeling High Servant's boot.

Ortega was close by, and picked it up, inspecting each side of the coin, then flipping it to the Mayor.

"A coin of broken trust," Ortega said.

"The Mayor is merciful!" the crowd chanted in unison.

The Mayor stood over Quinn, silent, stalling. Maybe even a little confused. It was then Quinn knew that whatever the coin was, it meant that the Mayor couldn't kill him. At least not yet.

"Low servants," the Mayor said. "Rise."

Three men rose. Quinn recognized two of them—Old Rich from the legion, and Marcus Jarvis. The third man was elderly, his face deeply creased, his hair thin and gray. The Mayor approached him first.

"Cooper Murray," he said. "The Great Survivor. Produce your coin."

Cooper reached into the back of his pants, drew out his wallet, and produced a silver coin. The Mayor inspected it, nodded, and returned it.

Then, he walked over to Marcus.

"Marcus Jarvis," the Mayor said, smiling. "Produce your coin."

Marcus didn't reach for his pocket.

"No," Beth said, not a scream, but a plea. Since taking a massive blow to the face, she'd remained dazed on the gym floor, watching it all unfold, but the plight of her father woke up a pained effort to talk through her broken jaw.

Quinn had taken the coin from Beth just hours earlier, and she had no doubt gotten it from her father. Marcus didn't have it, and while Quinn had never seen the consequences of not producing the "coin of broken trust" when asked, he figured they were dire and painful.

Just as Quinn prepared himself to watch Kate's father be executed, Marcus reached into his jeans and drew out a silver dollar.

The Mayor inspected the coin closely, pinching it in his thumb and forefinger. Then he turned to Old Rich. Rich's head was down, and his shoulders were shaking. The old bastard was sobbing right there in front of everyone.

"Clever," the Mayor said, returning the coin to Marcus.

"Richard Larson," the Mayor said. "Produce your coin." He was walking casually in Rich's direction. Rich looked up, his face twisted with grief.

"You damn well know I ain't got one," Rich said. "That traitorous fuck Marcus took mine in the parking lot of the legion, and didn't leave me no time to even try to get it back."

The Mayor stopped in front of him.

"You're a lucky man," the Mayor said. "I don't have time to punish you properly."

He punched Rich in the chest, his powerful fist smashing through the breastbone. When he lifted him up, Quinn saw the Mayor's fist on the other side, glistening with blood, strings of tissue and veins caught in the creases of his knuckles.

He held the old man up in the air. Rich's limbs twitched and bounced, but he'd died instantly, and all the movement was just his last few nerves firing before burning out. The Mayor flung the impaled man down, hard, onto the gym floor. The thud echoed.

He had enough power to kill a person with one brisk punch. If his power was that much more superior than Ronato's, Quinn wondered if he could actually be killed—or if he could even be hurt.

Quinn finally got to his feet, clutching his injured arm. "Whatever mercy that coin earned me, give it to Beth instead."

"And you said you weren't a martyr." The Mayor took his time deciding. Harlow waited. He had to deliver mercy, yet he was itching to crush the Griffin in front of them.

"The heavy debt of deserting Harlow must be paid," the Mayor said. "You would bear it in Beth's stead? Is that how you wish to spend your coin?"

Quinn nodded.

The Mayor walked up to him, letting the echoes fade between each step. The silence became the exhale of his approach.

"Then my mercy you shall have," the Mayor said. He thrust his heel into Quinn's lower leg, a thunderbolt of bootheel hitting the stiff, fragile bones below the knee.

Quinn felt the tibia break under the blow, the snap loud enough to make the servants near them flinch. He crumbled to the ground, groaning, biting back a scream. The Griffin might die, but he wouldn't scream. Not a chance.

"Beth Jarvis is absolved of her crime," the Mayor said. "Her punishment for deserting has been borne by her benefactor, the mighty Griffin. So at least one of you was saved by him here today."

"Fuck you," Quinn grunted.

"You have earned a clean death," he said. "A death befitting a hero of your stature. A death at the hand of a god."

"If you're a god," Quinn said, "you won't be the first one I don't believe in."

The Mayor raised the axe high above his head.

Quinn closed his eyes.

"Don't kill him." A familiar voice—Marcus's voice.

Ortega leapt to his feet. "How dare you—"

"Let him talk," the Mayor said. "Let's hear what was so important that it's worth the miserable life that he's clung to for so long."

"My apologies, Divine One," Marcus said. "This man defiled my eldest daughter. He poisoned the mind of my youngest, I'm sure of it. Kill him, and I will praise you, as you have cleansed my family of his stain. Yet he has much to offer you alive. He has the journal—started by my wife, stolen by Kate, taken outside of Harlow. No doubt she entrusted it to him, for how else would he find this place?"

"Is this true?" the Mayor said.

Quinn contemplated telling him to fuck off again, that he never saw Kate's journal. But that's where she kept the secrets of Harlow, and it was his honor and his honor alone that had kept him from unlocking those secrets. He'd buried all of that valuable information with her—information the Mayor didn't want out of his purview.

"Yes," Quinn said.

The Mayor strolled over to Trent. The axe rested on his shoulder, the way a fifth-grader might carry his beloved baseball bat.

"Are you truly innocent, boy?" the Mayor asked. "Did she trick you? Coerce you? Force you? Or did you attempt to desert Harlow of your own free will?"

Trent didn't look at the Mayor. Not once. He looked at Beth, and Quinn sensed a familiar and genuine light in his eyes. A light he'd once felt himself not too long ago.

"I love you, Beth," Trent said.

The Mayor took the back of his head in one hand. In the other, he held the axe. Not by the handle, but by the back of the axe's head.

"Did you follow her willingly?"

Trent finally looked him in the eyes. "Yes," he said.

The Mayor zippered the edge of the axe across Trent's throat.

Blood spewed forth in heaving gushes as Trent collapsed into the bonds of his chair. A bloom of redness widened on his shirt as Beth screamed through her devastated jaw. Chris Keller howled at the loss of his son, the sound muted by the heavy strands of duct tape over his mouth.

A smile crawled across the Mayor's face.

"I want the boy's body to rot in the darkness," the Mayor said. Again, Ortega obeyed, dragging Trent's limp body across the gym floor. He left a trail of smeared blood in his wake.

The Mayor returned to Quinn, who lay at his feet, his leg shattered.

"You'll need help retrieving the journal," the Mayor said. "I'm afraid your leg is catastrophically injured."

"I've dealt with worse," Quinn grunted.

"Oh, have you?" the Mayor said, and swung the axe.

The blade came down in a silver streak and struck Quinn just below the knee. His leg offered no resistance as the head of the axe moved through flesh and tendon and bone, smashing into the gym floor. Blood funneled out of the stump.

He heard nothing but the rapid breaths squealing from his shocked airway, and the thud of each crushing heartbeat. The Mayor's voice sounded distant, bottled up, coming from somewhere far away. He made out a few words—*Wound. Torch. Cauterize.*

Quinn looked at his lifeless lower leg and imagined it bagged up with the severed heads and yanked-off limbs as they cleaned up the gym for school the next day. Who would mop the floor? His leg looked foreign and blurry, the blood loss sucking the focus from his vision.

The hallway always needs a second mopping after fifth hour.

Hands grasped his arms. He looked down. A blue flame emerged from the silver mouth of a blowtorch. Ortega gently brought the tip to the gushing wound. Quinn thrashed, trying to get away from the bite of the fire, but he was too weak, and they held him steady.

Tissue sizzled and veins melted, their tips shrinking under the tongue of fire, shutting off the bleeding. The skin around his knee-cap blackened, and nerve endings turned to strips of ash. The marrow from his severed bone boiled and crusted over.

Quinn was not the Griffin. He was only a man, and could not help but scream.

CHAPTER 23

Beth woke up in a hospital bed. *Maybe I fell*, she thought. *I fell and had a bad dream.* Trent is alive. That poor cop wasn't gutted. My friends didn't eat human flesh.

Her father took her hand, startling her, and she tried to speak. Her teeth wouldn't separate, and knives of pain jabbed at her skull, just below her ears.

"Your jaw is broken," Marcus said. "Doctor Gaston says it's set well and should heal up fine."

Harlow's "hospital" was one floor, the old grade school building converted by Doctor Gaston, a Harlow resident. He was undoubtedly a High Servant to be trusted with Harlow's internal care. The Mayor's eyes were always watching.

She skipped trying to talk and pressed two fingers on the inside of her forearm, where the griffin tattoo was located—her way of asking about Curtis Quinn.

"He's probably not dead, or the Mayor would have made a show of it," he said.

"You saved him," she said. Her teeth vibrated, and she winced.

"Don't talk," he said. He wiped the sweaty hair from her forehead with a brush of his thumb and smiled at her. "I'm proud of you."

She looked away. How could he be proud of a failure?

"Stay with me, now," he said. "The Mayor didn't give you mercy because he's merciful. He's tempting you. Do you understand?"

She shook her head.

"Your mother lost her own father to him a generation ago," he said. "She was hellbent on bringing him down, and she died. Kate was hellbent on avenging her. She died. Now that we've been given this chance, I won't lose you to something as foolhardy as vengeance."

"What chance?"

"To live," he said.

"In shame."

"In peace," he answered.

She cut loose a dismissive laugh, a reflex she didn't think through. Her jaw clenched, and a wave of pain splashed through her.

"You took your chance," he said. "You learned your lesson and lost your friend."

"More than a friend," she said.

"Gone is gone."

"Who has to die for you to finally fight?" she said, hissing through her teeth.

"I have fought," he said, letting her hand drop. "Fought all these years for all my girls, and not a damn one of you has the sense to understand how he keeps us here."

He looked at the doorway, making sure no one was around, then lowered his voice.

"Harlow's not a cage," he said. "What keeps us locked up? A few stop sticks and a cornfield moat—you think that's enough to keep a whole fucking town under control? It's love that he uses against us. Duty. Loyalty. Our every emotion. That's his advantage. He can bank on us loving our children, wanting revenge for what we've lost, leaning on symbols to keep our families safe. He's a step ahead of us, always, because people who love are utterly predictable. The way you win? The way you live? Don't fight back. Struggle against the noose, and it tightens. You understand?"

He took his seat on the rolling recliner he had pulled up to her hospital bed. He'd said his piece and left it at that.

"You still saved him," she said. "You saved the Griffin."

He shook his head. "He's strong and capable. I'm hoping he can use the Mayor's obsession with that journal to escape. More than that, I'm hoping he'll have the sense to get gone and stay gone. The Griffin's been turned real, all right. Real enough to kill."

"The Mayor doesn't have to kill him," Beth muttered. "No one stood with Quinn. It never really mattered. The Mayor doesn't have to kill hope if it doesn't exist."

"All that bullshit's never been my worry," Marcus said. "Harlow is the Mayor's plaything, and once the Griffin is gone, shit's going to get awful boring for him."

"Then what?" she asked.

"That's my worry," Marcus said.

Quinn's calf was on a platter in the center of the table, bone-in, golden brown. His skin had a crust of salt and pepper. The leg was surrounded by stewed carrots, onions, and potatoes. A servant was cutting into it, putting a filet on both plates. The Mayor poured two glasses of red wine.

Gas lanterns lit the room. The walls looked like fossilized mud. Ties framed out the roof and walls, and the only furnishings were the table and chairs in the center of the underground space.

Quinn had lost track of time since he was dragged, one-legged, out of the gymnasium. It had been two days at least, maybe more. He was treated in the darkness, on a cot in the same underground labyrinth, the depths below the school. The painkillers were damn good, leaving a syrupy weight on his brain. His lower leg was capped with a thick, clean hat of gauze. His cuts and scrapes had the faint sizzle of antiseptic and were covered with bandages.

The Mayor gestured for the servant to leave. He sipped his wine.

"Eat first," he said. "Then talk. You must be famished."

He figured the Mayor got his rocks off by making people eat their own flesh. Resistance was what he craved. So, Quinn didn't hesitate—he slammed his fork into the meat and took a massive bite.

"Maybe I'm biased, but that tastes better than expected," Quinn said, talking with his mouth full, ignoring the urge to vomit—an urge that was purely mental. The meat itself wasn't much different from the rabbit meat his grandmother used to fry up, tough and greasy. He guzzled the wine, hoping it would mix with the painkillers for a delightfully numbing effect.

"You don't seem to put much stock in table manners," the Mayor said.

"Well, I did crash your party by chopping a motherfucker's head off, so chewing with my mouth open shouldn't surprise you."

The Mayor neatly laid his napkin across his lap and picked up the silverware in careful, measured fashion. He cut a dainty bite, placed it in his mouth, and savored it.

"You will deliver the journal," the Mayor said.

"You're scared," Quinn said. "All that power, and you're scared of a woman's scrawls in some tiny book."

"Nothing was ever built or accomplished without fear," the Mayor said. "Inspiration? Please. Inspiration and promises are nothing but polite threats. Look around. Fear moves everything. People go to work because they're afraid of going broke, they fuck their stale wives because they're scared of being alone, and they worship people like me because they're frightened to take responsibility for the world they live in."

He sipped his wine, then tilted the glass, staring at the shimmer of the wine's legs evaporating on the crystal. The act struck Quinn as counterfeit, something a Harlow bumpkin saw on TV and was trying to emulate.

"You're trying to be something you're not," Quinn said. "You're not fearless. You're the kid who roasts anthills with a magnifying glass." He leaned across the table, the scent of his own roasted leg pungent in the dank air. "I hated that kid."

"I am not ashamed of fear," the Mayor said. The wounded look was almost genuine. "When I was a child and my father took off his belt to whip me, I was afraid. Years later, when my stepfather came after me with his cock out, I was petrified. Then, as a young man working in mine nineteen when it collapsed, I was paralyzed by fear. I wanted to live.

"I was trapped with five other men, and to survive down there, I ate the flesh of those who'd died without hesitation. More days passed. I had to find those who were still alive, crawling through the dark to choke them in their sleep, because that's what needed to be done to eat. To live. Then, the universe rewarded my tenacity. I searched the tunnels in the dark for insects to eat. I scraped slime off the rocks, but it was too far down for any kind of moss, was it not? That must have been the source, the blessing that offered me a just reward for my tenacity. I ate the flesh of the Earth itself and achieved my power and my destiny."

The Mayor leaned closer, his head effeminately tilted. Still, it made Quinn recoil.

"Would that boy have survived without fear?" He picked up a thin, shining bone—Quinn's lower leg, picked clean. He dropped the bone onto the plate. The clink was thick and loud. "You laid down in the gym, unafraid to die. Failing your woman, but not caring. So you understand now, don't you? Stripped of fear, we are powerless."

"Powerless, fearless, legless. Are we done yet?"

"When you give me the journal," the Mayor said.

"Since I don't care if you kill me, what could you possibly threaten me with?"

"Not a threat as much as an offer," the Mayor said. "Decline, and you will watch Marcus Jarvis forced to desecrate the last of his daughters. And when Beth is dead, I'll let Marcus live. What's left of him, anyway. Then, I will plunge my hands into your belly and yank out your guts. You will die choking on them, and the last thing you will ever see is me laughing in your face. However, if you bring me the journal, I will make you whole again."

"Whole?"

"Your leg," the Mayor said. "I can give it back to you. That gift is mine to offer. You think Ronato was born empowered? I blessed him. I can bless you, too."

"Two legs aren't much good if I'm not allowed to walk away."

"I can't offer you freedom, but I can offer you an opportunity to win it back. I will give you fine accommodations for the next year. All the food and drink you need, and anything you need to train and prepare."

"For what?"

The Mayor smiled. "I will tell the town that you escaped. I will assure the flames of that rumor are fanned by many whispers. Next year, at the ceremony, you will make your glorious return at the height of your powers, with all your strength, all your anger. They will see your leg has returned, and suspect you share my gifts. Many will rise to support you. Then, I will then slaughter you and all those whose loyalty is weak."

The Mayor stared into the hypnotic swirl of a fresh pour. Red waves licked the glass. His eyes returned to Quinn.

"You have no idea what it took to make the Griffin flesh," he said. "Ben Cartwright gave his life to find you and stoke your flames. Carlos Ronato could have torn you to pieces but obeyed the order not to kill you, knowing it would cost him his life. All along, Kate meant to bring a savior to Harlow, but only I could finish what she started."

"You must get lonely down here," Quinn said. "I can't get you to shut the fuck up."

"Then answer me. The journal—yes or no?"

"Yes," Quinn said.

The Mayor reached into his jacket pocket. He placed Kate's journal on the table, the same one Quinn had seen her writing in each morning for the better part of ten years.

"Here. Just in case you think the journal is buried in a potter's grave, sealed in a plastic bag, safely tucked away next to her rotting body."

Quinn was experienced at keeping emotions from showing up in his face, but the surprise broke through. The Mayor noticed.

"It's all a love letter to you," the Mayor said. He pushed it across the table. "Please, enjoy. It's well done. She may even be telling the truth about loving you—and if that's the case, I have no doubts that the real journal, the one her mother started years ago, is either so well-hidden no one will ever find it, or perhaps even destroyed altogether."

Quinn picked it up. The fabric of the binding was warmed by her palms, each page bearing the ancient cells of her once-living skin. This was her secret relic, and it was all desecrated now. The Mayor's eyes had danced across each line first, staining them. Quinn would never be able to hear her voice when and if he chose to read it.

"A decoy," Quinn said, but it came out as a delicate whisper.

"Tell me again you can deliver the journal," the Mayor said. "The real one."

"I can," Quinn said. A lie, and they both knew it. "But I can't tell you where it is. Only I can get it."

"You're lying, but I won't argue. Serilda will escort you, lest you think you can escape," he said. "Sarah, to you and many of the locals. She is a loyal and powerful disciple. You executed her concubine, but she's had an eye on you all along. I'd send Ortega, but you killed his brother, and he's far more talented and committed to extracting revenge than you've proven to be."

The Mayor stood up, downing the last of his wine. He buttoned his jacket, straightening it, pulling the expensive, blended fabric of his suit taut, hugging his thin and knobby frame.

"You've been hiding who you really are, all for Kate. A noble illusion. Now you know the depth of your failure. Now you know how much you must have disappointed her, how disgusted she must have been with your feeble attempts to prove your love by throwing away the soulless fury she needed from you to survive."

Quinn's mind was a cauldron, too hot and messy for him to reach in and draw out a single word. The rage was old but familiar, an animal shaking at the bars, begging. He wanted to hurt the Mayor. Torture him. Kill him. Stop him.

"There's my little Griffin," the Mayor said. "Hurry now, and get the journal before I carve off a piece for dessert."

CHAPTER 24

Quinn rode in the front seat of yet another Tahoe. Serilda drove. His crutch rattled in the backseat as they bounced through the potholes of the Kinoka blacktop. The sun was freshly down, spreading an orange hue and a steady coolness that forced her to run the defrosters.

Serilda was a freak, supremely dangerous, but he knew what she was, and without the element of surprise, Quinn felt a measure of control. He was the one who could withhold information now. He was injured and broken, and she was imbued with whatever power the Mayor had the ability to give his trusted disciples, but he was the one telling her where to go.

"Which exit?" she asked.

They were at the on-ramp to the interstate. The cracked pavement was sealed with strips of black tar. The yellow paint on the shoulders of the median was faded, and grass and milkweed grew tall in the gaps.

"North," he said.

"Where are we going?"

"North," he repeated.

"North isn't a place, it's a direction."

He didn't respond, and she didn't press him. They headed north.

Once they were on the interstate, Quinn felt relaxed enough to close his eyes. They had a long drive ahead, and he had no desire to watch a series of cornfields and Cracker Barrels pass by. He needed to rest.

"Be honest, now," Serilda said. "How close were you to fucking me?"

He ignored her.

"What's the matter?" she asked. "Not used to such salty talk from girls? Not used to being scared of one?" She kept at him. "I bet you think I'm an awful driver. That right? Does it offend you that I don't know how to bake an apple pie? Did Kate know how?"

"You all keep poking that same spot, thinking it's sore," he said. "Poke too much, though, and all you do is vaccinate your intended victim against the pain. Torture is about variance. Expectation versus reality. It's not in the pain, but in the pauses between, in picking a different spot. Fucking amateurs."

He forced a laugh and kicked his seat back, signaling that he was taking a nap.

"When this is over, when the journal is in the Mayor's hands, I'm going to take you," she said. "You'll hate yourself for how hard you get when I do. You'll beg for me. I'll use you up day in, day out, but you'll still beg for it. You'll say please."

She reached over and placed her hand on his leg. He tried to swat it away, but it was like smacking a brick. She squeezed. Her fingers started to burst the capillaries, then pushed further. She could mash straight to the femur if she wanted to.

When she let go, he let out a burst of breath, relieved to be free of the pain.

"I'll mash your dick in my hand if you aren't sweet to me," she said. "So go ahead. Practice. Tell me you'll be sweet to me. Tell me you'll be gentle."

"I don't think you used to be this way," Quinn said. "But I don't blame you for ending up like this. Survival. I get it. There's a time we could have gotten along. Maybe more. I'll admit it."

Her steel gaze softened, just for a moment, and he caught a glimmer of the humanity she'd used so well against him during his time in Harlow, when she was Sarah.

"I can't hide the way I looked at you when I first met you," he said, "but it was all physical, just brain chemicals. Now? I wouldn't piss on you if you were on fire, and that's coming from a man who was once on fire."

She let go of him, giving the road her full attention.

"How far?" she asked.

"Wake me up when we get to the Dan Ryan," he said.

"Dan Ryan?"

"Chicago," he said. He didn't know where Kate had hidden her true journal, but he knew Chicago. He knew the ruthless men who wanted him dead, and what Serilda would look like to them—harmless, sexy, a possession of Quinn's to be either used or relinquished.

He figured it was time for an introduction.

Quinn guided Serilda through a convoluted route to Vic's Place, a South Side bar that looked like a dive on the surface, but the men drinking inside always wore suits.

Vic's Place was owned and operated by Tommy Garcia, who dabbled in profiting off of illegal poker machines before Illinois regulated its gaming system. He needed cash to expand, and Nico jumped at the chance to partner with him. The end result was Tommy getting fucked out of his share, and running his beloved bar as a laundromat for most of Nico's drug money.

Tommy was an honest crook, straightforward to a fault—the biggest reason he was broke and under Nico's thumb, but still breathing. When Kate went missing, Quinn sent Benoit to Vic's Place to ask him directly if Nico had anything to do with it. He gave Benoit a direct answer—no, Nico had nothing to do with the missing girl.

Tuesday nights were slow nights, and back in the day, they used to be money-counting nights after the bar closed. Quinn had spent many nights guarding the count and getting drunk with Tommy when the shift was over. If Tuesdays were still counting nights, that meant anyone inside wearing an outfit that cost more than three hundred bucks was probably on one of Nico's crews.

He guided Serilda around the block, hoping to scramble her orientation. The street was packed with residential parking, and only a couple spots were open. She drove past them.

"I can't parallel park," she said, and Quinn almost burst out laughing. Despite her superhuman strength and certifiable mean streak, Chicago traffic had turned her nerves taut. Ever since they joined the fray of the Dan Ryan, she'd sat up in the driver's seat, both hands on the wheel. In a town as small as Harlow, how often was a driver surrounded on four sides by impatient assholes? How often did they need to parallel park?

They circled the packed residential streets until they found two consecutive empty spaces where she could slide in.

"The journal is in this bar?" she asked.

"You'll find out where it is when we get to it," he said.

"You're stalling," she said. "Trying to figure out how to escape. Cute, that the Mayor hasn't broken you yet. He breaks everyone."

"Even you?"

Her knuckles turned white on the steering wheel. "Especially me," she said. "Or he wouldn't trust me to bring you back."

"Why don't you just leave right now?" he asked. "Leave the car at O'Hare, catch a plane. Would any of those hicks really find you in the Canadian Rockies? London? Japan?"

She stared through the dark glass. He thought he could open the door, grab his crutch, and hobble away, and she would still be there, hours later, wondering. Dreaming.

She turned to him. Her gaze could bend steel. "Run, and I shatter your one good leg and drag you back to him," she said.

She got out of the car. Quinn struggled with his crutch, fighting dizziness as oxygen returned to his system. He should have been drugged in a hospital bed somewhere, preparing for physical therapy when his stump healed over. Instead, he was dragging himself along, telling himself that the last moments of his miserable life were likely ticking away.

Yet, he always had a chance, the luck of horrible men. Karma wasn't a bitch as much as she was a comedian.

As they walked inside, Serilda said, "Ortega told me you didn't drink."

"Just because I don't drink doesn't mean I'm not an alcoholic," he said, and waited for her to open the door for him.

Vic's Place hadn't changed in over ten years. The dates on the Bud Light specials were different, and there were deeper creases in Tommy's forehead, but other than that, the place was frozen in 2005—the White Sox championship pennants, the ceremonial dollar bills from his first sale framed on the wall, the booths with slippery, fake leather that squeaked when you shifted in your seat.

When Tommy saw Quinn, the glass he was cleaning slipped from his hands and rolled down the bar. Tommy grabbed it, his hands shaking, as Quinn crutched over.

"Order me a whiskey," Serilda said, and took a seat in the closest booth. "The cheap shit is fine."

She wore jeans and a sleeveless blouse, her golden hair tied in a ponytail. Her arms were tanned and muscular. She was the most beautiful woman in Harlow. He wondered what depravities she'd endured in becoming a disciple, then decided he didn't want to know.

The bar was almost empty. A group of fresh-faced young guys sat in the corner booth, their hair slicked. Two of them had lush beards that were long enough to cover the knots of their ties. Two old guys played a game of pool. In the opposite corner of the bar, two young couples laughed, empty Heineken bottles littering their table. The guys were in cashmere sweaters and the brunette was holding out a selfie stick. Tourists visiting a dive for a social media memento and a cheap buzz.

"Tommy," Quinn said. "You've seen better days."

They shook hands.

"Yeah, every single one up to this one," Tommy said. "I could have gone a long time without seeing your ass again."

He couldn't hide his smile, but it quickly evaporated.

"Curtis, man," he said, shaking his head. "You know I gotta call it in, right? I got a family."

Quinn sized up the room. Serilda sat bolt upright, putting enough arch in her back to jut her chest forward. Was she doing it on purpose, or was using her body as a distraction a reflex? The suits at the corner table noticed. She looked away from them. Quinn could see her eyes roll, so she knew they could, too. All part of the game. She knew full well the thrill of the hunt, but only because she was a hunter herself.

"I know," Quinn said. "But make the call after you pour some whiskey."

"Still Macallan?" Tommy asked.

Quinn touched his tattoo, the Griffin, ready to fight, under the canopy of a willow tree. He'd asked Kate once why she loved willow trees so much. "If you saw the willows at my father's house, you would understand why they were so important," Kate had said.

He'd been to her father's house. He had a tree and a shed in his backyard. But not a willow tree.

"A shot of Jack Daniels for the lady," Quinn said, "and just a Coke for me, thanks."

Tommy made the drinks. Quinn kept gazing at the tattoo. The date she'd insisted on. The willow tree, the numbers. Five digits.

Not just a date. A zip code. Maybe she hadn't marked him as the Griffin—maybe she'd given him the map he needed to find it.

The men in the corner booth laughed.

"One of Nico's crews?" Quinn asked.

"A fresh one, too," Tommy said. "Fuckin' youngbloods, man. They tip for shit."

Tommy set down the drinks and picked up his cordless phone.

"When Nico gets word, he's going to call them first," Tommy said. "He'll tell them to wait, but I know those guys. They won't."

"Good," Quinn said. "Is your insurance paid up?"

"Yeah," Tommy said. "Premiums lowered over the years since you left. Fewer claims." He glanced over Quinn's shoulders, and his eyebrows shot up. "You're ten years older, one leg short, and that honey's with *you*?"

"More like I'm with her," Quinn said.

"Either way, she looks like a hell of a time."

"You have no idea," he said.

"What about your leg, anyway?" Tommy asked.

Quinn looked down. "You see it anywhere, you let me know."

Tommy stepped into the back with the phone and made the call. When he came back, he had turned pale and hung up the receiver with a trembling hand.

"I guess we'll find out now," Tommy said.

"What's that?"

"How a one-legged man really performs in an ass-kicking contest."

Serilda gulped her tumbler of Jack Daniels. "I miss getting drunk," she said. "The price we pay to evolve, I suppose."

"I wouldn't call whatever the fuck you are progress," he said, sipping his Coke.

"Neither of us can deny what we've experienced in Harlow," she said.

"Oh, I don't deny it—I just don't believe in fairy tales."

He glanced at the corner booth. The largest of the bearded men pulled a chirping flip phone from the inside of his sport coat, pressed the pickup button, and put it to his ear. As he listened, he began side-eyeing Quinn and Serilda.

Not much longer now, he thought.

"The Mayor cannot possibly fake what he is," she said.

"Everyone fakes who they really are," Quinn said. "He's a nerdy prick playing dress-up. The power he's got? I can't explain it. But that sizzle he's laying down with the steak? Demented, sure, but kind of brilliant. He would make an excellent televangelist."

The crew was talking to each other now. The slack was gone from their shoulders, tightening their postures. He could see the bulge of their weapons in the jackets of their custom sport coats. The bearded one was a lefty, the hilt of his pistol pressing against the gray fabric next to the right side of his ribcage.

"He's converted doubters before," she said.

"Hard to be a doubter when you're on the menu," he said.

"You presume yourself to be better than him?" she said. "Cute. He told me what you are. A man who kills without purpose."

"Survival is a purpose," he said. "As is a reasonable income. You live in Ratfuck, Illinois. Do you all get up in arms when someone steps on a cockroach?"

"So you're simply a noble exterminator?"

"Noble? Hell no. But cockroaches eat each other," he said. "Kind of like some of you assholes in Harlow. Like I said, survival."

The shortest one of the corner bunch stood up. His hair was long and greased over, but shaved to stubble around the crown of his head—one of those boy-band hairdos. He was the hothead of the bunch, no doubt. The one with the biggest beard grabbed his forearm, trying to talk sense to him.

"Humans have this compulsion to explain everything," Quinn said. He rattled the ice cubes in his almost-empty glass. The crew was debating—take on the mighty Curtis Quinn, or wait for backup?

"You know what I like about the Greeks?" Quinn asked. Serilda humored him, running her thumb along the edge of her glass, listening. "The Greeks saw the sun rise in the east and set in the west, and they claimed that Helios, the sun god, was riding his chariot across the sky. Spiders? Explained those pesky bastards with the story of Aranchne. But the moment astronomy and biology came along?

They ditched all that bullshit. Fuck it, it's fake, they said. So we speak about the Greek religion as mythology, wacky bullshit no one believes anymore. Yet here we are, two thousand years after Christ rose from the dead, eating wafers we pretend is the flesh of a god."

Tommy wasn't at the bar anymore. Quinn noticed him in his peripheral vision, gently urging the tourists to leave.

"Ignorance is the disease," Quinn said. "Faith is the symptom. We haven't evolved ever since."

"I have evolved," she answered.

"Yeah, and it's terrifying to see what believers will do because they think they know."

The sparkle returned to her eyes. She enjoyed the pushback, the danger, the uncertainty. *Immense power gets old fast*, Quinn thought. *You can only dunk on the toddlers so long before you crave a real game.*

A hand rested on Quinn's shoulder.

"I got a bet with my boys." He was the short one with the asshole haircut. "Are you Curtis Quinn?"

The game was about to begin.

"You lost your bet," he said.

"You're not Curtis Quinn?"

"Of course I am," Quinn said, just as he drilled the heel of his Coke glass into Boy Band's crotch. He collapsed, but Beard caught his arm. The skinniest of the bunch, the one with the mole underneath his right eye, caught the other arm. Boy Band squealed as his friends kept him from collapsing on the floor.

"Does it feel like you won?" Quinn asked.

Beard grabbed him. Quinn fought the reflex to snap his arm. He let him stretch the collar of his shirt and pull him out of the booth.

"Nico would like a word," Beard said.

Serilda tried to get out of the booth, but Mole pushed her down. She started laughing, and the suits stopped to look at her. "Crazy fucking bitch," Mole said.

By now, Boy Band was getting back to his feet. Quinn smiled at him, inviting the punch. He caught a fist in the teeth and couldn't help but laugh.

"You'll see what's funny when Nico gets ahold of you," Boy Band said.

"You were a lot scarier when you were a ghost and not a one-legged old fuck," Beard added.

"Oh, I'm not the scary one," he said. They followed his eyes to Serilda, who had reigned in her laughter. She was standing next to Mole.

"This tasty bitch your bodyguard?" They all laughed. Serilda rolled her eyes.

Then, with agility the eye could hardly track, she shattered the tumbler against the edge of the table, turning it into an oval of jagged glass. She jammed it Mole's crotch and gave it a quick twist. When she let it go, blood fell out of him as if a cork had been removed. He collapsed, but she caught his throat before he could fall. "I'm not nearly as gentle as him," she said, then shoved him across the room. Mole went airborne, clutching the blood-soaked fly of his trousers. He landed on top of the bar, bounced off, and smashed into the well of liquor bottles.

Quinn fumbled for his crutch as Beard tried to draw his gun. Serilda was too fast for him, grabbing his arm, twisting it until it snapped.

Not enough time, Quinn thought. *Only three of them? You've got about five seconds of interference left before you've got her full attention.*

"What the fuck?" A new voice, with a deep Chicago accent. Nico's son—Quinn knew it without looking at him. The whine was still in the little fucker's voice from when he was a twenty-year-old snot.

Michael Coletti wouldn't be dropping in for a drink all by himself. He had a crew, and for once, Quinn hoped they weren't as totally inept as they were a decade ago, back when they'd tried to torture and kill him.

Serilda yanked Beard's shattered arm, likely hoping to pull him in between herself and the guns now pointed at her. Instead, the arm came free, the tendons and skin ripping away at the clean break just below the elbow.

As the gunfire began, she threw the arm at them. Quinn almost laughed at the sight of the tattooed arm getting smoked by bullets, a slow-motion piñata exploding in the air.

He crawled, making sure he dragged the crutch along with him. The gunshots subsided. The haze of gun smoke hovered in the bar. Then, he heard the screams. The whip-crack of punches, the crab-leg crackle of bones breaking, the mewling cries of grown men who didn't understand what was happening to them, shocked that this bullet-ridden vixen was moving so fast, dissecting them with her bare hands.

Quinn was near the kitchen door. Tommy was ducked behind the bar.

"Is it still there?" Quinn asked.

Tommy was dazed, so Quinn repeated the question just as Michael Coletti begged for his life, his cries of "Please, no" turning into gargles. She was doing something awful to his throat.

Tommy couldn't speak. He just nodded. If she didn't kill him, Tommy Garcia had spent his last night at Vic's Place. Some shit just had a way of retiring you.

Quinn made it through the kitchen doors. A thicket of greasy smoke hovered in the air—Tommy had left some bar food in the fryers. Quinn hoisted himself up and hobbled to the walk-in freezer.

More stray gunfire. A scream. Glasses breaking. Tommy crying, pleading, talking to God, saying nothing but his name, hoping that God would use his omniscient powers to hear his prayers and answer them.

He didn't. Quinn sensed Serilda's hand in Tommy's mouth, ripping off his jawbone.

By now, Quinn was shutting the freezer door behind him. The inside had a lock, a panic room of sorts, one of Nico's paranoid ideas. Walk-in freezers doubled as storm shelters in most restaurants, with thick steel doors and insulated walls. This one also had a trap door hidden behind cardboard boxes of frozen chicken strips.

He opened it. The sewer escape wasn't glamorous or clever, but crawling through a pitch-black tunnel of liquid shit sure felt a lot like coming home.

CHAPTER 25

A s Quinn was crawling through the sewers underneath Vic's Place, Beth was riding home from the hospital with her father, with wires in her jaw and her mind muddied by drugs.

Marcus set a glass of water beside her bed.

"Think you'll sleep?" he asked.

She shook her head.

"Don't overdo it with the pain pills."

"It's not the pain that will keep me awake," she muttered through her swollen jaw.

"Should I leave a lamp on, then?" A question he hadn't asked since those first, rough nights after her mother had died.

She was too embarrassed to say yes, but Marcus knew and turned the lamp on before he left the room.

For the next few hours, she marched to the dull and never-ending drumbeat of pain, which she preferred to the blood-soaked nightmares she endured in the hospital, where Dr. Gaston's nurse was there to assure her it was only a dream.

...

Around 4:00 a.m., she took the keys to her father's truck and drove around Harlow with the windows down. The cold air helped numb the distant thud of a headache that lingered behind her eyeballs.

Once, she'd wanted to run. Now, she didn't. All she knew for certain was that she could not live in Harlow, could not accept it for what it was, could not let it close its jaws around her. Yet her father was right that to leave was to die, to fight was to suffer. So what could she do?

She could drive.

Chuck Godwin's light flicked on as she drove past. His farm truck doubled as a mail truck, a white magnet proclaiming him a U.S. Mail carrier clinging to the door. He'd deliver on time that day, just like every other, and wave to the whole damn town while he did it.

Jonny Thurston's light was also on. He was a farmer from a long line of farmers, but got into the welding business. He'd open up the metal shed that was on the lot across from the grain elevators before the sun even threatened to rise.

Jonny paid neighborhood kids ten bucks an hour to help him keep the place tidy, and lent one of his work vans to Tater Quandt. No one knew Tater's real name, but he was a thick man with a limp and always wore Vietnam veteran hats. He drove some of the local teenagers out to the horseradish farm on the south side of Harlow so they could hoe weeds for the day.

After a lap around town, the grayness of dawn started to gather momentum. Laura Esther was in her nightgown, shuffling out to get the newspaper, and recognized Marcus's truck. She waved. Beth liked her—most of the boys did, too. Her son, Buck Esther, was a star basketball player just two years ago, and always caught hell because Laura was a certified MILF, with long legs and luminous skin that seemed impervious to aging.

Once Buck graduated, Beth just assumed he went somewhere on scholarship. She remembered asking about him, but people would just look at the ground and say they didn't know. When Laura waved, Beth couldn't see the diagonal scar on the palm of her hand, but she knew it was there. She figured that she touched it every day, thinking of her son. There was no Mr. Esther. He was either gone or dead, and both were the same thing in Harlow.

Yet Laura was out with her fuzzy slippers picking up the newspaper. Beth saw her in the diner sometimes, having coffee with her friends, smiling, laughing.

That diner was just opening up—Joyce's. Joyce herself ran the place, up before probably all of them, baking biscuits, as many as she could. They still always ran out by lunchtime. Big plates slathered with sausage gravy churned out to people who would work the dig sites or farms. They'd weld or weed, teach or wait tables, scout or keep book at the outposts around town. They didn't work for the Mayor, or even for themselves. They worked for Harlow—not for what it was, but what it used to be. Every day was a rescue breath, a chest compression, an instinctive yearning to keep alive what the old had built and hoped to pass down.

They worked to outlast the Mayor. All this time, they kept watch, stewards of the tiny sparks even the Mayor could not extinguish. They waited, diligent and loyal, for them to catch fire or finally die.

Beth decided they would not have to wait much longer.

The First National Bank of Alpha, Illinois, had a green and white "FNB" sign that was far newer than the building. The mortar between the bricks was thick with moss on the northern facade, and the windows appeared at least twenty years old, with paint bubbling in the windowsills.

Quinn sat in a rented Camry, waiting for the bank to open. Less than two days earlier, he had emerged from a drainage tunnel in South Chicago. Rain pounded the city, and thunder bashed the sky. He washed himself in the teeth of the thunderstorm. After countless hours of marinating his wounded leg in dirty water, he needed a batch of antibiotics.

He found a payphone and dialed Doctor Carson Venhaus's

number from memory. Carson was a former trauma surgeon, a veteran of Desert Storm. Thanks to the significant mass of his student loans and a coke habit that was almost as big, Carson bounced around the Midwest. He had a talent for finding cash jobs and the good sense to maintain discretion. Carson became the doctor of choice for Nico Coletti and his crews.

After Nico attempted to "retire" him, Quinn was left with significant burns and no way to check into a local hospital. He would have died in a gutter, racked by shock and dehydration, before he'd let himself get arrested or let Nico find him, wounded and vulnerable.

Carson was the guy who got him through the worst of it, picking him up in a nearby alley. The flesh on Quinn's neck was scorched away, his arm and chest smothered in a variety of second- and third-degree burns. His hair was gone, his lips swollen and cracked apart, his eyebrows flash-fried. When he saw his reflection for the first time, Quinn thought, *Well, now you finally look the part.*

Carson took him to one of his impromptu clinics, a stand-up joint in a strip mall. Wasn't a burn unit, but Carson was skilled and determined, and made it work.

Quinn trusted him. Carson's loyalty was always to the patient—as long as they paid cash.

Within minutes of hanging up the phone with Carson, he had a prescription waiting for an alias at a nearby drugstore. After drenching his system in antibiotics, he worked on finding a car.

Once he was behind the wheel of a perfectly anonymous, pearl-white Camry, he'd stopped at a gas station and purchased a state map to chase down his hunch.

The wedding date Kate insisted on was the zip code of Alpha, Illinois, a town of nine hundred people near the Illinois-Iowa border. With the town map brought up, there wasn't much to analyze—the main street of Alpha was indeed called Main Street, but the other street that bisected it and crossed the railroad tracks was much longer. Willow Street. The bank was on the corner of Willow and Main. Other mom-and-pop businesses were on Willow, but

Kate wouldn't risk a bakery or bookstore closing down while hiding her most valuable asset. The journal was at the bank, likely in a safe deposit box, and he could think of no way to prove he had a right to its contents. He'd never signed a signature card. He had no access.

Still, he had to walk into the mystery she'd left for him, to trust her over his instincts, which railed against him—*if she left your name with them, maybe it showed up somewhere. Maybe the cops or Nico's guys have been watching, waiting for you to show up.*

Time to find out. He watched as a plump, short lady with a nest of gray hair sitting atop her head flipped the sign in the window from closed to open. Quinn took a deep breath and got out of his car. Wind clawed at his coat as he fumbled his crutch into place.

Inside, the lobby looked clean and recently remodeled. He could tell the drywall was new—he could still smell the mud job mixed with the pleasing, faintly toxic scent of paint. The framing around the windows was rather ornate, and he figured this for an old house that was converted into a bank sometime long ago.

Two tellers were chatting at the drive-through station. Another teller had her drawer open, busying herself with counting or records or whatever it was that tellers always did to look so damn busy. She gave him a smile, a rehearsed, how-do-you-do smile that probably got her a sterling rating on her performance appraisal when her supervisor checked the box for customer service.

But the smile stalled.

"You're him," she said. The other tellers were looking at him, too. A car in the drive-through honked its horn, startling them back to work.

"Lois," Quinn said, reading her nametag, "this may sound crazy, but I'm not a hundred percent sure why I'm here—I just know I'm in the right place. I'm him. I hope that's not a bad thing."

"You don't know why you're here?" she said, stumbling over her words, having to start over twice.

"I think I'm here for my wife's journal," he said. "I think she left it here, and if you know who I am, maybe you can help me."

She picked up the office phone, never taking her eyes off of him.

"Marvin? Yes. Can you come up here, please? And bring *the* picture. Yes, the picture. The one for box nineteen."

They waited for Marvin.

"That's the thing, mister," she said. "I don't know who you are. But we know what you look like. The scars and all."

Marvin looked like exactly what you'd expect a small-town bank manager to look like—an ill-fitting dress shirt, the cuffs rolled back over his hairy forearms. He gave Quinn the same amazed look that Lois had given him as he joined her at the counter.

"What's your name?" he asked.

"Does it matter?" Quinn responded.

Marvin placed a picture on the counter. He turned it so Quinn could see it—it was him, all right, sitting on the couch, vulnerable, smiling. He remembered the photo. She'd purchased a disposable camera at a drugstore no more than five years ago, saying that they should take more pictures, giving him some bullshit about photos having power, making moments into something you could never take away. He'd disagreed with her, but gently.

"Photos give you permission to forget," he'd said. Now, he knew that she probably agreed with him. She just wanted an excuse to snap a picture of him, and she did just that when they got home that evening. He was watching the news, fresh out of the shower, wearing shorts and a white T-shirt. She came out of the bedroom in her pajamas—nothing sexy, just warm and functional flannel bottoms with a long-sleeved top.

He heard the click, looked at her, and said, "I do have a bad side," then gestured at his scars. She just kept clicking, laughing the entire time, and he couldn't help but smile.

"Come with me," Marvin said. Quinn followed him.

"Unusual, to say the least," Marvin said. "Obviously against our bank's protocol, but safe deposit boxes are rather inconsistently administered around the banking industry. I'm the one who actually dealt with her back in 1990. Junior supervisor at the time. I'm bank manager now. Marvin Needle."

Quinn shook his hand, wondering just how the nerdy-looking Mr. Needle had survived grade school. He figured needle-dick was probably a high school bullying favorite.

The room was small, with a table in the middle. They had safe deposit boxes, but the number was in the dozens, not hundreds—only one wall had box access locks.

"She opened the safe deposit box, and asked for only one other person to get access," he said. "She said that even he—I mean you—wouldn't know you had access, so she couldn't supply a signature card. She was also quite candid, and said you had to change your identities often due to your career."

"So she just gave you the picture," Quinn finished. "And you're going to let me have the box?"

"Of course," Marvin said. "It was a sincere request. Whenever she stopped by, the ladies here seemed to get along with her splendidly. Said she seemed honest and a little bit scared, and besides, it wasn't like it was a ton of gold bullion or the secrets to cold fusion. She just had her notebook and some folders."

"She came here more than once?"

Marvin looked at him as if he were stupid. "She could come every now and again," he said. "Right when we opened. Someone would take her in here, and she'd write in that book of hers, right on the spot. Tuck something in the folder sometimes. I keyed her in at least three times myself. I think that's why the ladies in there were out of sorts—you being here, I think it means she's dead. Am I right?"

Quinn nodded.

"I'm sorry," Marvin said. He keyed out box nineteen and laid it on the table. From a larger set of keys, he opened the box.

"Want me to leave you alone for a few minutes?" he asked.

Lying before him was the journal, which was actually a full-sized, hardcovered memo book with lined paper, the kind you might use as a ledger. The spine was worn and the journal couldn't even close all the way—it was stuffed with extra loose-leaf pages, and he saw the border of a manila file folder that was tucked in the back. He could read the tab of the folder—Jarvis, Christine. Her mother. He also noted colored tabs. He leafed through and noticed they were medical records.

Taped to the back of the manilla folder was a laminated piece of paper. At the top was a logo in futuristic lettering: *CryoLock*. A welcome letter to Christine with a serial number and access instructions. The number and password was highlighted.

He placed his hands on the journal as if it were gospel. He looked up at Marvin.

"I'll just take it," he said. "Something tells me I should read it in private."

Marvin nodded, faking a smile, relieved to be cleansed of this little burden.

Quinn headed for the Camry, the stack of paperwork tucked under his arm, threatening to slip out as he crutched along. He got in the car and left immediately, forcing himself to wait before he read a single word.

After he was an hour east of Alpha, he stopped at a convenience store, one with heavy trucker traffic and a country diner, the sort of joint he'd once used as a meeting spot with Scott Benoit. He tucked his Camry into a small parking space, and among the mountains of trucks and bursts of diesel smoke, he opened the journal and started to read.

By the time he reached the end, all of Harlow's secrets were his, but Kate? She was not. She never was—Kate had seen him, and seen him clearly.

I can hear you in the other room, trying your best to exercise without waking me. All these years and your consideration for me, the way you treasure me every single day, refuses to change. Your love for me is almost maddening.

Almost.

On some days, I wake up thoroughly depressed by my past, and I fear for our child. Other days, I'm just so deeply grateful that I met you and that I found what little happiness I could scrape from this world, being a girl from Harlow, and all.

I have decided, Curtis. I decided long ago, I think, to absolve you from this, and to perhaps even absolve myself. I think I decided months ago, when you left for work after kissing me in the morning, like you always do—and I knew you had to smell the vomit of morning sickness on my breath.

I didn't waste any time. I went to the doctor and had a blood test.

That night, I didn't tell you. I told you I was sick and wanted to be left alone, that I didn't want to get you sick, and as usual, you respected my wishes.

The next day, I went to Planned Parenthood. I parked in front of it, but couldn't bring myself to go inside. Not unless I was truly sure.

I don't want to anger you—obviously I didn't go through with it. But I thought about it, and at one point I got out of the car and started walking inside.

You have to know something. I wasn't just deciding a baby's life that day. I was deciding Harlow's fate that day. I was deciding your fate, my sister's fate, my father's fate. I was deciding what, exactly, my mother had died for.

I knew on that day, if I didn't go inside, if I was bringing a baby into the world, that I could only do it if I admitted that I was ready for a life of duty, and not love. I had to admit that I wanted a child in my life. And I had to admit I was ready to let Harlow go, and let its imprisoned citizens suffer, and leave my family behind for good, if only to build a new one.

I had to decide that you were no longer the kind of man who could help me achieve that silly and dangerous dream of rescuing my sister and the innocents like her. I tell you not to be "that guy." Once, it was a way to prime you for the moment in which I'd unleash you. But now? It's because it's his resurrection I fear the most, because that man cannot rescue Harlow. He cannot be the Griffin.

You sleep too well, Curtis. That's how I know. You pretend to be this new man, all for me, but you have no guilt. You cannot hide the ice inside of you. Harlow needs a savior, and saviors are required to sacrifice. It needs a hero, and being a hero requires empathy and emotion.

To send you to Harlow is to trade one madman's massacre for another.

How could I let that man become a father? But, how could I let this child go? How can I let my family go? My mother's legacy? That's a lot for a girl to digest and consider. They don't ask you those kinds of questions on the Planned Parenthood forms.

So there you have it. I decided many lives that day, and I know I didn't bring you into that decision, but I hope you understand why.

I do not love you, Curtis. I'm sorry. But I love our child. And I can lie to myself and fantasize that maybe my sister will grow up to succeed where I have failed.

With that in mind, I don't think today is the day, but soon, I'll stop writing in this journal. Maybe one day, years from now, I'll have the strength to destroy it, when my mother's dream is dead. Wouldn't the Mayor love that?

Not today, but soon.

Until then, I'll live today, as best as I can, until I have no more days to give.

That was the final entry of the bound portion of the journal. He withdrew the manila folder, ready to sift through its contents, and a folded piece of paper fell onto his lap.

He picked it up and carefully unfolded it, the creases leading him to a handwritten note from a loose-leaf notebook, the left edge feathered with bits of paper from where it had been sloppily torn out. There was no date, but it was Kate's handwriting.

You're only reading this if I'm gone, and you somehow found this on your own. I can't put it past you, as difficult as the puzzle may be without me around to nudge you. I think you found Harlow and saw my father's yard, and realized where the willow tree would take you. That's the world speaking to us. I wanted to grow old, to have my Harlow nightmares fade enough so that one day, I could convince myself it was all a nightmare.

But you're reading this, so it turns out I am and always have been a Harlow girl. I'm a Jarvis, and proud of it. I reached beyond Harlow's shimmering blacktop roads and monochrome fields, but I still died in the dirt. I sincerely hope our child didn't die with me.

The world whispers to us, always, and we ignore it. Time and time again.

There's an honor in ignoring it, but an honesty in listening to the truth, even when it tells us what we don't want to hear. Honor gains its prestige from resistance. Honor is the hard way, swimming against the current, flailing against our morals. You have honored me by trying to be a good man.

But the truth?

The truth is you are a fucking monster, and I don't know if that can ever change.

That is the truth, and the truth is power that chooses no morality. The truth unleashes us.

I know the world whispers to you, Curtis.

I know it's whispering to you now, and the whispers are still as loud, long, and savage as they were when I met you. There is no one left to honor, Curtis. No one. I am gone forever, and I leave you with this—the truth has my blessing, my love, my consent.

So close your eyes. Don't speak. Don't think. The whispers...what do you hear? I think I know. I think that deep down, you know, too.

How long does the world have to tell you what you are before you'll listen?

QUEEN'S GAMBIT

CHAPTER 26

B eth stayed home until her jaw healed, doing the homework remotely. Teachers hand-delivered her assignments, and picked them up on Fridays to grade them over the weekend. She lost herself in schoolwork, hoping to forget about Trent, about the way the blood gushed from his open neck before he died on the hardwood floor.

Traitors did not get funerals. The town knew Trent's name once, and now, no one spoke of him. Chris Keller was still a High Servant, and Beth wondered if even he left the thoughts of his son behind to survive and hold status.

A month later, at the turn of December, Beth returned to school. Everyone treated her normally, as if nothing had happened. Smiles in the hallway. Laughter, talk of current events, pop culture, the latest music.

Everyone was addicted to pretending they lived a normal life. She hated it.

When school was out, she walked home and once again took her father's truck without asking. She drove to Cooper Murray's house, and he was standing on the porch to meet her before she even got out of the truck.

"I just made coffee," he said.

"I hate coffee," she said.

"I don't," he answered, and waved her inside.

Cooper was a farmer, his face hard and tan, a short, neat mustache dusting his upper lip. He wore a flannel shirt and jeans, what likely passed for evening wear in the Murray household.

"I'm sorry about Trent," he said.

Beth stared out the kitchen window, remembering how her father had grieved when they got the news about Mom. The way he refused to let his children see him cry, pushing Beth away when she went to hug his leg.

"My father won't fight," she said. "But I will."

"Low or not, your father was the best of us," Cooper said.

"Was," she said. "He lost my mother, my sister. He never fought back, like everyone never fought back."

"We have our reasons," he said.

"I don't care."

"First, you want to run. Now, you want to fight? Vengeance has a way of leading to grisly ends around here. You ain't the first who decided to push back."

"I'm here because I know better," she said. "I know I can't just challenge him to a fistfight. There has to be a way, and if anyone's thought it through, it's you."

"I haven't given it a thought in thirty years," he said.

"They called you the Great Survivor," she said. "What did you survive? Surely, you have to know something the rest of us don't."

"Forgive me for being crass at a bad time, but you got no goddam business getting me reminiscing about dead friends," Cooper said. "If all you got is a chip on your shoulder and a hole in your heart, I think it's best you leave."

She reached into her backpack and placed an orange plastic jar on the counter.

"Half the boys in school shoot this crap on the weekends for fun," she said.

Cooper picked it up, squinted, and checked the label. "Tannerite," he said.

"Harmless in small quantities. Just a little redneck fun on the weekends. No one would notice if we started bringing it in, little by little."

"You think we can kill the Mayor with a Wal-Mart explosive? Might as well attack him with firecrackers."

"I'm serious," she said.

"A plan Wile E. Coyote would be proud of," he said.

"I'll do this alone if I have to," she said.

He turned away from her and rinsed his coffee mug in the sink.

"You and that janitor started something, Beth. I fear it may be the wrong thing, and that people will die, but I don't know if I can stop you."

"I'm not the Griffin," she said. "That's a bunch of baloney my granddad made up. It put us all to sleep. I'm awake."

"Good luck, then," Cooper said. "I mean it. Best get home before your father worries."

"Say no," she said. "Say it to my face. Say you're too scared to fight."

"No," he said. "Happy? No. I won't fight. And don't ask again, because I'm never going to raise my guns behind you. Harlow already has too much death, and it'd pain me to see another young woman put on the pile."

"That's the thing about surviving," Beth said. "You get addicted to it. Too addicted to do anything other than clean up the mess when everyone else has fought and died for something."

The wrinkles in the old man's face deepened. "Shaun died for nothing," Cooper said. "Put down no different than a dog in a ditch, by my own hand no less. There's living and dying, and that's it. You think it makes you better than him if you die fighting? You color it the way you want, but you can't let the Mayor bury you and call it a win. Hard to proclaim victory while you're stuck in a grave. Even Jesus had the good sense to come back and check his work."

Beth caught herself chewing her thumbnail. She'd picked up the nail-biting habit over the summer, and it made her mending jaw ache, but she gnawed just the same. Cooper watched her, a man old enough to be comfortable with long silences. She took a step forward, ready to tell him off, then took a step back, meaning to leave and slam the door in his face.

Finally, she removed her thumb from her mouth and spit out the cuticle. "You're not the man I thought you were," she said.

"Neither is your father," he said.

CHAPTER 27

When Beth returned home, Marcus began reheating her dinner without asking if she was hungry. She settled in at the kitchen table, shoulders slumped, waiting to eat.

The microwaved hummed. Marcus watched the pasta bake twirl, arms crossed, waiting for Beth to speak. She didn't.

When he placed the food in front of her, she picked at it.

"Rough day?" Marcus asked.

"Normal day," she said. "Around here, anyway."

He placed a hand on her shoulder. She batted it away.

"Don't," she said.

He didn't press her. When she collected herself, she pulled her food back in front of her and ate until the plate was clean. He waited for her to speak, making no move to clear the dishes.

"I'm moving out," she said. "I'm eighteen now."

"You're broke."

"Scout work pays."

"Your scout work was a joke. A trap. If you push for a job, they'll put you on a dig site."

"Whatever it takes to get out of this house," she said. "I can at least get away from you constantly reminding me how much I've lost."

"We've both lost people," he said. "Your mother, my wife. Your sister, my daughter."

"And Trent," she said.

"You're my daughter. What hurts you, hurts mc," hc said.

"I can't figure out what's left of you," she said.

"Whatever's left of you, you're willing to throw away," he said. "I know you visited Cooper. I know what you want. Say the wrong thing to the wrong person around here, and you'll be the one getting carved apart in front of the town."

"I don't think I care," she said.

"I lost enough to this place," he said. "I won't let it take you, too."

"That's sweet," she said. "But what will you actually do about it?"

He said nothing as he started clearing her spot at the table, placing her silverware into the sink with almost no sound.

She stood up and waited until he could see her, shook her head so he could feel her disgust, then stormed away and shut herself in her bedroom.

She cried until the sun went down, thinking of Trent, of a time when she was younger and the size of the world matched her imagination. Now, the world was no bigger than Harlow, and everyone but her had adjusted to its compressive size. She couldn't breathe, suffocated as if the sweaty palm of the Mayor himself were pressed over her mouth. Finding just one ally like Trent would have been the deep breath she needed for the panic to subside, to think clearly, to consider a next move that wasn't blowing up a supernatural-powered cult leader with toy explosives.

When the crying ended, sleep found her, but its grip was loose. In her dreams, Trent's blood poured from his neck onto her hands as he begged her to help him. She was only eighteen, but already had a growing collection of ghosts.

When she opened her eyes, the room was dark, but a shadowy figure stood in her doorway. She screamed.

Her father turned on the light. He wore jeans and a flannel over-shirt. She glanced at the clock—it was only 11:00 p.m.

"Get dressed," he said.

"Why?"

"Because if I leave this be, you're gonna get yourself killed before I can save you," he said.

They drove to Thatcher Henderson's house, a ranch home on the east side of town, perilously close to the Harlow border.

The long driveway was packed with fresh snow. Two inches had gathered while Beth was asleep, and she was poorly dressed for the conditions. Snow packed into the mesh of her running shoes, and her toes numbed as they walked to Thatcher's outbuilding. Most of the farming houses had them, gargantuan structures that housed combines, four-wheelers, and tractors.

Marcus pounded on the door. Thatcher answered, his wrin-kles whipped red by windburn, his lower lip packed with tobacco. Thick sideburns looked like sagebrush beneath his Case Tractors cap. Behind him, at least a dozen men were gathered. Beers rested on a wooden picnic table.

"She got no business here, Marcus," Thatcher said. He went to close the door, but Beth tucked her foot into the gap before he could close it all the way.

"I insist," she said.

She heard the murmur of voices behind Thatcher, people asking who it was, and the unmistakable clack and clatter of guns being picked up and readied.

"We ain't risking no kid being here," Thatcher said. "Let alone one with your profile. You move that foot or you lose it."

Marcus stepped aside and waited for her to fend for herself. He'd given her this chance, and she wasn't going to waste it.

"I can help," she said.

"Your help will get us all caught and killed," Thatcher said. "Last call before I break your fuckin' foot."

"Thatcher." She heard a deep, creaky voice that cut through all the panicked noise. "Let her in."

Thatcher hesitated, but obeyed, unlatching the door. Once it opened wide, Beth saw the source of the voice—Cooper Murray.

Beth entered. Marcus followed. The floor was smooth, finished concrete. A woodstove was stoked up, warming the room just enough to keep it from being miserable. The men still wore their coveralls and flannel coats.

She recognized most of them. Thatcher's son, John, a sturdy high school senior with blond hair and cheeks that were inexplicably red all the time. John's classmate, Earl "Hamm" Jenkins, was there with his freckles and overbite and his father, Marshall. She recognized Winslow Bates, Mark Zimmer, Duke Evans, and four or five guys she'd seen around town, but didn't know all that well and didn't want to venture at guessing their names. Randy Davis paced while everyone else sat, a skinny, live wire of a man, always licking his lips and popping his knuckles—he lived each day as if expecting a fight to break out. And, of course, the oldest man in the room, Cooper Murray, wearing the kind of glasses that magnetically attached in the middle. It looked like a magic trick each time he put them on.

Everyone had a beer in hand, not only to cut the stress, but to give the scene a believable, country-boys-drinking-for-no-reason look should a High Servant show up.

"You bring your jar of Tannerite?" Cooper asked. They all had a laugh, Marcus included.

He put his hand on her shoulder. "Don't worry," he said. "We're on the same page. But the explosion we have planned? It's just a little bigger."

The rebels had a Ford F900 dump truck hidden in one of Cooper's outbuildings. Over the past few months, the farmers had been siphoning off small amounts of the tightly controlled fertilizers they were allotted in order to turn the truck into an ammonium nitrate-fueled weapon.

Cooper himself was overseeing the mixture, and he was blending shrapnel into the truck for additional stopping power.

"When did this start?" she asked.

The men deferred to Marcus. "When they brought Kate home," he said. "I talked to Cooper that day, before they even sent for me to finish her off."

"We have two problems," Cooper said. "One, we have no idea how we're going to get this close enough to the Mayor to blow his ass to outer space without taking most of Harlow with him. Two, topping off the truck is slow-going. When it comes to fuel and fertilizer, High Servants keep a tight lid on what we get and how we use it. At this rate, we won't have enough punch for how hard I want this thing to hit until well into next year."

"We was gonna wait until around Harvest to hit him anyhow," Thatcher said. "The Mayor tends to be around when Harvest is near. When they announce Harvest Eve, we have to be ready to take our shot."

"He'll be at the school," Beth said. "With the entire town there to take the Oath. Hit him then, and you'll kill everyone."

The men looked at each other. That was the debate they were having. If they had the opportunity, would they destroy the people of Harlow to kill the Mayor? Was that freedom, or his ultimate victory?

"You can't even be sure the explosion would kill him." Another familiar voice. A man in the corner, his head down, stooped over a Stag beer.

Chris Keller. Trent's dad.

Beth looked at her father. "I thought he was a High Servant?"

"He's been here since day one," Marcus said. "He knew Trent was in danger once he hitched himself to you."

The day Trent fell for her, his fate was sealed, and everyone seemed to know it. Perhaps even Trent. She couldn't let the thought weaken her in front of Harlow's motley rebels.

"He's right, though," Beth said, gathering herself. "You don't know the explosion would kill the Mayor for sure."

"You ever see footage of the Oklahoma City bombing?" Cooper said. "That evil bastard put a hole in the world with a truck half the size of ours. The Mayor's strong, but even he can't endure a blast like that."

"You can't be sure," she said.

"Perhaps," Marcus said. "But we know more about the Mayor than he realizes. That's why Kate's journal scares him. He had a mistress once, you know."

"Kate?"

"Your mother," he said.

She was young when her mother died, but all her memories were warm, full of smiles, the sunshine weaving through her mother's golden hair as they ran across the yard, kicking up dandelions.

"She would never let that monster touch her," she said.

"Not a monster—he's just a man with an illness," Marcus said. "And he's smarter than he is cruel. All this ritualistic bullshit? The cannibalism and ceremonies? Sure, he gets a kick out of it, but he's not doing it because he believes any of it—he's experimenting.

"Used to just be him having all that power," he said. "Then Ortega and Ronato lost their fathers in the mine when I was a boy. They shared the same mother, but she died young. Being Mexican and all, they had what'd you'd call ethnicity problems around these parts, but it seems that the Mayor rallied them to his side and endowed them with some version of the power he's got. Weaker than him, sure, but still enough to turn them into raging bulls that bullets can't kill."

"An axe in the hands of a madman sure did the trick," Randy said, and the room shared a chuckle.

"They've been around since you were a boy?" Beth asked.

Cooper nodded.

"You're—" She didn't finish, but Cooper did.

"Old? Yes, ma'am. Damn near seventy. Ronato and Ortega are pushing eighty or so, by my count."

"If that's an illness, it sounds like an illness a lot of people would pay to contract," Beth said.

"If only there was a cure," Marcus said. "There isn't. So we play the cards we're dealt. We remain patient until our opportunity arises."

"How long?" she asked.

No one answered.

"You're telling yourselves another story," she said. "First the Griffin. Now this. Both are fantasies. You'll never trigger that weapon."

"We don't need a hothead," Marcus said.

"No. But you need the Mayor out in the open where you can kill him with the fewest casualties," she said.

"That, we know," Cooper said. "You got anything to say that we don't know?"

She didn't have an answer.

Thatcher laughed. "It's okay, girl," he said. "We'll wait."

Boys, all of them, only old enough to buy beer and get gray hairs and pretend as if they had wisdom she could never know.

"The Griffin," she said, ending their laughter. "Maybe that could bait the Mayor into a mistake."

"You don't own that anymore," Cooper said.

"The janitor is the Griffin now," Marcus said. "For better or worse."

"We break him loose. Then he'll owe us. We use him as bait."

"He's already gone, Beth," Marcus said.

"The Mayor wouldn't kill him in secret."

"Escaped," Chris said. He remained hunched in the corner. She could barely hear him. "Killed Ronato, and now it seems that he outsmarted another—Serilda's paying the price for losing him, and she may never stop paying."

"The Mayor thinks he'll come back," Beth said. "He wanted him to escape. He wants the fight."

"What he wants is for us to get our hopes up," Cooper said. "He wants us to let our guard down, to wait for an imaginary rescue. I respect the janitor, but I won't bet on him. That old boy's tough, but I'd imagine that the combo of a stump for a leg and some good sense make it likely he sits this one out."

"Let's hope he does," Marcus said.

"Why?" Beth asked. "He's the Mayor's only vulnerability, the only chance to draw him out before Harvest."

"Kate had every opportunity to set him loose on Harlow," Marcus said. "If the man were a hero, she'd have sent him years ago. She left here looking for the Griffin, needing to find a savior. She didn't."

"What did she find instead?"

"A destroyer," he said. "And if we don't fix the Mayor ourselves, on our terms, and the janitor comes back? Then it'll be on his terms. A man like that don't lose sleep over innocent casualties."

"He saved me, and he didn't have to," Beth said. "He found his way here, all to avenge the woman he loved. He can't be a total monster."

"You've been wrong before," Marcus said.

She thought of Galen, how she'd felt about him before he revealed himself. The country smile, his good-natured drawl, the way he let her take naps and toasted her birthday.

Yes, she had been wrong before.

CHAPTER 28

T he cold bite of December turned into the even colder bite of January, then February. Beth went to school, smiled when necessary, and brought home As.

Before she left for school on the coldest day of the year, she stopped in the kitchen. Her father drank coffee and watched the snow fall through the window above the kitchen sink.

"We need to have another meeting," she said.

He shook his head.

"Nothing to meet about until the truck is finished," he said. "We got a few more months before Coop's happy with the payload, but we'll have plenty of bang by Harvest."

"If everyone dies along with the Mayor, he wins."

"Wins what, Beth? This ain't a game."

"It is," she said. "The game bad men play and always win. You said it yourself, that he imprisons us with stakes. It's not a game to us. It is to him."

He wasn't in the mood to argue and returned his attention to the window. What did he see out there? The serenity of a quiet sunrise? Memories of his long-dead wife? The soothing flutter of morning snowflakes?

She thought to ask him the question she had been afraid to ask since that day in the Henderson shed, after learning the truth and scope of their plan to defeat the Mayor. She thought to ask him about the idea that came to her the night before, a way to smoke the Mayor out of hiding and make himself vulnerable.

She knew he would talk her out of her idea and that he would dodge her question.

"I love you, Dad," she said. He kept his eyes on the frost-glazed glass and said, "I love you too, baby girl."

She went to school and readied herself for the game to truly begin.

School days were hypnotic—the bells, the roll calls, the hallway chatter, the bang of metal locker doors. Beth played the part of attentive student, but was always waiting for the day to end. She felt like an observed imposter at school, as if they could all sense her hunger to strike back against the Mayor.

She felt sluggish after another night of sleep thinned by nightmares. In most of them, she was hanging from the game hoist, watching as her classmates ate strips of her flesh while the Mayor laughed.

Trent was among those eating her flesh in these dreams, strings of skin and tendons dancing in his slit-open throat as he devoured a piece of her with greedy hands.

After sixth-hour English, Beth shuffled into the hallway. She had fallen asleep in class, gasping awake. All her classmates had taken the Oath. They knew the contents of her dreams. While their nightmares weren't identical, they were set in the same place, a gym they walked by each day, a constant reminder. Memories were the bars of Harlow that they could never bend away and escape.

As she headed for her locker, she saw students gathered, shoulder to shoulder, watching something. Kids never gathered like that to watch an act of kindness. She muscled through, even though her locker was in the opposite direction.

The scene was so familiar, she blinked hard to make sure she wasn't watching herself in one of her nightmares. Doug Albers towered over a lanky blonde girl. She clutched her books to her chest, afraid to make eye contact as Doug's right hand touched her waist. She couldn't slip away, but she was too terrified to do anything other than cower.

Beth recognized her—Corrine Garner, a cheerleader covered in freckles, a girl who was always smiling.

She's a young sophomore, Beth thought. At sixteen, they told you the parts of the truth, at least the parts that wouldn't drive you mad right away—that you can't leave Harlow, not ever. They give you your apprenticeship. A girl like Corrine would be worthless in a dig site, and didn't look like scout material. Maybe a waitress at the diner, a job at the bank, or worse, assignment to the son of a High Servant.

Doug Albers was not the son of a High Servant anymore. Morgan Albers had been dead for months.

"What the fuck are you doing?" Beth demanded, breaking loose from the gallery. Doug turned, and the rage in his face at the sight of her would have made her recoil during the first semester. But now?

"I said, what the fuck are you doing?" She flung her books away, a decidedly male act of aggression, the shedding of everything but rage. She stepped closer to him.

"Corrine's my girl now," Doug said.

"Says who?"

"Says me," Doug said. "You're off-limits. Word is the Mayor himself is poking you."

Laughter. She felt the heat gather in her cheeks, but she wasn't afraid. He'd given up valuable information and sealed his own fate—she was off-limits. That meant she could do whatever she wanted.

She took Corrine's arm. Doug grabbed her wrist.

"It's okay," Beth said to her. "Get to class."

With Doug occupied, Corrine made her move, slowly, ready to obey if Doug commanded her to stay put. He didn't.

"I'm about sick of you," he said to Beth.

"Careful now," she said, nodding at his white-knuckled grip. "Leave a bruise, and I'll have to tell my boyfriend."

He let her go. His every atom vibrated with rage. He wanted to choke her, to kill her. She saw the loss of his father in his eyes, but even worse, the loss of the status that came with it.

Shaking, he turned away, but Beth sensed opportunity. The Mayor didn't give a shit about Marcus Jarvis, Cooper Murray, or their merry band of rednecks. She was the last Jarvis girl, the daughter of his mistress, the sister of the woman who'd embarrassed him for a decade. If he couldn't have the Griffin, she was a fitting consolation prize—which is why she had settled on herself as the bait that would draw the Mayor out. The only question was how to imperil herself just enough to warrant the Mayor's attention.

Fate's answer? Doug Albers and his light-switch temper.

It's too soon for this, she thought. *The truck won't be ready until the fall. You need to wait. Waiting is the smart thing to do.*

She was ready to let it go, to try another day.

Your father would wait, she thought. Of course he'd wait. Her father curated knowledge, sharpening and oiling each piece of it, a tool prepared for the ideal moment of deployment. The toolbox of what he knew had become a burden, too heavy to carry alone, yet still, he would not unlock it and take out the pieces and lay them out just so, if only to show her what he carried, the weight that she never saw.

She'd grown tired of knowledge, of thinking, of wondering, of asking. All that mattered in life was who was willing to move, so she moved.

"I was there when your father died," she said.

Doug stopped. He didn't turn around, but he was listening with his back to her, a dare to continue.

"I remember him on his knees, just before the Griffin beat him into the mud," she said. "I remember thinking he was strong, right up until that moment, when he begged for his life, coughing out prayers to the Griffin between sobs."

"You lie," he said.

Come on, she thought. *Turn around. Don't you want to look me in the eyes?*

"You think I'm lying because of the bullet hole in his head?" she said.

He turned around. His mouth quivered as he tried to keep the urge to sob at bay. His entire face was a clenched fist, hard and creased and turned white with pressure.

"I begged the Griffin for justice," she said. "He handed me the Sheriff's sidearm."

She took a step closer to him. She was lying, of course, but there was enough truth there to keep her eyes clear and steady.

"I shot him in the head myself, and as your daddy twitched in the mud, I saw a secret weakness he'd long held back, a weakness I see in you right now as clearly—"

The punch arrived mid-sentence, and she made no move to dodge it. Her jaw had healed since Ronato shattered it, but she still had headaches from the stiffness, and it clicked in the morning when she brushed her teeth—so she was thankful when Doug's fist landed square on her nose.

She felt the crunch in her inner ear, and she was falling, falling forever. As an eclipse of unconsciousness passed over her, she felt a tear strike her face. Doug stood over her, the grief he'd worked so hard to board up inside of him now busted free, his fist cocked to strike again.

Beth spent the night in the hospital, her father at her side. Without a janitor to mop his way to her rescue, Doug had landed two more punches before his friends dragged him away. Neither did exceptional damage. Still, she had a mildly broken nose, a possible concussion, and swollen lips. The dark flesh of blackened eyes spread across her cheeks like storm clouds, purple and slow.

Despite the damage, Doctor Gaston called her exceptionally lucky, as her broken jaw had survived the punches and didn't re-fracture.

Marcus sat in the recliner of the hospital room, a dusty box laid across his lap. He had yet to ask her about what had happened, which meant that he already knew. What he didn't know was how intentional it was, what Beth was attempting to accomplish by baiting Marcus, and for once, she had her own piece of information to keep away from him.

"Ugh. I guess I finally look the way I feel," Beth said.

"Either way, I think you got an excused absence from school for a couple days," he said. He rolled his chair up to her side table. He opened the box and unfolded a cardboard chessboard.

"You want to be black or red?" he asked.

"I don't play chess," she said. "When did you start?"

"When did I stop, more like it," he said. "My dad used to play with me. We bought this at Wal-Mart one day on a whim. Four bucks, if I recall. He was no good. We learned the game together."

"I don't even know how the pieces move," she said.

"We got all day," he said. "But this isn't checkers, now. I remember you throwing your checkers tantrums."

She remembered. She'd double jump him and think the game was over, then he'd start stacking up her checkers, queening his own, until he'd won.

"This ain't about the double-jump," he said. "In chess, you can't do what the other person thinks you're gonna do. Whoever thinks the most moves ahead wins. Understand?"

She understood, and they began to play. For the first hour, he taught her how all the pieces moved. For the second, he let her make her own mistakes, setting traps she didn't know had sprung until it was far too late. During the last game, she truly thought she had him beat—she had captured more pieces than him and saw a way to checkmate him. Of course he checkmated her on the very next turn. All he could do was laugh.

After the chess, he gave her Jell-O from a cooler he'd brought along with him. He snacked on deer sausage and kept checking the clock.

"Got a hot date?" she asked.

"Curfew's six for me tonight," he said. "Unusual, but I think I know why."

A visitor. They both knew who to expect.

"I knew he'd come," she said. "Why else would I pick a fight with Doug Albers?"

She thought she'd surprise him, that she was finally one move ahead. He acted as if she'd just reported a weather forecast he'd already seen on the morning news.

"Truck's not ready," Marcus said, a hidden gravity dragging him into a hunched posture. "Or did you expect us to run the truck outside of Harlow and blow up a goddam hospital?" He shook his head. "Damn it, Beth. You can't go plannin' shit without telling me anymore."

The question she needed to ask him rose to the top of her chest and burned there. She couldn't keep it down any longer.

"You were loading that truck for a long time," she said. "You had your own plans for a long time. Yet, you let me run. If you told me you were planning to fight him, I would have stayed. Trent would be alive. So much would be different. Why didn't you tell me?"

He touched the scar on his palm, turning his hand over, starting at the white line for a long time. She caught his lower lip quivering, just once, no more, as he bit it still and waited to gather himself before he spoke.

"Your sister," he said, taking another breath to collect himself. "I see the best of her in you; the best of your mother. I wanted you to run. I believed you could. I fanned the rebellious streak in you, nudging you across that border. I saw how passion and anger was clouding your fear. And I was hoping you'd stay gone long enough for me to kill anyone who might pursue you."

He took her hand. For the first time, she touched his scar. A thick, white ridge laid diagonally across his hand.

"What we do from now on, we do together," she said. "No more secrets."

He nodded, then kissed the back of her hand.

"I know you have to leave," she said. "I wish you didn't have to. I don't know what I'll do when I see the Mayor. I don't know how I'll react."

"Just remember one thing," Marcus said. "The queen moves wherever the hell she wants."

CHAPTER 29

B eth watched the door for hours before she drifted off to sleep. A rap on the frame woke her. The Mayor stood there, dressed in a plaid shirt and dusty jeans. Full Galen Mettis garb. He had a bulky gift box pinned against his hip, and a small vase of flowers with a *Get Well Soon* balloon floating overhead.

She checked the clock—midnight.

"May I come in?" he asked.

"It's your kingdom," Beth said. "We're all just dying in it."

The Mayor placed her flowers on the windowsill. He put the box on the reclining chair, making it clear he intended to stand the whole time.

He dug into his pocket. "Your father's coin," he said, and placed it on her table, next to an empty Jell-O cup. "See that your old man gets it."

This was, indeed, Galen Mettis, his tone and vernacular switching from the regal speech that he'd used during Harvest. Whoever this was, he might have been someone real in the past, but that man was long gone. The thing in her room was harder to pin down than a shadow.

"When do I get my own coin?" she asked.

The question pierced him, and a wounded look crossed his face. The man was a hell of an actor.

"I'd never allow you to live out your days as a low servant," he said. "That's a fate for the weak and uninteresting."

She thought of Trent, but all her thoughts of him were now colored with blood. She wanted to scream at the Mayor, to claw at him, to hurt him. Then, she saw her father's sturdy hands moving his knight, just hours earlier. She heard him ask, "Why did I do that?" and she couldn't answer.

The storm of anger cleared, and she looked the Mayor in the eyes. "You find me interesting?" she asked, trying to sound hopeful, and pulling it off.

The Mayor hesitated, but couldn't conceal his delight.

"I always have, and I've done right by you from the start," the Mayor said. "Think back to your little escape. Think hard. You blame me for your capture, but if you just did what I said, what I suggested—if you went alone and didn't get greedy, you would have gotten away."

"You're lying," she said. The anger bubbled. She couldn't hold it down for long.

"You'll never know when I'm lying," the Mayor said. "But when I say something you don't want to believe, you'll find that it's often the truth. Such as this—I don't want you hurt. The younger Albers had no right to touch you, and with his father gone, I feel it's my duty to apologize on behalf of the Albers family."

She glanced at the box. The wrapping was meticulous, each corner tightly folded around the cardboard. Black wrapping paper with golden bursts. Fireworks. A red bow was knotted on top.

"You killed Doug," she said.

"Of course," he said. "He was an uninteresting boy, but his grief had turned him dangerous."

He placed his hand on the gift.

"Whatever piece of him is in there, I've seen worse," she said.

The Mayor laughed. "Like I said, you're interesting. Not like the others."

He lingered in her room, waiting for something. He was expecting her anger, expecting a fight. Surely, the gift was a piece of Doug Albers, something meant to disgust her, a menacing symbol of both his power and his affection, a threat and a proposition.

"You have yet to say one word about him," the Mayor said.

She opened her eyes. Now or never. She had to play the game and play it expertly, and that meant forcing herself to respond, not react.

"I expected your fury and disdain," he said. "But I had always long suspected that you two didn't truly love each other."

"I couldn't run alone," she said. "Now, I can't run at all. Maybe I never should have tried. My father kept telling me Harlow could be home, but I always wanted something more. Something...interesting."

He nodded. Once, he had longed for the same. Somehow, the universe had given it to him, and the worst of his impulses turned an impossible gift into a savage blade he used to carve out his own kingdom.

"What is it you want?" he asked. Now, he was hopeful. He wasn't acting. She had an opening. She held eye contact with him, but could show no signs of anger or disgust. She forced herself to think of something that she loved and was within her mind's reach.

The list was short. She thought of eating ice cream cake with her sister long ago, letting the warmth of the memory color her eyes.

"I don't know what I want," she said. "Not yet." She glanced at the gift box. "It's his heart, isn't it?"

The Mayor didn't answer. He looked almost ashamed.

"Take it away," she said. "Please?"

He nodded and picked up the box.

"You are indeed the girl I got to know in the truck on all those nights," he said. Now, he almost looked like an awkward teenager who'd brought a boneheaded gift to impress his date.

She struck.

"I want to see you again," she said. "I understand the late nights, not letting everyone see you. I know the power of absence. But if I need to see you again—"

"You will," he said.

"How?" she asked.

"I'll send someone for you," he said. "If this is what I hope it is, I'll help us find out for sure."

"Promise you won't force me," she said. "Only the weak have a need to take."

His body language shifted in agreement. He took Harlow many years ago, and it was effortless, perhaps even boring. In the years since, he had set about earning its soul, even if he only meant to break it in his hands.

"So wise at such a young age. I took your mother, so I could never trust her," he said. "Kate, I thought I had earned. She enjoyed every comfort. Still, she ran."

He was at the foot of her bed now. His eyes had turned hypnotic, and she didn't even notice he had gotten so close.

"I see the best of both of them in you," he said. "And twice their beauty."

He placed a hand on her lower leg, his fingers hot on the flesh of her calf. She waited for them to either glide up to the inside of her thigh, or dig in so hard they cracked bone.

Instead, he removed his hand.

"You will have to earn me," he said. "Fail at the task, and my interest in you—and your well-being—will diminish dramatically."

"How?" she asked. She meant the word to be full-throated, but it came out as a whisper.

"When I send for you, you'll know," he said. He tore into the gift, letting the paper fall to the ground. The ripping sound was loud enough to make her flinch, and when he was done, he held up a crystal bowl filled with tiny bottles of liquor, strands of ribbon dangling from their necks.

He placed it gently on her nightstand.

"The boy's heart was not mine to give," he said. "I gave it to his mother, and once I placed it in her hands, she was eager to prove her loyalty. After she finished eating, she took back her maiden name. I trust her implicitly."

His fingertips brushed her calf again as he walked to the door. His slender muscularity disappeared in the shadows of the hallway, where he looked gaunt and stricken. He watched her in the dark until she was sure she would scream if he lingered one moment longer.

She forced a deep breath and mustered the effort to wave at him with a steady hand.

He waved back, his toothy grin catching the glare of her room's fluorescent lights. The rest of him was a narrow slice of shadow. He backed out of view and was gone.

She heard no footsteps. He could be just around the corner, but that was her life now, wasn't it? With him just around the corner?

One thought gave her comfort—as long as he was close, he was vulnerable.

CHAPTER 30

T he snow melted under a cold, gray sky. Blackened slush gathered in overwhelmed gutters and the sidewalks were littered with crushed rock salt.

Beth followed her father through Thatcher Henderson's yard, her sneakers turning muddy and wet. She saw a buzzard circling near the outbuilding. She didn't even squint. This time of year, they got the sun's leftovers. The buzzard twirled, circling a cosmic drain, never once flapping its wings. She decided to not believe in bad omens, only the persistence of scavengers.

A fifty-gallon drum was sliced in half and outfitted as an over-sized grill. Smoke churned from the tube welded into the hood. She smelled hickory and fat, and her stomach rumbled. She hadn't eaten much in the two days since her return from the hospital. Chewing gave her a headache, and her appetite had yet to return.

Marcus rapped on the door. All the men were gathered under the guise of a barbecue.

When she returned home and told Marcus her plan, he didn't say much, but he couldn't conceal his crestfallen look, one that confirmed what Beth suspected—that she was right, and her plan

was the best option in a short list of shitty ones to attack the Mayor
away from a concentration of Harlow citizens. Yet it was also the
plan that threatened her own life the most.

Marcus called them to order and had Cooper update them on
the status of the truck.

"I want a bang big enough to start another universe, and I'll keep
filling her to the gills, but right now? She's ripe enough to get my
blessing," he said.

"Good," Marcus said. "We may have our chance in the near
future. One that minimizes casualties." He looked at Beth, her cue
to explain her idea.

She told them about Doug's attack, about the Mayor's visit in the
hospital room. She repeated everything he said, almost down to the
word, but the punchline that got everyone's attention was that he
had promised to send for her.

"You don't need to search for him, or hope he pops up," she said.
"Watch me. All day, all night. I wouldn't be surprised if he visited
me himself, but if he does send for me? You'll know, clear as day.
You follow me, you find him."

Silence, until Cooper spat tobacco juice on the concrete.
Thatcher didn't object. All of them wanted to spit at the thought
of it. She knew then she was in a room of good men, and not chess
players, and thought of the buzzard.

"Marcus?" Cooper asked.

"We watch her close," he said. "The Mayor will likely toy with
her head some and let her go. Then we'll have the location we need
to pop."

"And what if he don't let her go?" Randy said, jittery as ever.
"What if he takes her somewhere busy, like lunch at Joyce's or
some shit?"

"He won't do that," Marcus said. "He wouldn't be seen in public
as a regular person. It's unlikely that he captures her in secret. If we
watch Beth, it's the best opportunity to get a shot at him. We just
have to be ready for anything."

"Bullshit," Randy said. He had a line of empty Pabst cans resting on the picnic table next to him. "Bull-fucking-shit. This is a trap, this is."

"We vote," Marcus said. "I'm making clear—you're not voting to kill my daughter. I just want to know if you think this is the best option, and if we agree, I believe she's brave enough to operate in harm's way. If she has a chance to give us a chance, I know she'll take it."

"Randy's right," Chris said. Months after Trent's death, he still looked malnourished and sleep-deprived, fat bags bulging underneath his bloodshot eyes. "The Mayor's gonna make us eat this, somehow."

"We knew the risk going in," Marcus said. "I vote yes." Their leader, Beth's father. Casting the first yes vote would clear their consciences to agree. Saying no to him now was disagreement, not deference to his family.

"Father of the fuckin' year," Chris said. "I seen too many children bleed, my own among them. I say we take the fight to him. Lure him out somehow to fight us, full front. Let Cooper drive that truck up his ass while we tangle with him. We go down with the ship, not a little girl. I vote no."

Marcus turned to Cooper. "How about it, Cooper?" he asked. Beth knew what he was doing—if Cooper, the Great Survivor, agreed, the yeses would fall in line.

Cooper hesitated, looking at Chris Keller, either sizing him up, or giving the man's argument more weight than expected.

"Chris's right. Maybe if we just leak out these little meetings, the Mayor'll come," Randy said. "We'll have shotguns waiting for him. The truck'll be icing on the cake."

"He'd just send Ortega," Cooper said. "And that would be enough to end this."

"The janitor killed a disciple," Chris said. "Without a gun. Who's to say we can't kill a disciple while armed to the teeth? We ain't never fought one, not in my lifetime. They're tough as a two-dollar steak, but we can chew it, I imagine. Then the Mayor will have to come and face us."

"And then he wins," Cooper said. "The Mayor isn't a disciple. You understand? He's something more. He makes the disciples, and he'd never allow someone to equal himself in power."

"How the fuck would you know?" Chris said.

"I know," Marcus said. "My wife told me. Just before she died. She was his queen and learned his secrets—at least the ones he'd risk telling. He can copy his power somehow, but a much weaker version of it. Wish I knew how."

"He calls me the Great Survivor," Cooper said. "Marcus knows why. Do the rest of you?"

Randy raised his hand, a half-drunk adult acting like he was in grade school. "Red Rock," he said. "I don't know exactly what happened, but I always heard that Red Rock is where it started."

"Where it ended, more like," Cooper said. "Harlow as we knew it, anyway. I wasn't even supposed to be there, but the Mayor needed a Great Survivor."

"Why?" Thatcher asked.

"Too many uprisings," he said. "He could quash them, but he wanted something more from Harlow, and for that, he needed a witness."

"Don't, Coop," Marcus said. "We come this far. Spook 'em now, and it does us no good."

"They should know," Cooper said. "Before the vote to have your girl in harm's way for the greater good, a vote that's pretty fucking heavy to cast, they should know why a different kind of fight—the one they're used to—won't work."

The men were rapt, their beer cans gathering frost in the cold of the barn—a cold that overwhelmed even the flickering rage of the woodstove. Beth gave the listeners as much attention as Cooper himself—she could tell who had heard the story before, and who hadn't, even as she heard it unfurl for the first time.

"I was thirteen," Cooper began, and no one said a word until he was done.

"First thing to know, the men who rose up against him didn't know the somebitch was bulletproof. They knew he was strong and fast, thrashing mean as a kicked-over snapping turtle, and weren't going to take any chances. But he was hard to pin down. Never made it a point to show up in public all that often. Rumor had it that he liked to sit on Red Rock Point and look down over Harlow, especially at night.

"Those same rumors had him with vampire ears and blood on his teeth; they said he could hear every whisper in Harlow from up there.

"I don't believe those, but I do believe the ones about him being the survivor of a mine collapse in the early 1900s, forced to murder and eat his compadres, emerging as the lone survivor. The town shunned him, but he never got the hint to leave. Eventually, they lynched his ass, not knowing he had the powers he had. He took the men that lynched him and put them in the mines to die starving.

"Since that day, he spent his time getting his grip on the town's power structures—power that dissipated as the mines went dry and the world slowly moved on. The handles got easier to grip.

"One man he couldn't grip was Dalton Jarvis. He drummed up a posse. Ten men, all hunters, farm boys he could trust. All married, too. Hell, small town like this, wasn't a man over the age of nineteen who wasn't married or engaged. My old man was one of them, Ted Murray. Just by chance, I went into our old shed that night and saw my father lining up rifles on the open tailgate of his truck. Guns everywhere. I thought it looked like deer camp, but deer were out of season and my old man wouldn't hunt without me.

"He grabbed me by the collar and dragged me out of the shed, told me to mind my mother at the picnic. He gave me ten bucks to shoot squirt gun rifles at targets for prizes—he knew that was my favorite game, and told me I had to make it last all night.

"Farming towns always have some kind of fall celebration after harvest is in. Back then, before the Mayor's Harvest started that very next year, ours was the St. Francis church picnic, and it was on that night the men decided to take the Mayor down.

"One reason was because they felt their wives were safe at the picnic. They all had volunteer shifts to run, and when they were done slicing pies or doling out chicken dinners or selling raffle tickets, they all played bingo. The seamstresses in town worked all year on quilts to give away as bingo prizes, and the whole town would see the quilts up for grabs pinned to a clothesline.

"The Mayor had yet to get a taste for public theatrics, so the wives were safe playing bingo until they closed down the picnic at midnight. They'd sit on a bench under spotlights, laughing and picking away at funnel cakes, lamenting their close calls and switching cards when they went too long without threatening to win a quilt.

"The trucks pulled up at Red Rock Point, spotlights pointed at the naked hill where an observer could see the picnic's glow just beyond the lower tree line. The Mayor wasn't there, but they kept their lights on the point all the same, because something colorful was in the dirt. Floral patterns and checkers and starburst shapes, pinks and yellows and reds and deep blues.

"Dresses. Each man recognized his wife's outfit, the one they were wearing when they headed off for the picnic.

"Only one dress was missing. Dalton's wife, Janet. Panicked and afraid, the men turned on him, thinking him a traitor that sold them out to save his own family. Yet no man was brave enough to pull the trigger as Dalton pled his case. He wore them down and convinced them that the Mayor was playing a game, hoping they'd turn on each other, and they needed to band together to either save their women, or extract bloody vengeance.

"The Mayor watched all this, of course. He stepped out of the shadows and told them their loved ones were hidden underground, lost in the dark, and only he could find them. He said the first man to kill Dalton would enjoy his wife's safe return, and the rest wouldn't be so lucky.

"They held fast, though. Think of what a man Dalton Jarvis must have been for their loyalty to not break in that moment, for their trust in him to trump the fear the Mayor was laying down on them. They turned their guns on the Mayor and fired. They knew the fucker was strong, but that's when they discovered he was bullet-proof. When a man's gun is shown to be useless in his hands, prior-ities change, and fear suddenly finds a shorter path to your heart.

"They had no choice and turned their guns on Dalton Jarvis. His body was shredded with bullets, everyone racing to land a killing blow and win the Mayor's favor. You couldn't tell who shot him first without a video replay, so the Mayor told them all they'd enjoy the fruits of Harlow as his first High Servants, and get their wives back, if they chose to bend the knee.

"They did. The Mayor stepped into the shadows and returned with an old-fashioned military duffel bag. The green fabric looked blacked and wet in the moonlight. He dumped out its contents, and ten heads rolled down Red Rock Point, wives reunited with their kneeling husbands.

"He killed them with his bare hands. Some fought back, while others remained on their knees, hoping it was a test, hoping he would let them live. But he never intended to let them live. He wanted the light of hope in their eyes before he took it away from them. Even all those years ago, killing bored him. He could have slaughtered the whole town anytime he pleased, but if he did that, he'd never own it.

"That's why he went to my house and woke me up and took me there, telling me the story of what he'd done to my father and his friends.

"'What is a man without a witness?' the Mayor asked, showing me the massacre. Guts and limbs strewn in the dirt, white shards of bone poking from dismembered corpses, catching moonlight. 'A man is only what others decide him to be.'

"He put his hand on my shoulder. 'If I am to fulfill my destiny, Harlow must know my mercy—but they must always remember my wrath.'

"That was the year the Harlow Griffins died. The gym floor was torn up, the school's crest stripped off and thrown into the dumpster. The Harlow Orphans were born, and I was one of them.

"We had no church picnic the following year, but we had a ceremony. The orphaned sons and daughters took the first Oath, and we ate the flesh of Father Andy, the St. Francis parish priest. The Mayor put all the bingo quilts in the church and burned it to the ground.

"I lost my parents and the Mayor put the screws to Harlow. I can't lie and say I didn't think about eating a shotgun every now and again. I couldn't have been alone in that mental gutter, but a funny thing happened—I kept hearing a rumor around school, about the Mayor tearing down the Griffins because he was afraid of them, that a Griffin was destined to come and destroy him and deliver Harlow from his evil grasp.

"Of course I thought it was bullshit, and of course I knew the bright-eyed kid who started those rumors. He was an orphan himself, but one smart enough to start fighting the Mayor at his own game—Dalton's own son, a man who stands before you now, a man whose daughter is willing to risk her life so we can win this fight.

"And that is the fight we're in now, gentlemen. The Mayor knows he can rip us apart, and it bores him. If he even catches a whiff of what we're up to, he won't just show up and kill us. He'll try and find a way to rip us apart, to weaponize our love, to poison our loyalty, to turn our morality against us. He thinks himself a god, and we're in the Old Testament. Harlow is full of his Cains, Abels, and Abrahams, and he's writing his commandments in first draft.

"That's why we have to get him now. One day, he'll raze this place like Gomorrah and move on. So I vote yes, and if any of you have a no vote caught in your throat because Beth here is young and pretty and can't do the job, swallow it now. She's a Jarvis. She'll start the fight—and we'll finish it."

Cooper's tale and vote left a long silence in its wake. Marcus broke it.

"Like I said, I vote yes," he said.

"She's your girl," Thatcher said. "We'd all understand if we had to wait for another way."

"She's not willing to wait," Marcus said. "You know my choice would be anything that doesn't risk her, but she's had a hell of a time staying out of harm's way around here."

Beth nodded, wanting to absolve him, knowing her father's heart was breaking, but his logic had long held dominion over his emotions.

"Harm's way it is, then," Thatcher said.

The votes fell in line, and as they did, Beth felt the heaviness of responsibility build inside her, a gathering storm she hoped she could weather when the time finally came.

A NOBLE ILLUSION

CHAPTER 31

Quinn laid his crutch across the barstools of the Blue Door Saloon. Tourists ate pub food lunches. They were sunburned and wet from their time on the beach, which was just outside the door. He ordered a Macallan. It was 10:00 a.m.

His stump ached. He'd endured a long day gimping around with his clunky prosthetic until he gave up and went to the crutch. He did just enough rehab to get around. A dull ache rumbled from his stump every time he took a step onto his fake lower leg. Other times, the tingling shadow of the limb that was would make him want to scratch a foot that was no longer there.

He came to Destin, Florida, half-healed and a hundred percent drunk—a return to drinking that was part therapy, part send-off. He came to Destin to get drunk and die.

The Blue Door was a tiny spot just off the beach, attached to one of the McResorts that were all the same—bad lighting, no televisions, and expensive, with the salty smell of the ocean mixing in with the chlorine stench of the poolsiders who came in for cocktails.

Quinn had visited most of the dive bars in Destin, but they had pretty bartenders programmed to receive maximum tips. He needed help from someone else, the kind of person you don't know you've found until you've found them.

The bartender here was a promising prospect. He wore a tropical shirt, most buttons undone, gray hair thick across his chest. His face was wrinkled down to his skull, his skin so deeply tanned, he'd never find the melanomas.

Quinn unfolded a stack of handwritten pages. Kate's journal. The rest of the package—the folders, the medical records, the notes her mother took—were all in the hotel room. He intended to burn them when the time was right, along with what was left of his worthless body.

For now? A second Macallan and his daily reading.

How long does the world have to tell you what you are before you'll listen?

Even now, when Quinn thought of Kate's death, he thought of his lost baby girl, and couldn't spark the same rage he felt when the news was fresh. The memory of anger isn't anger. It's a bad photocopy. The mind had a way of wrapping things in scar tissue, time spooling around the hurt, padding it like rings on a tree.

He couldn't pinpoint the moment when he stopped being cold, focused, and terrifying, but Nico saw Quinn's capacity to soften long before Quinn himself did.

Nico was one of those faux-cultured types, the guys that acted smart by reciting quotes from books they'd never read. Whenever they were primed up for a job, he would say, "How can a man die better, than facing fearful odds?" He always fucked up quotes and their sources, but it made him sound fancy to his lieutenants and hitters and foot soldiers. Before the last job, he recited the same quote.

"You don't even say it right," Quinn had said. "You don't even know where it's from."

"It's just a saying," Nico responded. "Confucius or some shit."

"The poem *Horatius*," Quinn said. "He holds the bridge. He faces fearful odds, and dies, for the ashes of his fathers and the temples of his gods. We're dying for money. Your money."

"You plan on dying?" Nico asked.

"Everyone can plan on it," Quinn said.

He should have put a bullet in Nico's face that day, before the shipyard job. He knew something was off, years of instincts building up a black residue that made him capable of pulling the trigger as easy as taking a morning piss, giving him a keen sense of the way men sweat and twitch and flick their eyes when something's up. He should have killed them all. But he didn't.

Whatever it was that made him bury his every dark instinct for a woman who never even loved him was just starting to bubble to the surface.

I have sinned against you, Curtis. I've kept secrets from you, and those sins, like yours, are permanent. You don't have to tell me any stories for me to know it. It's etched on your skin, it's in the way you touch me and care for me, as if you can make up for your sins, for all the lives you've taken or ruined.

I watch you sleep sometimes. Weightless, dreamless, steady. You are a machine, flushing out guilt and memories—they are inconvenient to your efficiency. Humanity is a burden, and you have no room for it, but you continue to pretend, to struggle against what you are. I still can't love you for it.

She wanted victory at first—a partnership between them, storming Harlow, freeing her family. Then, she wanted vengeance. The weight of knowing she was being searched for and might one day die at the hands of the Mayor and his loyalists filled her with a rage that she would outsource in the journal, telling Curtis to avenge her, to kill the Mayor and anyone who stood with him. Then, she took it all back. She realized the impossibility of killing the Mayor without innocent causalities and had decided on peace with her child. She had moved on. She was pregnant, and the world felt big again, and Harlow faded. Danger faded with it. She let her guard down, and the Mayor landed a fatal blow and pinned the Griffin mantle on a man who looked the part, but was weak and crippled even before the axe fell upon his leg.

Quinn pushed his empty glass forward, requesting a refill, and folded up the pages.

The bartender poured.

"You're no tourist," the bartender said.

"You're no bartender," Quinn answered.

"I pour, I get paid. That's the definition of bartender the rest of us have all agreed upon."

"You seem like a Marine," Quinn said.

"You seem like a guy who'd notice," he said. He held out his hand. "Tony Cardone."

Quinn shook it. "Jack London."

"Ah, the famous author?" Tony said. "What are you, about a hundred and thirty years old, give or take?"

"You got me," Quinn said. "I'm an asshole."

"Of which variety?"

"The kind that sees the beck and call of the glorious and infinite ocean and wishes to walk into its waves and never return."

"I hate to break this to you," Tony said, "but that's not the ocean. It's the Gulf of Mexico."

Tony poured two Macallans. "I'm gonna put this one on your tab since you're hellbent on dying and all." He knocked it back in one swallow.

"A man don't own a shirt like that unless he's got a boat," Quinn said.

"Guilty as charged, but I'm more of a drunk than a fisherman."

Quinn swirled his drink and watched the Macallan lick the glass, then dissolve away.

"I need a captain, not a fisherman," Quinn said. "I can't tell you who I am. I can't tell you all the reasons why. But I'd like a ride to someplace deep, a place where my body can't be found."

"Okay, Mr. London, shit done got too serious too fast. I haven't even had lunch yet and you're winning 'batshit tourist of the day' by a mile. You need to speak to a professional."

He reached out to grab Quinn's glass and found his wrist ensnared in Quinn's massive grip. His fingers dug into Tony's ligaments, which were as taut as piano strings, dancing under the flesh as he yanked his hand away.

Quinn let him. "I am speaking to a professional," he said, gesturing at Tony's upper arm, which was covered by a pattern of palm trees and coconuts against red fabric. "Death before dishonor."

Tony sighed. He lifted the sleeve to show Quinn an eagle, a Marine-ink favorite. He could only make out a silhouette on Tony's deeply-tanned skin.

He turned his own arm over and showed him the Griffin. "Let me tell you a story about tattoos," he said.

Getting drunk was the only area of Quinn's life where he showed no signs of rust. He settled into the rhythm of his final days, drinking at night to dull his thoughts and drinking in the morning to keep delaying a hangover he never intended to experience.

He had decided these were his final days, because like it or not, he was the Griffin. Men like Cartwright would eventually come looking for him. Nico Coletti already had a long-standing bounty on his head, and he was now running with one leg and the warm, familiar haze of getting drunk every damn day.

If he just fell off the face of the earth, the Griffin would live forever, and Nico would die wondering how Curtis Quinn had eluded him.

Death before dishonor.

Tony understood all too well. Quinn's wishes clicked so seamlessly with Tony's disposition that Quinn wondered how often Tony himself had contemplated suicide.

Still, he couldn't convince Tony to charter Quinn's final boat trip without telling him all the ways he had failed the woman he loved—and when that didn't work, he told him about the Mayor.

Quinn waited for Tony to finish his shift. He sat on the beach, his ass buried in white sand. The ocean met the horizon on a black and starless night, creating a mouth of darkness that ate the world. He drank Macallan eighteen-year, straight from the bottle.

Tony's fishing charter banged against the dock, a vessel named *Enyo*. A goddess of war, destroyer of cities. He toasted her.

Behind him, the yellow eyes of lit resort balconies shimmered. The dark of the beach could not be pierced by the glow, and he had a long and silent piece of sand to himself.

Flashlights danced around the dock a couple hundred yards away, kids looking for crabs. They would put their victims in a bucket and show their parents and smile and then the crabs would die.

He checked his watch. Tony should be strutting down to the dock any minute. He still had half a bottle to take on the trip.

"Don't get cold feet now," he said, and tipped it.

When he lowered the bottle, a woman stood in front of him. The surf lapped her bare feet. She was panting and forced a smile. Her teeth were white enough to see in the dark.

She had been running, but the sand ate the sound of her footsteps. Her cover-up rippled in the breeze. She sat near him, but not next to him.

"What's your name?" she asked.

"Jack London," he said. She believed him. "Don't tell me, your name is Enyo."

"Sorry to disappoint you," she said. The wind caught her ponytail. She kept pushing it out of her face. "I'm Alexis."

"And what trouble brings you my way tonight, Alexis?"

She stammered, and then shut up altogether.

The girl smelled of sex and wine coolers. She was unkempt and running, saw a scary-looking brute with a bottle, and stopped to make friends. Even in the low light, the math was simple.

"What brings you out here?" she asked. "You can drink anywhere."

"A woman," he said.

"Married?"

They did take vows. "The Griffin remains loyal to one mate, even after death," Kate had said. Loyalty to her beyond death. More than a marriage.

"No," he answered. "She left."

"Why?"

"She saw me for what I truly am," he said. "I think you do, too. That's why you stopped. Isn't it?"

"Maybe I'm just friendly."

"That's probably what got you into whatever it is you got into," he said. "I'm drunk. I'm twice your size. It's dark. You're alone."

"Yeah, I should know better, I've seen *Dateline*. But I can handle myself." She batted away her hair again. "Sometimes."

"Yo, this ain't gonna be the Love Boat." Tony was behind them. Tonight's tropical shirt was a pastel blue invaded by parrots. "Time to shove off, matey."

He didn't wait for Quinn to get up, walking right past them, heading for the docks. Quinn planted his palms in the sand and struggled to his feet. His crutch was useless in the sand, but he was determined to board the boat without it—his way to die standing.

"Please," Alexis said. "I can't go back there."

"Call the cops, honey," he said. "If you can't tell, my ass-kicking days are long gone. I'm one leg short."

"These guys have money," she said. "And the cops know me around here."

He handed her the bottle.

"Chug that and take a long swim. Stuff your pockets first. Become the cliché you were always meant to be."

Tony whistled.

"That's my ride," Quinn said.

He left her on the beach. When they shoved off, Quinn saw her silhouette, sitting where he left her, with three shadows moving in her direction.

"I see you met Alexis," Tony said. "She's the third-most popular tourist attraction around these parts, right behind the ocean and the beach."

"If she's a pro, why's she working without muscle?"

"She usually does," Tony said. "Don't know what the hell she got into this time, but we got a busy night planned, wouldn't you say?"

The boat ripped through the night. He couldn't see the beach any longer. Soon, the resort lights faded.

No clouds. No stars. A womb of darkness.

Not a womb, he thought. *Not birth. I'm in a grave. I'm home.*

Tony shut off the boat, submitting it to the mercy of the waves. Now accustomed to their rhythm, Quinn found them soothing, even as the hull dipped and crashed.

"A bit rough, but we're in deep, distant waters, my friend." Tony turned on a light and began to rummage through the under-seat storage.

They had agreed on what would happen next—Quinn would put on a weighted vest and sit on the edge of the boat. Tony would point a sawed-off shotgun at his face and obliterate him and any potential of dental record identification.

That is, if anyone found him. He would sink, and with the vest, he would stay sunk, even after his body bloated and rotted. Drowning victims tend to float after a couple days, but soon, the gas and rot would subside. The ocean would feed on him, leaving nothing but bones.

A dead Curtis Quinn was a dead Griffin, but a vanished Curtis Quinn? That was the only way to stalemate the Mayor.

"There it is," Tony said. He removed a bottle of Macallan twenty-five. Older, mellower, far more expensive. A worthy send-off. He poured two glasses without spilling, even as the boat swayed underneath them.

"Fuck it, right?" Tony laughed.

Quinn took the glass and knocked it back.

"Why are you in a hurry?" Tony asked. "Going somewhere?"

"Yeah. Down," Quinn said.

"I been thinking a lot about this Mayor you told me about," Tony said.

"Don't," Quinn said.

"Don't what?"

"Sounds like you're ramping up a philosophical argument for life."

"Maybe it's the opposite," Tony said, and the jovial tone drained away from him. Now, in the dark, a mask was lifted, something he covered with Jimmy Buffett shirts and an endless stream of banter.

"When you told me about this guy, I knew I had to help you," he said. "You ever lose anyone to cancer?"

Quinn shook his head.

"That's some evil shit, man. So, imagine you get a brain tumor. Imagine they find the tumor, right? They know what's wrong with you. They can see it. They know where it's at. They even know how to destroy it. So, how the fuck does that tumor kill you?"

He waited for an answer. Three waves smacked the boat.

"That's not rhetorical?" Quinn said.

"Cowardice," Tony said. "When the scalpel doesn't work, the only treatments they have fuck up your healthy tissue. So they don't do them. Even when you ask them to do it. Even when you beg them. They fucking kill you because they're afraid of killing you."

"Can we at least skip to the part where you mention Enyo?"

Tony laughed.

"She couldn't kill Zeus," he said. "He was too powerful. The god of gods. So she and Ares set about destroying all his creations. They traded the scalpel for full-brain radiation."

Tony brandished the shotgun.

"Ain't no king without a kingdom, brother. Your woman thought you were the scalpel, but you're not. So what? It don't mean you're not the solution."

"I don't know what I am," Quinn said.

"Shit, no one knows that," Tony said. "You know what you are? What everyone thinks you are, fair or not. You know what your woman saw? Same thing Alexis saw."

"A man who can hurt people," Quinn said.

"I'd bet on a different horse," Tony said.

"What, then?"

"Turn this boat around, find Alexis, and ask her," Tony said.

"Why'd you charter this trip just to come out here and talk me out of it?" Quinn said. "What is it you see in me?"

"I see a man who's sick of running," Tony said. "And it takes one to know one."

He laid the shotgun on his lap and reached into the side pocket of his cargo shorts. He laid a piece of paper on the seat next to him and scribbled out a signature.

"I'm done running," Tony said. "Not by choice, either. What I wouldn't give to die fighting, brother."

He folded up the paper.

"What's this?" Quinn asked.

"Registration for the boat," Tony said. "My last PET scan had more spots than a fucking Dalmatian, and they won't do shit. They use the word 'can't,' but it's 'won't.' Fucking cowards."

He gripped the shotgun.

"Oh fuck," Quinn said. "Tony. No."

"You can follow me down into the abyss," Tony said. "Or, you can turn the boat around. It's not too late, brother."

"Put the gun down," Quinn said.

Tony turned the shotgun around, the black eyes of the dual barrels tucked against the flesh of his lower jaw.

"Wait," Quinn said, scrambling to keep him talking. "Not too late... for what?"

"To figure out that you're not what you've done—you're what you do next."

"Tony—"

"Death before dishonor."

Tony pulled the trigger.

Quinn fitted the vest on Tony's near-headless body and tossed him overboard. He picked up the shotgun.

How long does the world have to tell you what you are before you'll listen?

The resort lights were specks of gold on the distant and black horizon. He sat in the boat, the shotgun across his lap, the vessel swaying with the gentle waves that underscored a perfect summer evening.

He closed his eyes and saw Kate, her blond hair, her blue eyes, her smile. Quinn began to sob, grieving her truly and completely for the first time. He refused to let it take its course and burned away the tears with the heat of anger, screaming out, "What the fuck did you want from me!"

The gulf held no answers. The wind shrugged at the question. He stood up, plunging the shotgun into the underside of his skull.

"What did you want?" he said, a whisper this time. "Or did you even know? Were you just as scared and confused as me?"

The wind lapped against his face, drying his tears.

How long does the world have to tell you what you are before you'll listen?

He turned the boat around.

Quinn went to Piper's Cove and asked the front desk to help him locate Alexis's condo. He didn't expect her to be there, but it was a start.

She wasn't home. He asked to get inside, giving them a story about being a concerned stepfather, so they let him in as long as he had a security escort.

Inside, he found her picture. She was arm-in-arm with an older woman he presumed to be her mother. Alexis had brown eyes and chocolate hair, a real stunner. She could have made ten times as much in Chicago, perhaps ended up as an exclusive for Nico's outfit. Maybe even Nico himself.

He thanked security and walked along the strip. The search went slow—he used his crutch, trying to preserve his energy. Walking on his prosthetic sapped him. He hadn't rehabbed properly, hadn't exercised, and wasn't eating anything remotely useful to his body.

Resorts stood side by side against the backdrop of the beach, all of them sporting goofy-ass tropical names. *Sunny Waves. White Sands. Sunny Sands. Piper's Crossing. Sandpiper Sands.*

He flashed the picture around. The buzz of alcohol didn't last long. If he had one talent, it was his constitution, the way his blood could scrub toxins from his system. Adrenaline helped burn it away.

His stump ached. No one had seen the girl.

He doubled back to the same front desks. This time, he changed the question. Was a group of young men staying at the resort? Were they obnoxious? Did they use fancy credit cards or otherwise smell of money?

At White Sands, a front desk girl with *I'm from Alabama*! on her name tag and the accent to match rolled her eyes, and Quinn knew he'd found them.

"Twelfth floor," she said.

"Which room?"

"I really shouldn't say," she said.

"The alternative is me knocking on every door," he said. "I think my niece is with them."

"You said stepdaughter just an hour ago."

"Niece, stepdaughter." He leaned closer. "She's in trouble. What do I have to say? She's my sister. My wife. She's the President's daughter."

"I think I should maybe call security," she said.

"Tell you what," he said. "Let's allow cooler heads to prevail. I'll try her cell a couple more times, and if it's no dice, I'll call the cops myself. Deal?"

She accepted. He stepped outside, looped around the exterior of the building, and went back in via the beach entrance. No key card required.

The elevator stank of saltwater and body odor. Sand dusted the tile underfoot, making his boots crunch. He wore heavy, steel-toed Red Wings, one of them laced tightly to his prosthetic. With jeans on, no one would notice he was crippled. He stepped out of the elevator and slowly walked the hallways, listening at each door on the beach side of the building. If they had money, they wouldn't accept anything less than an ocean-view suite.

He found them in about thirty seconds. Laughter, the television turned up too loud, the clink of glass in the garbage can.

He cast aside his crutch and knocked on the door.

The man who opened the door was wearing swim trunks. He was barefoot, and had a barbed wire tattoo painted around a swollen bicep. He wore a muscle shirt and had tightly cropped, sun-damaged hair.

The layout of the condo looked to be identical to Alexis's. A long, narrow hallway, leading into a small kitchen, which opened into a living room. The sliding door was open, and having the hallway door open created a draft. The humidity whipped through the room and carried the smell of the ocean and coconut oil.

Beyond Barbed Wire's shoulder, he saw two other men, early twenties. Frat bro assholes. A skinny kid in cargo shorts and a polo shirt held a deck of cards. The other one was black, but he wore a white asshole's uniform—pink T-shirt, boat shoes with no socks, plaid shorts.

The bottle of Macallan he'd given Alexis was resting on the coffee table. The assholes were drinking it out of paper cups.

He heard the distinct click of a doorknob lock. The bedroom. A fourth guy was in the condo, taking his turn with Alexis.

Allegedly, of course.

Quinn processed all this before Barbed Wire said, "Can I help you, sir?"

He had practiced courtesy and a greasy smile. Quinn figured the kid would make an excellent stockbroker if he survived the night.

"Party's over, asshole," Quinn said. "Get her dressed and drag her out of there. I'll take her home."

He wasn't a kid that was used to pushback. An only child, most likely. Spoiled. It wasn't enough to take what he paid for from Alexis—paying for things meant nothing.

"I think you have the wrong room, sir," he said.

By now, the other two were standing, attentive and alert, watching them.

"You're so polite," Quinn said. "My apologies for being a tad, shall we say, blunt. Let me try it again. Will you pretty please, with sugar on top, escort the girl into the hallway so that I may take her home?"

"I'm starting to get pissed," he said. "You got the wrong room."

"Yeah, motherfucker, you got the wrong room!" The skinny one, of course. The mouth of the group, and probably the wallet, too.

Barbed Wire tried to close the door. Quinn caught it.

"I don't typically ask three times," Quinn said. "But I'm going to make an exception. The girl. Yes or no?"

His grip loosened on the door, and he couldn't maintain eye contact with Quinn's fiery gaze. As usual, the guy with the barbed wire tattoo was a pussy.

Quinn stepped into the condo and brushed past him. He didn't bother with the bedroom door, knowing it was locked. Instead, he headed to the living room, taking careful notice of any sounds coming from behind him. Barbed Wire meekly followed. No aggression.

Not yet, anyway.

"Macallan?" Quinn said. "Appears to be an eighteen-year vintage. May I?"

No one objected. He sat on the couch. The skinny one stood near the balcony's sliding door. Barbed Wire blocked the hallway. The black guy strolled into the kitchen.

A headboard started banging against the wall. The boys looked at each other. Quinn grabbed the bottle of Macallan by the neck.

He filled a paper cup to the brim.

"Who the fuck is she to you?" the skinny one said.

"Nobody," Quinn said. "Then again, everyone is a nobody to me. Including you assholes. The only difference is, you motherfuckers have already lied to me tonight, and you're spreading out, eyeballing each other. Having this nonverbal discussion about try-ing to whip my ass. But none of you have the balls to make the move, right? I'm big and scary, face full of scars, wearing a boot on one healthy foot at a fucking beach resort. I get it."

He picked up the cup and sniffed. "I'm gonna miss this," he said. "Two hours on the wagon, and here I am, already tempted."

"Look, asshole," the black guy said. "You can leave out the door, or out that motherfucking window."

"That's good, kill me, make it a murder case. They'll find and question Alexis. She'll be easy to find, I bet. She's unconscious, right? Fuck, you'll have to kill her, too. Won't stop the rape kit from finding your jizz."

"We paid, though," Barbed Wire said. "It's not rape if you pay."

The other two gave him a *shut the fuck up* look.

"Paying's not enough for assholes like you," Quinn said. "Paying gets old fast. Too easy. You can only get off by taking. Usually, rich fucks get away with it, too. But not tonight."

"You're so tough, huh?" Skinny Guy said. "You gonna take on all of us, tough guy?"

"Yes," he said.

He stood up, still holding the paper cup.

The black guy opened the kitchen drawer and found a knife. Only a steak knife with a flimsy blade and a plastic handle.

"Terrence, don't," Barbed Wire said. "Just everyone relax, okay? We just give her to him. You're just taking her home, right, buddy? We had to get her out of here anyway."

The tension drained out of them. They never had it in them to attack him. He sensed it from the start. Relenting was the right play, and they put up just enough resistance, just enough of a fight, to talk about how lucky Quinn was to walk out with his ass intact after the ordeal was over.

That's exactly what would have happened if they were dealing with any reasonable person, if they were dealing with a hero, if they were negotiating with a savior.

They were not.

He threw the whiskey at Terrence's face. Then, he moved on the skinny kid, shoving him two-handed over the railing. He screamed all the way down, a symphony punctuated by moist organs disintegrating on concrete.

Terrence waved the knife around, his vision blurred. Barbed Wire was stuck behind him in the tight quarters of the condo.

Quinn moved on them, his approach cautious. Terrence waited, then lashed out with an overhand stab, clumsy and slow. Quinn caught Terrence's wrist, turning it, cracking it, shoving the knife into the bottom of his jaw, up into the roof of his mouth.

Not a killing blow, but a stunning one. Terrence released his grip on the knife and Quinn was now armed. The serrated blade did more ripping than cutting, but it was enough to create a ragged opening in Terrence's throat. A pink slit opened in black skin as blood poured out of him.

Barbed Wire was running now, but wouldn't you know it, the fourth frat bro opened the bedroom door and entered the hallway. They ran into each other.

As Barbed Wire tried to get to his feet, Quinn was behind him. He took him into a chokehold and drove the knife deeply into each eye socket.

He saw the fourth friend for the first time. He was naked and sunburned, tan lines deep along his waist. He sported a hard-on that had yet to wilt, and pubic hair shaved to the stubble. Barbed Wire's blood rained down on him. Sunburn's hard-on slapped against his inner thighs as he scooted backward toward the door. The closed door—one he would never get open in time.

Quinn drove the steel toe of his boot into the base of the hard-on. Sunburn reflexively sat up, clutching his crushed testicles, and Quinn met his eye with the tip of the steak knife, then punched him in the larynx to crush it and silence him. Eyes, throat, genitals. His usual targets for making quick work of assholes who only fought the kind of fights they saw in action movies. Sunburn collapsed to the hallway tile, twitching, his face turning a deep shade of purple.

Quinn stepped over him, into the bedroom. Alexis was naked and passed out. He packed her clothes, covered her in a sheet, and in the emerging chaos of a splattered body near the resort pool, he had no problems getting her to the boat under the cover of darkness.

The next day, Quinn sat on the hood of his rented Camry, drinking a bottle of Gatorade under the blazing Georgia sun. The brush grew high and thick in the ditches, and the side road hadn't seen regular traffic in a long time.

The car door opened. Alexis was awake. Quinn hopped down, wincing as his prosthetic slammed into his stump. He took a fresh Gatorade from a small cooler and handed it to her. She tore off the cap and drank it with a greed for fluids reserved for the dying or badly hungover.

"Where are we?" she asked. She had the sheet wrapped around her and looked like hell.

"About three miles from civilization," he said. "You'll walk north to find that civilization, which amounts to a gas station, the kind with untrustworthy chicken salad sandwiches and empty fuel islands."

He pointed to her clothes, which he'd folded neatly and placed on the hood.

As she dressed, he turned away.

"I know you think I got myself into that mess," she said.

"I don't think anything."

"The skinny one paid me," she said. "In cash at my place. He invited me out. Seemed to have money. I liked him, and hadn't partied at the beach in a while."

"I don't care," he said.

"I do," she said. "I want you to know."

He gave up and let her talk.

"I knew they put something in my drink and I ran. I didn't have anywhere to go, just away from them. I found you. I'm glad I did."

"They aren't," he said.

"You hurt them?"

"Something like that. You done yet?"

Once dressed, she finished her Gatorade. He handed her another.

"One for the road," he said. Then, he handed her an envelope. "Tony's charter boat. The deed is signed. You sign it, and it's yours. You can make more renting that out than your body."

She was suspicious. No one did nice things for her, and it was baked into her body language. She took the envelope anyway.

"That way," he said, pointing north.

"I can't thank you enough," she said.

"You shouldn't," he said, walking away. He paused at the driver's side door. "You saw me and stopped," he said. "You can see now what I look like, what I am."

She listened. The unseasonably hot spring winds flapped at her greasy hair. She brushed it away, same as she did on the beach.

"Why?" he asked.

"You looked like you would help me," she said.

"I killed them," he said. "I didn't have to. I killed them, and their deaths didn't un-rape you."

"I said you looked like you would help," she said. "I didn't say you looked like a hero."

Her gaze cradled him. He remained frozen at the car door, looking at her, and she let him, and smiled.

"You said your woman saw you for what you really are," she said. "So what? She's gone. You're not. The gas station's three miles away—but I don't have to walk. And you don't have to be alone."

Her voice rode the wind, thrumming a warm place in his chest, a feeling he hadn't had in a long time.

She nodded, brushing away her hair, reluctant to turn and walk away.

"What's your real name, Jack London?"

"Curtis," he said.

"Thank you for saving me, Curtis." She tossed a silver object that glinted in the newborn sun, a perfect throw that he caught just before it smacked against the top of the Camry. He opened his hand to find a Zippo lighter with the black-and-white yin-yang symbol set in the body.

"I don't smoke," he said.

"I just quit," she hollered back.

He watched her walk away. She was getting away from him, or he was letting her go. He could have let Kate walk away from him all those years ago, but he ran to catch up with her. What worlds awaited at Alexis's side?

He wondered if she would look back at him. She didn't. Most of him was glad.

He finally got in the car. He turned on the engine to chase away the silence, but it was all too loud now, his every thought a thunderclap, his voice finally rising above all the others. He touched his Griffin tattoo.

How long does the world have to tell you what you are before you'll listen?

For the first time in his life, he listened.

He flicked open the top of Alexis's lighter and ignited it. A thick flame with a wide blue base sparked to life. He watched the fire— an old enemy. He took his left arm and turned it, the Griffin tattoo facing his lap. He brought the tip of the flame to the ink etched in his flesh and kept it there until it bubbled away, the years of his marriage dissolving, the Griffin's eagle-beaked face scorched to black. The flame opened a pocket of slick, pink tissue, cleansing away the heavy ink that had poisoned him for so long.

The smell of cooked flesh rode the curls of black smoke. The pain was nothing; the pain was everything. The pain was focus, an old friend, a reminder not of who he was, but what he was missing.

Quinn felt like himself again. He felt like a soldier.

Now, all he needed was a war.

CHAPTER 32

A new millennium began, and the world did not end. The engine of that world, computers, didn't miss a beat. Beth watched it all unfold on the news and thought it silly that the all-powerful computer could be tripped up by something as trivial as a new date, like an old lady who puts the wrong year on her checks for two months before she finally gets it right. It all made Harlow feel like even more of a forgotten world.

The cold Midwestern winter turned into a cold Midwestern spring. Yards turned swampy with a slow thaw and ensuing rains. The sky was gray forever, and all the trucks were baptized by mud. But spring didn't last long in Illinois. The sun returned with a vengeance, angry at all those who had celebrated its disappearance last October. Humidity rose from its wet grave and tried to strangle Harlow.

Beth thought the Mayor would act decisively and visit her within a few days, but days turned into weeks. Weeks turned into a month, then two months, and still the Mayor did not send for her. She spent her first few days at home moving her bedroom to the northeast corner of the house, her sister's old room, so that whoever

was on shift could see the driveway, the front door, and her bedroom window from across the freshly planted cornfields. She went
to school, taking the same route every day. She kept a predictable
rhythm so that she was easy to watch.

Soon, the corn would heighten under the gaze of summer sun,
and watching her at home, from a distance, would turn far more
difficult. With each passing day, she relived that night in the hospital room. The Mayor's lack of interest in the months since made
her feel jilted, and the feeling disgusted her, as if some deep and
biological part of her yearned for his affection.

In early June on a Saturday night, she sat on the couch, reading
one of her father's books. She never left the house, never made herself difficult to track, and she often fell back on reading. Her father's
bookshelf was a curious assortment of philosophy and mythology
and war texts she never bothered to browse. The King James Bible
was sandwiched by the *Tao Te Ching* and *Mythology: Timeless Tales of
Gods and Heroes*. One shelf was all Greek names that meant nothing
to her until she began reading the texts: Epicurus, Seneca, Marcus
Aurelius and his *Meditations*.

At first she thought Aurelius's meandering sound bites were
impenetrable and nonsensical, but she backtracked to read the
introduction. He never meant anyone to read the words within.
He was talking to no one but himself, a powerful emperor working
each day on humility and making the right choices. He was writing
a journal that no one was ever meant to find.

As she browsed its pages, gravel crunched in the driveway. Her
father had just left to pick up groceries, and had promised to bring
back pizza. She thought he might have doubled back because he
forgot something, maybe his wallet.

She closed the book and peeked out the window. Black, immaculate paint sparkled in the June sun. A massive Tahoe idled in the
driveway, its windows tinted.

When she heard the knock at the door, she flinched so hard, she
dropped the book.

That knock meant the time had finally arrived. She took a deep breath, slotted *Meditations* back into the shelf, and answered the door.

Ortega stood outside, gripping the skinny arm of someone next to him. The other man had a bag over his head, his hands bound behind him.

"The Mayor sends for you," Ortega said. He threw the bagged captive into her living room. Beth had no choice but to step out of the way. Ortega entered, holding a pistol by the barrel, holding the handle out to her.

"Take it," he said. She obeyed. No harm in being armed, even if she knew bullets were useless against the disciple.

"Now is your chance to earn your place at the Mayor's side," he said. "Kill this prisoner, and I'll take you to the Mayor, and your life will never be the same. A life of comfort and freedom, one you can only deserve once you prove your loyalty."

Ortega removed the bag.

You will have to earn me, the Mayor had said. He knew all along— he knew she meant to trap him, he knew how to tease her, and he knew she couldn't pull the trigger.

Trent looked up at her, his face dirty, his eyes set deeply in his malnourished face. She could almost feel how the light made his pale skin ache—the boy hadn't seen the sun in a long time. His throat—the same throat she saw laid open at Harvest so many months ago as he bled to death on the gym floor—was smooth and undamaged. No scar tissue. No signs of violence.

"I don't know how," Trent croaked, sensing her confusion. "I wasn't all the way gone, I don't think, and he brought me back from it. Like waking up from a nightmare and finding a worse nightmare."

She pointed the gun at Ortega. It was all she could think to do. He laughed.

"I told the Mayor that of all his silly games, this was the silliest yet." Ortega stepped closer to her. "If you don't kill this boy, I don't know what the Mayor will do, and I find delight in surprise. Don't you?"

"Beth," Trent said, his tone as comforting as it was when they would split cold-cut sandwiches at lunchtime. "You have my permission. I did die that day. Give me warm sleep over the hell I've experienced since, and I'll love you even more."

He tilted his head down, ready to receive the bullet.

The Mayor did not expect her to shoot him, but here she was, holding the gun. The obstacle had arrived, if only she were brave enough to pull the trigger.

She turned the gun on Trent. The bullet would enter the top of his head, travel through brain tissue, and slam into the tip of his spine. He would feel nothing but the release of pain and fear that had built up for so long.

"Could it be?" Ortega said. "The first Jarvis with a spine?"

Ortega's taunts only served to steady her grip. Her finger was tight against the trigger—a few more pounds of pressure, and she could take the fight to the Mayor.

What would she lose? She had grieved him. She hadn't moved on from Trent, but what girl ever truly moved on from her first love? If she wanted a serene life imprisoned in Harlow with Trent as her doting husband, she could have had it. She didn't want it.

He didn't want it, either. All this started because they couldn't tolerate the illusion of happiness.

"Happiness isn't something you go out and find," Trent said, sensing her hesitancy, knowing he could not look up and make eye contact. "Happiness is something you take with you...and I'll be with you, always."

She was on the cusp of crying, and that wouldn't do. Tears would hinder her vision, her hands would shake, her emotions would take control. She had to beat the sorrow, get ahead of it, take control of it. She willed it into hiding.

As Ortega laughed, she stared into the brown hair that she'd once ran her fingers through. Stared at the boy she'd once kissed, a boy she could have loved truly and rightly in any other world.

And then she pulled the trigger.

The click jolted her. She dropped the gun, thinking it had fired, the sound of the butt thudding into the carpet drowned out by Ortega's hearty laughter.

"You continue to surprise me," he said. "I thought the Mayor had it wrong for once. Another lesson learned."

He picked up the weapon. Beth knelt down and took Trent into her arms. The embrace did nothing to quell his trembling, and he cried, quite literally, on her shoulder.

"The boy is a weakling," he said. "The Mayor wished to deny him the mercy of a quick death. Now, he lives knowing the girl he loved would see him dead, if only to glimpse the Mayor himself."

She kissed Trent on the temple with a maternal softness. He was a boy she'd loved, but he was still a boy, and she was a woman now. Harlow had choked away the softness of adolescence.

She rose to meet Ortega's eyes.

"Your brother was weak," she said. "Or at least, his neck was."

Ortega maintained his control, but she caught a flicker of rage. Only a spark, but it was there—she couldn't goad him into hurting her and incurring the Mayor's wrath, but she could piss him off, and that was just fine by her.

"Weakness?" he said. "He could have shredded your precious janitor. True strength lies in sacrifice, and the Griffin had to be forged. Ronato was the anvil, and you were the hammer. You see that now, don't you?"

She stepped forward, putting her hips and body into the most vicious punch she could muster. She couldn't reach his jaw and settled for his chest. Her knuckles might as well have landed on granite. Her pinky bone split upon impact, a boxer's break. She clutched her injured hand, hiding the pain with held breath.

Ortega grabbed her wrist. The broken bone pressed against

the flesh on the top of her hand, creating a lump that had already turned a shade of bluish green.

"Be at Red Rock Ridge at nine o'clock tomorrow morning," he said. "The Mayor will proctor your final test, and I bet you pass with flying colors. Your whore of a mother once did."

Ortega mashed his thumb into her broken bone. She screamed and heard a *pop* as he set it into place. The pain clouded her vision, turning her dizzy. She backpedaled, collapsing on the couch, waiting for the sting to subside.

When she looked up, Ortega was gone. Trent had gone to the kitchen and filled a rag with ice. He pressed it on the back of her hand.

"I'm sorry," Trent said.

"For what?"

"I don't know," he said. "Sometimes it feels like you should be sorry for something and you don't know what."

He looked at her, and something vital was missing from his eyes. She sensed his love, but it was buried in darkness, struggling to surface.

"I missed you," he said, shaping the words in such a way that she knew he didn't expect her to respond in kind. She had already missed him, and moved on.

The world always did.

CHAPTER 33

T he Harlow rebels were meeting for the final time. They all sensed it—the sunken postures, the long silences, the distant eyes. The end was coming for them, or the Mayor, and at Red Rock Ridge, of all the places.

And every one of them thought it was a trap. Beth wasn't so sure. The Mayor was bored, and leaving himself vulnerable to attack was the type of game she wouldn't put past him. It was the best way to provoke a fight, perhaps with enough danger to entertain him in the process.

Cooper wasn't present at the beginning of the meeting. Marcus didn't explain it, saying only, "He'll be along shortly."

The second order of business was the newcomer, Trent. Chris ran to his son, tearfully embracing him, but after the reunion, Chris sat in his usual spot, straddling a picnic table bench near the Henderson clan. Trent sat next to Beth and looked at his father with vacant eyes, retreating into himself as everyone questioned his presence. They had all seen his throat laid open, and to be back now? By the Mayor's hand, no less? Was he a disciple? A High Servant? An informant?

"The boy's reappearance is meant to scare us," Marcus said. "Will you give him permission to scare us? The choice is yours."

Silence.

"Our reaction is to think it's a trap, to hide, to stop what we're doing and go back to normal," Marcus said. "How can we turn this to our advantage?" Listening. Nodding. Echoing their speech to keep them talking.

Marcus was a listener. He reaffirmed the words that required affirmation and ignored the ones that didn't. His speech carried weight because he chose to use it far less than men filled with fear. Scared men talked a lot. He let them.

For the first time, she realized that the group did have a leader, and it wasn't Cooper or a mythical Griffin—it was her father.

The conversation turned to the dig sites. Three of the four had recently been shut down, the workers either reassigned or absorbed into the ranks of the High Servants. The final site, Dig Site Four, closest to Red Rock, was shut down two days earlier.

No more digging in Harlow.

"Maybe the Mayor was looking for something," Beth said. "Maybe he found it."

"He's not looking for anything," Trent said. "He wants to watch us dig some big, useless fucking holes. Torment. That's it. That's what he digs for."

"Arbeit Macht Frei," Marcus said. No one else knew what it meant, but Beth did: *Work will set you free*. The words were posted above the Soviet gulags, muddy prisons she'd learned about while browsing his books.

"Something's in them tunnels," Thatcher said. He gestured to his son, Cody. Thatcher was a farmer, but his boy was assigned to Dig Site Three.

"We lost two men on Dig Site Three," Cody said. "Butch Imming and Kenny Billings went down for their shift a couple weeks ago, and by the end of the day, no one had seen or heard from them. The site got shut down the next day."

"I've heard about the accidents at the dig sites," Marcus said. "Chatter at the diner."

"Accidents tend to kill you," Cody said. "Not make you go missing."

"That ain't the Mayor's doing," Cooper said. He was leaning against a combine tire, arms crossed, listening. "Rumors of growling in the tunnels, claw marks on the walls."

Beth had heard nothing of the rumor, but she saw it in their faces—all of them had heard something.

"Can't be no Griffin," Thatcher said. "Head of an Eagle, shouldn't it sound like a fuckin' bird?"

"And so the Griffin shall come," Marcus said. "And see in and through the darkness, and clear its throat, and breathe fire in Harlow's name."

The line was familiar. Marcus had said it before when she was younger, but she was too young to remember the context. Her sister was alive. She remembered the light through the kitchen window, and him sitting at the table, holding his coffee mug. Who was he talking to?

Kate, she thought. *He repeated it to her all the time. To make her remember.*

"Ain't no goddam Griffins in this room," Cooper said. "But we do got a traitor. That we do."

He stepped into the center of the room and held up his index finger. A piece of Scotch tape was dangling from the tip.

"Simple anti-tampering measure," he said. "Tape busted, some-one's been in the honeypot. In this case, the back of the Ford. I didn't want to jump to conclusions, but now that the Mayor has been kind enough to make an appointment at Red Rock to show us his throat, all ripe for the cutting, I'm almost certain that truck won't pop. Someone's mucked up the mix. We can't be sure how much of it is fertilizer, and how much is kitty litter."

Now it made sense. The Mayor knows the truck is sterile, makes himself vulnerable, the traitors reveal themselves. Massacre ensues.

"That settles that, then," Thatcher said. "Let's go home."

"Wait," Beth said. "We can't. Not when we have him where we want him."

"It's the other way around, young lady," Thatcher said.

"He thinks that truck is useless," she said. "He's laid out a script for us to follow, but for once, we're the ones who are a step ahead. All we have to do is make sure that truck has enough punch to kill him."

"In less than twelve hours?" Thatcher responded. "Took us months to sneak that much fertilizer into the load, and if Coop's right and one of us here is a traitor to the cause, we ain't surprising shit."

"It's him," Trent said, nodding in his father's direction. "It's my Dad."

Chris didn't deny it. He stared at the floor, the color gone from his face. Trent went to him. By the time he crossed the room, Chris was sobbing.

"I'm sorry," he said. "I couldn't lose you twice."

Trent embraced him.

"No one blames you," Marcus said. "A child in this town is the thickest of chains. But we need to know everything. We need to know what the Mayor knows."

They waited for him to gather himself, and he told them—the Mayor knew an attack was brewing, and that a truck bomb had something to do with it, but nothing else. So, he showed Chris his miraculously living son, and made a deal.

"The fertilizer is useless," Chris said. "Been spiking the load with lime."

"The fuckin' fruit?" Randy said.

"If only," Cooper said. "Lime weakens the nitrogen. Mix in enough, and it's neutralized completely. The truck's useless."

"Not entirely," Marcus said. "If he's expecting a fight, then we give him one. We can send word that we're occupying his attention. The youngest among us can run with their families, and alert the town on the way out. It would take him years to round up everyone if he bothers to do it at all."

"I was already planning on killing my old ass over this, so I'm with you," Cooper said.

They took a vote. Everyone raised their hands in favor. Everyone but Beth.

Marcus wasn't angry. His eyes were full of curiosity, not disregard. "The lady dissents?"

"She dissents," Beth said. "No one will run away, as they should. They're too scared. You guys will all die for nothing. What then?"

"Then provide us with a better plan," Marcus said.

"Same plan," she said. "Same truck. Only we make it explode."

Marcus laughed. "And how do you propose we do that?"

"The dig sites," she said. "Explosions to get through granite rock shelving and dig deeper and further. They aren't using cotton candy to do it."

"Oh my God," Marcus said. "The nitroglycerine."

"The word around town is that the dig sites are closed, so we sneak out the nitro, load up the truck. Turn the Mayor to dust."

"I'll be damned," Cody said. "That'll work. I seen the shift books, and they got a couple day shifts watching the fence, and typically only one guy at night."

"If the dig sites are compromised and people are going missing, maybe it's more than security," Marcus said. "Maybe it's being watched by a disciple, or the Mayor himself."

"We can still do it," she said. "Ortega and Serilda are the only two disciples left. If the Mayor crawls out of the shadows to patrol a dig site—fat chance—that's only three. And there are four dig sites. We send a crew to each one. Even in a worst-case scenario, at least one crew should have an easy run."

"If the shit hits the fan at any one of them, we're fucked," Marcus said. "The Mayor will notice the nitro is gone and he can put two and two together. Hell, we don't know if that blast will even kill him. Maybe nothing will kill him. This is almost all risk for a sliver of reward."

"That's life in Harlow," she said. "He's too cocky to back out and not show up. Even if he thinks the truck will pop, he'll think he can survive it. I know it. All we have to do is come away with the nitro. Cody, do they ever run security at night?"

"Last fall, a few nights. Not sure why. Flashlights and pacing around the trailer and equipment. I heard they take turns covering for each other so they can sleep during the overnight shift."

"They upped security when the janitor was in town. That's my wager," Cooper said. "But Beth's got herself a hell of an idea—so it appears we need four crews."

"Hell, I know everyone at Site Three," Cody said. "I'll run that crew."

"And I'm going with my boy," Thatcher said.

"Site One for me," Cooper said. "Close to my property. Not uncommon to see me cajoling about in those woods."

"Anyone have experience at sites two or four?" Marcus asked.

"Four," Drew Murray said. "Worked it for the past year. Although I'm scared shitless and don't want to run a crew."

Everyone looked to Cooper. If his grandson went to Site Four, the last of his living kin would be separated from him, but the old man nodded once. Drew knew the site, so it had to be done.

"I'll take you," Marcus said. Then, to Cooper: "I'll watch out for him."

"Thank you," Cooper said. He clapped his grandson on the shoulder. "You listen to every goddam word Marcus says, you hear?"

Drew nodded.

"That leaves Site Two," Marcus said.

No one spoke.

"I'll do it," Beth said.

"You're not going," Marcus said.

"I knew you'd say that," she said. "Typical man."

"Typical father."

"You can't keep me out of this. Not now."

"Please—you've done enough," he said. "Stay behind. If no one comes back from this, you can still run."

"Running doesn't work," Trent said. Then, to Beth: "I worked Site Two."

"I know," Beth said. "That's why I can't do it without you."

Marcus grabbed Beth's arm. His unshakeable facade cracked, along with his voice, as he whispered to her. "Please don't. I've given up too much already."

"I'm not yours to give up," she said.

"Your mother and sister—"

"Are gone," she said. "Gone is gone, right, Dad? But they're not gone to me. I won't fail them." She touched his arm. "And neither will you."

Taller than her, older, weathered by the loss of his wife and eldest child, unflappable, immovable, yet when she touched him, tears shimmered in his eyes.

He nodded once and gathered himself. He had men to lead.

So did she.

CHAPTER 34

D ig Site Two was hidden in the woods near the Kinoka
blacktop, familiar territory for Beth thanks to her scouting shifts with Galen.

Not Galen, she thought, always correcting herself. Galen was a
part the Mayor played. The man didn't exist.

She stuck to the shadows, on the edge of the brush. Familiar
razor wire was gnarled along Harlow's border. Trent followed
close behind her.

Chris Keller waited on a utility road a half-mile away. He had
Trent's Jeep idling, and one of Thatcher's trailers was untethered
just behind the Jeep. If they found the nitroglycerin, he'd hook up
the trailer and bring it into the compound for a load. If not, he
didn't have to shed the trailer to assist with an escape.

Chris's inclusion was something Trent insisted on, and the men
reluctantly agreed. Trying to hit four dig sites at the same time
stretched their numbers. They needed all the help they could get,
whether he was an Honest Abe, or a reformed traitor.

Beth's plan was to walk the perimeter, outside of the fence,
looking for signs of a night patrol before entering the compound.
Trent refused to leave her side. She didn't want to walk the dark of

Harlow's edges alone, so she accepted the company. A chain-link fence surrounded the site, topped off with more coils of razor wire. The gate was locked shut.

She checked her watch—just past 1:00 a.m.

They circled the dig site's fence, listening the entire way, hearing nothing. Trent's key still worked in the gate's padlock.

"Four trailers," Trent whispered. "Last I was here, the supply trailer was northwest. I'll check that one."

"I'll take southwest," she said.

"I think that's the break room trailer," Trent said.

"Good," she said. "Maybe I can steal someone's lunchbox."

They slipped through the gate.

The dig site was mounds of dirt and rock, the heavy equipment almost glowing in the dark, its yellow paint catching the overhead moonlight. The beasts were quiet and still, yet they pulsed with menace, like dinosaur models in a museum. She saw no sign of flashlights and heard no footsteps.

She saw the trailer on the corner of the lot, and went for it. The loudness of her footfalls shocked her, so she sacrificed speed for stealth, quieting her movements until she arrived safely at the trailer door.

Once inside, she clicked on her flashlight, keeping her palm over the front, hoping to use only as much light as she needed.

Space heaters were located underneath picnic tables. Some left-behind flannel coats were on the hooks that lined the wall. A bank of lockers rested against cheap wood paneling.

She moved to the back. The refrigerator kicked on, startling her. A desk was tucked against the back of the trailer, and a calendar hung nearby. A winter coat was hanging on the back of the chair, possibly stripped because the evening was rather mild, a welcome departure from the cold snap that had kept its claws dug into the spring thaw.

She checked the calendar. Patrol shifts were written into the oversized boxes. *Truby, 0800-2000. Carter, 2000-0800.* Eric Carter was on shift, a name she knew. A newlywed, new baby, but where was he?

She opened the fridge. A lunchbox was inside. She checked it and found a can of Coke and a sandwich tucked into a Ziploc bag.

Eric was definitely on shift, patrolling the dig site, and doing a piss-poor job of it.

She exited the break room trailer and cut across the middle of the dig site, and for the first time, she saw the fruits of its design—a massive hole cut into the center of the site. According to Trent, they'd tapped into the heart of one of the mine structures down there, and had it cleared out to where you could take a walk in some of Harlow's old mines if you had the balls.

The Mayor insisted that some men have the balls. They called them canaries—men who were tasked to walk through the mines and do curious tasks like take photographs of rocks, bring back samples, slowly log the twists and turns of the old, underground structures.

Workers usually lowered themselves into the tunnels via a construction elevator, but she noticed the platform was gone. Someone had gone down and had yet to come up.

Orange fencing was staked in place to keep people away from the perilous edge. She walked up to it and peered down. Darkness. She closed her eyes and listened. Nothing. But if someone was down there, she needed to find the nitroglycerin before they came up.

Beth saw the last trailer tucked into a dark corner of the site, offset from the equipment and graveled areas. She headed for the door, remaining in the thickest shadows, keeping her footfalls gentle and silent.

She heard footsteps, and hoped it was Trent. A flashlight clicked on.

Eric swung the beam across her spot near the heavy equipment. She ducked, a reflex—and a bad one at that. Movement was easier to spot. She should have remained still, closing her eyes to reduce the chances of them reflecting in the dark.

She ducked behind the hauler's tire, which was taller than her. Eric's flashlight beam lingered.

"Max, that you?" Eric said. "You forget your coat again? Or you just trying to give me a heart attack?" He laughed. "I swear, if you're wearing a Griffin costume, I'm gonna shoot."

He's armed, she thought. So was she—the one thing the rebels weren't short on was guns. She had a .38 revolver stuffed into the waistband of her jeans. He got closer to the hauler. She circled as he came around the corner. If she looped around quietly enough, she could get behind him, draw, and fire before he even realized his head was disintegrating under the assault of a close-range bullet.

She reached behind her jeans to draw the pistol—but it was gone.

"What the fuck?" Eric said. The beam angled down as he bent over to pick up her dropped pistol.

She fought the urge to run. She couldn't bridge the empty space between the hauler and the trailer without getting his attention, and she couldn't outrun the flashlight.

She squatted down, making herself small enough to duck underneath the hauler's belly.

He circled the hauler once more as Beth held her breath. Satisfied, Eric began to walk away. As he did, he keyed his radio.

"I found a gun by the hauler. Thirty-eight. Anybody drop one?"

She listened. Four negatives came back. *Five people*, she thought. *This isn't a patrol. This is defense.*

"Can you guys come up, then? We may have a situation."

"Ten-four," a crackly voice said.

Come up, she thought. *They took the platform. They're in the tunnels. And they're coming.*

If five men were patrolling site two, the other sites had to be similarly defended. They'd get no nitro tonight, not without a bloodbath that would decimate their forces and ruin their ability to surprise the Mayor.

The right play was to try and escape without incident, to regroup and counterpunch. That's what her father would undoubtedly do, and Cooper didn't become the Great Survivor by making unnecessary waves.

The platform motor cranked up. She had to leave and hope that Trent would be wise enough to bail out and wait for her in the woods near the gate. She started creeping away from the hauler as Eric headed for the break room trailer.

Suddenly the overhead pole lights burst on, illuminating the entire compound. The work lights surrounding the massive hole sizzled and popped. She was exposed and visible, and had no choice but to run.

"Hey!" Eric screamed.

Beth didn't look back, bolting into the shadows as Eric gave chase. The gate was fifty yards away. Just beyond, the woods. She could lose him there.

Lose him? They'll have five men searching in less than ten minutes, and with a few radio calls, they'll have a hundred High Servants.

Then she heard Trent's voice, booming and assertive. "Hey! What the fuck are you doing?"

Beth stopped. Trent had stepped out of the shadows to intercept Eric.

She couldn't let Trent sacrifice himself for the second time, but as she listened, it was clear that he didn't intend to sacrifice himself, or fight, or escalate the situation. He had another plan in mind. She saw Eric in the dusky light of the work lamps, pointing the gun at Trent, visibly shaken. He had seen Trent's throat cut like everyone else, and was quite literally seeing a ghost.

"I asked you a question," Trent said.

"Someone's here," Eric said.

"You're goddam right, someone's here," Trent said. "A disciple is here. Me. The Mayor's mercy brought me up from the darkness, and his grace empowers me. I know what's happening in these dig sites. Do you?"

Eric didn't bother to question his authority. Why would he? Trent was dead, and the only one who could heal him was the

Mayor. In Eric's eyes, why would the Mayor do that if not to make him into a disciple?

"No sir," Eric said. "They say the Griffin's been taking men in the tunnels, but we ain't seen jack shit for a couple weeks."

"The Griffin is just a story," Trent said. Eric nodded.

The platform reached the end of its destination, and four men stepped off. Trent's story wasn't going to hold up forever.

Beth needed to act.

Cut the lights, she thought. *Trent will run. By the time they get the lights on, he's gone. Disappeared. Truly Mayor-like. Very disciple-ish.*

She moved along the fence, remembering where the amperage box was posted. *You know it'll be padlocked.*

She fought the urge to scream "Shut up!" at herself and kept moving.

"Absolutely, sir. Just a story," Eric said.

"And we get to write the ending to that glorious fiction!" A female voice, shouting in the distance.

Trent squinted, seeming to physically shrink in the glare of the lights. A woman led three men off the platform. Beth knew her only casually, the way that everyone seems to know everyone else in towns like Harlow. Everyone called her Sarah, but the rebels knew she was a disciple named Serilda.

No one had seen her around town in months, and the reason was clear—Serilda was now disfigured. The right side of her face appeared freshly burned, black curls of blistered skin set in pink tissue that shone with moisture. Her hair was gone, her right temple burned to the bone. The left side of her face was mostly intact, her blue eyes bright and alive, the unburnt part of her mouth curling into a half smile.

"This one says he's a disciple, ma'am," Eric said.

One of the bearded grunts spat in the dirt. "I saw that little fucker's throat cut same as ya'll," he said. "Between me, you, and the lamppost, that's the Mayor's work if I ever seen it."

Serilda circled Trent, sizing him up.

"So you're the one?" she said. "Can't be. The Mayor just cut you loose. What are you doing here?"

"I used to work here," Trent said. "Came to see how deep she got. Pride of ownership, and all."

She grabbed his arm. Her fingers ratcheted in, and Trent groaned.

"You're the Mayor's toy," she said. "But I'm still allowed to break you."

"You're the toy," Trent grunted. "All of you are his toys."

She swung Trent by the arm, flicking him effortlessly into the door of the trailer, twenty yards away. The hinges blew out of the rickety door as Trent smashed through it.

"Enough!" Beth screamed, walking into the glare of the lights. "I brought him here."

"You," Serilda said. "No. It can't be you. Small. Weak. Pitiful."

She signaled to the High Servants. They dragged Trent out of the rubble of the trailer door, just as Beth finally located the nitro—a roll-off storage pod stamped with black lettering was set alongside the trailer. She couldn't make out the words from that distance, but saw a picture of fire, and took it to mean "no open flame." She had located the treasure at the pinnacle of her failure.

"If it's you, then where's Max?" Serilda asked. "And Butch Imming? And Ken Billings?" So, workers going missing in the tunnels wasn't a rumor, and they didn't know how or why someone was lurking underground, picking people off.

They threw Trent down at Serilda's feet. Blood gushed from a cut in his cheek, and he held his arm tight to his ribcage, his shoulder injured. She kicked him, her foot thudding against his breastbone. He spun in the air and crashed down, gasping.

Beth attacked, knowing it was futile, running at her, screaming. Serilda sidestepped her with infuriating grace and slammed the meat of her palm into Beth's back, spiking her into the ground face-first.

Beth's fractured hand sent a harrowing pain up her arm. She fought through it and got to all fours, blood dripping from her chin.

"Little girl, all alone," Serilda said. She pressed the heel of her boot to the back of Beth's neck, pressing her face into the gravel. "What happened to our men?"

Serilda released the pressure of her boot. Beth rolled onto her back, catching her breath, the blood thick at the back of her throat.

"Me," she said. "I killed them in the tunnels. I'm the Griffin."

Serilda pulled Beth's hair, snapping her head back. Beth smelled the blackened flesh. The burns wept clear fluid.

"The Mayor is eager for the Griffin's return," Serilda said. "He has invited him. He welcomes the fight."

"Then take me to him," Beth said.

The men laughed. Serilda quieted them with a stern glare. They followed her eyes to Trent.

"Shoot the boy in the guts," she commanded them. "Let's see if our little Griffin wannabe is the Mayor's equal. Let's see if she can save him."

The bearded High Servant kicked Trent over. Beth caught Trent's eyes, and he winked at her. He was once as scared as her, a frightened boy running away from a world he didn't understand. Now, he was about to die, winking at her, and here she was, smiling at him. With the fear gone, Harlow could only kill them, and nothing more.

The High Servant stood over Trent and drew his pistol. Trent kicked him in the lower leg. The bearded man yelped and collapsed as the other men circled him, drawing their pistols. Beth finally recognized the bearded man's face—Pernell Baumgartner, who looked like he'd aged a decade since she saw him slicing the cop into steaks at the school gymnasium.

"Don't all shoot at once," Trent said. "You might kill me on accident."

"I got this," Brad said, hobbling to his feet. "Little prick," he added, limping over, gun in hand. The other men stepped back, allowing him to extract revenge for his injured leg.

Before he could raise his weapon, the lights died. The compound went dark. The overhead bulbs retained residual heat, creating orange embers that looked like stars that had fallen too close.

A deep, metallic *chunk* sound echoed, metal on metal, followed by the sound of a man collapsing onto the gravel.

Chunk.

Chunk.

Between the claps of metallic thunder, bodies crashed to the ground.

Panic. Confusion. The High Servants scattering. *Chunk.* Another body down. She heard the gravel crunch as he skidded across the rocks at full speed before coming to rest.

Doesn't sound like gunshots, she thought. *Of course it doesn't. You grew up on hunting rifles and common pistols. This is suppressed gunfire, picking them off in the dark, brutal tactics from wars you've never known.*

Brad ran—she knew it was him from the way his gait limp-scraped against the gravel. She imagined him panicked and unable to see in the dark. He smacked into the hauler's tire and fell down. *Chunk.* She heard a disgusting, gurgling sound. He wasn't getting up after that one.

Darkness. Stillness. She heard Trent's labored breaths as he tried to find her. She reached out and took his hand.

Brad choked on his own blood, dying in the night with one final, wet cough. Serilda's boots slammed against rocks as she sprinted away.

"Let's go," Beth whispered. They wheeled around, heading for the gate. She clicked on her flashlight, knowing it would give away her position, but she needed to orient herself and make sure they were headed in the right direction.

The beam struck the monster from the caves, green eyes alive in the dark. She fought the urge to scream as the hulking shadow came for them, lifting the green eyes from his face. A mask?

No. Night vision goggles, she thought.

"Turn that fucking light off," he said.

The janitor. Curtis Quinn.

Black grease camouflaged his face, and he carried the biggest rifle she'd ever seen, its nose fattened by a suppressor the size of her forearm.

"Take cover in the woods," he said. "I'll be along shortly."

"Serilda ran off," Beth said. "Afraid of the Griffin—afraid of you. Come with us. We need you."

"She's not running," he grunted. "She's trying to turn on the lights."

"You can't fight her," Beth said.

"I'm not going to fight her," he said. "I'm going to kill her."

A loud series of clicks echoed in the woods—breakers flipping back on. The overhead lights came to life, one after the other, illuminating the whole dig site again.

The High Servants were dead, and Beth didn't know if they'd been hit by bullets or small missiles—Brad Reynolds had a hole in his chest big enough to fit a soda can.

"You came back," Serilda said, strolling into the light. No fear or anger in her voice, but relief. Beth half expected her to try and hug him.

"Each day, I serve my penance," she said, touching her destroyed face. "Each day, I refresh these wounds, as the Mayor commanded. A reminder of the janitor, the same scars he bears. A reminder of how a cripple slipped away from me."

"You know what she is, right?" Beth asked him.

"Yes," he said. "But she doesn't know what I am, and I suggest you take cover before I teach her."

Quinn knelt down and placed his gun on the ground—a Barrett .50 caliber rifle. The Barrett was an old friend he hadn't visited in a long time, but in preparing for his mission, he had spent weeks getting reacquainted with his favorite rifles, the highest-caliber sidearms, and explosive ordinance. He had rehabilitated with a cocktail of highly illegal performance-enhancing drugs to fuel his dogged work ethic, and used illegally obtained prescription drugs—Adderall, mostly—to stay awake, focused, alert. His prosthetic was a Revo, expensive, specialized—the same prosthetic used by Olympic athletes for its dexterity and high-grade durability. He had unlocked all the secrets in Christina Jarvis's cryogenic safe deposit box. He had researched and mapped out Harlow's entire history, including schematics of the mines that underscored the town.

The king was invulnerable, but the kingdom? As fragile as a house of cards.

"Don't put the gun down," Serilda said. She looked coiled, wearing dusty jeans, boots, and a flannel shirt with the sleeves rolled up, her ponytail twisting as she paced.

"I'm not putting it down," he said, unscrewing the suppressor. "I'm just not concerned about staying quiet anymore."

"And why is that?"

"You'll see," he said, standing up, reasserting the rifle in his grip. "Or maybe you won't."

She held out her hands, welcoming his attack. "Please, by all means," she said. "Remind yourself of your futility. Then I'll remove that fake leg of yours and drag you back where you belong—at the Mayor's boot."

Quinn shook his head, more amused than disgusted. "That's the thing." He took aim. "You're all talkers. You're playthings in his little game of make-believe. Just a scared girl playing pretend."

"Shoot me, then," she said. "You should know by now what happens if you squeeze the trigger."

"Oh, I'm not going to shoot *you*." He eased the rifle a few degrees to the right, aiming past her. She followed the sightline to his new target—the nitro.

She didn't know that it was Quinn who'd packed all the nitro into a single storage container. She didn't know that he'd sensitized it into a hazardous state using space heaters from the break room trailer to reach an unstable temperature where concussive force could detonate it.

And after he pulled the trigger, Serilda didn't know anything at all.

The explosion connected with Beth's instincts before her mind. She dove to the ground as a concussive wave skimmed her, the air pleasingly warm. A curl of bright orange twisted into the air, then bent back into itself. Smoke reached for the stars.

"You okay?" Trent was lying next to her. He reached out with his healthy arm and touched her shoulder. She nodded.

Headlights turned onto the dirt road. Beth and Trent ducked into the woods. The Jeep crept up to the edge of the open gate. The fire roared in the dig site. The hauler exploded, and the air turned pungent with the stench of melting rubber.

Chris was behind the wheel of the Jeep, his face covered in blood. "Hop in," he said. "We have to—"

The thunder of a gunshot cut him off. Trent screamed as his father's head disintegrated. He ran to the Jeep and opened the door; his father's limp body fell into his arms, the blood from his decimated skull soaking Trent's chest.

Quinn was on the other side of the Ford, clutching a handgun she doubted she could even lift, a chrome monstrosity capable of making Quinn's hand appear small. No simple feat. He holstered it.

Trent wailed, holding his father's corpse.

"Why?" Beth asked.

He studied her in the light of the towering fire. "Chris Keller sold you out," he said. "He's loyal to the Mayor."

"We know," she said. "That's why we had a chance to surprise the Mayor tomorrow. Chris was scared and tried to make things right, and you killed him."

"You got the last part right," he said.

"If you came here to help us, you're not off to a good start."

"I didn't come here to help you," he said. "I came to end this."

"End the Mayor?"

"No. Harlow," he said, again measuring her with his eyes, focused, intentional. "I can't kill him, but I can kill everyone here. I can leave him nothing else to rule."

"That's depraved," Beth said.

"He's depraved, but no one else here is," he said. "That's why nothing ever changes."

Trent tumbled out of the Jeep, gathered himself, and then sprinted at Quinn. "You son of a bitch!" he screamed, a sound so guttural, so full of grief and terror that Beth saw Shaun Murray caught in the razor wire once again, a vision she hadn't experienced in a long time.

Quinn stood his ground and let the boy punch at his midsection. Trent was exhausted, injured, a bare wire of emotions, his adrenal glands cooked dry. Once punched out, Quinn took him by the collar, dragged him back to the Jeep, and pushed him in.

"Leave," he said. "Now. If you're smart, you'll leave Harlow before it's a hole in the ground."

Trent grabbed the steering wheel and steadied himself. "I won't leave her," he said.

"She's coming with me," Quinn said.

Trent looked at Beth, his eyes asking for her decision.

"Go," she said. "Do like he says and leave Harlow."

"Not without you," he said. "Never without you."

"Go, Trent," she said. "Go! Before I say something we both won't forget."

The Jeep's headlights flooded the woods as Trent executed a three-point turn and headed down the dirt road.

"Let's go," Quinn said.

Beth didn't budge. "You said Harlow would be a hole in the ground," she said. "What did you mean?"

"You rednecks wanted to blow up the Mayor," he said. "But you're thinking too small. Harlow is stripped bare underground. Mines everywhere, and the dig sites make it easy to access the whole system. I've spent weeks burying plastic explosives in tunnel junctions."

He reached inside his tactical vest and withdrew a detonator. "And I'm finished with the job. I hit this button, Harlow disappears."

"You can't be like this," she said. "People think you're the Griffin."

He rolled up the sleeve on his left arm and grabbed her wrist, directing the beam of light onto the remains of his tattoo. Nothing remained but a patch of white tissue blotched with curls of pink. More burn scars.

"The Griffin is the one toy he wants to play with before he leaves this place, the one thing your family got over on him."

"Then why haven't you blown the place up yet?"

He looked away, through the trees. "They'll be here soon," he said. "High Servants. Ortega. Maybe the Mayor himself. This is the most vulnerable spot, the dig site closest to the school. I want to bait them here. If the collapse of the town can't kill the Mayor, maybe it'll trap him underground forever—the best result we can hope for."

"Results?" she said. "Go, then. Blow it all up. Save your own crippled ass. My sister—"

"Kate didn't love me," he said. "She thought I was a monster. She loathed the fact she had to use me, and eventually thought me so atrocious she wouldn't even risk sending me here."

"I can see why," Beth said. "She was afraid you'd kill everyone. And you're doing it."

"Then leave," he said. "This town won't live to see another day, either by the Mayor's hand, or mine. I choose mine."

"Why?" she said. "If you wanted Harlow to suffer and die, you didn't need to come. All you had to do was wait."

"I can help you," he said. "Come with me. The one thing your sister wanted to do was save you, and here I am. We'll be out of here in ten minutes. Hit the button. Behind us, ashes. I'll drop you off somewhere and you can start a life. A real one."

"A haunted one," she said. "We can get others out. Maybe even my father. He's alive, I know it."

"Life is nothing more than choosing what to leave behind," Quinn said. "Nothing here is worth saving."

"You're wrong," she said. "Dad was right. He said you weren't a hero. He said you were a destroyer."

"I don't disagree, but this is a one-time offer. Come with me—or stay and die trying to save everyone. A futile task. Heroes are for stories, not towns like this."

"Stay," she said. "Help me. If things go wrong, you've got the button. I can't do this alone."

"You can try," he said. "If you're that stupid."

"I know it's hard. I know my sister failed you," she said. "I won't."

He shook his head and walked away from her. Beth followed.

"When people see the Griffin, they'll fight," she said.

"Like they rose up to help me at Harvest?" he said. "The only person in Harlow who believes in fairy tales is you."

She tried to grab him. He brushed her away, aggravating her broken hand. She hissed in pain.

"Broken?"

"Broken hand, broken nose. I broke my jaw. Cuts and scrapes and stitches. I'll have more scars than you when it's over."

"Kate was right," he said. "You're stubborn."

"She talked about me?"

"Wrote about you," he said. "She decided to leave you here. She thought trying to save you would end up killing you."

She thought of Kate, tussling her hair, calling her "nugget," letting her win games of Abalone.

"I know how angry you are," he said. "You think she left you."

Beth turned from him. She expected tears, but none came. Still, she felt a burning in her chest. Anger, or sorrow? She couldn't tell the difference anymore.

"We were going to have a kid," he said. "She wanted it to be a girl. She wanted to name her Beth."

The thought of her sister holding a newborn squeezed the breath right out of her. Kate was gone, but never left her. She never would. She put herself in that hospital bed and imagined a writhing newborn placed in her arms, and she would whisper, "Your name is Kate, little girl."

Earning that moment meant not just surviving, but keeping her soul in tact along the way, unlike the man in front of her.

They reached his vehicle, a salvaged SWAT van outfitted with off-road tires and a brush guard. The body was flat black with random streaks of dark green, a spray-painted camo job.

"I never chose this," he said. "I never wanted to be the Griffin, and you don't have to carry your family's bullshit any longer. By now, anyone who wanted to fight is dead, hurt, or found out. Be smart. Get in the truck."

She looked at him, clear-eyed, the wave of sorrow boiled away just as quickly as it had arrived. She shook her head.

Quinn looked down at his boots, measuring his next move. He shook his head and turned away to open the truck door.

He didn't get inside.

"You'd rather try to save everyone? To fight a battle you can't possibly win?"

She nodded, clear-eyed, with no hesitation.

"Here," he said, tossing her the detonator, an aluminum box with a silver switch. The sliders on each side locked the switch in place so it wouldn't accidentally trigger.

Then, he went to the passenger side of the truck, and returned with a thick folder of documents and what looked like a carry-along cooler.

"These belong to you," he said, giving her the paperwork. "Your mother's notes and medical records. Your sister's journal."

The folder was softened by time, creased by use. Touched by her mother's hands. Her sister's.

He opened the cooler. From inside, he withdrew a metal drawer with a thick, metallic carrying ring. The metal smoked, the icy metal frosting in the humidity.

"This belongs to you as well," he said. "Your legacy. Not mine."

He hopped into the truck and rolled down the window.

"Harlow's in your hands," he said. "If you of all people decide to flip that switch, then I believe it deserves to die."

He fired up the engine. The SWAT van's growl eclipsed the crackle of the massive fire that had spread from the smoldering dig site.

"Where will you go?" she asked.

"I don't know," he said. "Doesn't matter to you anymore."

"At least give me a ride to the end of the road. I can walk from there."

He nodded. She joined him in the truck, and he was struck by how small she looked. Her bony hands rested on the frosted metal drawer, one of them swelling from a boxer's break.

The journey was short and silent. He let the truck idle, waiting for her to get out.

Beth opened the door. He tossed her an empty duffel bag. "It's a long walk. Stash the gear so you can read on the way."

She held up the drawer, no bigger than a shoebox, so light it felt as if it were empty. "What is this?"

"A fairy tale," he said. "Skip to the end of the journal, and you'll see why I shouldn't have it."

"But Kate chose you," Beth said.

"She shouldn't have," he said. "She loved you too much to see."

"See what?" she asked.

"How long does the world have to whisper what you are before you'll listen?" he asked.

She dismounted the truck, never once thinking he would leave her behind. But he revved the truck and drove off, cutting through a field, heading for Kinoka Road.

He'll turn around, she thought. He has to—he was right, she couldn't do it alone. It was stupid to fight, and she couldn't save anyone. But the van bounced through a ditch and soon its taillights were red eyes slowly closing until they were gone.

Beth was alone in the dark. She had a long walk back to Cooper's house, and dreaded arriving there. Only then would she know the depth of their failure and the number of casualties from the other dig sites, if there were any survivors at all.

He was right about one thing—the walk provided her plenty of time. She clicked on her flashlight, dimming it with her fingers, and started to read.

CHAPTER 35

T he van powered through the light strip of brush that separated two cornfields near the dig site. The Kinoka blacktop was ahead, the place where his misplaced efforts to be a hero almost got him killed.

He felt relieved to put the journal in Beth's hands, a secret burden he'd carried for months. Not just a burden, but a temptation, and a dangerous one—a temptation he could only blot out by leaping off the wagon and drinking copious amounts of hard alcohol.

His hands were not the right hands. They never were. The right hands rarely had blood stains and powder burns.

He neared the blacktop. Vengeance and destruction drove him into the tunnels. They choked those men, buried those explosives. They shot Chris Keller in the temple.

Yet, something continued to lurk—Beth's clarity of purpose and disregard for her own survival infuriated him. Not because of the stupidity of it, but because of jealousy. He was innocent once. He'd believed he could save the world and everyone in it. He was thirteen and was going to be a lawyer one day.

He became a soldier instead, and never stopped fighting. For what? For who? Lost in the jungle, then the streets, and now, the dark.

He arrived at the blacktop. Turn right, and the rig he had outfitted to hold weapons, explosives, and lodging would churn right over any stop sticks and blow through any roadblocks without slowing down. Then, he'd just keep driving. Drive to Chicago and die trying to keep the fires of vengeance burning, or drive down to the beach. Take the boat ride he'd always meant to take.

Or do what he came to do. Watch as Beth learned what he'd learned, her struggle with how to make it work. Help her with that struggle. He had prepared for this. A good soldier is ready for any contingency. He had his Hail Mary bag. He had a plan.

Yet, the urge to run was thick in his veins—an urge Kate had sensed in him, a cowardly thing she hated about herself, and saw in him.

He didn't know which way the wheel would spin when he got to the road, but all he had to do was watch his hands and he would know for sure. He would know what he was, and if there was ever any moving on from it.

He got to the Kinoka blacktop and stopped. He closed his eyes, feeling the steering wheel, waiting for it to turn itself. It didn't.

He opened his eyes. The moonlight illuminated the contours of the road, and he had his headlights off to conceal his movement.

No one could stop him if he just turned right. Called off the whole insane and suicidal operation.

Then he saw a shadow in the road. Slender shoulders, long hair, a flowing dress. A woman walking. Not Beth.

He twisted on the headlights and saw Kate—her blue eyes, her smile, the dress she'd worn under the willow tree. Her wedding dress. She looked eight months pregnant.

He exited the truck, but by the time he looked back into the cone of light, she was gone.

The blown-up dig site wore an orange halo as it burned, a false sunrise. In the other direction, miles away, over the tree line, he saw a fat tail of smoke dissolving into the stars, and a woman in white walking in that direction. He blinked. She remained. Kate waited for him.

"No," he said. "Fuck no. That's not real."

Of course it wasn't. He was watching himself act like the violent scumbag he always was, but a rebel lurked. The rebel was the reason his right arm was sore and itchy. The rebel had stocked the truck with smoke grenades he never intended to use. The rebel had painted his one true love on the palate of his vision, a love who had rejected him—but he could never reject her in turn. He did love her, and a pure and true love didn't require reciprocation, only surrender.

"Fuck it, then," he said. "Fuck everything."

He turned off-road, hiding the truck in the tree line, its brush guard scraping against razor wire. He saw Kate in the woods, and knew he was cracking. The long nights in the tunnels, the cocktail of drugs for pain, for focus, to get twenty-two hours out of a day with no need or regard for sleep. The steroids and growth hormones to accelerate his recovery from physical therapy and ease the transition into his Revo prosthetic. He was cracking under the weight of it all, but nothing was heavier than trying to do the right thing.

He couldn't lift it by himself. Neither could Beth.

"I hear you, baby," he whispered. "I'm right behind you."

He left the truck and followed her.

THE GRIFFIN

CHAPTER 36

Quinn stepped into the brush and snipped through the razor wire with cutters he kept stashed in his tactical belt. Dead leaves clung to the branches of the oaks overhead, blotting out the moonlight.

No matter. He had walked in darkness for months now, and had worn his night-vision goggles so often that he saw the world in green, sometimes in broad daylight. He tipped down the goggles and allowed his internal compass to guide him through.

He emerged on a different farmer's soybean tract and saw a fire in the distance, washing out his night vision. He stowed the goggles and crossed the field. Another country road, another field. Roads and fields, fields and roads, territory no one would ever want to fight for, all of it on the precipice, one button-press away, dust collapsing into dust.

The fire was not a dig site. He knew all the dig sites, and in his infiltration of Harlow's past, he had uncovered evidence of other dig sites, now filled and closed.

The Mayor made them dig, but when he wanted to truly break them, he made them fill it all up again, erasing their sense of progress, accomplishment, and value. A psychotic and maligned bumpkin from a few decades ago had erased his insufficient self and replaced him with an amalgam of cruel acts and villainous flourishes. He spoke like evil men in movies and comics and tortured according to what he had found interesting from Nazi Germany, Communist Russia...and the Old Testament. Quinn now sensed the dog-eared pages in the man's actions, and hated him. He wasn't a true foil, he deserved no respect, he was nothing but a void—one amplified by powers that made him impossible to kill. Quinn could never dig up the feeble man he used to be and break him, and the thought infuriated him.

He neared the fire. A truck. He got closer. Marcus's truck, the cabin blackened, the flames dying, nothing left to chew on. The metal was distended, twisted, the wheels blasted off. The truck had exploded.

He looked inside and saw the remains of two bodies. Or at least, the pieces of at least two bodies. Around the truck, a half-dozen men were gunned down. Quinn recognized many faces, but didn't remember their names. None of them were Marcus.

He inspected the scene and pieced it together—a truck fleeing. High Servants open fire, the driver is killed. The truck stops. Wounded men try to escape on foot. They are shot in the field. The servants come to investigate, to finish them off. More gunfire.

The real surprise—Marcus had a Hail Mary of his own. Quinn saw pieces of shrapnel and the twisted metal of a pressure cooker. Marcus had fashioned an IED in case they got cornered.

Someone whistled behind him. Quinn spun around, drawing his Desert Eagle. Not the most nimble sidearm, but he wanted a blend of handling, stopping power, and visual intimidation.

He saw no one. Another whistle escaped the shadows. He backed away, seeking cover near the truck. Then he tipped down his night-vision googles and saw the source.

Marcus.

Quinn found him sitting against an oak tree, clutching an

abdominal wound. His hands were black, his skin pale. He was sweating, his head steaming in the cold, pre-dawn air. A rifle laid beside him, a thirty-aught-six, a weapon for hunting, not war, and Quinn figured that was how he'd remotely detonated the pressure cooker without getting shredded himself.

"You came back," Marcus said. A weak smile softened his pained face. "Fuckin' idiot."

"I smelled you before I found you," Quinn said. "Your intestine's nicked. You're going septic."

"Gee, hadn't noticed," he said. "Beth?"

"She's alive," Quinn said. "Not for lack of trying to get herself killed. I bailed her out of a scrape at site two."

"She leave?"

Quinn shook his head.

"No one's left," Marcus said. "No one with the gumption to fight, anyway. I heard plenty of gunfire in the distance, long before the bullets started hitting us."

"Some of it may have been mine," Quinn said.

"They were shootin' guns," he said. "I bet those suppressed cannon shots I heard were yours."

"Think you can walk?" Quinn asked.

"Hell of a question coming from a one-legged man. You are still one-legged?"

Quinn showed him the Revo prosthetic.

"What about that left arm of yours?"

He obliged him, showing the torched-off scar tissue of what used to be a griffin tattoo.

"I got no interest in living," Marcus said. "I do got an interest in dying right. That means helping Beth. I figure you're with me on that?"

Quinn turned away, looking at the truck. No answers lurked in the flames.

"All this time, I was afraid a man like you would read that fucking journal, then come here and kill everyone."

"The thought crossed my mind."

"Lose your nerve?"

"Beth," he said. One word was enough.

"She's got her mother's disregard for survival, that's for sure," Marcus said.

"And she lacks her sister's keen sense of judgment."

"You're a damn moron," Marcus said. "She wrote that journal when she meant to use you, and she was taught that love is weakness. Because in Harlow, it is."

"Beth doesn't think so," he said. "She still wants to save everyone. She wants to save you. So I gave her the journal, and I brought along a long-lost secret from the freezer."

Marcus considered the implications for two long, raspy breaths.

"You *were* gonna kill everyone," Marcus said. "If she agreed to leave, that is."

"That's right," Quinn said. "She stayed. So now it's a different kind of fight. The kind you fight with myths and legends."

Marcus nodded, a man who'd spent a lifetime protecting Beth, never once considering what she could mean to Harlow. She was a daughter, not a son, and daughters were always protected from everything, even expectations.

"Let's go make a myth, then," Marcus said.

"Myths are stories," Quinn said. "I think I've got a hell of a story, and I think you can help me tell it."

"Help me at least make it that long," Marcus said. He braced his arm on the roots of the oak, trying to push himself up. Quinn grabbed his arm and steadied him. As he got vertical, a tangle of guts poked out from between his fingers. The stench from his torn intestine was acrid and overwhelming. The old man was screwed, but he was a tough, smart old bastard who wanted to live long enough to author his own ending, and Quinn had seen enough death to know that a fierce spirit could keep death at bay for a long time.

"You'll survive on your own," Quinn said. "What you're going to need help with is climbing a big fucking ladder."

The sky purpled, a precursor to the looming dawn. Beth arrived at the mouth of Cooper's driveway, and was greeted by Cooper's severed head mounted on a spike, right next to his mailbox. The old man was ready to die at the wheel of a truck bomb, but he held the open mouth and terrorized look of a man who'd wanted to live, and to see such fear on his face broke apart the memory of the steady, unflappable man she'd come to know.

She had walked for hours by then, reading the journal, learning all the things her family had wanted Quinn to know—and he had given it to her. She couldn't waste it, she knew her limits, and she was ready.

The first order of preparation was to expect no survivors at Cooper's farmhouse. The pillars of smoke told that story. Dig sites blown up, trucks burning. Thatcher's house and outbuildings on fire. While the innocents slept, High Servants were on guard, and when the call came down to purge the rebels at the dig sites, she knew who had more men. And more guns.

So she walked by Cooper's head, knowing the message—if the Great Survivor's time was up, what chance did anyone else have?

On the porch, she found the bodies, shoulder to shoulder. Blood and bullet holes. The men from their meetings. Anyone with a will to fight. But there were too many bodies, and only when she used her flashlight did she see the truth.

Not just the rebels, but their families. Wives. Children. A stack of bodies on Cooper's porch.

She expected to see her father, but didn't. Hope flared inside of her—that he was alive, that she could still win, even alone, against the forces arrayed against her.

She heard a shovel bite into dirt. The sound echoed off the tin shed. She tracked it, leaving the bodies behind, heading along the side of the house. Trent's Jeep was parked in the back, and he was knee-deep in a fresh grave. The headlights skimmed over his sweat-soaked head as he continued to shovel.

He had already completed two graves, neat squares in the ground with a pile of soil beside them.

"Trent," she said. He ignored her and shoveled again. She got closer and touched his shoulder. He stopped. His face was covered with filth and anguish.

She moved to take the shovel from him, and he was too weak to fight her. The callouses on his hands were broken. Blood stained the wooden handle.

"The Mayor killed my mom," he said, gesturing to the first grave. "Your heroic Griffin killed my dad." He kicked at the fresh grave's wall. "This one's mine."

"Stop it," she said.

"That's the point," he said. "It's the only way to stop it. I can't live with this, even if I run away. You can't wash Harlow off you. You have to burn it."

She felt the allure of the detonator dangling from the back loop of her jeans, clipped on with a lanyard. Fire was at her beck and call.

She showed it to him and told him what Quinn had done.

"He would have killed everyone?"

"I stopped him," she said. "Maybe I can stop the Mayor, too."

"Stop him from what?" he said. "You saw the porch. How many dead? How many over the years? The citizens who are sleeping right now, they'll wake up like nothing happened. They'll find out who died and drink their fucking coffee and go to work and pretend like nothing happened. They'll just be glad it wasn't them."

"Maybe," she said. "But maybe I can show them something. Something they've never seen before."

"This town's seen it all," he said.

"Not yet," she said.

An orange sliver peeked out from the trees to the east as the sun began to rise. The sky turned the color of embers, unable to decide if it was a fire put out or one just beginning.

That was when they heard Marcus Jarvis screaming.

CHAPTER 37

Beth and Trent drove the residential streets of Harlow with the windows down, creeping closer to the shouting voice of her father.

The town always rose early. Windows were squares of light in the murky dawn, newspapers resting on driveways and brought inside. A skin of frost clung to the grass and roof tiles.

Did they know what they had slept through? Would they dare to ask why the diner was so empty that morning?

Marcus shouted again, but she couldn't make out what he was saying. Fractions of syllables, none of them coming together, except for one word—*Griffin*.

She parked the Jeep on the shoulder and turned it off.

"We're close," she said. "Let's walk. Easier to listen."

She hopped out of the Jeep. Trent followed—he would follow her anywhere, but it was more out of habit than duty. The boy she knew was still in the grave he'd dug for himself. He thought he could wring happiness out of Harlow, but when he went to squeeze, it squeezed back. He'd come to terms with his loss one day, or he wouldn't. The grave would always be waiting.

"How do you do it?" Trent asked.

"Do what?"

"Keep going," he said. "After your mom. Your sister. You know when we find your dad, it won't be a happy ending."

"Take one step," she said. "Then another. Same as you're doing now."

She kept going.

"The water tower," he said. They saw glimpses of white paint through the screen of the mature oak trees that sprouted from the oldest yards in Harlow. She was finally close enough to hear Marcus clearly.

"Judgment has come to Harlow!" Marcus shouted. "The Griffin has arrived, and another disciple is dead. Fight with him now, or suffer for the rest of your days!"

He kept going, the same message, different variations. The Griffin had arrived. Serilda was dead. Ortega and the Mayor were next, and it was time to fight alongside the Griffin or be lost forever.

They were not the first ones to reach the water tower. Ortega paced in front of a squad of High Servants, each of them holding rifles in their hands, eager for the command to shoot.

Marcus was perched two hundred feet in the air, leaning against the catwalk's railing. The maintenance ladder had been torn away from the tower's spine, leaving no way to get to the top.

Yet it also meant he never intended to come back down safely. Beth saw the morning light reflect off of his abdomen—he wore something shiny and tight, a cummerbund of glossy red.

Shrinkwrap? she thought. *He's hurt bad, and the shrinkwrap is holding his stomach together.*

Like most small towns, the water tower was its defining feature. A thick cylinder with a tin roof, four legs holding it high in the air. White paint, blistered all over. Black letters: HARLOW.

Only the familiar lettering was obscured by a white flag with a red figure on it. A Griffin. An old flag from the high school, before they were the Orphans. The fabric was stained with Marcus's bloody handprints, and she wasn't sure how he'd secured it to the surface of the water tower, but the Griffin was there for all to see, an eagle's head crowned with white feathers, a red body, gold accents in its claws and tail.

He screamed as he had screamed all morning, the wind just right to carry his voice across Main Street and toward the nearby houses. Faces peered from windows. Farmers and dig site workers—always the first ones up—stood on porches in their bathrobes, bearing the morning cold to look up at the always-quiet Marcus Jarvis screaming like a lunatic.

A small crowd gathered. Word spread. Everyone in Harlow could see the flag on the water tower if they cared to find a sightline, and Marcus's voice was impossible to ignore as it broke the morning serenity.

Ortega watched, doing nothing. His instinct was surely to kill and silence Marcus—a low man standing higher than all others, a quiet man delirious with joy, preaching a secret gospel in public for the first time, his words given gravity because anyone close enough to see his wounds knew he was spending his final breaths on this, the heralding of the Griffin.

Yet the Mayor had made it a point to invite this, to relish the confrontation. He had gone to great lengths to manufacture a dramatic conflict with the Griffin, all to make him real in the eyes of Harlow. Only then could he strike him down.

Beth thought it impossible that her father would play into the Mayor's hands.

"Dad!" she screamed. Marcus paused, looked down, and saw her. She couldn't make out the smile, but sensed it, and then he looked away, back at the horizon, and called out once more: "The Griffin walks among Harlow! Hear the call! Follow and be free!"

The crowd grew larger. More men on porches, this time joined by their wives, who had finally progressed their hair and makeup to a level acceptable for public consumption.

All while Beth stood at the foot of the tower, obscured in the crowd. She was covered in grit and blood, swollen with bruises, her hair sticking together, a bundle of dirty ropes.

"What is he doing?" Trent said.

"I don't know," she said. "Quinn is gone."

"The Mayor hides," Marcus screamed. "He's just a man. He needs you to believe he's something more, but he's not."

Muttering from the crowd. Marcus had scored his first point—the Mayor was nowhere to be found. He knew the power of absence, but he also knew the power of making an entrance. She didn't wait for him to arrive as much as she braced herself.

Marcus slammed his palm against the tin flesh of the water tower, leaving more bloody streaks on the white fabric of the Griffin flag.

"The Griffin—"

"—is welcome in Harlow!" The Mayor finished his sentence for him, waltzing down Main Street, as if he'd been there all along. "Perhaps an introduction is in order?"

As the Mayor got closer, the citizens outside in their driveways and porches and standing on the sidewalks all got on their knees. Housewives doubled their robes up, softening their kneecaps against the crooked concrete.

The Mayor looked at Beth. His warm breath turned into puffs of frost. She tensed. Her muscles coiled. She wanted to fight.

He sensed it. Anger was impossible to hide from anyone, but a man like the Mayor could sense even the slightest ripple of discomfort, and poke at it until it cracked open.

He smiled at her as he approached his loyalists—a kneeling Ortega, kneeling High Servants. He touched Ortega's shoulder, and the disciple rose, a full foot taller than the man he called his master.

"Thank you, my friend," the Mayor said. "Your day has come at last. Vengeance for your brother. The quenching of an overdue thirst."

Ortega bowed his head in acceptance.

Above them, Marcus was fading. He leaned on the rail. His words had slowly deflated, and now he struggled to find the strength for his voice to carry.

Yet, he somehow found it.

"And so the Griffin shall come." He labored, taking a long pause. The Mayor nodded along, urging him to continue. "And see in and through the darkness, and clear its throat, and breathe fire in Harlow's name."

The Mayor shook his head. "The Griffin...always on the way, never here."

"Let me begin with the low man," Ortega said. "Let me show his daughter his guts."

"By the looks of him, perhaps a familiar sight," the Mayor said. He looked up at Marcus and waved with a sarcastic and feminine twiddling of his fingers.

Beth took a step forward, but Trent grabbed her shoulder.

"Not the Mayor," Trent said. "Remember? Not him."

"Marcus Jarvis!" the Mayor called. "Produce your coin!"

Marcus reached in his pocket. When he removed it, his middle finger was extended.

"Ah, here it is," the Mayor said, removing the silver dollar from his own pocket. "I kept it safe for you since you have forgotten the value. Wouldn't want you losing it on the street, now, would we?"

He let the coin dance between his fingers and over his knuckles. Then, he let it rest in his palm and squeezed. When he opened his fist, the silver was bent and warped. He let it fall. The coin struck the sidewalk and tottered into the gutter.

"Mercy has its limits," the Mayor said.

Then, he leapt into the air, the strength of his legs defeating gravity. He rose, his body lean and graceful. He matched the height of the tower, landing softly on the catwalk far above them.

"That's a new one," Trent said.

The Mayor couldn't fly, but leaping two hundred feet from a dead stop did plenty to remind the crowd of his power. Marcus looked at the Mayor, then back down among the people. Beth found his eyes once more, and he shook his head. *Whatever the Mayor's about to do,* he was saying to her, *don't stop it.*

Tears bit at the corners of her eyes. She tried to swallow, but her throat was dry.

Trent took her hand, opening her stone of a fist, intertwining his fingers into hers, a feeling she hadn't known since the morning of the day the Mayor cut his throat.

"Marcus Jarvis, the Griffin's herald!" the Mayor proclaimed. He applauded. No one joined him. The town continued to kneel. Marcus got to his feet, pushing himself away from the rail. The two men glared at each other for a long moment—and then Marcus raised his fists, taking a boxing stance.

The Mayor couldn't conceal his delight. He stepped forward, and Marcus tried to punch him. The Mayor caught his fist and crushed it, bones snapping as easily as kindling. Marcus did not scream.

The Mayor took him by the throat and picked him up.

"The Mayor is merciful!" the Mayor called.

The crowd repeated it: "The mayor is merciful!"

"Is the Griffin merciful? Because I refuse to kill this man," the Mayor said. "He is a treasure, and his family has long entertained me."

He dangled Marcus over the railing of the catwalk. Marcus's feet kicked as he held the Mayor's wrist, trying to keep the pressure off of his throat.

"I refuse to kill him," the Mayor said, "but the ground will not, and the ground will kill this man if the Griffin doesn't intervene."

"Don't watch this," Trent whispered. She didn't listen.

"Do you hear me? I'll even count it down for you to make it easy, oh mighty Griffin. Three."

Beth's heart crashed against her breastbone.

"Two."

Marcus stopped struggling. His feet weren't kicking. He released the Mayor's arm. The Mayor held him by the neck and prepared to drop him, but the Mayor could take nothing more from him—the damage was done, and his death was certain.

"One," he said.

The following moment unfurled forever, silent and cold. Beth waited. They all did.

"Zero."

The Mayor released him. Marcus fell, paddling at the air until he smashed against the concrete.

She made herself look. Her father's head was spread across the pavement, the skull fragments loosely connected by mushy tissue. Blood ran over the sidewalk, then into the street, turning into a stream that crawled for the gutters. Legs and arms were broken, laying in haphazard directions, freed from the prison of ligaments and biological order.

Her father was gone. The mess on the ground wasn't him, and it wouldn't ever be him. Gone was never really gone.

The Mayor swan-dove off the water tower, twisting in the air, landing nimbly on his feet.

"Can someone clean that up?" he said. "Maybe a janitor?"

Ortega laughed. The servants followed suit.

The citizens, trapped on their knees, did not.

"Nine o'clock," Beth said.

The laughter stopped. The Mayor approached her.

"What did you say?"

"Nine o'clock," she said. "Red Rock Ridge. You said you'd meet me there at nine." She held up her wrist and tapped her watch, never taking her eyes from him. "I need some time to get ready."

"For what?" the Mayor asked. "I know what you and your little band of merry men wanted to do, and all those merry men are dead."

"I'm not," she said. "And maybe they weren't the only people who wanted to fight."

He considered her offer, licking his lips in thought.

"You want me to meet you at Red Rock in an hour?" he asked. "To fight me?"

"Send Ortega first," she said. "I'll bring you his head. And I won't be alone." She turned to the small crowd. "If you're sick of kneeling, if you're sick of taking the Oath . . . if you're sick of watching your friends and family carved up and killed, then I won't be alone!"

Silence. Everyone obediently waited for the Mayor to speak.

"I like it!" he boomed. The Mayor spoke to all of Harlow. "Spread the word. An early Harvest Ceremony commences this morning. You will take your Oaths, and I will give my final blessing. The scouts will be disbanded, and you may all leave Harlow forever."

A murmur from the crowd.

"He's lying," Beth said. "He'll do anything to keep you as his audience. Don't you understand? His power means nothing without witnesses."

"If you believe her," he said, "then please, stand with her at Red Rock." He turned to Ortega. "Beth is to have free passage to Red Rock this morning." Ortega nodded. "As will anyone else who wants to join her."

He addressed the people once more. "At nine, anyone who is not in the gymnasium for Harvest has rejected me," he said. "My mercy has limits, but Ortega's wrath does not."

He rejoined Ortega, his boots crunching against the pavement, leaving smudges of Marcus's blood behind.

"When the clock strikes nine, kill them all," the Mayor said, glancing at Beth. "And bring me her head."

She saw hunger flash in Ortega's eyes.

The Mayor checked his watch. "All of you, pass word to your friends and neighbors. Make your arrangements. You have two hours to assemble," he said. "But when Harvest begins, Harlow is no longer under my protection."

The sun gained traction as the morning firmed up, and those early-morning onlookers rose from their knees and scrambled home.

Beth knelt by her father. She reached out and took his hand, sticky from the pool of blood that surrounded his crushed body. Two of his fingers were haphazardly broken. Still, she held him.

"I love you," she whispered.

"The body stays," the Mayor said. He turned to Trent. "Go on, boy," he said. "Scamper to Red Rock. You'll get to die for her two more times than you got to fuck her."

The Mayor moved to stand behind her. "You disappoint me," he whispered. "Your father knew better than to pick a fight, no matter how hard I tried to entice him. I thought you'd play a more worthy game."

Beth placed her father's hand on the pavement and brushed away the wetness in her eyes. She rose to face him. He was taller than she remembered, probably because she knew him in the darkness of shift work, seated in a truck. He had a way of making himself look small when he was Galen Mettis, but the Mayor walked taller, his shoulders back—the walk of an impregnable fortress.

"I don't care about his body," she said. "Leave him to rot. Dad wouldn't care. And that's why you could never beat him."

The Mayor smiled. "Would you like to know your father's last words? He whispered them up there, when my hand was around his throat."

She didn't give him the pleasure of saying yes, but didn't deny him the opportunity to say them uninvited.

"He said it was better to rule your own spirit than to rule the world," he said.

She believed him.

"But that is what all this is, Beth—do you see that? My body is indomitable. But what about my spirit? What are my limitations? My weaknesses? What is my purpose? We are not equal in body, or potential. I am evolved, and you are not. But our minds are equal. Doubt. Boredom. Longing. Anger. We speak to ourselves. Our feelings come from those whispers. Listen long enough, and you get to the truth. The depths of our depravity, the height of our purpose. I have plumbed those depths here, but in preparation for something greater than both of us."

"I don't care," she said. "You're a kid with a magnifying glass burning anthills. You're a man. A man with an illness. Born with the one in your mind, but the one in your body? You contracted it. My mother figured it out. My sister wrote it all down. And I read it. I know the truth."

She thought that just once, the facade would slip, that she would see the frightened boy from the mines behind the faces he had constructed. But his face remained impassive.

"He gave the journal to you, then," the Mayor said. "He's here. And perhaps he can now show me my limits. Perhaps he can set me free."

"He was here," she said. "He's gone now. He won't show you the Griffin's neck just so you can cut it."

"Then go to Red Rock Ridge," he said. "You were important, but now you are merely a weakness of mine, a favorite toy, and I want you to know that when I see your severed head, I will grieve. Harlow will see how much I cared for you. Their loyalty will deepen when they see my sorrow. And that is when I will slaughter them all."

He squeezed her face with one powerful hand, clamping her cheeks against her molars.

"I am a corrective," he said. "I will rectify the lies perpetrated by gods and propagated by man. Harlow's sacrifice is necessary, but it will not be in vain."

The Mayor kissed her on the top of the head before he let her go.

"Goodbye, Beth," he said, stepping over her father's corpse.

She watched him leave. He strolled down Harlow's main street, appearing to savor each step, taking it all in for the final time. His blessing would be death, and perhaps the citizens already knew it.

Only when he was out of sight did the onlookers dare rise from their knees. She watched them shamble home, the burden of what they'd witnessed pressing on their shoulders.

To fight was to die unless she could show them otherwise, and she could not show them if they marched to the gymnasium, wagering their lives on the word of a madman.

CHAPTER 38

B eth stood at the pinnacle of Red Rock Ridge. Illinois had
a reputation for being flat, but farther south, the terrain
gave way to the sandstone sculptures and bluffs in the
Shawnee National Forest. They'd learned about the Garden of the
Gods in fifth grade. She remembered the photos, the gold of the
sun above a canopy of woods and shards of rock even higher than
the trees, and imagined what gods would walk there. She asked if it
was a place they could visit, and the teacher shook her head, knowing the truth that they were too young to understand.

Red Rock held no such beauty. A dirt road gave way to a well-
worn path to the top of a half-hill. The clay-rich soil was a dull
red color, and at the top of the hill, it was a short, twenty-foot
drop into the creek bed below, and then more rolling hills. Woods
flanked them on each side. At the top of the hill, the highest point
in Harlow, they were as high as the oak canopy, and with the leaves
gone, the reaching branches looked like netting against the skyline,
a trap ready to spring. From here, they could overlook the center of
town and see Harlow rooftops peeking out of a blanket of low fog
the sun had yet to burn away.

Trent sat in the dirt, his arms wrapped around his knees. The flesh under his eyes was swollen from a lack of sleep. He watched the dirt road, waiting.

"No one's coming," he said.

She checked her watch—twenty to nine. "We still have time," she said.

"We do—you and me. If we leave now. The way we always wanted."

"That dirt you're sitting in?" she said. "Do you know how much blood was spilled in it?"

"You think adding ours to the mix makes a difference?"

"I'm not forcing you to stay."

"I believe in you," he said. "But I'm the only one. No one else is coming to fight."

"I don't need them to fight," she said. "I need them to see. If Ortega is alone, if the Mayor isn't here, that's exactly what we wanted—now I just need them to see."

She watched the dirt road. The trees that flanked the ridge clearing swayed in the morning breeze. Dead leaves fell. She checked her watch again.

If no one came, they were at the school, kneeling in the gymnasium. The Mayor among them, holding court.

She touched the detonator, making sure it was still dangling from her belt, comforted by its presence. From the ridge, she could watch the whole town fall into the earth. Quinn had told her the eastern edge of Harlow had the most tunnels underfoot, near the school. The Mayor was there, and she could make it his tomb, buried under the bodies of those he meant to rule.

"What are you doing?" Trent said.

She had removed the detonator from her belt while she considered pressing the button. She held it with both hands, reverent of its power.

"I don't know," she whispered.

They sensed a distant rumble. It grew closer and louder as they waited, watching the mouth of the dirt road.

A Ford truck emerged from a mouth of trees and rumbled toward the hill. High Servants sat in the truck bed, their rifles slung over their shoulders. Ortega's crew.

The truck stopped. The passenger window lowered, and she saw Ortega's smiling face. He raised his arm and tapped his wrist—time was almost up.

She let her thumb glide over the detonator's release sliders. Click them back, flip the switch, and watch Ortega's face contort as he realized his lord and master was being consumed by the depths from which he'd emerged all those years ago.

Not the ending she had in mind for Ortega, but it was the only consolation prize available to her under the circumstances.

Ortega stood at the foot of the hill, his crew behind him, their cheeks swollen with tobacco. Overalls were faded by a summer of labor and sun. Mesh hats were crowned with the white stains of perspiration salt.

"It's nine o'clock," Ortega said. He glanced over his shoulder. No one. The dirt path was still empty. He shrugged, as if to say, *what a shitty break, kid.*

"I know it pains the Mayor to give you up to me," he said. "He thinks me heartless. Merciless. Depraved. He thinks I'll tear you apart, but I am a warrior. I know one when I see one, and here you are. Honoring your word. Staying to fight. I respect it. So I'll kill you quickly. A warrior's death."

He started to climb the hill.

The detonator trembled in her unsteady hands, her thumbs against the lock sliders.

"If you can't do it," Trent said, "give it to me."

Ortega drew closer.

She squeezed the body of the detonator hard enough to wring the blood from her knuckles, turning them white, but could not push the button.

She spiked the detonator into the clay-hardened dirt instead. The corner struck a stray rock, and the homemade contraption cracked apart. She expected wires and screws and chipsets inside the now-broken plastic housing, but saw none of that. And even as Ortega drew ever closer, a falling guillotine of a man close to his most treasured target, he could not draw her attention from the examination of the detonator's inner workings—most interestingly, a silver disc with a small tail of wire, and a coin-sized lithium battery taped to it.

She knelt down and picked it up, holding it by the wire. A tracking device.

"Beth," Trent whispered. The tenor of his voice had changed—the fear was gone—but he wasn't looking at the silver disc. He was looking past her, over her shoulder.

Ortega's ascent stopped. He turned to see, and the fear that once belonged to Trent now belonged to the High Servants when they saw what was about to unravel at Red Rock Ridge. Their eyes pleaded with Ortega, begging for an order, for comfort, for protection. None came. He was frozen, watching, unable to fathom how his own master's threats had failed in Harlow for the first time, trumped by nothing short of a legend come to life.

Curtis Quinn walked the dirt road with a hundred Harlow citizens behind him. The sleeves on his skintight tactical shirt had been cut away. The melted Griffin remained a pool of scar tissue on his left arm, but on his right, a Griffin tattoo spanned the entire canvas of his muscled flesh. This was no small and regal creature—this Griffin had the demeanor of a sprinting, snarling dog chasing prey, everything condensed, slicked back, the eyes narrow and squinted from effort. The wings were pinned to its back, its haunches coiled for the next bound. But the beak was open, as if it was screaming, and it ended around the middle of his forearm, so that when he stretched his arm out, it looked like his hand was coming directly out of its mouth—a hand that hovered over a holstered Desert Eagle hand cannon.

And that is where the fire would come from.

Quinn never knew exactly how he would weaponize the Griffin, but he had long been a man that planned for every contingency. Each time he survived a stealth mission into the tunnels of Harlow, leaving buried explosives and missing persons in his wake, he scheduled an appointment to add more size and color to the sleeve tattoo.

The Jarvis family spent decades cultivating a myth, and he reveled in watching it come to life on his arm, wondering if he'd ever get the chance to wield it. To reveal himself and embrace the role the Mayor had wanted him to embody was not victory, but submission. Still, becoming the Griffin held the cold clarity of vengeance and confrontation, ideas he understood, battles he always thought he would win.

This was not that battle. Not anymore. He drove a dying Marcus Jarvis to the water tower and helped hoist him to the top, then climbed back down. He watched and listened, hidden in the murk of dawn and the shadows of quiet houses who didn't know their fates were being negotiated before they even turned on the coffee maker.

And when Beth was gone and word began to spread—the Mayor's promise of freedom, the Harvest, Harlow's final day of captivity—that was when he ripped away the sleeve of his form-fitting tactical gear, stepped into the streets, and began walking.

Blinds peeled. Onlookers gathered. An old man was drinking coffee on his porch and asked him, "Where's the Griffin off to this morning?"

"Red Rock Ridge," he answered.

The old man put his mug down.

"Wait three minutes for me?" he asked. "I need a jacket."

Quinn waited for him, giving others time to witness what was happening. The old man, Marvin Richter, came outside in jeans and a leather bomber jacket, and walked beside him.

Others followed. Married couples who'd lost children to the allure of leaving Harlow. Star-crossed lovers who could never be together, separated by the status of high and low, the doling out of marital permission. Older citizens who didn't want to die in Harlow. Mothers who didn't want their children to take the Oath, pulling those same children along—they wore puffy coats and wool hats and didn't know the danger of taking that walk. Those who finally saw the cage bars that held them in Harlow, and sensed the awful fate that awaited them at Harvest. Those who wanted to fight all along, but not alone. Those who believed all along, and those who had just converted at the sight of Quinn's tattoo.

By the time they turned away from Main Street and headed for rural Harlow and Red Rock Ridge, Quinn had their number at just under a hundred.

They left the road and trudged across the cut-down cornfield and entered the woods. Red Rock was a long walk, but with a shortcut across Cooper Murray's acreage, they could make it there by 9:00 a.m. His grandstanding as the Griffin had drawn a hundred followers, and in a town of six hundred, he should have been thrilled with the result, but he wasn't—hundreds of others were headed to the school, and the Mayor would kill them. Beth wanted to save everyone, and that meant she would want to confront the Mayor at the school—and that's only if they survived Ortega.

The war for Harlow was tricky to fight, but in the battle of Red Rock, he had one more strategy to ambush a superior enemy.

Quinn emerged in the clearing at the foot of Red Rock. Ortega bounded down the hill as his High Servants exchanged befuddled glances. Quinn kept walking, his hand resting on the heel of his Desert Eagle.

Half the High Servants kept a white-knuckled grip on their hunting rifles, afraid to move. The other half raised them and took aim at not just Quinn, but the followers behind him.

"They don't have enough bullets for all of us!" Marvin barked. Even at the sight of the guns, no one had peeled off, no one stopped, no one hesitated.

Soon enough, all the weapons were pointed at Quinn.

"Put your guns down, fools," Ortega commanded. "The man's a trained killer, and most of you have missed a buck from forty yards."

The command to stand down was an obvious relief to them. They rested their rifles against the truck as if absolving themselves the weight of a concrete block.

Quinn waited. Ten paces separated him and Ortega. He turned to the crowd that was gathered behind him. "Get back," he said.

"You fear for their safety?" Ortega said, mocking him. "You led them to their doom. No ornate punishments today, only death."

"You first," Quinn said.

"Single combat, then?"

"I didn't come all this way to debate you," he said. "Let's fucking go."

Ortega smirked. "Indeed—but you, I won't kill," he said. "You, I'll cripple. You'll watch them die. You'll watch me tear her head from her pretty neck. Then, I'll drag you to the Mayor. I'll be the one to deliver what he himself never dreamed he could possess— the carcass of the Griffin, made small by my hands. Maybe some will be alive to witness how he executes you."

Quinn monitored his breathing—calm, steady. But his jaw was clenched, muscles as hard as wire. His hands were balled into fists. Rage. Good. Just what he needed, a feeling he'd missed, the fire that made it easy to pull a trigger, to break a neck, to launch a rapey frat bro out of a high window.

Beth stood at the top of the hill, suddenly forgotten. Trent was gone. She must have hurried him away, urging him to safety while she stayed behind.

Quinn made eye contact with her. He nodded, subtle but curt. In that nod, a question was buried: *Did you read the journal? Did you open it? Do you believe?*

She nodded back.

Ortega pounded his chest—one fist, two sharp blows to his breastbone. All the disciples embodied the Mayor's taste for theatrics, the thirst to show off their supernatural abilities. This time, he wouldn't give in and let Ortega show off his bulletproof resistance.

Quinn reached for his tactical belt and snapped it free. The gun fell away from his hip. He tossed it aside. Disarming himself was something Ortega didn't expect. His brow furrowed, and during that tiny window of confusion, Quinn charged at him.

You're gonna regret this, he thought, and jumped into the air, giving up the target. He wanted to take a shot to the torso, not the head or neck. Ortega obliged him, punching him in the breastbone with the concussive force of a crashing truck.

The blow spiked him into the dirt, whiplashing his head against the ground. Dizzy now, the overhead clouds swirling. He tried to blink himself back to clarity.

Ortega flexed his fist. "Kevlar," he said. "Clever, but not quite clever enough."

The voice was distant. Quinn's ears rang. He rolled over, pressing his palms into the dirt to push himself up.

"Your savior has executed you. He's brought you all to the slaughter," Ortega said. "This is the weakling you died for?"

He turned to Quinn, who continued to struggle against the drumbeat of pain in his chest. He couldn't expand his lungs enough to take a full breath.

"This feeble man...this is your hero? This is your leader?"

Quinn's vision came into focus. He turned his head and saw what he was hoping to see—a blurry figure that Ortega was ignoring. He tried to speak, but the syllables came out in a warbled grunt.

Ortega leaned over, cupping his hand to his ear, a mocking gesture. "What did you say?"

Quinn cleared the dust from his throat and found his voice. "I'm not their leader," he said. "She is."

Ortega turned around. Beth was standing right behind him.

She unleashed a clumsy punch into Ortega's stomach, and the impact sounded like the full-throated thunderclap of a summer storm. Air shot from Ortega's body in a harsh *chuff* as he launched into the air, then through it—ten yards, then twenty, still rising, until he smashed, back-first, into an oak tree.

She looked at her fist, then Quinn—*did that really work?*

"Go on, then," Quinn said.

She approached Ortega. He sat against the tree, his chin covered in coughed-up blood. He tried to get up, and she shoved him back down. He reached out, trying to grab her, and she took hold of his arm and punched the crook of his elbow. The bones shot out of his skin as the arm snapped in two, and he screamed.

She let him scream, waiting patiently for his pain to subside before she struck him again.

The thought of my mother's death never fails to break my heart. Imagine it, Curtis—after all you've read, after all you learned. Imagine you're a young mother in her thirties in a small town with a loving husband. You have a pre-teen daughter who adores you, a five-year-old who worships you, a husband who would die for you.

And you ask him to do worse than that—to give you up. To stop loving you so that you can fully and completely pretend to love another. And you bed down with the Mayor, and give in to his advances, and out-act him at every turn, all for his secrets, to know how he bestows his power among the disciples.

The ruse takes years. All doubt removed. The Jarvis matriarch, a loyalist, a concubine. He yearns for a son, but you sabotage his every effort. What did that take? How many falls? How many nights alone in the dark, finding ways to hurt yourself and the seed inside of you?

Until finally, he relents and gives you not only the power of a disciple, but something more. Something once-removed. The power of a Queen.

Because now you know the source, if you cared to ask a doctor about her condition. Now you know how confused those doctors were, how the prion disorder appeared to be a strain of deadly Mad Cow disease, but the proteins were bent in impossible ways. Now you know the cannibalism was a way for him to experiment with sharing his disease, discovering ways to transfer and weaken his gift, to make sure disciples were strong, but not strong enough to challenge him. He thought the power would heal her womb and give him the son he wanted.

She saw the doctors hoping they could find out what afflicted her—and what could cure her. A cure meant a way to disarm the Mayor.

But no cure existed. It was a dead end, and soon, the Mayor would expect a son, or she would bear his wrath.

She killed herself at home. Her instructions were meticulous, and my father obeyed.

Imagine having the power only dreamed of in comic books and popcorn movies, but your calling was higher—to buy time and hope for a cure that could diminish his strength, and to give up your own life so that a Griffin could be born.

So your husband rigs up a sawed-off shotgun powerful enough to blow your brains all over the wall of your kitchen, and only your daughter has the will to carry out the explicit instructions to do what her father isn't strong enough to do.

I didn't run away from Harlow, Curtis. I was on a mission. I took a cooler full of my mother's brain tissue to store it away—so that one day, perhaps a cure for the rare disorder would emerge, and with it, a way to battle the Mayor. But she had also given me the key to forge a Griffin from the gift she left behind.

You are not the man for this power. To possess it requires humility, the governor of a conscience, a judicious soul. You do not possess those things. Your rage is buried, your storm clouds are permanent.

Harlow requires a hero.

My mother's suicide note is tucked away in these pages. I've read it many times, as short as it is:

"Always remember—all cruelty springs from weakness. I love you girls, and when the world whispers to you, I hope you listen."

Listen to the whispers, Curtis. Listen, and make me proud.

Quinn watched the crowd. Their stunned demeanor shifted into a communal relish of their tormentor's imminent defeat, all at the hands of a five-foot-six, hundred-pound teenage girl.

"You are not the Griffin," Ortega said, his voice glazed with pain.

"No, I'm not. I am Christina Jarvis's daughter," she said, and punched him in the chest again. "I am Kate Jarvis's sister." Another punch. A cracking sound with wetness behind it—she was caving in his sternum.

She waited, letting the waves of pain crash through him. Ortega choked and gagged, clutching his fractured chest.

"I am Marcus Jarvis's vengeance," she said, and struck his chest one more time. Her fist broke through bone, plunging inside his chest cavity, like an axe stuck in a tree stump. She yanked it free, her fist covered with the purplish-red of oxygen-depleted blood. Ortega twitched. His face tightened into a mask of suffering. Thickened blood escaped him in a slimy trickle. His life slipped away, taking the tension with it. His face turned slack and serene as he slumped against the tree, sliding against the bark as his corpse crunched into dead oak leaves.

Quinn's breath returned. The pain submitted to the drugs and adrenaline coursing through his system. He approached Beth, who looked at her own bloody hand, disbelieving—not just in her abilities, but in the decisiveness of her violent action.

She had taken a life in anger, and had every right. Quinn knew the look of that regret, but only in other people.

"What you feel right now," he said, "it won't go away. You'll lose many nights of sleep over it. So I'm told. I never did. But that's why it had to be you, do you understand?"

She nodded. "What now?"

"We leave," he said. "A hundred saved lives will have to do." "But the Mayor..."

"The Mayor would kill you just as easily as you killed Ortega," he said. "He's careful about doling out his power. He always made sure a disciple was four generations removed from the source. You're a tier above them, but still below him."

"So many others—"

"Are good as gone," he said. "Now it's our job to make the Mayor gone."

"If he's too strong for me, then how?"

"Just like I planned," he said. "We bury him."

"How do you know it will work?"

"I don't," he said.

"Then we will have killed hundreds of people at the Harvest, and not the Mayor."

"What kind of final blessing do you think he was talking about?" Quinn asked. "You think he's really going to let them leave? He knows Harlow is lost. He's going to kill it on his terms. I say we kill it on ours, and take a shot at sinking him with it."

"I can't let all those people die," she said. "Not when I have the strength to at least try and save them."

"I won't let you do this."

"You know I can just chest-punch you into the woods and do whatever I want, right?"

"Look at them," he said. "They won't leave now. They'll follow you. You can lead them out of Harlow, to freedom and safety, or into battle. They'll die. You'll die. What's your choice?"

She looked at them. The awe never left their faces. Marvin gave her and Quinn a comical thumbs-up gesture.

"Before we argue anymore about this," she said, "let's get everyone out of here. Between the Jeep and the Ford, we can shuttle at least ten at a time."

"Superslab is the closest road out of here," he said. "If you get across the Sugar Creek Bridge, you'll be far enough."

"Far enough for what?"

"We have a chance to trap him forever," he said. "It's a chance we need to take. Let me take it."

He unclipped a cargo slot in his tactical belt, removed the true detonator, and tossed it to her. She caught it.

"I said only you would know when to hit the button, and I meant it."

"I will," she said, "once you're across the bridge with us."

He shook his head.

"Oh my God," she said. "You're going to the school. You're going to face him."

He unslotted what looked like a walkie-talkie from his belt and pulled out an oversized antenna, a bolt of silver in the morning light.

This receiver will beep as long as it has that little disc's signal," he said. She took the disc out of her pocket. He took it, handing over the receiver. "When it stops, you'll know I'm underground. I'll have the Mayor with me. That's when you push the button. No hesitation. Understand? Harlow dies, and the Mayor with it."

"You do realize that they're going to live in fear if we can't definitively kill the Mayor," Beth said.

"They're used to living in fear," he said. He looked off into the woods—his truck was close, a six-minute jog. Four more minutes to drive to the school. She'd have everyone out soon after that.

"I don't know if I can do it," she said.

"You will," he said. "Good people are the easiest to predict."

She smiled. "That's why I knew you'd come back to Harlow."

"Don't give me that hero shit," he said. "Your sister said something in her journal about me listening to the world, whispering to me about what I really was. So I did, and you know what it said? I'm a thug. A henchman. A hitter. Disposable. I'm a layer between what's important and what's dangerous. So you wait until that little blip disappears, and then you press the goddam button."

She looked at the dirt, but it held no answers. He saw Kate in her, long before the world had sanded down the shine in her eyes and dampened the hope in her voice. Beth still had the head-shaking, bulletproof hopefulness of an eighteen-year-old. She finally looked up at him, and he knew it would be the last time he'd ever see her.

She nodded.

He nodded back, the matter decided. He brushed past her, heading for his truck. She caught his arm and pulled him into an embrace.

"Thank you," she whispered. "Kate would have been proud of you."

He considered it. Maybe she would have. But he had an hour left to live, give or take, and that was plenty of time to do awful and violent things of which she'd never approve.

He was a killer and a thief, a destroyer, a mercenary, but he knew full well that the insulation between what's important and what's dangerous was a thug to some, and a hero to others.

He could afford no such delusions. Not now. He couldn't let a soul distract him from the work at hand, even if he planned to die within the hour, when a soul would be all that he had left.

CHAPTER 39

Quinn parked his van near the bus barn and prepared for conflict.

He unzipped the Hail Mary bag. Inside, a second tactical belt, this one with elastic loops. He changed out his belts and tucked his Hail Mary smoke grenades into six slots on the left side of the belt. On the right, he holstered a Smith & Wesson 460 Magnum revolver. Five shots, each bullet as thick as a fat man's finger. He sacrificed the handling and familiarity of the Desert Eagle, but no other handgun could send a high-grain bullet with the speed and stopping power of the S&W.

The recoil was palm-bruising on the range, and the recommended setup was with a scope and shooting braces—the perfect NRA asshole setup, so that you could brag at the diner that you blew the heart out of a buck from two hundred yards with a pistol.

He packed no other ammunition, knowing he'd never have time to open the chamber to reload. Even the hammer action required between rounds was too much time to think he'd ever get more than one shot at the Mayor with the weapon. Yet the Mayor always invited that shot, just like his disciples. He liked to show off his bullet-resistance, to prove his strength, to show how futile the gesture of trying to kill him really was.

But the Mayor had never been shot with something that could rip through the trunk of an oak tree from twenty yards, and wouldn't expect that kind of punch to come from a handgun, even if it made Dirty Harry's magnum look like a toy.

He slotted the nine-inch barrel into the holster and headed for the west entrance of the school. Once at the door, he peeked through the slat of tempered glass. He saw five men standing outside the chained gym doors, looking through the school's main entrance.

Waiting. Of course. They were probably expecting Ortega, but the Mayor was expecting a Griffin.

Quinn intended to deliver. He opened the door.

The creak of the hinges echoed on the hallway. The High Servants turned and saw him. Only two had rifles. They didn't raise them. Instead, they put them aside.

In a town like Harlow, there were no faces he hadn't seen, but he didn't know their names. Even if he had, it would not cause him hesitation. They were loyal due to fear, and with the Mayor gone, they'd likely drink beer together and and lose their every violent inclination. They were decent men trying to survive, but Quinn was the last man in the world who gave a fuck about their inherent goodness. They were in the way, and if they didn't step aside, they would die.

"Mayor said the Griffin would come." The leader wore a John Deere hat and well-worn jeans, the denim the color of a summer sky. They were all similarly dressed, looking ready to farm, not fight.

The shortest of them had blonde fuzz clinging to his balding scalp. He yanked the chains off the doors and threw them open.

Through the threshold, Quinn glimpsed the gymnasium. Bodies were strewn about the gym floor in parts. The hardwood Quinn used to mop was glossy with blood. The survivors were in the bleachers, their heads down, their hands folded in prayer.

The Mayor was on the stage, receiving Oaths. His arms were slick with blood all the way to his elbows.

"Ortega is dead," the Mayor announced. "He and his brother have proven weak in the face of the Griffin's assault. But is he worthy to face me? My sons, I beg of you—bring his body to me. Then, I can take his spirit."

That's why they put their guns aside, he thought. *The Mayor thinks I ate the tissue. He wants to show the onlookers what I really am before he kills me.*

The sacrificial lambs were five unarmed rednecks in heavy boots and restrictive jeans, men who had perhaps been in some high school scraps, grab-ass fights where no one poked eyes or snapped fingers or shattered testicles. No one whose first instinct was to go for the kill.

Five of them against Curtis Quinn, the Coletti family's rabid dog, a man who added the filthiest fighting tactics and a thirst for blood to his instructor-level skill in Marine martial arts, a discipline of lethal hand-to-hand combat capability.

He didn't intend to waste his Hail Mary bullets, so he waited in the farthest reaches of the hallway, allowing the tightness of the quarters to prevent them from surrounding him. To his left, a bank of lockers. To his right, a bare concrete wall from which stray hoodies and jackets hung, left behind during the cold mornings that turned into hot afternoons. Such was the fickle weather of southern Illinois.

They came for him. He stepped forward, closing the gap with a casual walk. Their faces were stripped of anything resembling a killer instinct, or a belief they could subdue him. They wanted to run away, to sit in their dens with a Stag beer and watch a football game with the head of a deer hanging on the wall.

The leader charged him, catching a knee in the gut. Quinn tossed him aside, causing a metallic crash against the lockers. The door of one locker swung open. He took the second man, caved in his knee, clamped his head into a guillotine lock, and brought the back of his neck up into the metal corner of the locker.

The neck snapped before the corner could puncture the base of his skull, shredding his cervical spine.

The other three tried to pile on. Punches, kicks. Untrained. Feeble. Quinn remained calm, backing to the opposite wall where the coats were hanging. The Revo flexed, bending just enough to support his movement, providing a stiff and stable base from which to strike.

He landed a punch to a flannel-covered sternum, grabbed the back of the man's head, and jammed him face-first into the coat hooks. One brass hook drove through his eyeball. Quinn bashed the back of his head, driving the hook deeper, fracturing the eye socket, finishing off the kill.

He yanked a hoodie off the wall, flipped another assaulter over his shoulder, then wrapped the fabric around his throat, using the sleeves as handles, pressing his knee into the back of the man's neck, pulling back, choking, breaking.

Quinn stood up. Only then did he notice his face was swelling, bruised, having been punched repeatedly. He towered over the last two assailants. The men hesitated, waiting for the other to go first, a prisoner's dilemma.

Quinn reached into the open locker. He brought out a math textbook—always the heaviest ones—and a ballpoint pen.

He launched the textbook at the men and charged them.

Seconds later, bones were broken and over thirty holes were opened up between them, all in soft tissue areas. Their eyes were gone. The short one had blood leaking from his punctured ear as he twitched on the tile; the other had the pen buried through the undercarriage of his jaw, the tip stuck in the roof of his mouth.

The first man, the leader, was still alive. He mumbled, returning to consciousness after slamming against the lockers seconds earlier. *You think it's all a bad dream*, Quinn thought, the adrenaline hot in his veins, the hunger roiling in his chest. He felt steady, alive.

The man rolled over, his John Deere hat askew, but somehow still planted on his head.

Quinn dropped the heel of his boot into the man's face, crushing it against the tile. He repeated the heel-strike, the Revo sturdy in support of his furious stomping. He didn't stop until the skull was in pieces and gray matter was stuck to his sole.

He left the bodies in his wake and entered the gym to the Mayor's mocking applause.

CHAPTER 40

Quinn crossed the threshold and entered the gym.

The Mayor was shirtless, lean, covered in tiny bullet holes. His arms were drenched in rich, dark blood all the way up to his biceps from plunging his powerful limbs into the bodies of his enemies. His hair was matted with tissue, white chunks sticking in his hair like oversized dandruff.

Hundreds were dead, their bodies littering the gym floor. Quinn smelled spent gunpowder. A few dozen living remained, trembling in prayer, cowering in the bleachers.

The crowd had turned on him, and he'd made an example of them. Fired weapons meant that even High Servants had turned their guns on the Mayor.

"Show me your leg," the Mayor said.

Quinn hoisted the leg of his cargo pants to show the bend of his Revo prosthetic. The Mayor shook his head.

"You found the journal," he said. "Yet you did not partake in the power it held?"

"You won't get the show you wanted," Quinn said. He looked at the last of the Harlow residents, cowering on the bleachers. "And this isn't the adoring audience you expected."

"I've already broken them," he said. "Hope breaks in many ways, you see. It's a fragile thing. I just wanted to break you at the same time."

"You wanted to break the Jarvises," he said. "But you won't. Beth is gone. Far away from here."

"After what I've done here?" he said. "Harlow will remain close to her heart forever. As it will my own for what is to come next."

"There is no next for you," Quinn said, drawing the magnum revolver. He let the massive gun dangle at his side. His muscles twitched, moving the Griffin's feathered body on his tattooed arm, primed to strike.

"You know nothing but what those cunts thought they knew, scribbling in their little books," the Mayor said. "You know nothing of what comes next."

The Mayor smiled and walked toward him, almost strolling, savoring each delightful moment before the execution.

"Turns out, I do," Quinn said. He raised the gun. The Mayor made no move against him, ready to absorb the bullet. And why not? It was just a revolver. Just another bullet.

He fired. The pistol snapped back, his powerful hand still too weak to contain the recoil. The sound was that of God himself ripping open the universe to start anew, and left his ears with humming, tinny and distant.

The bullet struck the Mayor just below the sternum. The high-grain bullets would penetrate oak trees and blow up pumpkins on his makeshift shooting range. They'd leave a frisbee-sized exit wound on a normal human. But the Mayor? The damage was minimal—yet it was still damage. Blood spurted from the wound, squirting through the Mayor's hands as he tried to cover it. The look on his face was utter shock.

He fell to one knee. He screamed—primal, guttural—the first glimpse of the man behind the character he had created. The Mayor removed his hands and let the wound bleed, holding them out to his sides, a Christ-like pose.

The bleeding stopped. The hole shrank, healing in real time. The slug squirted out of him, rejected by his empowered body.

Quinn never meant for the shot to kill him. He only meant for it to distract him, and as the Mayor recovered, he was pulling pins on smoke grenades, rolling them to every corner of the gym, under the bleachers, tossing them onto the stage. Six in all, pins removed, leaking smoke, then vomiting thick, yellowish clouds into the humid atmosphere of the gym.

As visibility obscured, Quinn looked at the traumatized crowd huddled in the bleachers.

"Run," he said.

He found the thickest plume of infant smoke and stepped into it, hiding from the Mayor.

"You never fail to entertain," the Mayor said, walking through the vapor. The wound on his torso was already a memory.

Quinn used the cover of the smoke to head for the boiler room door, but as he approached, he saw the Mayor's shape emerging in front of him.

A man who was born in the dark pit of a collapsed mine, one who chose to live and dine in the muddy confines of the old tunnels, was not deterred by the reduced visibility of the smoke.

Quinn couldn't make it to the boiler room door now—the Mayor had intercepted him. So he prepared to fight. He felt the weight balanced perfectly on his prosthetic and his normal one, a familiar stance from his training, years of knowledge he only had to unearth during the past year. He stayed light on his bad leg, putting most of the bounce in the solidity of his one, healthy anchor. He had trained to be nimble, just in case—but he would not be nimble enough.

"No one to watch," the Mayor said. "But that doesn't mean I'll do it quickly."

The Mayor was a blur. Quinn couldn't keep pace, got turned around trying to dodge, and was gut-punched by a blow he couldn't even see. The Kevlar packed into his midsection, which was already bruised by the show with Ortega just a half hour ago.

The blow was powerful enough to lift him off his feet.

He skidded across the gym floor. He took a breath and felt fluid in his lungs. Broken ribs, punctured lung.

This isn't going well. That was a playtime punch. This fucker can shatter Kevlar if he wanted.

He saw the boiler room door. All he had to do was beat him underground, and make him follow.

If not, he could put the tracking disc on the gym floor and smash it, sending a false signal to Beth to detonate the underpinnings of the town. Useless, maybe—but worth a shot, and better than nothing.

He had no time to reach for the disc. Before he could take a second breath, the Mayor was upon him, an animal leaping out of the smoke, landing a massive blow that crunched the Kevlar against Quinn's back. More broken ribs. Heat rode along his nerve endings, turning to a pins and needles feeling in his healthy leg.

Then he felt the Mayor's powerful hands around his ankle, and he was airborne, swung forcefully up into one of the gym's overhead windows, a trip of at least thirty feet.

Quinn smashed through the glass and bashed into the metal bars behind the panes, falling backward onto the top bleachers, pinballing all the way down. By the time he hit the hardwood floor, he felt the open cuts on his face. Pain finally pushed through the massive barricade of drugs.

The Mayor picked him up by his Kevlar vest. Quinn finally decided to try a few punches and kicks, which were as futile as kicking a boulder.

"Let's see how hard I can hit you without killing you," Mayor said. He whip-cracked a punch into Quinn's face just as he released him. Quinn flopped onto his back and spit out pieces of fake teeth. He hadn't had his original ones for years.

"Ah, good. Now, I wonder, can you handle just a bit more punishment? Or do you want me to take your head off? I am merciful, janitor. I will end this if you beg me."

The Mayor waited for Quinn to drag himself to his feet, then slugged him once more, harder. He felt the joints in his jaw stress to the point of nearly shattering. A smaller man with a thinner neck would have been paralyzed.

The blackout lasted only seconds, as most blackouts do, but in the solitude of his mind, it lasted much longer, a vision as still as a pool of water. No sound, just images—a willow tree, Kate's blue eyes, the scribbled pages of a journal...her desecrated body.

Quinn opened his eyes. He tried to get to his feet, but couldn't. He lingered on his knees. He reached into his pocket, his hand shaking, trying to remove the disc. Fluid poured into his lung.

The Mayor took him by the wrist, his touch delicate. "You were worthy," he said. "But you failed. I will find Beth, and do her worse than I did your wife and son. I promise you that."

He squeezed. Quinn's wrist crumbled under his grip, snapping and crackling. He bit back a scream and waited for the deathblow.

Then, he saw shadows in the smoke, an army of silhouettes. *The demons of hell are ready to welcome me*, he thought, and smiled.

The Mayor drew back his fist. The shadows emerged from the smoke and crashed into him—a mob not of demons, but of the Harlow survivors that had taken up fearful prayer in the gym.

They hadn't run. They'd stayed, ready to die fighting beside the neighbors and friends and family they'd lost. The Griffin couldn't save them—so they chose to try and save him.

The move would cost them their lives. As the Mayor took them apart, Quinn dragged himself to his feet and stumbled toward the boiler room door. He heard squelching and snapping behind him as the Mayor killed his attackers.

He fell down the wooden stairs of the boiler room's secret door, but was no worse for wear, since he was already approaching one hundred percent fucked up.

He limped through the dark. Lost in the pitch-black of the old tunnels, he heard the echo of a switch—and bulbs with creaky filaments came to life.

The Mayor was following him. Quinn searched for the entrance to the Mayor's lair, a turn-off that took them deeper into the mines, a long and shadowed path to victory.

CHAPTER 41

Beth sat in the Jeep, staring through the windshield at the people she had led to freedom. They milled about, waiting, the nearest town miles away. They laughed and hugged, the reality of freedom setting in, perhaps prematurely.

But they had seen her slaughter a disciple. She had power that eclipsed theirs, and it made them feel safe.

Trent sat next to her, the receiver in his hands, a steady blip emitting from the speaker.

Beth remained transfixed on the horizon, staring out the truck window at Harlow. From Sugar Creek Bridge, she saw trees, the roof of the school, the water tower.

"What you did…" Trent said, trailing off, unsure how to finish. Finally, he did: "It couldn't be done."

"It wasn't truly me," she said. "Now I've got the same poison as the Mayor."

She sensed movement on the blacktop—a truck in the distance, closing fast.

"High Servants?" he asked.

"A street crew to pick off the stragglers," she said. "Now they're after us. After me."

"What do we do?"

She exited the truck.

"Beth—"

"I'll be fine," she said.

"It's not you I'm worried about. What about everyone else? We're on foot here."

"Take cover down the slope," she said. "Under the bridge if you have to."

He knew better than to argue with her and fired up the Jeep.

The tunnel felt eternal. Quinn found himself leaning against the wall, his breath rasping, his collapsed lung turning into an anchor.

Come on, you son of a bitch. Come deeper with me.

"Scurrying away in the dark of the underground like the cock-roach you are," the Mayor cried, his words echoing as they pounded off the tunnel walls.

Quinn could go no further. He turned around and saw the Mayor drifting in and out of the pockets of light created by the bulbs— dark, then light again, dark, then light again, coming ever closer. The tunnel was no more than eight feet wide, eight feet high.

He checked his watch. Over three minutes since he'd popped the first smoke.

The Mayor was almost upon him. Quinn's right hand was limp and useless, his wrist shattered down to the soft tissue.

He plucked the last grenade from his belt.

"Smoke won't save you," the Mayor said.

He yanked the pin and launched the grenade. The Mayor watched it travel over his right shoulder, landing far behind him.

"It's not smoke, asshole." The Semtex grenade erupted, and a deep rumble shook the tunnel. The bulbs swayed, the rafters vibrated as the tunnel began its collapse behind the Mayor, sending forth a tidal wave of dust that swallowed him.

The Mayor emerged from the dust. The collapse stopped, incom-plete. The ties held.

For now, he thought. *Hurry, Beth. Don't lose your goddam nerve.*

The Mayor wiped the thick layer of soot from his face as the lights cut out. Quinn popped a flare, the orange tongue lighting the Mayor's approach.

Quinn smiled through his shattered mouth. He dropped the flare and gestured at the Mayor with his left hand—*come on, then.*

It was over, one way or another.

The truck stopped at the mouth of the bridge as Beth stared them down, standing in the center of the road. Four men exited a jacked-up Chevy Silverado, all of them holding rifles.

"Hi, Charlie," she said. Charlie Rensing was the man you called to remove dead trees or cut down overhead limbs. The town of Harlow paid him each year to trim tree limbs that threatened the power lines.

He was joined by Nick Dugan, Harvey Fellowes, and Blake Ayres, but Charlie was the eldest, and they all remained a step behind him. Charlie was who she had to focus on.

"Beth Jarvis," he said. A smile emerged in the brambles of his wiry beard. "Jackpot."

"Just who we was looking for," Blake added.

"Charlie, we're leaving," she said. "I got a hundred people out, and we need your help."

They laughed. Charlie pointed his rifle. "I don't see nobody," he said.

"They're hidden for now," she said. "Until you put your guns down."

"You're coming with us, girlie," he said.

"You don't get it. It's all over. We have only two vehicles for all these people. We are moving on from Harlow, and need your help."

"What you need is to get your ass to Harvest," Charlie said.

"You know what's happening there," she said. "They're already gone, but this time, the Mayor is going to join them."

More laughter.

"Last warning," Charlie said, staring down the barrel of a Remington.

"Beth!" Trent shouted. She saw him at the end of the bridge, holding the receiver over his head, waving it.

She reached for the detonator. The sudden movement must have started Charlie—she heard the snapshot of a rifle and felt a sting in her neck. She instinctively slapped the spot, as if it were a mosquito bite and not a slug fired from thirty yards away.

Charlie chambered another round and fired, center mass. The bullet struck her chest, opening a hole in her shirt, but doing no damage.

"You're a disciple," Charlie said, breathless.

"No," she said, walking toward them. "I'm not."

They dropped to their knees and lowered their heads—a force of habit.

She stopped before them, men kneeling in front of her, offering themselves for slaughter or submission. Her choice.

When Charlie looked up, she was holding the detonator. She pulled the sliders back, unlocking the switch.

"There are no more disciples," she said. "No more servants of any kind. No Mayor. And no more Harlow."

She flipped the switch and tossed it aside.

They felt a distant rumble underfoot, and smoke began to rise on the horizon. She held out her hand to the kneeling servants. Charlie took it, and as he got to his feet, he began to sob.

"I'm sorry," he said.

She hugged him.

An implosion was much slower and less noisy than the pyrotechnics on television, but with the critical joints of Harlow's underpinnings blowing apart, the collapse was a process more than an event. The water tower was already gone, and the rooftops began to follow.

Behind her, the survivors emerged from the bridge's slope, now gathering to watch the destruction in the distance as Harlow disappeared. She joined them, with the former High Servants following her across the bridge.

It was impossible for the entire town to simply sink away, but Beth could tell from the lurching, echoing sounds that Quinn's plan had done enough catastrophic damage to wipe a great deal of Harlow from existence. The hollowed-out mines sucked most of the roofs and treetops out of the horizon.

Trent tried to hold her hand, but she pulled it away, fixated on a young mother, Kari, who was bawling into her husband's chest.

Beth went to them and touched Kari's shoulder.

"We're going to be okay," Beth said.

"It's not that," Kari said. "It's the most beautiful thing I've ever seen in my life."

The survivors insisted on watching it end before they'd let Beth take them away, waiting until the slurping, collapsing, and crunching sounds came to a final stop.

It was a long, long time before it did.

Just before the looming detonation, the Mayor pressed his hand on the tunnel wall.

"Did you think you would trap me down here?" he said. "These are my tunnels. You aren't taking me deeper, but farther. Just outside this wall is the hillside in the woods. When you're dead, I will claw my way out, only I'll emerge two days faster than Jesus himself."

The Mayor moved to stand face-to-face with Quinn for the final time.

"It was fun while it lasted," the Mayor said.

The orange flicker turned his face into a demonic shadow. Quinn braced himself for a face-collapsing punch, one that moved faster than the high-grain bullets shot from his magnum.

But as the fist moved through the air, Quinn could see its movement instead of the imperceptible blur he expected. He reacted, his reflexes now faster than the Mayor's as he reached up with his healthy hand and palmed the Mayor's fist. The fist felt tiny in his hand, not much bigger than a baseball. As he squeezed it, the Mayor's eyes bulged in shock.

Denial at first—the Mayor threw another punch with his other hand, and Quinn allowed it to land in the center of his cheek. Felt like a good, old-fashioned punch from a little man trying to be a big man. A barroom brawl punch, one that was untrained, that didn't come from the hips. It barely registered.

The Hail Mary grenades had worked—the smoke in the gym wasn't meant as cover. The smoke was an aerosol medication.

"What did you do?" the Mayor pleaded. "You...poisoned me. The smoke."

"I cured you," Quinn said. "Maybe not a cure, really. Maybe just temporary symptom relief."

The Mayor had a mutated form of Mad Cow, a prion disorder from the same family of diseases. Mad Cow had no cure; the disease was too rare to investigate or invest in treatments, but some off-label medications had proven promising in providing symptom relief. Quinn'd had no idea if the medications that his old friend Doctor Carson Venhaus had mentioned would work on the Mayor, but he'd taken the time to make sure his smoke grenades had a massive aerosol dose of Fenozepam—a treatment for fungal infections that just so happened to work off-label for rare prion disorders.

According to the studies, there was a thirty-five percent chance that the Mayor would be affected by the drug, at least temporarily—but that's all Quinn was hoping for. A few moments with the man the Mayor used to be, weak and vulnerable.

He stepped forward and punched the cowering Mayor across his jawline. Another in the center of his nose. The electricity of vengeance overwhelmed him, fueling each punch. The Mayor was still durable—Quinn didn't feel jawbones break and noses turn over at the crest of his fist like he normally did—but it was hurting him all the same.

The Mayor was now just a skinny man trying to hit back. Quinn didn't bother dodging, absorbing every blow, letting the Mayor feel the futility that his mutated form had inflicted on so many others.

The Mayor fell to his knees and knew he was defeated.

"Vengeance is yours now," he said. "Does it taste like you thought it would?"

Quinn loomed over him.

"Yes," Quinn said.

"Killing me won't bring her back."

He grabbed the Mayor by the temples and pulled him close. "She brought *me* back," he whispered, his lips almost touching the Mayor's ear. "And that's why you're about to die."

Quinn shoved the Mayor's head away. He drew his pistol in his healthy hand, but shooting with his left hand would not do—the Griffin tattoo was on his right arm. He worked the gun into his pale, weakened right hand, the circulation choked by crushed bone.

The gun felt like a concrete block. Fluid loaded his crushed lung. Shards of teeth had shredded the flesh of his tongue and mouth.

He held the gun steady. The mouth of the barrel hovered over the Mayor's heart.

The striations in his extended arm made the Griffin look lethal, huge, and hungry.

Then, the Griffin breathed fire.

The slug chewed through the Mayor's torso, spraying cardiac tissue on the muddy wall behind him. The twisted corpse lulled for a long moment, then slumped to the ground.

Exhausted and satisfied, Quinn sat. Then, he laid down, letting the cool earth suck the heat from his sweating neck.

Finally, he sensed the town's destruction, the explosions giving the tunnels the voice of an angered monster, deafening. The flare died. His new, dark world shook apart around him. The dust of the mine sprinkled onto his face, followed by pebbles. As the rumble rose, the debris picked up in its intensity and size. He felt a heavy stone smash into the right side of his decimated ribcage. One of them might have plunged into the tissue of his lung, because the back of his throat filled with blood.

But he hadn't taken the Mayor as deep as planned. They were far from the school, and even in the midst of the explosions, the ties held. Eventually, the rumbling stopped.

The mine's digestion of him stalled. He'd be sealed in a dark grave alongside the Mayor. The thought made him laugh. His breath rasped. He wouldn't die of thirst or exposure—he was going to drown as his lungs collapsed and took on fluid, a sinking boat in the center of him.

The gun had three shots left, but one was all he needed. He took it in his left hand, and felt no fear. Instead, he was filled with a serenity he'd never experienced.

He had saved Beth and destroyed the Mayor. Vengeance was toxic, but addictive, and he snorted one last line of it, thanks to the good luck of bad men.

He put the barrel in his mouth and prepared to take his place among the buried.

CHAPTER 42

A fter Harlow was gone, after its survivors were scattered
at gas stations and rest stops to begin new lives, and after
the sun had set, Beth and Trent drove and drove, not
knowing where to stop. They ended up in Colorado.

They stopped at a Love's travel plaza that felt bigger and more
populated than Harlow itself, a concrete tundra with hissing brakes
that smelled of diesel. Only when she went inside and saw the newspaper did she even remember the day of the week, the way that the
world had agreed to a system of time and measurement—a world
that always felt distant and cosmic.

She bought them some shitty gas station food—a microwaved
burrito for Trent, poorly warmed hot dogs for her. They ate in the
car, watching trucks and weary travelers come and go.

After the meal, they sat in silence. He waited for her, ready to
follow her, as all the others did before she set them off to forge their
own lives. It was his turn.

"I have to go," she said, "and I can't take you with me."

He argued with her. He pleaded with her. He professed his love
for her, and at one point got angry—how many times did he risk

his life? How many times did he do something stupid to try and be with her when he could have just walked away?

"We could have been together," she said. "Anywhere else in the world. I know it. But I can't be sure if we love each other. I needed you, and you needed me, and now we don't need each other anymore."

"That's bullshit," he said. "I don't care what happened in Harlow. I only care about you, nothing else, not even myself."

"That's the problem," she said. "Can't you see that?" She leaned over and kissed him on the cheek. "I think we both need to be a little selfish for a while."

They didn't have cell phones, or home phones, for that matter. So he told her where and when she could find him again, if she wanted.

She told him goodbye, and he let her go, forcing himself to not look back. He needed to get in the car and just drive.

"Beth," he called out.

She had no choice now. She looked at him, the love of her young life, the deep sadness creasing his face. They were artifacts of a lost world, a place where their parents and friends had died.

"I do love you," he said.

She nodded, and they lingered in silence. He walked away before she could drive away. She imagined him staying at the gas station for hours, scouring the brightly lit convenience store for the girl he already missed.

But that girl was gone forever.

Quinn sat in the dark, the unfired gun at his side. He was surrounded by soot and rock, the cold floor biting through his clothes.

He coughed up blood and felt himself fading. Every breath was a loud wheeze as air whistled out of a sagging lung and shards of bone. He thought of the ambient light of the woods beyond the dirt wall of the mining tunnel, close enough to fantasize about, but eclipsed by rubble he couldn't move, even if he were healthy enough to live longer than roughly five more minutes.

He closed his eyes again, hoping for Kate, to die looking into her eyes. She came to him and spoke the words from her final journal entry snaking through him in the dark.

The truth unleashes us.

He thought he would drift away, but her words wouldn't let him. Kate wouldn't let him.

Beside him, the Mayor's corpse was limp in the dirt, a reminder of what he was dying for. Yes, it was revenge, and it was petty and useless, just pick your cliché—but maybe it wasn't the end of something.

Maybe it was the beginning.

He opened his eyes. He fought to get to one knee, and felt the wetness on the right side of his body, his left lung working harder than ever to keep oxygen flowing into his system. He reached into the nearby rubble, searching for a jagged, heavy rock he could wield with one hand.

He found one.

Quinn crawled to the Mayor's body, feeling for it in the dark. He raised the rock over his head, and brought it down, sharp edge first, on the side of the Mayor's skull. He struck the temple once, twice, a third time before it finally split with a wet, hollow sound. He tossed the rock aside and felt around until he scraped up a fistful of goopy brain tissue from the Mayor's remains.

He took a breath, the longest he could muster. He braced himself as best he could, and then he began to eat.

ONE YEAR LATER

CHAPTER 43

T he Harlow disaster was unpacked over the course of months, and with every rock the investigators moved, the more the details made no sense. No motives, no explanation.

Reporters and news vans took up permanent residence in one of the farming fields outside of town, and of course the farmer himself didn't care—Cooper Murray was dead.

As hard as it was to have a Jamestown in the infancy of the Internet age, this was about as close as this generation was going to get—a mystery they'd be trying to figure out for years, the truth obscured by conspiracy theories and manufactured lore.

Beth Jarvis was one of the few who knew the truth. Like all news stories, this one burned out. Just so happened it lasted weeks instead of hours—good legs for a news story nowadays.

On the one-year anniversary of Harlow's demise, Beth returned to Red Rock Ridge. She climbed to the hilltop, where she and Quinn once looked out at the town, debating its fate.

The cranky bastard was right. People had to die, and most of them did. Didn't make it any easier or any less sad. Beth was just happy the Mayor was among that number.

She noticed something out of place—a young willow tree, planted out of the reach of the oak tree's canopy, where it could get sunlight.

She knelt by the tree, pressing her fingers into the soil. It felt rich and moist, a whole section dug out of the thick clay of the dirt trail and replaced with a truckload of topsoil. The tree had to be planted that high on the hill so that it could overlook all of what Harlow once was—and only one person could have come back to finish planting it.

The town was gone, but she could close her eyes and remember. She saw Harlow roofs, the Griffin flag obscuring the town's name on the water tower, the mature oaks that flanked the houses in the older part of the town. She remembered the explosion, how the ground trembled and the sound was low and hollow, a great beast clearing its throat.

She opened her eyes. The air still tasted dusty, and no one would unravel what happened there. Not ever.

Only when she heard the snap of twigs behind her did she break from the paralysis of the moment. She turned around, and Trent was making his way up the hill.

He looked revived compared to the boy she'd left at that gas station, a fresh weight in his face, clear eyes, a familiar smile.

They both smiled, unsure of what to do. Hug? Kiss? Shake hands?

She broke the awkwardness of the moment and drew him into an embrace. Then she took his hand and led him to the crest of the hill.

They sat there in the twilight and caught up on their delightfully boring, normal lives, complete with shitty part-time jobs, cheap cars that broke down all the time, and the challenges of living alone. Perhaps more accurately, living with secrets.

Then they had their quiet time. They looked off into what used to be home. She said a silent goodbye to her father—and knew that Trent was likely doing the same for his parents.

"Quinn's alive," Beth said, gesturing to the willow tree.

"How?" he said.

"With him? 'How' doesn't apply."

"If he's alive, you don't think the Mayor..." he said, letting the sentence trail off, afraid to finish it.

"No," she said. The Mayor didn't survive. He couldn't have survived. Yet she had lived a year thinking Quinn was gone for good, so—

She had no choice but to let that thought die. If the Mayor survived, he had a new world to contend with, a connected world that was harder to contain and even harder to rule.

"Let's go," she said.

"Where?" he asked.

"Anywhere we want."

They slowly moved east together. Her dream was to live at least a year in New York City, and his dream was for them to go to college and graduate together.

As they chased their modest dreams, she thought of Curtis Quinn and his unlikely survival less and less as time went on. But some days, she'd see a willow tree or a news story about the mysteries of Harlow, and remember him—the man who'd once cast a Griffin's shadow that eclipsed a self-proclaimed king.